I0633507

THE LAST BREATH OF A
DYING TOMORROW

DEFIANCE
BOOK 7

JASON KRUMBINE

Published by Lantern Key Books

ISBN: 978-1-971197-06-7

Originally published in 2023 by Jason Krumbine

First Lantern Key Books Edition: December 2025

Books in the Defiance Series

Defiance
Hand of God
Act of God
The Test of Truth
The Price of Paradise
The Value of Terror
The Last Breath of a Dying Tomorrow

Subscribe to my newsletter and I'll let you know as soon as the next Defiance book is ready to read.

Sign Up Here
https://onestrayword.beehiiv.com/subscribe

THE LAST BREATH OF A
DYING TOMORROW

previously...

One hundred years ago, the United Planetary Alliance (UPA) was attacked by the Unity, a parasitic, single-minded species from a lower dimension that consumes and absorbs every universe it comes into contact with. Something about our universe has made it difficult for the Unity to establish a presence. Since their initial attack, they have been making covert moves against our universe.

The Veneer Empire was a former member of the UPA until the Unity's attack. In the aftermath, they withdrew from the UPA. No one has heard from the Veneer since. Unbeknownst to the citizenry of the UPA, the Veneer established a relationship with the Unity that resulted in the development of several new technologies, including ships and weapons. Intelligence experts believe within the UPA Security Council that this was the cause behind the Veneer Empire's ultimate collapse.

The Natuzzi are members of the UPA. They are notoriously xenophobic and do not allow for any presence of non-Natuzzi on their planet. They exist in a police state. The government controls all information. They are allowed no access to outside resources and provide nothing to the UPA at large. The Natuzzi also have a strict belief system that suggests they are the center of the universe, and all other life in the galaxy is irrelevant. To suggest otherwise or participate in any kind of intimate relationship with a member of a species that is not Natuzzi is considered High Treason and punishable by death.

The Defiance is an eighty-year-old starship that was built as a response to the threat of the Unity and is an asset of Admiral Philip Wanamaker and Directive Fifty-Two which is responsible for protecting the UPA from threats too dangerous for the public to know. Directive 52 operates at the upper echelons of the top-secret community and works independently within the governing body of the UPA.

Recently, it was discovered that Lt. Commander Nax is actually a member of the Natuzzi Royal Family. He was found guilty of High Treason against the Natuzzi people. His mother, the queen, chose to show mercy and condemned him to life in prison. However, he was attacked by a religious fanatic and left for dead.

While on a covert mission to rescue Nax, Captain Gavin Mitchell, and Commander Cayden Keane were captured by a Natuzzi warship and summarily executed by being jettisoned into space.

With her captain dead, the Defiance is now under the command of Broderick Cooper. He was assigned to the Defiance at the behest of UPA President D'Ambra. His agenda is unknown, and his allegiances are suspect.

Queen Xie, the leader of the Natuzzi people, decided that the UPA was a threat to the Natuzzi way of life. To protect her people, she acquired a weapon built by the Veneer Empire in conjunction with the Unity. The weapon was known as the Tyrant of Paradise, the first planet killer this galaxy had ever seen.

Queen Xie was assassinated by unknown parties, bringing the war between Natuzzi and the UPA to an abrupt stop before it could even begin. Her first-born daughter, Gouren Ril, has ascended to the throne. Her focus has been on building a lasting peace between Natuzzi and the UPA.

The Unity has infected Ensign Erin Calloway. It is unknown when this occurred as her assignment onboard the Defiance is the first time she's been off planet. But rather than consuming her entirely, remnants of Calloway's personality have remained.

Upon the activation of the Natuzzi weapon, it sent out a signal. It was a signal undetected by anyone in our galaxy save for one person: Erin Calloway. This signal triggered the next stage of Calloway's evolution, and she began merging her physical presence with the Defiance.

When the Defiance and her crew are confronted by the Natuzzi weapon, Calloway defends them by forcibly uploading the consciousness of Emily Westin, an undercover agent of The Church of Eternal Clarity, to the Natuzzi weapon, disrupting its original programming.

The Natuzzi weapon is no longer under the control of the Natuzzi people. Its current whereabouts are unknown.

1

THE ATLANTIC

CURTIS LANGFIELD WAS LOST in the dark, figuratively and literally.

A two-time Imperium Nebula award winner, he had been one of the most popular and controversial reporters in the United Planetary Alliance. He celebrated his fiftieth birthday three weeks ago. But after all the years spent in the different gravity wells across the UPA searching for truth, uncovering the stories no one wanted to be told, Curtis Langfield easily looked fifteen years older. The bags under his eyes were dark and heavy, a sharp contrast to his pale, sun-starved skin. He couldn't remember the last time he had been under a real sun. It had to have been over five years, at least. And since he had been back to his home, Earth? Easily twice that. To be fair, though, he had three ex-wives waiting for him back there, looking for any excuse to suck the last of his life from him. After hopping around the galaxy, any planet suddenly seemed very small, regardless of how many landmasses there were between you and the people you wanted to avoid.

He hunched now. Langfield used to have impeccable

posture. He carried himself with pride. He stood at a hair over five feet, eight inches. But his reputation had made him larger than life. Regardless of who may have towered over him, he had always been the tallest person in the room. Now, it didn't matter if he was sitting or standing; there was a hunch in his shoulders that he couldn't get rid of. It made him look sickly. He couldn't stand looking at himself in the mirror.

What little hair he had retained was completely white at this point. It looked thin and wispy, as if a stiff breeze could come along and simply blow it all away. Fortunately, there weren't any breezes on the *Atlantic*.

Langfield had been the one to expose the Aurrod senator for his backdoor dealing with the Oxean Syndicate. He wrote the story that exposed the election fraud on Uboklu Four and brought down the Speaker of the House as well as three different planetary governors.

Curtis Langfield didn't just speak truth; he brought truth to the people. He was the light shining in the darkness.

He looked up from his empty drink, trying to spot the bartender. Everything was in a blurry haze, and what wasn't blurry was obscured by the darkness that was encroaching on his field of vision.

It had been getting worse for weeks. Maybe even longer. Of course, he hadn't really noticed because of the drinking. Kusalax ale tended to add a blurry haze over everything for him. It was three weeks ago, during a sober day, because despite everything, he still had to turn in *something* and be sober when he wrote. It was then, staring at his terminal, trying to write a piece on the Aurrod Ambassador and whether or not she had actually meant it when she had called half the Natuzzi population a failed Mionzi abortion, he realized that the blurry haze was not only still present, but actively getting worse. He had to increase the font size on his terminal by almost two hundred percent before he could read the garbage he had written. It got exponentially worse after that.

He couldn't make out people's faces unless they were standing close enough for him to lick their noses. Distances were essentially a blurry abyss. In addition, color was disappearing from his vision. He couldn't see reds and yellows anymore. Greens, purples, and blues were getting faint now, too.

Midianga's Disease. It was sexually transmitted and was nearly a public health crisis among the Stravin. It was completely treatable and preventable. It was a three-part vaccine over six months, which seemed like a perfectly reasonable price to pay to avoid going blind after having a one-night hookup. The larger problem was that the pharmaceutical company that produced the vaccine couldn't actually keep up with the demand, which was how the rest of the Alliance discovered the Stravin were a bunch of sex-crazed horn dogs.

Fortunately, Midianga's was only supposed to affect less than one percent of the human population. If you did get it, it was even easier to treat than the standard garden variety herpes. For humans, it was only a one-shot vaccine.

Unfortunately, since it was so rare that a human contracted it, the Atlantic didn't keep the medicine on hand to treat it. The closest facility that had it was the *Smithsonian*. This meant it would be almost two months before it would reach the *Atlantic*.

Best case scenario, the doctor told him Langfield would be stuck with the blurry vision until the treatment arrived. Worst case, he'd actually go blind for three weeks.

Three weeks in the dark.

The thought kept him from sleeping too much.

The doctors assured him that there wouldn't be any permanent damage. But he didn't trust them. Partially because he had a distrust of anyone in the medical profession but mostly because he had managed only one decent story since getting kicked out to the *Atlantic*.

Doctor Ruâne Pàngal, a Bethari, had been the station's top surgeon. He was considered one of the best in his field. He was on the *Atlantic* as part of the Bethari delegation, running an elite surgical internship. He was also selling prescription drugs on the side and sleeping with half of his students. Langfield had stumbled onto the story while looking for a new prescription for his sobriety meds. It was a trashy story. Too close to the exploitive garbage that the cheap tabloids fed off. But by virtue of being who he was, Langfield had managed to elevate it into a story about systemic abuses within the medical field out here in the dark, lightyears away from a planet and months away from any kind of escape or legal help. In a moment of brilliant sobriety, he managed to reach out to a few other deep space stations and assembled a few choice quotes that helped support the narrative.

It was still a trash story, though.

It had destroyed Pàngal's career. Or, at least, it had tainted it enough that Pàngal couldn't stay on the *Atlantic*. Despite Pàngal's crimes, there were still plenty who had liked him, none of them had gone anywhere, and they were still plenty pissed off at Langfield. So he didn't put it entirely past them to be hiding the medicine he needed. Unfortunately, he couldn't prove anything since he couldn't actually *see* anything. And since he couldn't see anything, he couldn't prove anything.

Langfield tightened his fingers around the glass in his

hand, letting his fingertips dig into the smooth grooves along the edges.

He was stuck out here in the darkness.

The problem, the *real* problem, was the *book*.

The book was what kept Langfield out here. The book was what kept him afloat, financially at least. Between the advance and royalties, he could live out the rest of his days comfortably. He just didn't have any place to live out those days.

The book had given and then taken.

The book had made him *persona non grata* with his network and among half the Alliance.

The book had gotten him labeled a crazed conspiracy theorist.

That damn book.

Langfield scowled and lifted his glass, only to be reminded that it was still empty. He slammed it back down on the counter and called out for the bartender. Or, at least, that's what he thought he did. He couldn't tell if his words were making any sense, and he couldn't tell if anybody had even heard him. He looked around; squinting sometimes made it easier to make out shapes in the distance, but he couldn't tell if anybody was coming toward him.

He vetted every source. He had cross-checked every lead. Every fact in that book had been tripled-checked and then quadruple-checked. There hadn't been a single thing he had put in it that wasn't true.

And still, all it took was five minutes from the former president of the UPA to completely discredit him.

That. Damn. Book.

Langfield's personal datapad sat on the bar next to him. He tapped the screen, and it came to life. He had the magnification cranked all the way up, and still, he could just barely make out the time. He needed to get back to his quarters. He had an appointment for something tomorrow. He couldn't remember what. But he knew that he needed to be moderately rested for it. He squinted at the time on the datapad and decided that maybe he had just enough time for another drink. He did some quick math in his head and nodded. Yeah, he could pull that off. Four hours of sleep, sobriety pills, and a couple of Dicci caffeine pills could get him presentable.

He cleared his throat and raised his hand, trying to flag down a distant figure he thought was the bartender. Maybe he would avoid any more Kusalax ale. A glass of Boveran blood wine sounded good, actually. Maybe two glasses.

There was a chirp from his datapad, announcing that he had a new message. It was probably garbage. That was the only mail he got these days. Langfield ignored it and focused on the shadowy figure behind the bar that was finally making its way toward him.

The datapad chirped again, more loudly. In fact, it was a different alert. He looked down at the screen; he hadn't programmed that alert. He scooped up the datapad and held it close to his eyes as the message automatically opened.

He couldn't make out all the details. The screen was too small. He would need to open it on his terminal back in his quarters. But there were words, key phrases, that he could make out. It was like his brain was prewired to hone in on those words. It didn't matter how blurry or out of focus everything else was; he could pick out those details almost immediately.

There was a voice, somebody trying to get his attention. It was the bartender finally making his way over to Langfield, but he waved him off. Suddenly he didn't care about another drink.

He turned and slowly slid off his barstool, his legs unsteady. But muscle memory got him to the exit of the bar. He might have bumped into a person or two, but he didn't notice, and honestly, he didn't care.

He needed to get back to his quarters. He needed to read all of this.

He kept focusing on the words:

Classified.

Top Secret

Redacted.

Captain Gavin Mitchell.

Security Council's Eyes Only.

And then his failing eyes managed to focus on something that made his blood run cold with fear and excitement:

Species 4876.

2

STARBASE 64

"THIS IS *OUTRAGEOUS*!"

Johanna Dupree took a deep breath and fought against every instinct in her body that told her to lunge across the small table and slam her fist into the face of the slight Phaw ambassador. She glanced down at her hands and saw that they were already flexing into familiar fists, despite the mental effort she was making. She pressed her palms together as if praying and said, in a voice that betrayed none of the frustration she was feeling, "Ambassador–!"

The Phaw Ambassador didn't give her the opportunity to continue. He slammed his three-fingered palm down against the table's surface, causing it to shake so much that Dupree was genuinely concerned it would fall apart.

"I have never been so *insulted*!"

Dupree winced slightly. As the Phaw ambassador got angrier, his voice reached decibels that weren't pleasant to most humans. It was part of the UPA's problem with the Phaw in general: they were nearly impossible to speak with. The Phaw spoke with an almost tinny echo that was simply unpleasant to hear in the best of times. And in the worst of times...The Phaw were generally considered one of the most quick-tempered species in the quadrant. And when they got angry, they were not only nearly impossible to understand, but the decibels their voices could reach in their heated states had been known to cause hemorrhaging in the ear canals of most species. The translation collar located around the ambassador's long neck did a lot of work to keep the pitch of his voice under control, but there was only so much it could do.

Dupree took another deep breath and lowered her voice in the hope that if she presented a calmer disposition, the Phaw ambassador would match her energy. "Ambassador Haiduk–"

Ambassador Haiduk rose to his feet, his body uncurling as it rose to its full height. In the cramped quarters of the small meeting room, the Phaw ambassador seemed even larger than usual. He jabbed one of his thick fingers at her; its pointed claw buffed to a dull edge but still no less intimidating. "If you think that I'm going to talk to that–"

In that instant, Ambassador Johanna Dupree dropped all pretense of diplomacy. She got to her own feet, the palms of her hands pressed firmly against the table's surface as she leaned forward and craned her neck up to meet Haiduk's gaze. "If the next words out of your mouth are another derogatory slur about Master Moogai's race, I swear by all that is holy; I will shove you out the nearest airlock myself."

For once, the Phaw ambassador didn't say anything. He stood there, his three-fingered hands curled inward, staring at Dupree. Like most Phaw, he was tall with long, gangly limbs with a surprising amount of strength. There was something about his body, his presence, that gave the impression that he was about to tear through the ridiculously small meeting room at any second. His skin was leathery, the color of ancient stone, and stretched out across his frame like a dried-out canvas. His eyes were oval-shaped, occupying almost a third of his face. They were black and frequently mistaken for not having any pupils. But in bright fluorescent lighting, you could just make out their dim outlines.

The two almost square holes above his narrow mouth flared, and tiny puffs of smoke drifted out.

Images of the earliest diplomatic attempts with the Phaw rose unbidden through Dupree's mind. They were horrific images, and Dupree had lost a week's worth of sleep after looking over the historical files that had been prepped for her. But she didn't blink.

The Phaw ambassador scowled, briefly displaying the razor-sharp teeth that lined his mouth and stormed out of the meeting.

The room shuddered as the door slammed shut.

Dupree didn't move for a moment, waiting to see if the Phaw ambassador would return. When he didn't, she finally exhaled and dropped back into her seat. She rubbed her forehead tiredly and looked at the short, almost squat-like figure of the Ulriharad space wizard seated with an apologetic smile. "Master Moogai, I'm sorry."

The pale figure, dressed in dark brown robes, had a face that could only be described, at best, as dour. His skin was thick and plentiful, clinging to his face in heavy folds that seemed reluctant to move. Despite this, the Ulriharad Wizard's eyes were unusually wide and expressive, which was for the best since the wizard spoke sparingly. In response to Dupree's apology, he simply tilted his head forward. He slowly got to his feet and wordlessly left the room.

Johanna Dupree was alone in the small meeting room. Again.

3

—————

"THIS IS the third time this week." Otis Patrice gave off the appearance of a man with the patience of a saint. This was a lie. It was a carefully constructed facade that he had built and cultivated over his sixty-plus years to make sure that no one, not even his own wife, was aware of how much of a nervous wreck he was on the inside. But like all good spouses, Dupree knew what was really going on inside her husband.

"I know how many times it's been," Dupree replied. "I've been careful to keep track, seeing as I've been present at each incident." She sat at her desk in the quarters provided for her in the residential habitat ring. To her right, there was a window with a view of the Dauerfrost Nebula in the distance, its soft yellow glow undulating across her living space. She sipped at a glass of Huna wine, wincing slightly as she eased back into her chair. The pain in her lower back, a nearly ancient injury that refused to fade away, tended to flare up in times of stress. "And it's four."

Patrice gaped at her from across the lightyears. She

avoided his direct eye line, twisting her chair slightly so that she was staring at the corner of the view screen.

"*Four*?"

Dupree took another long sip of her wine before answering, hoping that he would simply let the matter drop. He didn't.

"Four?" he repeated.

Dupree sighed and set the glass down on the desk. She leaned forward, folding her hands together, and locked eyes with her husband. "There was a get-together at the beginning of last week before the talks officially started."

"A get-together?" Patrice repeated as if trying to pull some deeper meaning from the three words.

"An informal get-together."

"Informal."

"It was Eddie's idea," she said.

"Is that supposed to make me feel better?"

She shrugged. "He thought we could try to start the talks on the right foot."

Patrice raised a dubious eyebrow. "The Phaw aren't known for their dinner parties."

"Then it was a good thing that it wasn't a dinner party," Dupree replied with a small smile. "Eddie suggested that we hold a small event–"

"Now it's an *event*?" Patrice interrupted. "A second ago, it was an informal get-together."

She continued, ignoring him. "Eddie suggested we hold a small, informal event to welcome the Phaw delegation."

Patrice made a snorting sound.

Dupree rolled her eyes. "It wasn't a bad idea. The Phaw don't like visiting places they haven't already conquered."

"So hors d'oeuvre and Huna wine were supposed to make them feel welcomed?"

"Well, it was actually Avrora wine from the vineyards on Vastum Eight," Dupree corrected. "And yes, that was the idea."

"Avrora wine is illegal in the UPA."

"Are you calling me to nitpick every little decision I make?" She asked him. "Because I already have Takacs here doing that, and I have to say, it's not something I'm looking to get in surround sound."

He held up an apologetic hand. "Sorry."

She nodded. "Apology accepted." She helped herself to another sip of wine. "Anyway, Takacs gave me an earful about the Avrora wine."

"I'm sure he did," Patrice smirked.

Dupree shook her head. "He was just upset, thinking he had been left out of any bribes that had been placed in order to get the wine on the station."

Patrice rubbed his eyes. "Please tell me you didn't say that to his face."

"Of course not," Dupree replied. "I just strongly implied it."

"Johanna..."

She waved a hand. "You wanted to know about the welcome party for Ambassador Haiduk."

"And now it's a party?"

"It lasted all of fifteen minutes before Haiduk took notice of Lt. Commander Cohad and stormed out, threatening to eviscerate half the station if Mr. Cohad ever stepped within ten feet of him again."

"What happened?"

Dupree took a long drink from her wine. "Well, Lt. Commander Cohad is a Knoksian, so I'm sure you can understand Ambassador Haiduk's delicate state of mind when being in the presence of...Well, I have too much self-respect to repeat any of it. Still, I think if you use your imagination, you can piece together a variety of colorful derogatory epithets that Haiduk shared with us."

Patrice rubbed his face tiredly. "Johanna..."

"It's fine."

"It's *fine*?" He shuffled around in his seat. "This literally sounds like the opposite of fine."

"It ended up being a great party after the Phaw delegation left," she said. "I learned that Glynda plays the Backlon saxophone and is remarkably good at it."

"You threatened to kick the head of the Phaw delegation out of an airlock today."

Dupree shrugged.

"That's not fine."

"It's not a disaster, either."

"Then what else would you call it?"

"A great start."

"A great start," he muttered, shaking his head.

"The Phaw are extremely aggressive," she started.

"I know *exactly* how aggressive they are," Patrice cut her off.

Dupree shot him a look that, even across the lightyears, he knew better than to argue with. He held up his hands, signaling his temporary surrender.

Dupree cleared her throat and helped herself to more wine. "As I was saying, I threatened Ambassador Haiduk with having him tossed out the nearest airlock. We all know this is an empty threat. The ambassador is easily ten times my weight. And, even if I could somehow actually move him, he's still faster and stronger than me. Also, I was in the room alone, as per the Naonzo Agreement."

"These are all great points that are making me feel so much better," Patrice replied dryly.

"The fact is," she continued, choosing to ignore the sarcasm, "the Phaw don't understand an empty threat. As far as they're considered, a threat is a *threat*, regardless of how it may have been intended. And instead of responding to that threat with escalation, Ambassador Haiduk *left* the room." She held out her hands as if resting her case.

Patrice didn't say anything for a moment. Finally, he took a deep breath and exhaled slowly.

"You were very lucky."

Dupree smiled. "I'm married to you. I know exactly how lucky I am."

"Haiduk could have easily decided to disembowel you right then and there."

"I am very much aware of that."

"That's what happened to the last negotiator the Phaw were willing to talk to."

"I read all the files," she said. "Front to back checked the footnotes, read the acknowledgments, the afterwords, the supplemental reports, then started back at the beginning and went through them all over again."

"Administrator Takacs reached out to me earlier today."

Dupree frowned. "If Takacs has a problem with the way I'm handling things, he can drag his skinny ass down here and tell me to my face."

"His primary concern is making sure his starbase isn't ground zero for an interstellar incident," Patrice said.

"What do you want me to say? You want me to say that I'll march up to the command deck and tell Takacs that if he has a problem with how I'm conducting my negotiations, he can have it out with *me* instead of trying to get me in trouble with my husband? Because I will definitely do that." She started to get to her feet.

"No. I definitely do not want you to do that." Patrice sighed. "I'm just worried about you."

"I know." She sat back down and reached out, pressing her fingers against the screen. She tried to pretend she was caressing his face, but it was a poor substitute. "When do you think you'll make it back out here?"

"I don't know. Another two weeks? Maybe three? The Antid Delegation is being...picky again," he replied.

"Picky?"

He shook his head. "It's stupid."

"I'm sure it's not."

"You're trying to negotiate a peace agreement between one of the most violent species in our quadrant and the Ulriharad."

Dupree shrugged. "It's a job."

"The last time the Phaw agreed to meet with the Ulriharad, it resulted in the subjugation and enslavement of the Ulriharad for nearly fifteen years."

"I'm sure the Antid Delegation is just as difficult."

"They refused to meet today because we were serving Bressier fish for lunch," Patrice replied flatly.

Dupree stared at him for a moment before bursting out laughing.

"It's not funny," he said.

"I'm sorry," she said after she calmed down. "But it's a little funny."

Patrice grunted but refused to acknowledge it beyond that.

When she had stopped laughing, Dupree leaned forward again, bringing her face close to the screen. "Two weeks?"

"If I'm lucky."

"I have a feeling you're going to be lucky."

"I think you're confusing that with *getting* lucky."

She smiled. "I love you."

He smiled. "I love you, too."

The screen went blank as the connection was terminated.

Dupree leaned back in her chair again. The pain in her lower back flared up briefly, but she barely noticed it.

She caught her reflection on the dark screen and was amazed that she had managed to snag a man like Otis. Her once-dark hair had gone completely gray. She wanted to hack it all off, the pixie cut was all the rage in the UPA these days, but Otis wouldn't hear of it. He insisted her hair was one of her defining features.

Dupree ran her hands down the sides of her face. She was almost ten years younger than Otis, although she didn't feel it. Too much of her misspent youth had been spent on Zapus Four, where the heavier gravity, almost twenty percent more than Earth's, had done a number on her body. She *felt* a decade older than she was, and although Otis would never say it, she was pretty sure that the gravity on Zapus Four had made her *look* older, too. Maybe not older than her husband, but pretty damn close. She examined the dark circles underneath her eyes and decided that perhaps it would be better for everyone involved, including the section of the galaxy that bordered Phaw space, if she actually made an effort to get enough sleep tonight.

Dupree got to her feet, turning off her console. She intended to head directly to the bedroom and call it a night when her comm chimed. She considered ignoring it, but then she noticed the alert on the console informing her who was on the other end.

Dupree cupped her hands around her mouth, took a deep breath, and then answered her comm. "Ashley."

"Ambassador." The voice over the speaker sounded like it belonged to a much younger woman. In fact, Ashley Skouras was fifteen years Dupree's senior.

"I hope you're calling me with good news."

"Well, I'm certainly calling you with news."

"This doesn't sound like it's off to a great start," Dupree muttered and dropped back into her seat.

"It's not that bad," Skouras said.

"Then how bad is it?"

"Probably worse than you would like. But I don't think you have to worry about an interstellar incident taking place."

Dupree rubbed her tired eyes. "What happened?"

"Haiduk's recused himself from the rest of the meetings."

Dupree frowned. "Recused?"

"I'm paraphrasing it into something that won't make it worse than it needs to be for you," Skouras said.

"Might as well rip off the whole damn band-aid."

"There's no indication that they're going to cancel the talks completely."

Dupree perked up. "That's good."

"Haiduk's people–"

Dupree scoffed at the description of the Phaw delegation. It was primarily comprised of Haiduk's three wives and a Quay. The Quay, who had no other name or identifier that Dupree was aware of, was a member of one of the lower castes in the Phaw society. No specific gender had been assigned to the Quay, and despite their best efforts, Dupree and Skouras had been unable to determine what it was. The Quay appeared to be limited to performing basic administrative tasks for the higher caste members. The reality was, near as Dupree could tell, the Quay were more slaves than anything else. Some had administrative jobs, such as assisting the Phaw ambassador. Others were less glamorous.

However, it was most likely Haiduk's second wife that Skouras was referring to. The Quay weren't allowed to communicate with non-Phaw, which meant that Haiduk's second wife had acted as the go-between when they weren't at the negotiation table.

"What did Number Two say this time?" Dupree asked. Nobody bothered to tell Dupree or her team if the wives had any proper names. Dupree and the rest of the diplomatic team had simply taken to referring to them as Numbers One, Two, and Three. It didn't matter; all three were impossible to tell apart. The only way they knew there was any distinction was that Haiduk himself had specified that his second wife would act as his mouthpiece.

"The usual, actually," Skouras said. "The ambassador was deeply offended by your words, your tone, your general existence. You know, so on, so forth, etcetera, etcetera."

Dupree frowned. "I don't get it. If it's the same crap as the last three times, what made this one so different?"

"I genuinely don't know," Skouras said. "Number Two went on her usual rant and then ended it with the declaration that Haiduk wouldn't be showing up at any more meetings this week."

Dupree leaned forward, drumming her fingers on the desk. "That's weird."

"Any weirder than anything else they do?"

"And she didn't give any explanation?"

"When I asked for one, she said something that wouldn't translate and then hung up on me."

"She cursed you out."

"That's what I was thinking."

Dupree leaned back in her chair. "They're only here for one reason. If they're not going to participate in the talks, what will they do?"

"Take a long nap?"

"Well, I mean, it's not the worst idea I've ever heard," Dupree said. "Have any of them left their ship?"

"Nope."

"This is weird. What did Master Moogai say?"

"I haven't spoken to him yet."

Dupree nodded. "Good."

"What do you want me to say?"

"Nothing."

"Nothing?"

"We'll deal with it in the morning."

"Are you sure about that?"

"No," Dupree admitted. "But I'm too tired to figure anything else out right now. Besides, there's literally nothing else for the Phaw to do around here. They're not going to come on board and sample the cuisine or take in one of the Aurrod operas. If they're determined to clock out for the rest of the week, they're basically going to stay cooped up in their ship."

"Okay." Skouras didn't sound entirely certain.

"Check with station communication and see if they can tell whether or not the Phaw ship has received any transmissions since our last meeting."

"What are you thinking?"

Dupree shrugged. "I don't know. I think it's weird that Haiduk's response to me threatening to toss him out of an airlock is to go hide away for the rest of the week."

"I suppose he could have disemboweled you. Would that have been better?"

"Your humor is not appreciated," Dupree said.

"I think we both know that's not true," Skouras replied.

"I'm going to bed. Try not to wake me."

"I'll do my best. But if Master Moogai insists on sharing the good word of Yahyef, The Eternal Wise One again...."

"Good night, Ashley."

"Good night, Ambassador."

Dupree closed the channel. "Shit," she muttered. Haiduk bowing out like this wasn't something she had considered. She couldn't decide if it was a worse possible outcome or not.

She got to her feet and was halfway to her bedroom when her door chimed. She rubbed her hands across her tired face. "Clearly, somebody's determined to make sure I don't sleep tonight," she muttered.

Dupree crossed her quarters and opened the main doors to find a familiar old man standing outside in the corridor.

Dupree exhaled slowly in surprise. "This is an unwelcome surprise."

"Good to see you, too, Jojo." The old man tilted his head and gave her a smile that was more of a grimace than anything else.

She pointed at him. "Don't."

The old man held up a hand. "Sorry. I didn't come back to pick at old wounds."

Dupree folded her arms. "Then why the hell are you here, Jim? Last I heard, this is a little out of your way."

Doctor Jim Rabkin nodded, his bushy eyebrows furrowing together. "I suppose I could have called you over subspace, but I had a feeling you wouldn't take my call."

"And you thought showing up on my doorstep unannounced would be better?"

Rabkin nodded. "Well, I also thought it would be better

to ask you in person why you didn't bother to put in an appearance at Mitchell's funeral." He shrugged. "I figured it was the least I could do for my old friend."

Dupree's face was set in stone. "To be honest, I wasn't entirely certain I'd be welcome at my ex-husband's funeral."

4

NATUZZI

KINLIN NAX WATCHED the sun slowly rise over the horizon and felt nothing.

As a young child, he found the Natuzzi sunrise almost magical. It was a cascade of colors spilling across the sky, igniting his fertile imagination. Vibrant red, pink, and yellow rays stretched out from the Natuzzi sun as if the sun was pulling itself up little by little during those early morning hours.

It was a beautiful, breathtaking thing to behold.

No matter how late he had stayed up the night before, Nax would be awake to see the sunrise the next morning.

Now, though, Nax watched those colorful rays stretching out from the sun, seeking purchase in the amber sky, slowly pulling the Natuzzi sun into its rightful place, and he felt absolutely nothing.

Instead of a promise of untold wonders and magic, the sun blocked out the stars above and was simply another reminder of how trapped he was.

Nax looked down at the wheelchair he was confined to.

Trapped in more ways than one.

He looked back at the sunrise, his sharp eyes catching the glint of a starship breaking orbit and heading off to unknown sectors. He felt an ache in his heart that threatened to break his soul in half as he watched the starship disappear.

Trapped.

Bitterly he turned his attention from the stars to the spaceport in the distance and its hastily constructed addition. He had been watching for the last three weeks as it was quickly erected from prefabricated materials shipped on an expedited schedule. They starkly contrasted with the graceful architectural wonders that populated much of the Natuzzi skyline these days. The three buildings were almost ugly in comparison. They lacked any sense of design or style. They were functional to a fault.

Nax knew, even before the logo went up, he knew. He couldn't believe it, of course, and until the UPA logo was placed, he thought the buildings were a product of a fever dream, a side effect of the medication he had been prescribed to help deal with the pain of his nearly mortal injuries.

But no, it was real.

Nax glanced around the empty apartment assigned to him, far away from the palace and the planet's capital. At least, it was as real as anything else he might have observed.

He had tried to inquire about the structure, but none of the medical aides assigned to him would share any news. He wasn't sure if this was because they didn't know anything or, more likely, they had been instructed not to share anything. Considering none of the consoles in his humble apartment had any access to the Natuzzi data feeds, he found it safe to assume it was the latter.

Kinlin Nax may have been alive, spared an ugly and barbaric execution, but he was clearly still a prisoner.

He watched as a shuttle took off from the spaceport, the UPA Fleet logo impossible to make out from this distance, but the shuttle's design was unmistakable. The buildings, while still being constructed, were obviously nearly done and, more importantly, occupied.

The United Planetary Alliance had a presence on Natuzzi.

Even if there had been anyone for Nax to speak with, he would have been speechless.

He searched his mind, trying to recall a passage from a history book he had read nearly two decades ago, and he shook his head, giving up. Historical information like that was most likely available on his consoles. It didn't matter, though; he knew the quick answer: It had been hundreds of years since anyone other than the Natuzzi had established any kind of presence in this sector, much less this planet.

Nax leaned forward, folding his hands under his chin, watching the construction drones put the finishing touches on the UPA buildings.

"What have you done?" he whispered.

"Happy birthday."

Nax turned his chair around at the sound of the new voice.

The woman who stood inside his apartment was tall and slender. She was dressed in what could have been mistaken for a simple blue gown, save for the small diamonds that sparkled gently from the hem that hovered just below her knees. The gown's sleeves were intended to be worn long, but the woman had rolled them to her elbows, creating an illusion of casual familiarity that her body language warned against. Her orange skin had grown slightly lighter since he had last seen her. But, of course, that last visit had been two decades ago.

Nax searched her eyes before saying anything. He wasn't sure what he was looking for, and he was even less sure that there was anything he wanted to find.

"Birthday?" Nax said.

She nodded and stepped out onto the balcony with him. "You've lost track of time?"

Again, Nax paused before answering, reading her body language. Time changed everyone, and he suspected that his sister had changed more than he could have possibly imagined.

He turned back to the UPA buildings in the distance. "It would seem I have."

Gouren Ril folded her arms and gently nodded her head. "You've found something else to keep your attention?"

"No," Nax replied. "The passage of time simply hasn't been a concern."

She watched him, studying his profile. "Time has treated you well, brother."

Nax tapped at the arm of his wheelchair and said nothing.

"That has less to do with time and more to do with unfortunate circumstances," Ril said.

"Unfortunate circumstances." Nax made a sound that could be, if generous, described as a laugh. "What are you doing here?"

Ril arched her brow. "What am I doing here? Has your memory been damaged along with your sense of time?"

Nax didn't reply.

"The doctors say that you're doing well," she continued after a moment.

"I would imagine that's subjective."

"According to your physician, you had lost nearly a third of your blood," Ril said. "The knife was tipped with poison and pierced one of your lungs. You nearly died."

"Nearly."

"Our ancestors were watching over you," Ril said.

"It would seem that somebody was," Nax agreed.

Ril took a deep breath and took the empty seat in the corner of the balcony. "If you'll pardon my forwardness, brother, but I'm sensing some hostility."

He glanced at her from the corner of his eye.

She held up her hand. "I'm not the one who condemned you to a nearly forgotten dungeon where a religious zealot lay in wait to kill you."

Nax simply grunted and turned his focus back to the UPA structure. One of the construction drones, finished with its assignment, disappeared as it descended to the ground.

"I am the one, however, who found you on death's door and made sure to keep you from crossing over that threshold," she added.

"So I've been told," Nax said.

"Ah." Ril nodded. "So you've been told."

"It was apparently the one thing my nursemaids were allowed to communicate to me."

She shrugged. "It didn't seem fair to let you wallow in an unnecessary mystery."

"How magnanimous of you," Nax replied. "And what has our mother said about this? I can't imagine that she's pleased with your actions."

When Ril didn't respond, he turned to look at her, misreading the expression on her face.

"She doesn't know yet." Nax nodded. "Of course. That's

why I'm hidden away out here. Set aside, perhaps, as a weapon for you to use against her?" He gestured at the UPA addition to the skyline. "It's nice to know that despite the obvious changes, there are still some things that can be counted on."

Ril crossed her legs, pressing her palms against the silky surface of her dress. "Not exactly." Her voice suddenly had a coarseness to it that Nax couldn't identify.

Nax raised his brow in confusion. "How so?"

Ril avoided his gaze for a moment, choosing to watch the twin moons of Natuzzi disappear for the day. She took a deep breath and slowly exhaled. She turned back to Nax and said, "The Queen is dead."

Nax just stared at her, unresponsive. "Well, that is certainly unexpected."

Ril arched her brow. "This wasn't the reaction I was expecting."

"As you already pointed out, the Queen and I weren't on good terms."

"And now she's dead."

"So, in a way, our relationship has improved dramatically," Nax replied.

Ril pursed her lips, studying him carefully, "That seems a bit, cold. She was still our mother."

Nax shrugged. "She also condemned me to a forgotten dungeon."

"The attempt on your life hadn't been authorized by her."

"Is that supposed to make me feel sad that she's no longer with us?" Nax asked.

Ril shrugged. "I'm not sure. Apparently, your time away has...altered your emotional responses."

Nax scoffed under his breath. "What happened?"

"That's what I was going to ask you."

"How did the Queen die?" Nax clarified.

Ril plucked at the small stones across the hem of her dress. "She was murdered."

"Murdered." Nax nodded. "By whom?"

"That is..." she paused for a moment, studying the back of her hand, "in dispute."

Nax frowned. "Dispute?"

Ril exhaled and rubbed her hands together. "There have been no less than three different groups claiming credit."

"Obviously, she wasn't as popular as she believed herself to be."

"Or perhaps she was just popular in a different way," Ril suggested.

Nax paused for a moment, studying his sister. "If we're going to comment on unusual reactions, I would be remiss if I didn't comment on yours."

"I've been living with this news longer than you," Ril said. "Also, I'm the queen now."

"Long live the Queen," Nax murmured.

"Yes. Long live me."

"May you live longer than the previous head that wore the crown."

She tilted her head to the side, looking at him. "There's clearly something on your mind. You might as well say it."

"I'm just...processing," Nax replied carefully.

"Processing," Ril repeated.

"If the queen is dead, what am I doing out here?" he asked, gesturing to the apartment.

"Despite your stay of execution, you're still considered public enemy number one. Although," she glanced out at the UPA buildings. "There are others competing for that title."

Nax leaned forward, folding his hands across his lap. "Then perhaps I should rephrase: Why am I still alive?"

Ril turned back to him in surprise. "I beg your pardon?"

"What benefit is it to you to keep me alive?" Nax asked. "After all, I had been shoved into a forgotten dungeon with a murderous, religious zealot. Letting me die would have done nothing for you or against you. There would have been zero effect. In fact, an argument could be made that leaving me down there would have helped you establish your new administration."

Ril frowned, staring at him with open disdain. "Brother, you have an interesting way of showing gratitude. Is this something else you learned during your time away? Because I can't say I care for it."

"Gratitude."

She pointed at him. "You would be dead right now had I not come for you."

Nax just stared at her.

Ril folded her arms. "A 'thank you' wouldn't be considered out of order."

Nax sat back in his wheelchair. "Thank you," he said. His voice was devoid of any real sense of gratitude.

She clutched a hand to her heart in mock gratitude. "That's all I ask for."

"I'm still a prisoner."

Ril dropped her hand. "Of course you are. In case you've forgotten, you've committed terrible crimes against the people of Natuzzi."

"I fell in love with a woman."

"Who was not of Natuzzi." She wagged her finger at him.

"That's still frowned upon. Our mother's death hasn't changed that."

Nax gestured at the UPA structures. "But some things have changed in the wake of the queen's passing."

"Yes, some things," Ril replied, sounding slightly strained.

"So if I'm still a prisoner, why not just leave me in the dungeon?" Nax asked.

"You don't appreciate the view?"

"I prefer my bars to be literal and not metaphorical."

Ril shook her head. "You're here as a gesture of good faith."

"Good faith?"

"The UPA Fleet wants to establish a base here to facilitate Fleet vessels moving into Veneer space," Ril said.

Nax looked at the hastily constructed buildings. "And you agreed to this?"

"We were on the verge of a war that we had no chance of winning," Ril replied defensively.

"Not according to the queen," Nax pointed out.

"Yes, well, her weapon of mass destruction was less controllable than advertised."

Nax turned back to her. "What happened?"

"The weapon returned to Veneer space," Ril explained. "At last report, it has established a stationary orbit around Veneer Prime, essentially becoming a new moon."

"That doesn't explain what happened."

She held out her hands, palms up. "It gives you the same information that I have."

"So the Alliance is here."

"The Alliance is here." Ril nodded and looked up at the sky. "In fact, your old ship just departed for Veneer space this morning. Perhaps you saw it."

Nax remembered the departing star from the sunrise earlier. "The *Defiance*..."

"Yes," Ril replied as if suddenly remembering the ship's name. "I didn't speak with any of them personally, but as I understand it, they asked about you."

Everything clicked into place.

"A gesture of good faith," Nax said, not bothering to hide the bitterness in his voice.

Ril got to her feet. "There's no need to be upset about it."

"I'm still a prisoner."

"Of course you're still a prisoner," she replied. "But better a prison like this than trapped in a cell drowning in your own blood."

"A cell is still a cell whether or not the bars are visible."

Ril sighed. "You're going to have to accept there's no chance of you leaving Natuzzi again."

"Perish the thought," he replied. "After all, I may fall in love with another offworlder."

Ril stood in the opening between the balcony and the rest of the apartment, her back to him. Her shoulders sagged. "You don't have to be a bastard about it."

"I thought you were the queen," Nax said.

She turned back to him, her eyes blazing. "I am. And while I don't agree with many of the messes our mother created, I can't say that I disagree with the judgment against you."

Nax didn't speak for a moment. "I see." He looked down at his hands. "And what is the nature of the good faith gesture?"

"The UPA wanted to know that you were being treated humanely."

"Humanely," he echoed hollowly.

"They also insisted on a liaison."

Nax looked. "A liaison?"

She gestured at the apartment's front door as it opened.

A familiar blonde-haired woman stepped into the apartment. She smiled at Nax. "Well, aren't you a sight for sore eyes?"

Nax returned the smile. It was the first genuine sense of joy he had felt since returning to Natuzzi. "As are you, Sadie Sadler, as are you."

5

THE DEFIANCE

BRODERICK COOPER STARED at his reflection in the small mirror, focusing on the badge on the left side of his chest. The extra pip, rounding the total to four, stood out like a sore thumb. There wasn't anything unusual about it; it matched the other three pips perfectly. But the fact that it was there simply felt *off*. He could feel, impossible as it seemed, the extra weight of that fourth pip.

Cooper took a deep breath and glanced down at the communicator sitting on the counter. "Captain's log, supplemental."

The red light indicating that the recording had paused, turned green. Cooper picked up the communicator and stepped out of the bathroom.

"I don't know if I like being a captain." He looked around the bedroom, which was more spacious than he thought it would be. It still seemed like a stranger's room. His duffel bag lay in the corner between the bed and the wall, still packed. Despite having been on the *Defiance* for nearly three months, he hadn't bothered to unpack. Cooper set the communicator down on the bed as he grabbed his boots and pulled them on. "I should rephrase that. I don't know if I like being captain of a *starship*. There's a sense of...." He trailed off, resting his elbows on the back of his legs as he stared at the blank wall across from his bed. He should put something on that wall. "I don't know what to call it. Lack of permanence. Is there a word for that? A starship is constantly moving; it has no home, no berth, and no permanent residence. The starship *is* home."

Cooper got up, grabbed the communicator, and stepped out into the living room of his quarters. Here there was a single window looking out into the emptiness of space.

"I don't like it."

Cooper folded his arms, searching the void of space for something familiar, the dim light of a distant star, but, of course, when you're traveling faster than light, there was nothing to be seen.

"This is supposed to be my home now, I guess," he continued. "But I don't like it. A home should have, at the very least, a sky to look up into." He sighed. "And I guess that's the problem with space; there are no skies."

He stared down at his communicator.

"Pause recording."

The indicator light turned red.

"There are no skies in space?" Cooper repeated. He looked up at his reflection in the window. "That sounds stupid. Are you an idiot now? Are you going space crazy already? Three months and you're losing your damn mind?" Cooper shook his head. "Dumbass," he muttered. "Resume recording."

The indicator light turned green.

Cooper turned away from the window. "I think when I had envisioned my first command, it was going to be something more administrative. I had my eyes set on the Belarus station. Or maybe even one of the FitzRoy class science ships. Instead, somehow I'm in charge of a damn *spy* ship." He shook his head again. "I hate spy shit. For some reason, it was a constant point of contention between my dad and me because I wouldn't read those stupid spy thrillers he was always harping on about. He grew up reading Frank Fletcher, and apparently, he spent every day of his adult life anxiously waiting for the moment when I would be old enough to be introduced to the womanizing spy known as Felix Flint. I was sixteen when I read the first one and immediately pegged the entire series, nearly twenty-one books and twice as many damn movies, as infantile, sexist, racist, populist trash. My dad wouldn't talk to me for almost a week after that."

Cooper paused. He stared at the communicator in his hand, an image of his father so clear in his head that he had to smile.

"Now I'm living one of those stupid books. My old man would be so proud of me." Cooper ran a hand across his face tiredly.

"Damn it," he muttered.

Around him, the ship groaned slightly. He didn't react this time. The groaning, rattling creaks of the ship had become almost background noises at this point.

"I guess my problem is," Cooper continued, "I can't tell if I'm supposed to be a captain or a spy. And if I'm somehow supposed to be both, how can I manage that? Whatever criticisms I had of Captain Mitchell, he clearly knew his role on this ship and managed it successfully. Or, at least, that's what the crew believed. There's always the possibility he didn't know what he was doing either, and that's why he's dead, and I'm not.

"Pause recording." Cooper looked at the comm again.

"Damn it, I am an asshole." He pinched the bridge of his nose and took a breath before continuing. "Resume recording. I don't know what the hell I'm doing. That's nothing new, I suppose. Most first-time captains don't know what they're doing either. I'm trying to do my best to project an air of confidence to the crew. I don't know if it's working. I think most of the crew is still under the impression that I stole this command from Mitchell. I don't know what I can do to correct that impression. I don't know if it's worth the effort, either.

"Stop recording."

The indicator light turned off, and Cooper hesitated for a moment before swiping his thumb across the screen and deleting the audio file.

"Stupid," he muttered. He slipped the communicator into the pocket on his upper arm and grabbed the datapad from his desk.

He paused in front of his door one last time, adjusting the collar of his uniform. Satisfied that it was about as good as it would get, he opened the doors and stepped out into the corridor, where he immediately nearly ran into an immovable object.

Cooper jerked back at the last second into the door of his quarters and looked up in surprise.

"Mr. Zemble."

The Elwat tilted his head in greeting. "Captain."

Cooper took a second to compose himself. "Good morning."

Zemble took a step back. "I surprised you."

"Well, I certainly wasn't expecting you outside my quarters," Cooper said.

"I thought this would be a good time to go over some issues before the meeting."

"Issues?" Cooper asked, stepping out into the corridor.

"Administrative," Zemble clarified.

Cooper nodded. "Right. Administrative. And you thought it was better to just surprise me outside my quarters?"

"My mistake was that I didn't anticipate the possibility of you exiting while attempting to use the call button."

"Your only mistake?"

Zemble arched his brow but didn't respond.

Cooper waved the datapad at him. "I trust that, despite your promotion to first officer, you still have access to the ship's communication systems, yes?"

Zemble nodded. "I see how I might have made a second mistake."

"I'm glad I could help you come to this realization, Commander."

"In my defense, I didn't want to come across as nagging."

"Nagging?'"

"It's a term often used to describe an individual who is constantly harassing another individual to do something."

Cooper rolled his eyes. "I'm familiar with the term."

"I thought as much," Zemble replied. "But I didn't want to run the risk of making another poorly timed assumption."

Cooper gave him a sideways look. "You seem to be extra..snippy today, Mr. Zemble."

"Apologies, Captain."

Cooper waved off the apology. "You haven't said anything out of line, yet."

"I like to see how far I can push against that line before I actually cross it."

"Make a note, then."

"Yes?"

"You're getting pretty damn close."

Zemble nodded. "Noted."

Cooper gestured down the corridor. "What administrative issues have got you so concerned you felt the need to arrive at my quarters unannounced before my shift starts?"

"To be fair, you are the captain," Zemble said.

"Oh? Am I? When did this happen?"

Now it was Zemble's turn to give him a sideways glance.

Cooper coughed into his hand. "I thought we were building a safe space where we felt comfortable enough to be sarcastic to one another?"

"You did?"

"Clearly, I'm reconsidering the thought now."

"I don't know that I feel that comfortable with you yet, Captain."

"Yeah, it didn't feel great to me either. What's your point about me being captain?"

"You are essentially always on shift."

Cooper's shoulders sagged for a moment before he straightened out as they rounded a corner. "Yeah, that's definitely going to get some taking used to. So, what's on your plate, Mr. Zemble?"

Zemble held up his datapad. "Duty rosters."

"Duty rosters?" Cooper looked at him with mild disbelief. "I thought this was heading in a very different direction."

"And what direction was that?"

"Something less mundane than duty rosters."

"I did warn you that it was administrative."

"What's wrong with the duty rosters?"

"Specifically, you keep doing them."

They reached the lift, and Cooper tapped the call button. "I'm sorry?"

"Typically, it's the first officer's responsibility to construct the duty rosters," Zemble explained.

"And you're upset I'm taking work off your plate?"

The lift arrived, and the two men got on board.

"I'm not upset," Zemble said.

"Deck Six," Cooper said, and the lift started to rise. "You showed up unannounced outside my quarters to confront me about it."

Zemble clasped his hands in front of him. "I'm not confronting you."

"What do you call it?"

"You're the captain."

"It was a joke earlier when I said I had forgotten."

"You have other responsibilities," Zemble continued.

"I'm aware of what my responsibilities are, Commander," Cooper replied, his voice getting testy.

"Apparently, you're not, though," Zemble said, ignoring the change in Cooper's tone. "You're the ship's captain, and at any given moment, you have at least fifteen different things competing for your attention."

"Right now, it just feels like one."

"You haven't checked your calendar for the day," Zemble said.

"You have a point beyond complaining that I'm not giving you enough work?"

"I'm not complaining that you're not giving me enough work," Zemble said. "I'm trying to bring it to your attention that you're giving yourself too much. Let me take care of the duty rosters."

"It doesn't take me that long."

"That's not the point."

"It also allows me the opportunity to get familiar with the crew," Cooper said.

"You've been captain almost three months," Zemble said. "At this point, you're as familiar as you're going to get."

"Is that why you're bringing this up now?"

"It's one of the reasons."

"What's another?"

Zemble looked at him. "I don't need my captain distracted with administrative paperwork when he needs to be focused on more important things."

"Such as?"

"We're the first UPA ship entering Veneer space in almost a century," Zemble said. "There's the potential for at least one or two diplomatic disasters a day."

Cooper held up two fingers. "Second."

"Excuse me?"

"We're the second ship," Cooper said. "The *Reliant* crossed over two days ago."

"What happened?"

Cooper shrugged. "I don't know."

"They were supposed to be a day behind us."

"And now they're two days ahead of us," Cooper said. "We're supposed to rendezvous with them outside the Kuma system."

Zemble grunted. "Perhaps if you weren't so busy with duty rosters, you would have thought to share this information with me sooner."

"Maybe," Cooper conceded. "Or maybe I figured it wasn't relevant to you doing your job."

The two men stared at each other for a few seconds before Zemble grunted again and turned his attention back to the door.

"I didn't anticipate this relationship being so antagonistic," Cooper said.

"It's nothing personal."

"Oh?"

"Apparently, I have a habit of picking fights with all of my immediate superiors."

"Picking fights?"

"Pushing boundaries is perhaps a more politically correct way to describe it."

"I think it's what I'll put in the log."

"Point is," Zemble continued, "you really need to let me take care of the duty rosters."

Cooper sighed. "Look, I understand your concerns. But..." Cooper paused. "Permission to speak a little freely with you, Commander?"

"I think that's supposed to be my line," Zemble said.

"The duty rosters are the one thing on this ship that I feel like I can do without screwing anything up," Cooper said. "I was not prepared for this command."

"I don't think anyone would be," Zemble said.

"Our upcoming mission is essentially a series of first contact missions," Cooper said. "I don't know the first thing about first contacts. I got a solid C in Professor van Sickle's course back at the Academy."

"Congratulations," Zemble said. "I failed it completely."

"You failed it *completely*?"

"There's a reason I wasn't on the command track," Zemble said.

"If you don't mind me asking...?"

"Apparently, you're not supposed to use first-contact situations as opportunities to spread the word about Jesus Christ."

Cooper gaped at him. "You did what now?"

"I wrote a paper."

"A paper?"

"I thought it was a particularly well-written paper," Zemble said.

"And in this particularly well-written paper...?"

"I posited that evangelical missionaries were ideal candidates for first contact scenarios."

"And Professor van Sickle failed you?"

"Aggressively so."

The lift reached deck six, and the two men stepped off.

"Wow," Cooper said. "That is...not what I expected at all."

"Duty rosters are not first-contact situations, though," Zemble said, bringing them back on topic.

"No, they are not," Cooper agreed.

"Permission to speak freely?"

"You're right. Now that I hear it, it is your line. Granted."

"Now's as good a time as any to stop hiding behind excuses like that."

Cooper chewed the inside of his cheek. "I'll take it under consideration. Now, since you've opened this door."

"What door would that be?" Zemble asked, suspicious.

"We need a new Chief Tactical Officer."

"You already have one," Zemble replied.

Cooper looked at him; his lips wrinkled in disapproval. "Mr. Zemble, I'd rather not have my First Officer pulling double duty."

"I'd rather be surfing the twin black holes of Fazanama Five."

Cooper raised his eyebrows. "I'm sorry?"

"I thought we were sharing things that would never happen."

Cooper pointed at him. "You brought this on yourself."

"It's clearly something you've been considering for some time now."

"And you've given me the perfect opportunity to address it. As I understand, we have a couple of viable candidates to take over the position."

Zemble made a grumbling noise of discontent in the back of his throat. Cooper ignored it.

"Dyslin, Kucharski, and Sokol are qualified," Cooper continued. "And, as I understand it, Dyslin's long overdue for a promotion."

"Dyslin's long overdue because he doesn't have any people skills."

"Apparently, neither do I," Cooper said. "And yet, here I am. Seems to have worked out pretty well for me."

"I haven't seen you emotionally cripple a lieutenant because they loaded a weapon's locker incorrectly," Zemble said.

"That..." Cooper paused for a second. "I'm sorry; what happened?"

"Lieutenant Kahn requested to be transferred after it was determined that he was suffering PTSD after that interaction with Dyslin."

"Fine. Okay. So not Dyslin. That still leaves Kucharski and Sokol unless you're going to tell me they're awful people as well."

"They're fine people. Excellent officers."

"Great. Then tell me which one should get the job."

"Neither one of them has security clearance."

"Security clearance."

"Don't tell me you forgot about that, as well."

Cooper snorted and shook his head. "You really have this sass thing down, don't you."

Zemble grunted. "It's a blessing and a curse. Neither Kucharski nor Sokol will get the necessary security clearance."

"And why's that?"

"Because while they're both excellent officers, Sokol has a cousin who runs with the Blysk mercenaries out of the Alazar system, and Kucharski used to be married to a Sweezakaalan prostitute."

Cooper dropped his face into his hands.

"Like I said, I have the job under control."

Cooper looked up at him. "Seriously? That's what you want to go with after giving me grief about the duty rosters?"

"You should take it as a good sign that I was able to address that issue with you while still being able to maintain my responsibilities as Chief Tactical Officer."

"Except you're not," Cooper said.

"I'm sorry?"

"My concern isn't about security clearances," Cooper said. "In fact, I don't give a damn about security clearances. Security clearances are an obstacle until they aren't."

"Interesting point of view."

"My primary concern is running this ship." He pointed at Zemble. "Your focus is split because you're trying to do two different jobs."

"Doesn't mean I'm not doing them well."

"Actually, it does," Cooper said. "Part of the reason I took over the duty rosters is that I noticed they weren't getting done until the last minute."

"They were still getting done," Zemble said defensively.

"I had people coming to me wondering where they were supposed to be stationed because the rosters were getting posted late."

Zemble grunted. "Thirty minutes is hardly late."

"It is if it's thirty minutes past when it's supposed to be posted," Cooper said. "We're in the middle of space, Commander. You've logged more hours out here than I have; I shouldn't have to explain to you that if things don't run on time out here, the consequences could result in all of us floating out into the void."

"That's an...extreme take."

"It's space, Mr. Zemble," Cooper said. "It's my personal opinion that extreme is normal out here."

"You're not entirely wrong," Zemble grunted.

"In addition," Cooper continued. "While we were in orbit at Natuzzi, I had three different reports of contraband being found offloaded from the supply shuttles. That sounds like something my Chief Tactical Officer should have been on top of. Specifically, it should have been my Chief Tactical Officer delivering that report to me instead of a Lieutenant who apparently has 'people issues.'"

Zemble didn't say anything, and they walked in silence for a minute.

"You knew I was going to say something to you about the duty rosters," Zemble said eventually.

"I had a suspicion, yes."

"You gave me enough rope to hang myself."

"I find that it can be easier to get my point across if I can have the other party make it for me," Cooper replied.

Zemble nodded. "Well played, Captain."

"Thank you."

"What happens next?"

"Well, we still need a new Chief Tactical Officer, and you already torpedoed my top three choices," Cooper said. "So, guess what?"

"I have to find three new choices."

"Sure. But we only need one. So if you pick the right one the first time, we don't need the other two."

"Interesting technique."

"It worked selecting my first officer."

6

"JAXSON."

"Hang on." Warrick knelt on his bathroom floor, wrestling with the twin heating coils he had pulled from the wall.

"*Jaxson.*"

"I'll have it working in one second."

One of the cables suddenly sparked, and Warrick jerked back, nearly falling over into the cooling bathwater.

"Jaxson. Please. *Stop.*"

Jaxson Warrick finally stopped and turned to face the green-skinned woman standing in the doorway of his bathroom. He pointed the end of one of the heating coils at her. "You said-"

"I know what I said-."

"You wanted-"

"I know what I wanted," she replied. "I was the one who said it."

"I'm just trying-"

Commander Trella Langlois pressed her hands together as if starting to pray. "I want you to stop."

Warrick frowned. "You want–"

"This cannot turn into a *project*."

"A project?"

"Don't play dumb. You know exactly what I'm talking about."

"It's not going to turn into a project."

"Jaxson, you've dismantled the entire heating apparatus of your bath. It's a project. I love a good engineering project. But I didn't come over here for an engineering project." Langlois unzipped the front of her uniform, stopping just below her sternum.

Warrick looked down at the heating coils in his hands, and then he looked back up at the green-skinned woman who had one hand on her hip and the other pulling suggestively at the open front of her uniform. "Right. I don't know what I was thinking."

Warrick tossed the coils over his shoulder and jumped to his feet.

They kissed as they pulled at each other's clothes, stumbling back towards the bed. Langlois managed to kick off one of her boots and then tripped over it. Warrick caught her, and they tumbled to the floor, just short of the bed, bumping into the nightstand as they fell. The two tumblers on the nightstand rolled off, shattering against the floor.

"Sorry," she said breathlessly, rolling on top of him, her fingers working the zipper of his uniform.

"It's fine," Warrick replied. "I never liked those glasses. They were a gift from some Carzalan pond scum."

Langlois lifted her head slightly to look him in the eyes. "Carzalan pond scum?"

"Finkus Spizzich'ino."

She shook her head. "I don't know the name."

"He's a loan shark from Vilas Prime."

She scratched the side of her head. "I'm sorry, but I'm having difficulty tracking this story."

"He owed me money," Warrick explained.

"The Carzalan pond scum loan shark owed *you* money?"

Warrick frowned. "Why is this what we're talking about?"

"Right, fair enough." Langlois shrugged the top of her uniform off.

The comm on the nightstand chirped.

"That's not me," Langlois said. "The *Reliant* knows not to bother me."

Warrick grumbled a Vulderran swear under his breath as he reached for the communicator.

"Seriously?" she said. "We're supposed to be in the middle of something. You know, technically, you are off duty."

"Yeah? How does that work for you?" Warrick asked.

Langlois sighed and slid off, propping herself up against the bed. "Fair point."

"Go ahead," Warrick said, thumbing the comm on.

"Sorry for bothering you, sir," replied a voice from the other side. "It's Ensign Dweck."

"Dweck, do you know what time it is?"

"Uh, yes, I think so."

"You think so?"

"No."

"No?"

"I mean, yes, I know what time it is, sir, Commander, sir."

Langlois laughed silently and shook her head.

Warrick rolled his eyes. "This better be important, Dweck."

"Well, uh, we seem to have, a, uh, problem in the forward fusion cannon."

Warrick waited for him to elaborate, and when he didn't, he said irritably, "Is it a problem that really needs the chief engineer right now? Because I really wasn't planning on getting out of bed until my next shift started. In fact, last time I checked, I had a department of fairly competent officers. If microfilaments in the fusion cannon need to be descaled, I would hope that one of you could figure out how to do that without me looking over your shoulder."

"It's not an issue with the microfilaments in the fusion cannon, sir."

Langlois rested her head on his shoulder and twirled her fingers around his long beard.

"Then what is it?" Warrick asked, clearly growing more distracted by the moment.

There was no response from the other side.

Langlois worked her fingers down from his beard towards his chest, and Warrick was suddenly aware that the ensign on the other end still hadn't said anything.

He grunted and pulled back slightly. "You still there, Ensign?"

"I'm really not sure what I'm supposed to say, sir."

Warrick frowned. "Well, here's a novel idea, if there's a problem that you can't solve, why don't you just tell me what it is or, better yet, take some initiative and figure it out yourself?"

There was another long pause. "Sir, Commander, *it's* happened again."

It took a long second for Dweck's words to pierce Warrick's lust-ridden brain, but when they did, it was like being doused with a wet blanket.

Langlois felt the change in his body. She sat up. "What?" she mouthed.

"Shit," Warrick muttered.

"I shouldn't be showing you this," Warrick said.

"Okay. I'm not sure how I'm supposed to react to that," Langlois replied.

They were both dressed in their Fleet uniforms. Warrick stopped them in the corridor outside the doors to the forward fusion cannon.

"This is considered...." Warrick paused, looking for the right words. "Top secret."

Langlois arched an eyebrow. "Top secret? Oh, this should be interesting."

"I'm showing you this out of professional courtesy."

"Professional courtesy," she repeated with a strong note of doubt.

"And also probably because I couldn't come up with a reasonable story for you not to be curious after hearing what you heard."

"Technically, I didn't hear anything," she pointed out.

"You heard enough."

She tilted her head in agreement. "That's true."

"Enough to nag me until I told you anyway."

"Nag you?" Langlois clucked her tongue disapprovingly. "I don't nag. I'm not a nagger. I've never nagged anyone." She waved a hand down her body. "Do you see this body? I don't need to nag."

Warrick held up both of his hands, eager not to get himself stuck in an argument he wasn't going to win. "Professional courtesy."

"Professional courtesy."

"From one chief engineer to another," Warrick said. "Keep this out of your logs and to yourself." He paused and then added, "Please."

She folded her arms across her chest. "Well, now I'm *really* curious."

"Seriously, I'm warning you, if even a hint of this ends up in your logs," Warrick said, "we're both getting court-martialed."

Langlois gave an impatient groan. "*Enough* with the foreplay already. I'm primed. I'm *ready*. Let's do this."

Warrick waited a second and then pointed down the corridor to the lift. "If you want, you can just return to my quarters and pretend none of this ever happened."

"Stop it." She pushed past him, slapping her hand against the control panel next to the doors. There was a loud groaning noise as the double doors slid open. She looked at him and shook her head. "It's truly amazing that this ship hasn't fallen apart yet."

"Well, hang on," Warrick said, gesturing for her to step inside. "You ain't seen nothing yet."

Langlois started to fire off another retort, but the words died off as she stepped into the room.

Located against the exterior hull of deck eight, the forward fusion cannon was a complex series of chromium plasma tubes connected to a neogenic capacitor. They ran the length of the room, and when the ship was in active combat, the temperature in the room was known to reach one hundred and twenty degrees Fahrenheit.

Today, however, things looked very different.

"What the actual *shtik drek*," Langlois gasped, gaping at the inexplicable sight before her.

The entire fusion cannon array was *gone*. It had been

replaced with something...else. Something that was attempting to pass itself off as the fusion cannon.

Langlois was dumbfounded in every sense of the word. Her mind tried to wrap itself around the notion of what she was seeing. It tried to catalog it and then apply a rational set of physics laws to it. But whatever was happening before her refused to allow itself to be placed into a box that would allow for any traditional understanding.

It was an oily black substance that appeared to be constantly moving, undulating, as tendrils crisscrossed back and forth, creating a black skeleton of what, presumably, was intended to be the fusion cannon array. It seemed to be excreting from the hull itself. Everything that Langlois understood to be true about the universe and its very nature suggested that the substance was organic. Except that if it was organic...

Langlois slapped her hands on either side of her face and dragged them down her cheeks. "*Ayin kafin yan.*"

From across the room, Lt. Jared Carole looked up from a plasma tube that was slowly being formed by the black substance. Each new black thread caused the tube to come into sharper focus. He looked at Langlois, then made eye contact with Warrick and raised a wordless eyebrow.

"Don't worry about it," Warrick said.

"Sure," Carole replied, coming from around the nightmare image of what was now the fusion cannon. "That sounds like something that won't get us in trouble."

There were only two other engineers in the room, Ensign Dweck being one of them. Each of them carefully scanning a section of the cannon that was being rebuilt by the black tendrils.

"Trouble is relative these days," Warrick said, eyeing the unholy nightmare taking place on his ship.

"Sure," Carole agreed. "But assuming we survive this, I don't want to have my record tarnished by your questionable command decisions."

"I don't understand," Langlois said, her voice barely above a whisper.

"Join the club," Warrick said.

She started to reach and touch the nearest surface, but Warrick caught her hand before she did.

"I wouldn't do that," he warned her.

"Why?"

Warrick hesitated a second before answering. "Honestly? Because there's a fifty/fifty chance you wouldn't survive the experience."

Langlois took an extra step back. "Now I have more questions."

Warrick turned to Carole. "Well?"

"Same as before," Carole replied, holding the datapad in his hand. "The entire thing was broken down, and she's been reassembling it."

"How long?"

Carole checked his datapad. "About twenty minutes. I don't have any hard data on this, but I feel like she's moving slower. As if there's something tripping her up about the assembly of the cannon."

"Maybe she shouldn't have taken it apart in the first place," Warrick said.

"That seems like a sound suggestion," Carole said. "You have an idea how we might pass it along?"

Warrick glared at him.

"I wasn't intending that as a joke," Carole said.

"I know," Warrick said. "That's what makes it worse." He turned back to Langlois, whose expression hadn't changed. "Well?"

"Well, what?" she asked. "I feel like I'm in the middle of a damn fever dream." She watched as the exterior shell of the cannon started to take shape and then abruptly stopped. It slowly disassembled, the tendrils unraveling like a loose thread being pulled. She watched as the interior circuitry followed suit. When everything had been stripped away, the tiny tendrils paused, their tips flickering back and forth in the air as if considering...*something*. Then, moving forward again, as if held by invisible hands, the tendrils slowly began rebuilding the cannon from the inside out. "What is happening to your ship, Jaxson?"

7

COOPER LOOKED up as Warrick entered the conference room and took his seat across from Zemble.

"Nice of you to finally join us, Mr. Warrick," Cooper said.

"Sorry," Warrick replied. "But I've been trying to keep this ship from turning into a floating pile of Unity sludge."

"And how's that working out?" Cooper asked.

"I'd say not great," Warrick said. "But I guess technically, we're not a collection of Unity sludge floating through the vacuum of space yet, so maybe I don't know what I'm talking about."

"Maybe," Cooper agreed. "What's happened now?"

Warrick leaned back in his seat. "The forward fusion cannon is currently being reassembled."

Cooper pursed his lips and raised an eyebrow. "Is this going to be a problem?"

Warrick shrugged. "Well, we still have the rear fusion cannons and a full complement of torpedoes that haven't been affected yet. But, realistically, I'd like to avoid running into anybody who might want to shoot at us."

A brief expression of uncertainty passed across Cooper's face. "As would I."

Cooper took a moment to compose himself and then addressed the rest of the room.

"Okay, let's start with the elephant in the room," Cooper said. "You're my new senior staff. For those of you who just got promoted, congratulations. I would hope you all know each other, considering most of you have been stationed on this ship longer than I have, but I don't believe in making assumptions. That being said, I think everybody here has done the math and realized that Commander Warrick is our Chief Engineer. So, we'll start with somebody else." Cooper gestured to the large Elwat on his right. "This is First Officer Commander Zemble."

Zemble glanced around the table and simply grunted.

Cooper turned to the dark-skinned woman sitting on Zemble's left. She was in her thirties, slender, with sharp, almost angular features. "Lieutenant Lea Tully, our new Chief Helmsman."

Tully gave a sarcastic salute. "Hi there."

Cooper gestured to the next officer down. He was a Knoksian. He had a lanky form, dark purple skin, and two antennae extending from beneath his jet-black hair. "Lieutenant Commander Askon is now the head of our Science Department. As I understand it, the *Defiance* has been missing a Chief Science Officer for some time now, a situation I believe to be borderline criminal. I find it questionable that Captain Mitchell–"

Zemble grunted again.

Cooper pressed his lips together tightly and inhaled through his nose. "It has been suggested to me that I spend too much time publicly criticizing your former captain and that it would perhaps better endear me to the crew if I stopped." Cooper took a deep breath and placed his hands on the table's surface. "Fortunately, I don't particularly give a damn what you people think of me. Last time I checked, I'm the captain, and you're not. If you don't like the fact that I have problems with how Captain Mitchell ran this ship, you have two options: request a transfer or build a time machine and go back in time and tell Mitchell to do a better job."

Cooper looked around the table, waiting to see if anybody would respond.

"That's not exactly what I had in mind," Zemble said under his breath.

"Yeah, well, expectations were made to be disappointed." Cooper turned to Askon. "Mr. Askon, I've heard nothing but amazing things about you. As far as I'm concerned, this promotion is long overdue."

Askon tilted his head forward. If he was at all bothered by the tone in the room, he didn't show it. "Thank you, Captain."

Cooper turned his attention to the left side of the table and focused on the woman in the white coat at the far end. "Doctor Marlize Dheer."

"I'm not the Chief Medical Officer for this ship," she said, cutting him off.

"You're about to be."

Dheer looked at him in surprise. "I beg your pardon?"

Cooper held the tablet. "Doctor Rabkin has put in a transfer request, and I'm inclined to approve it. Unfortunately, while I can't deny that he's a valuable resource in our current situation, I'd rather not have a doctor on board that I will have to fight with every ten minutes. So when he returns from Captain Mitchell's funeral, he'll be tasked with bringing you up to speed. As for when he's actually going to be leaving us, I haven't decided yet. I'm waiting for an appropriate opportunity to present itself."

"You think that's likely to happen the farther we get from UPA territory?" Zemble asked.

Cooper shrugged. "I won't lie; I considered signing off on the transfer and shipping the rest of his belongings out to him."

"But?" Zemble asked.

"But nothing," Cooper replied. "I considered it and then changed my mind."

"Are we allowed to ask why you changed your mind?" Warrick asked.

"You certainly are," Cooper said. "But I'm not required to give you an answer." He tapped the dull gold badge over his left breast. "I'm the captain."

"That's not the word I would use," Warrick muttered.

Cooper ignored him. "Okay, so that's everybody. Excluding, of course, a new Chief Tactical Officer and a new third shift commander. Apparently, my pool of options around here is limited," Cooper said. "Everybody's concerned about bringing on new officers and how they might react to the ship being taken over by some human/Unity hybrid creature." Cooper looked around the awkwardly silent table and frowned. "That was supposed to be a joke."

"Was it supposed to be a funny one?" Warrick asked.

Cooper ignored him and clapped his hands together. "All right, now that introductions are out of the way and we're all on the same page. Let's get started."

A projection of a giant planet materialized above the table. Veneer Prime.

"So, thanks to our new treaty with the Natuzzi, and given

the recent events, the President has decided it's time for the UPA to reach out to the Veneer."

"Nobody's heard from the Veneer in almost a hundred years," Warrick said. "And not for lack of trying. They've just made it very clear they're not interested in talking."

"It's actually much worse than that." Cooper gestured for Zemble to take over.

"About twelve months ago, long-range sensors suggested the entirety of Veneer Prime went dark," Zemble said.

"Dark?" Dheer raised an eyebrow.

"No signals in, no signals out," Zemble clarified. "Their entire digital infrastructure went silent. Other planets within the sector reached out to Veneer Prime without response. Fleet Intel has discreetly reached out and received reports from within the sector, and they all say the same thing: Nobody's home on Veneer Prime."

Dheer looked back and forth between Zemble and Cooper. "What does that mean?"

"That's what the president wants to know," Cooper said. "Among other things. Without any clear power structure in place, the Oxean Syndicate has been moving to expand their operations beyond the Neutral Zone and into the remains of the Veneer Empire."

"Remains of the Veneer Empire?" Warrick raised his eyebrows. "That escalated damn quickly."

Cooper held out his hands, palms up. "We're not sure there's a better way to describe it. We've managed to locate a small handful of Imperial ships, but according to the chatter, their fleet is on the verge of being abandoned. Without any communication from their home planet, they've been unable to coordinate anything, and they have no way to replenish any of their ships' resources."

"And has it occurred to any of these impoverished vessels to simply go home?" Askon asked. His voice had a soft, angelic ring to it.

"Intelligence believes they're afraid," Zemble said. "And, honestly, I don't blame them. If my home world suddenly went dark, I'd be pretty scared, too."

"This has to do with their alliance with the Unity," Warrick said. "Right?"

Zemble and Cooper shared a look.

"Yes," Zemble said slowly. "That's what Directive Fifty-Two believes."

"And the president?" Dheer asked.

"I don't know what the president believes," Cooper replied flatly.

"That's an interesting way to phrase it," Dheer said.

"Do you think there's a better way to answer your question?"

Dheer paused for a moment, studying Cooper's expression. "Does he know about the Unity?"

The silence that followed, while brief, was still longer than it needed to be.

"I don't know what he does or does not know," Cooper said.

"That seems..." Dheer trailed off.

"It's not my place to ask the President of the United Planetary Alliance if he's been kept current with any highly classified dossiers involving high-level threats against the UPA. You can see how that might be...*awkward* at best."

"Yeah," Dheer said. "I think so."

"I think what Doctor Dheer is trying to get at is that you were dispatched to the *Defiance* at the behest of President D'Ambra," Zemble said. "It seems reasonable to assume that you've passed along a detailed report of what's happened on this ship."

"I thought I was clear about how I felt regarding assumptions," Cooper said tersely. He looked around the table, making eye contact with every officer. "I'm not here to tattletale to the president every five minutes. I might have been given this assignment because of the president, but that doesn't mean he's my priority. My priority is this *ship*, this *crew,* and our *mission*. If any of that overlaps with the president, so be it." He paused and then added, "But thus far, it hasn't."

"Nice speech," Warrick said.

"Well, I thought so," Tully added. Everybody looked at her, and she added, "And I actually mean that sincerely, not sarcastically." An embarrassed expression passed across her face.

"Here's what we can be certain the president knows: the Veneer Empire is in disarray, and if somebody doesn't plant their flag over there, the situation will only get worse," Cooper said.

Dheer leaned back in her seat. "That's interesting."

"How so?" Cooper asked.

Dheer shrugged. "I wasn't aware the UPA had entered a state of territorial expansion."

Cooper gave a tired sigh. "None of you are going to make this easy, are you?"

"I thought I was doing a pretty good job," Zemble replied.

Cooper snorted under his breath and turned back to Dheer. "I think everyone would prefer to start with offering help before taking on a more aggressive approach."

Now Dheer was genuinely surprised. "Is the president

actually considering the option of annexing the Veneer Empire?"

"Well, right now, it's not like there's an actual Veneer Empire to annex," Cooper said. "And I have no idea what the president is considering. I don't know how else to get this through your thick skulls, but the president and I aren't best buddies. In fact, I think I've had a total of three conversations with him."

"That's three more than I'm going to get," Warrick said.

Cooper started to open his mouth when Tully cut in. "Who are we offering help to?" she asked.

Cooper chose to take the out. "The Veneer, hopefully. And if not them," he shrugged, "Anybody else in their sector that might be interested in establishing a calming, authoritative presence."

Tully opened her mouth and then closed it.

"You have something to say, Lieutenant?" Cooper asked.

She shook her head. "No, sir."

"You're senior staff now," he said. "If you have something to say, you shouldn't be afraid to say it."

Tully paused and then looked at him, frowning. "I was thinking that your answer didn't help dismiss the notion that we're an advance guard for expanding the Alliance's borders."

Cooper shook his head. "I genuinely don't know how Mitchell put up with you people." He gestured for Zemble to continue.

The projection of Veneer Prime disappeared and was replaced with a star map of the sector known as the Veneer Empire.

"The Veneer need very specific atmospheric conditions to survive," Zemble said. "Because of this, despite the fact that the Veneer Empire occupies one of the largest sections of our quadrant, there are only six planets they can survive on outside of a sealed habitat."

Six planets were highlighted in the star chart.

"The rest of the Veneer Empire is made up of sixteen unique races," Zemble continued. "All of whom relied on the Veneer for a variety of resources necessary to their survival. Much of this administrative work was conducted out of Veneer Prime. With their home world dark, the other five planets are unable to keep up with the needs and demands of the Empire. Thus, the Oxeans."

"And us," Askon added.

Cooper nodded. "And us."

The projection of the star map disappeared and was replaced with three ships: the *Defiance*, *Reliant,* and the *Lexington*.

"At the president's directive," Cooper said, "the three of us have been dispatched on what's being called a fact-finding mission. Our end destination is Veneer Prime. But we're encouraged to reach out and engage with the other occupants of the erstwhile Empire along the way."

"And what will we do when we reach Veneer Prime?" Dheer asked.

"Hopefully, get some answers," Cooper said. "Best case scenario, we find a planet that's slightly out of sorts and willing to talk to us about rejoining the UPA."

"And worst-case scenario?" Tully asked. "Isn't the Natuzzi weapon supposed to be there? That's where long-range sensors last pinged it, right? In the vicinity of Veneer Prime."

Cooper didn't say anything.

Tully raised her eyebrows. "Am I out of line here? I mean, this thing nearly destroyed us the last time we encountered it. What happens if we run into it again? *When* we run into it again?"

"Unfortunately, I don't have an answer for you," Cooper said.

Tully pressed her lips together. "With all due respect, Captain, that's not the sort of thing that inspires confidence."

Cooper glanced at Zemble, but the Elwat just shook his head slightly. "It's a...complicated situation," Cooper said.

"Complicated?" Tully replied.

"In that, it's a problem for tomorrow," Cooper said.

"When do you think you might want to start workshopping solutions for tomorrow's problem?" Tully asked.

"When we get to it on the to-do list," Cooper replied coolly.

Tully arched an eyebrow. "There's a to-do list?"

"Of course, there's a to-do list," Cooper said. "I may be an asshole, but I'm not a disorganized one."

"And 'dealing with an inevitable confrontation with the unbeatable Natuzzi weapon' is on it?"

"It's not a Natuzzi weapon," Zemble interjected. "It was built by the Veneer with the help of the Unity."

"I think it's just easier to call it the Natuzzi weapon," Tully said. "After all, they were the ones that unleashed it on us."

"It's on the list," Cooper repeated in a tone that suggested the topic was closed.

Dheer cleared her throat. "Not to make anything worse, but if we actually make it to Veneer Prime, none of us are exactly skilled diplomats."

"True," Cooper argued. "That's not our job, though. It's not the *Reliant's* either. The *Lexington* is waiting for a UPA Ambassador to join them before heading out. Once that happens, they'll be taking a more direct route to Veneer Prime."

"And what route are we taking?" Warrick asked.

"The scenic one," Cooper replied.

"The *Reliant* left ahead of us," Zemble said. "We'll be rendezvousing with them at our first stop: Dais'u."

The star chart faded away and was replaced with a planet and its three moons.

Zemble continued, "It's a small planet in what's called the Kuma System. Home to the Chice." He paused, looking around the table. When no one reacted, Zemble grunted and continued. "The Chice are not the native inhabitants of Dais'u. They established a presence about three hundred years ago when their generational ship arrived, after a thousand-year journey from the Mataora Galaxy."

"Now, *that* is a scenic route," Warrick said.

"The Veneer didn't have a problem with their presence as the Chice were able to live on the surface of the planet without any environmental assistance; they were able to harvest the jikkeobana spice mines that littered the planet," Zemble continued. "Jikkeobana spice is apparently used in three hundred different Veneeran meals. The Veneer thought it was a reasonable trade-off to let the Chice live there as long as they mined the spice for them."

"How magnanimous of them," Dheer commented.

"When the Veneer closed their borders a hundred years ago, the Chice were extremely vocal about their displeasure with that decision," Zemble said. "Because of their proximity to the border, they had developed some longstanding relationships outside of the Veneer Empire. The closing of the border was going to deliver a devastating blow to their economy. They protested regularly and even tried to circumvent the Veneer border patrol. They petitioned the UPA for asylum, even going so far as to request to be annexed from the Veneer Empire into the Alliance. This continued for about five years before the Veneer decided they had had enough. They took out the Chice's subspace relays and established a military base on the third moon of Dais'u. And that was the last anyone heard from the Chice."

"It's the opinion of the Foreign Affairs Committee that the Chice would make for an ideal first contact," Cooper said. "They were already predisposed to join the UPA, and we believe they would be more than willing to share with us any firsthand knowledge of what's been going on in the Empire of late."

"That was a hundred years ago," Tully said.

"I'm sorry?" Cooper replied.

"It was a hundred years ago," she said. "We're basing this mission on their reaction a hundred years ago. There's no telling how they may feel now. I mean, what's the average lifespan of the Chice? Would any of them even remember that they wanted our help?"

"According to our records–" Zemble started, pulling something up on his datapad.

"Outdated historical records," Tully interjected.

Zemble shot her a brief look before turning back to his datapad. "The average lifespan of the Chice is about two hundred years."

Tully opened her mouth and then closed it. "Okay, well, shit." She glanced awkwardly at Cooper. "Sorry, sir."

Cooper waved a dismissive hand. "You actually raise a valid point."

Tully looked at him, surprised. "I do?"

Cooper nodded. "This means there are most likely people down there that remember the UPA not doing a damn thing to help them."

An uncomfortable silence fell across the room.

Cooper looked around the table, letting his gaze linger briefly on each individual. Then he nodded as if they had made a collective point. "There's another reason we're stopping at Dais'u. Mr. Zemble?"

Zemble made a displeased grunt but didn't argue beyond that. He tapped his datapad, and the projection changed. For a brief moment, it appeared that Dais'u had gained an additional moon. Zemble quickly disabused the table of that notion. "The Natuzzi weapon made one stop before appearing at Veneer Prime, and that was here."

Tully whispered an obscenity under her breath.

"According to long-range sensors, it was in orbit for approximately twelve hours," Zemble continued. "There was some kind of exchange between the weapon and something on the planet. Sensors were unable to determine the nature of the exchange."

"What does that mean?" Tully asked.

"It means," Dheer answered for Zemble, "that we don't know if the weapon was engaged in a fight or it opened a line of communication."

"Twelve hours is a long time," Askon said. "If it was some kind of energy-based combat, based on our limited data, there might not be anyone for us to meet with."

"There's nothing to suggest the planet has suffered any kind of attack," Zemble said.

"But there's also nothing to suggest that it hasn't," Cooper countered.

The uncomfortable silence fell back across the table.

Warrick abruptly smacked his hand against the surface of the table. "Well, this sounds like it's got all the hallmarks of a great party. One that's going to end up with a bunch of us very drunk on M'reth ale or dead. When is this shitshow supposed to get started?"

Cooper nodded at Tully.

She swallowed, taking a moment to compose herself before answering. "We're making good time. It looks like there's a plasma storm forming about six parsecs out, but I don't anticipate it being a problem for us."

"The *Reliant* should be arriving shortly," Zemble said.

"So hopefully, they can get the first impression out of the way," Dheer said.

"Something like that," Zemble replied.

Warrick snorted. "First impression, my ass."

"You have something you'd like to share, Commander?" Cooper asked.

Warrick shook his head. "No, sir. The *Reliant* is a fine, shiny ship commanded by a nice shiny crew."

Cooper frowned. "If that's supposed to be some kind of insult, I'm afraid I'm out of the loop."

"That's probably a good place for you to be on this one," Zemble said.

"What about the military base?" Dheer asked. "The one the Veneer installed? What kind of welcome can we expect from them? Considering the purpose of that base was to keep the Chice in line, I can't imagine they'll be too happy to see us."

"Our intel suggests that it's been abandoned," Zemble said. "Along with the rest of their outposts this close to the border. The Veneer just don't have the resources to maintain a strong presence out here."

"So they'd rather not maintain one at all?" Dheer asked.

"Something like that."

Cooper clapped his hands together. "Right. Okay. That's the mission. Please don't disappoint me."

"That's a worse speech than the last one," Warrick said.

"We have thirty-six hours before we reach Dais'u," Cooper said. "I suggest everybody here takes that time to familiarize themselves with any intel we have on the Chice and their adopted planet."

"Outdated historical records," Tully reminded everyone.

Cooper managed to keep from rolling his eyes. "Dismissed." Warrick got to his feet and started to follow the other three out. "Everybody but you, Mr. Warrick."

8

Cooper gestured to the empty seat when Warrick didn't sit back down.

The chief engineer gave Zemble a questioning look, and the Elwat pointedly ignored him.

Warrick slowly sat back down.

Cooper straightened the datapad on the table, his fingers running along its smooth edges. He said nothing for what felt like a long moment.

Warrick fidgeted in his seat uncomfortably.

Cooper scratched the side of his nose. "You'll forgive me, but I'm not sure how to start this exactly."

Warrick leaned back, running his fingers through his long beard. "Well, I spent a summer in the gardens of Xi'ngtora on Vulder Prime. They liked to start uncomfortable conversations with a heartfelt song. Put everybody at ease."

"Did it now?"

Warrick shrugged. "When the Senior Garden Chef I was seeing decided it was time for us to part ways, she started belting out a tune from a Vulderran opera about the six holy suicides."

"And were you put at ease?"

"After a fashion."

"What kind of fashion?"

Warrick cleared his throat and shifted in his seat again. "Let's just say the social engagement went in a different direction before we landed at the end destination she was looking for."

Something in Warrick's tone got Zemble to look up finally. "I've heard this story before."

Warrick frowned. "If I told it to you, I had probably been drinking too much M'reth ale."

"She was engaged to a ministry butcher," Zemble said. "He walked in on the two of you."

"Yeah, well, not every culture appreciates a good lock," Warrick said. "Either way, we ended up going our separate ways."

"There's an outstanding warrant for your arrest in the Desolis System," Zemble said.

Warrick held up his hand. "Which the UPA doesn't recognize. I asked. Also, it's a trumped-up charge."

Zemble snorted and turned back to his datapad.

Warrick turned back to Cooper. "Vulderran women are very...intoxicating."

"Okay," Cooper said.

"There are things that happen," Warrick said, "when you're engaged intimately with a Vulderran woman."

Cooper grimaced. "Is this really the kind of conversation you want to have with *me*?"

Warrick opened his mouth and then closed it. "No," he admitted sheepishly.

"Good," Cooper said.

"I just didn't want you to think I'm running around the galaxy with an arrest warrant for no good reason," Warrick said. "It was a *very* good reason."

Cooper held up his hand. "Please stop."

Warrick nodded. "Sure, okay."

"Given all that," Cooper said, "I don't think I'm going to open with a song."

"That seems fair enough," Warrick agreed.

"That being said," Cooper continued, "you've already provided me with a convenient opening."

Warrick opened his mouth and then wisely shut it again.

Cooper folded his hands atop the table. "I understand you're entertaining a guest."

"She's not a Vulderran," Warrick said.

Cooper frowned. "I'm aware that she's not."

Warrick nodded. "Good. Because I didn't want you to think I was the kind of officer that would bring a Vulderran woman onboard without clearing it with you beforehand. That's the sort of thing that could cause problems for the crew."

"Interesting way to phrase that," Cooper said. "Considering that you didn't let me know you invited the chief engineer from the *Reliant* over for a...*social engagement*."

Warrick glanced over at Zemble, but the first officer was focused on his datapad again. "Okay," Warrick said. "And if you don't mind me asking, where did you hear that?"

"That's not exactly the response I was hoping for."

"What kind of response were you hoping for?" Warrick asked.

"Considering that you just spent five minutes going on about the time you slept with a Vulderran woman who was engaged to a ministry butcher, I thought, at minimum, you'd do me the courtesy of not jerking me around."

Zemble made a noise under his breath.

Cooper's mouth tightened into a thin line. He took a

deep breath through his nose and slowly exhaled. "I'm not trying to pick a fight here, Mr. Warrick."

Warrick glanced at Zemble again and then turned his attention back to Cooper. "That's not what it feels like."

"If I wanted to pick a fight," Cooper said, his tone abruptly hardening. "We would be having this conversation in the *brig*."

"No, we wouldn't," Zemble said, looking up from the datapad with an expression of infinite patience.

Cooper shot him a look.

"It's not against regulations to have a visitor from another Fleet ship," Zemble said.

"It might not be against regulations," Cooper said, turning back to Warrick. "But I would think it'd be *polite* to inform your captain when you're entertaining the chief engineer of another ship. I like to know who's on my ship, Mr. Warrick. Especially when they're invited onboard by a member of my *senior staff*."

Warrick didn't say anything, and it looked like it was taking an effort for him to keep his mouth shut.

Cooper sighed and rubbed his forehead. He pressed his hands against the edge of the table. "I'm not trying to be an asshole, Commander."

"You should consider trying a little harder," Warrick said.

"You don't understand," Cooper said, looking at him. "I don't have to *try* to be an asshole. It comes to me naturally. I'm putting in the effort to be *nice*. Sure, I won't throw you in the brig, but that doesn't mean I'm not above having a conversation with you in the brig before I let you know that you're not going to be residing down there permanently."

"Captain," Zemble started.

Cooper held up his hand, cutting him off. "Never mind.

Point is, you brought somebody onboard my ship, and you didn't have the common courtesy to give me a heads up."

"You want me to apologize?" Warrick asked.

"It would make for a nice start," Cooper said.

Warrick sat there silently.

Cooper pressed his hands against the table again to keep from balling them up into fists. "Right. Okay, then." He cleared his throat and swiped a finger across his tablet. Langlois' profile appeared. "Commander Langlois has quite the resume." The admiration in his voice was genuine. "Three different doctorates from the Elon Institute, and she has tenure at the Chesson Science Academy, which I understand is rather hard to come by. She taught Advanced Quantum Mathematical Theory there for almost six years before Doctor Teutsch convinced her to join the Fleet's R&D Division, where she worked on the quantum drive. Completed three successful test runs on it, one of which happened to be on the *Reliant*, and actually managed to get promoted from R&D into the field, straight to the chief engineer spot on the *Reliant*." Cooper looked up at Warrick. "A bit of a step up from a Senior Garden Chef?"

Warrick chose to ignore the jab. "Are you thinking of offering her a position? Because you need to know, right now, there's nothing that's going to get her to leave the *Reliant*. Also, you already have a chief engineer unless there's an unexpected twist to this whole thing."

"Oh, there's a twist, all right. Just not the one you're expecting. What I'm thinking is," Cooper said, turning off his datapad, "that, despite you not clearing it with me first, it's not a bad idea to loop her in on our situation with Ensign Calloway and our ship."

A Vulderran swear escaped Warrick's mouth.

Cooper looked at him firmly. "And this brings us back to

the issue of you not bothering to give me the basic courtesy of keeping me in the loop."

"You seem to be doing a fine job on your own," Warrick said.

Cooper shook his head. "I can't believe this," he said quietly. "All right, let's skip to the end here. Our...developing situation with the *Defiance* is...delicate. I think we can both agree on that?"

Warrick nodded. "Delicate. Sure."

"It's a need-to-know basis," Cooper continued. "And outside of the crew of this ship, I'm not entirely certain there are many people who need to know." He waited a second to make sure his words fully sunk in. He gestured to his datapad. "Commander Langlois is a smart woman. Smarter than you, I'd wager. Hell, probably smarter than this entire crew combined. I think it's an excellent idea to consult with her on this problem. But she's not a member of our crew, and eventually, she will have to return to the *Reliant*. I want to ensure that the *Defiance*'s...*problems* stay onboard the *Defiance*." Warrick opened his mouth, but Cooper raised his hand, cutting him off. "I'm not looking for a response, Commander. You've made your position clear. At this point, this isn't so much a conversation as it is me letting you know that I'm not an idiot, and I'm paying attention to what's going on on my ship." He got to his feet. "Do us both a favor, and don't pull a stunt like this again."

Cooper left the conference room.

Warrick stared at Zemble, who was pointedly looking at his tablet.

After a minute, Zemble asked, "What?"

"I feel like that's what I should be asking *you*," Warrick said.

Zemble looked up at him. "Is there something specific you're expecting from me?"

Warrick shrugged. "Hell if I know anymore."

"He's not wrong," Zemble said.

"Doesn't mean he's right."

"Actually, it does."

"What exactly is the plan here?" Warrick asked. "Are you supposed to be running interference for him?"

"You wouldn't have pulled a stunt like this under Mitchell," Zemble said, sidestepping the question.

"We wouldn't be in this situation if we still had Captain Mitchell."

Zemble snorted.

"What?" Warrick asked.

"That's an unrealistic expectation," Zemble said.

Warrick leaned forward. "Just so I know for future reference: Whose side are you on around here?"

"We're all supposed to be on the same side," Zemble replied.

"Doesn't feel like it."

Zemble got to his feet. "Maybe consider that the next time."

"Next time?" Warrick asked.

Zemble didn't bother to clarify.

9

COOPER WAS WAITING down the corridor from the conference room. "Well?"

"You could have handled that better," Zemble said.

Cooper fell in step alongside Zemble. "I suppose I could have," he agreed, clasping his hands behind his back.

"But you didn't."

"But I didn't," Cooper said.

Zemble didn't say anything as he ruminated on that for a moment. "You really are an asshole," he concluded.

"I try to tell people that," Cooper said, "but they never really believe me until they experience it for themselves."

"What was the point of being an asshole back there?"

"You didn't like the brig bit?"

"I didn't like the brig bit," Zemble said. "The brig bit is the sort of thing that gets captains bumped back down to commanders."

"I thought about using an airlock instead," Cooper said.

"That would have been worse."

Cooper nodded. "I suppose it would have. Maybe I would have gotten a better result."

"What was the result you were looking for?"

"I wasn't sure."

"That...doesn't inspire confidence."

"I would have known it when I saw it," Cooper said.

Zemble grunted. "Okay." He didn't sound convinced.

Cooper shrugged. "Warrick already has an attitude with me."

"He has an attitude because of how you keep dealing with him," Zemble said.

"Maybe." Cooper shrugged. "Or maybe because he joined the Fleet so late in life, he built up a lot of bad habits that nobody really noticed because Mitchell pretty much gave him free rein."

"He's had other commanding officers," Zemble pointed out.

"I'm aware," Cooper said. "They all said the same thing: He's brilliant but *difficult*. The *Defiance* is his second-longest assignment. Interestingly enough, his longest was the *Providence*, where he was stationed with Lieutenant Commander Nax."

"So maybe it wasn't Mitchell who was acting as a buffer," Zemble said.

Cooper nodded. "Maybe. Either way, Warrick no longer has that buffer, and he'll need to learn to behave."

"Or else?"

Cooper shrugged again. "Commander Langlois would make for a nice chief engineer."

Zemble looked at him in disbelief. "You're not serious, are you?"

"Well, thanks to Commander Warrick, she's already looped in, and I don't think I'd have to work that hard to convince her to take the position." Cooper rapped his knuckles against the corridor wall. "The *Reliant* may be state of the art, but we're a floating mystery in space. There's not a scientist or engineer worth their salt who wouldn't jump at this opportunity."

Zemble stopped in the middle of the corridor and held up his hand, bringing Cooper to a halt. "Warrick's itching for a fight, and your plan is to give him one?"

"My plan, such as it is, Mr. Zemble, is to run this ship to the best of my ability," Cooper replied. "If that results in crew members picking fights with me, well...." He shrugged. "That seems like a problem that's easily fixed."

Zemble stared at him for a moment, not entirely certain what to say. "I don't know that I agree with that policy."

"Fair enough," Cooper said. "I'm not entirely certain I'm on board with it, either. But let's see how it plays out before switching gears."

Zemble started to say something and then stopped. He turned and resumed walking.

"What were you going to say?" Cooper asked, following him. "You were going to say that's not how Mitchell would have done it, weren't you?"

Zemble didn't respond.

Cooper shook his head. "I really wish you people would stop invoking Mitchell like he's some kind of patron saint of captains," Cooper said.

"He cast a large shadow."

"That just means he was large enough to blot out a brighter light."

They reached a split in the corridor.

"I want three new options for our new Chief Tactical Officer," Cooper said, pausing before splitting off from Zemble. "We also need a new third shift commander."

"You don't think Sadler's coming back?"

"I want somebody I can trust," Cooper said. He held up three fingers. "I want three options."

"I don't know that we have three."

"Like I said before, all you really have to do is pick the right one on the first try, and then you don't have to worry about the other two," Cooper said over his shoulder as he turned down the opposite corridor.

Cooper was lost in his thoughts. He reached the lift and tapped the call button. The doors immediately slid open, and he was surprised to see Tully standing there.

"Captain," she greeted him, her hands clasped behind her back.

Cooper nodded at her. "Lieutenant. Heading up to the bridge?"

"Yes, sir. That is the plan," she replied.

The doors slid closed, and the lift resumed its upward trajectory.

The two quietly rode the lift for a few seconds before Tully abruptly reached out and tapped the hold command.

Cooper frowned, an almost anxious expression passing across his face. "Lieutenant–"

Tully turned to him, pressing her hands together. "How was I back there?"

"Back where?"

"In the meeting," she said. "I'm worried that I might have stepped over a line."

Cooper glanced at the hold command on the control pad next to the door. "I think you're stepping over a line *here*."

She took a step towards him. "Okay, well–"

He held up his hand. "I told you, I was very clear about this."

Tully's expression turned serious, almost mockingly so. "Oh, you were clear. *Very* clear."

"And yet," he gestured at the hold command, "here we are, holding up the lift, just the two of us."

"Well, I wanted to make sure it wasn't too much."

"Too much?"

"Back there, in the meeting," she clarified. "I thought that maybe I was being too difficult."

Cooper snorted. "Too difficult seems to be the default setting for this crew."

"I just wanted to make sure that, you know," she took another step toward him, "I hadn't stepped over a line."

"I'm pretty sure you strongly implied that I was an idiot."

"See, that's what I'm saying," Tully said. "Is that too much?"

"Did you make it a habit of implying that Mitchell was an idiot?"

"Broderick–"

Cooper visibly winced at the use of his first name.

Tully took a step back and held up her hands. "What? Am I not allowed to use your first name now? Because last night, it wasn't a problem."

Cooper rubbed a hand over his eyes. "Apparently, I wasn't clear enough."

She looked around the otherwise empty lift. "It is just the *two* of us here."

"Exactly, there's just the *two* of us in this *lift*."

"I feel like I'm missing something crucial here."

"Optics," Cooper said.

"Optics?"

"Appearances."

"We are literally *alone* in this lift."

"Onboard sensors are logging our presence in this lift you're holding."

"I'm pretty sure onboard sensors were logging my presence in your quarters last night," she said.

"Nobody's looking at those," Cooper replied. "Privacy is still a thing unless there's a reason for it not to be."

"I don't see why that doesn't work here."

"Because why are the two of us holding this lift?"

Tully stared at him, her mouth a gape. "Oh my goodness. You cannot be serious. There are dozens of legitimate reasons why one of us would be holding this lift."

"Nobody's going to think of those," he said. "I told you how this was going to work. How this *had* to work." He pointed at his badge. "I'm the *captain*."

"You've made that very clear."

"You're one of my *subordinates*."

"Yes, that's the point. I have a thing for men in command."

A thought occurred to Cooper. "Wait a minute, were you waiting in here for me?"

Tully folded her arms, offended at the suggestion. "That is an insane thing to suggest."

"You were just waiting in here for me," Cooper said. "Just riding this lift up and down until I got in. Or worse, you were holding it."

"You keep saying that like it's against regulations to hold the lift."

He threw up his hands. "That's because it is!"

Tully was surprised. "Seriously?"

"Seriously." He pulled out his datapad.

"What are you doing?" Tully asked.

"Pulling up the regulations specific to holding lifts," Cooper replied. "Because clearly, you don't believe me."

She placed her hand across the screen of the tablet. "Okay, well, point made."

Cooper looked at her. "I don't feel as though the point has been made."

"Well, I'm not looking forward to you quoting Fleet regs to me. Okay? It's definitely a turn-off."

Cooper sighed. "Lea–"

She held up her hand, cutting him off. "Wait, I just want to make sure we're clear on this. You're allowed to use my first name, but I'm not allowed to use yours?"

Cooper shook his head. "I'm the *captain*."

"This is not how I thought this was going to go," she admitted. "Your use of your title is supposed to be; I don't know, sexier? Somehow, though, you're making it the opposite of that."

"Stop it," he said. "I told you when we started this, there were going to be *rules. Specific* rules."

"Yes, I know. I heard you."

"And yet, here we are, holding the lift," Cooper said.

"To be fair," she said with a mischievous smile, "you didn't say anything about not holding the lift when you were laying out the rules."

"This isn't funny."

"I'm not trying to be funny," Tully replied. "Ask anybody who knows me. It just comes to me naturally."

"Yes," Cooper replied flatly. "That sounds like a great idea. I should definitely go around asking about you with other crew members."

"I know for a fact that's something that captains actually do," Tully said. "And they manage to do it without suggesting they're sleeping with any of the people they're asking about."

Cooper winced again.

"Come on," she said. "It is literally just the two of us."

He rubbed his eyes. "I can't believe this."

Tully placed her hands atop his and pulled them away from his face. "You know what? I'm not going to lie; you're kinda cute when you're stressed out like this."

"Stop it," Cooper said.

"It's doing something for me. What, I'm not entirely certain. But it's definitely something."

She stood up on her tiptoes and kissed him.

Cooper sighed. "This is inappropriate."

Tully let go of him and turned back to the control panel. She released the hold command, and the lift started moving back up towards the bridge. She gave him a sly smile. "Yes. That's the point."

The lift arrived at the bridge before Cooper could respond.

10

Zemble stood outside Cargo Bay Two. He stared at the closed doors, debating with himself whether or not to go inside.

It didn't really matter if he went in. At this point, Calloway could theoretically be reached from any point in the ship.

But based on his previous experiences, it was just easier to do it in Cargo Bay Two.

Zemble closed his eyes and muttered a prayer under his breath. He wasn't sure where God fell on the issue of a human/Unity hybrid slowly taking over the ship, but he imagined, He had to have found it interesting enough to pay closer attention.

Zemble tapped the control panel next to the oversized doors, and they slid open.

He stepped into the cargo bay.

It was dark, although not so much that he couldn't see.

At some point, all the original lighting had disappeared. Elsewhere on the ship, Calloway was clearly taking great pains to maintain the original appearance. But here in Cargo Bay Two, she was going for something…different.

The lighting was gone. That being said, it wasn't dark. Zemble couldn't figure out how the cargo bay was being lit, and neither could Warrick or Carole, not that either one of them spent nearly half the time that Zemble spent in there. There was a soft glow coming from everywhere and nowhere.

The cargo bay felt a little bit smaller every time Zemble visited. He had checked the dimensions of the bay and the surrounding space, and everything matched up, except that his senses told him Cargo Bay Two was just a little smaller every time.

The floor and the walls were the same shade of black. It was an absolute black that gave a sense of vertigo upon entering the cargo bay. The brain insisted there was no floor; there were no walls. Every time his mind screamed that he was stepping into a gaping void from which there would be no escape.

But his feet always found purchase. And if he reached out with his hand, he would feel an actual wall next to the cargo bay doors. It was still the cargo bay, more or less.

Mostly less, though.

Zemble took a second, as he always did, to stand in the doorway and allow himself to acclimate to the space. When he felt the sense of vertigo retreating when he felt his mind giving up the panicked screams, he finally stepped forward, and the doors slid closed behind him.

It felt like being swallowed whole.

The contents of Cargo Bay Two had been moved, redistributed throughout the ship, and, in some cases, unloaded completely. There was nothing left in the cargo bay, but it didn't feel any more empty.

Random shapes rose out of the floor, extended from the walls, and descended from the ceiling. Every time Zemble visited, the shapes were different. There seemed to be no rhyme or reason for their appearance or disappearance. They resembled nothing familiar. In fact, they resembled nothing at all. There was nothing in any of the figures that anyone would immediately identify as a familiar geometric shape. The shapes were unrefined, amorphous blobs that seemed to be natural extensions of the cargo bay until they weren't.

Zemble never saw the shapes appear or disappear. They would be there on one visit, and on the next, they would be something different.

He tried to ask about them, but Calloway wouldn't, or couldn't, answer him.

Today, though, was different.

There was a single shape in the middle of the floor. It rose out of the void of the floor seamlessly. It looked vaguely like an obelisk of some kind. There were dark blue veins etched into it, making spiral patterns that were dizzying to look at if he stared at them for too long.

This wasn't the first time the blue veins had appeared.

A week into their stay at Natuzzi, the blue veins had made their first appearance. Like everything else in the cargo bay, they were inconsistent. Sometimes the blue veins would cover the walls, like a maze designed by a blind man. Other times there would be a single dark blue vein that ran through the center of the cargo bay, cutting it in half perfectly.

Then other times, there would be no blue veins. Just the darkness. A terrifying void with no beginning and no end.

Zemble found the dark blue veins to be strangely reassuring. They provided an anchor point where there would otherwise be none.

He took a hesitant step towards the obelisk shape, careful not to get too close. He couldn't be certain, it was impossible to judge the dimensions of the cargo bay now, but it seemed to sit in the exact center. Zemble walked around it slowly, his eyes focusing on the edges of the veins. He found it easier to stay centered if he didn't look at the spirals directly.

He quickly realized there was a pattern to the spirals.

On each of the six sides of the obelisk, a dozen spirals ran together to create a long rectangle. Once he became aware of the new shape, the sense of the spirals disappeared, and he found he could focus directly on them without any sense of displacement.

"Fascinating." Zemble took another cautious step forward.

Something at the corner of his vision caught his attention. He turned, but there was nothing there. Just the empty darkness of the cargo bay.

But with his focus pulled from the obelisk shape, he watched it out of the corner of his eye, and he noted it *moved*.

Zemble turned back to the shape.

Nothing about it seemed any different. The spirals were still in place, and as near as he could tell, the obelisk hadn't actually moved. Its shape hadn't even changed.

But at the edge of his field of vision, he had clearly registered some kind of movement. He was certain.

Or at least, he was as certain as he was of anything else in this cargo bay.

"I learned something new today."

Zemble wasn't an easily startled person. He prided himself on his ability to be constantly aware of his surroundings. But, as they said in the Bible, pride always goes before a fall.

An Elwat swear escaped Zemble's mouth at the sound of the voice behind him. A cold, crawling sensation made its way up his back. He turned slowly, taking the time to compose himself.

"Erin," he greeted the small woman standing a few feet away from him.

At one point, Erin Calloway was a vibrant, enthusiastic young woman, full of life and energy. She had wild red hair that was impossible to tame and a personality that insisted she would make a memorable first impression.

Now, though, Erin Calloway made a very different memorable first impression.

The color had been completely drained from her skin. She was pale, chalky, unhealthily so. But it was impossible to determine what was healthy for her now. Her once vibrant red hair was now as black as the cargo bay around her. It lay flat against her skull as though it was leaking through her pores; for all Zemble knew, it was. A vague impression of a Fleet uniform covered the rest of her body. But it was like somebody had started copying the design and got bored almost immediately. The outfit was black, like her hair and the cargo bay, and it clung to her body less like clothes and more like another layer of skin. Zemble noted, absently, that the dark blue veins were appearing on Calloway now, giving the impression of seams along her uniform.

It was her eyes, though, that disturbed him the most. They were completely black. No pupils, no irises, nothing for Zemble to focus on, to connect with. Just black, yawning pools of darkness that leaked out from the corners of her eyes like spidery veins, slowly working their way either up to her black hair or down her neck to her uniform.

Calloway had appeared out of nowhere and everywhere, as she always did. Sometimes he would catch sight of her rising from the floor or melting free from the wall. More often, though, she simply appeared when he wasn't looking. Zemble decided he preferred it that way.

He glanced at the obelisk-shaped thing behind him. It didn't move.

"What did you learn?" Zemble asked. "How to reassemble a fusion cannon area?"

Calloway walked across the surface of the cargo bay. He kept expecting her feet to make a sound, but they never did. Instead, it was as though with every step, she pulled all the noise, what little there was in the cargo bay, towards her. She looked in his direction but not at him. He could feel her gaze moving through and around him as if he was nothing more than an inconvenient obstacle.

"No," she replied. Her voice had a tinny, hollow echo to it.

"That's not something I want to have to report back to Warrick," Zemble said.

Calloway seemed unconcerned by this as she moved, making a slow circle around the obelisk-shaped thing. "I learned that you are an orphan."

Zemble grunted.

Calloway glanced up at him, her black eyes focusing on him. "Did I say something inappropriate?"

"After a fashion," Zemble grumbled. "How did you learn this?"

"It's in your file."

"No, it's not."

Calloway paused as if reviewing something. "According to medical records, you do not share any similar genetic markers with the individuals listed as your parents."

"That's…" Zemble trailed. "Why did you look that up?"

Instead of answering him, Calloway turned back to the obelisk-shaped thing. She held out her hand, hovering over the surface of it. "We are moving towards the weapon. Why?"

Zemble noted her avoidance of the question and decided to let it slide. "We're heading in that direction."

"That is what I said."

"Our destination is not the weapon," Zemble said.

"And yet, we are heading towards it."

There was something in her voice that Zemble hadn't heard before. "Are you concerned?"

Calloway lowered her hand and looked up at him. "Why don't you want anyone to know you are an orphan?"

Zemble's lips curled into a frustrated frown. "Because I don't like sharing all of my personal details with everyone."

"Interesting," Calloway said. "I used to do that? Share personal details?"

"Keane said you had a problem with oversharing."

"It bothered him?"

"No. I think he found it funny."

"Did it bother you?" she asked.

"Not much bothers me."

"That does not answer my question."

Zemble grunted. "You're one to talk about avoiding uncomfortable questions."

A ripple passed through the obelisk-shaped thing, and it abruptly melted back into the floor.

Zemble was startled by this. The cargo bay hadn't made

any changes in his presence since their encounter with the Natuzzi weapon.

"What is it?" Zemble asked.

Instead of answering him, she asked, "Are you afraid?"

The question took him by surprise, and Zemble hesitated before answering. "Of what?"

"Our destination? Your inability to combat the Unity? Life?" She looked at him and blinked. "Of me?"

"That's...a lot to unpack."

"I hear what's being said," Calloway continued. "On this ship, I hear everything now."

"That sounds like an unwieldy burden."

"I'm not sure what a burden feels like anymore," Calloway replied. "The crew is afraid of me."

"The crew doesn't understand you."

"And they fear what they don't understand?"

"That's a pretty universal reaction," Zemble said. "It's also reasonable for them to have concerns as you're rebuilding the ship underneath them."

"And what about you? Are you afraid of me?"

Zemble hesitated before answering. It wasn't a long pause. Only a second, possibly less, but nonetheless painfully obvious.

"I see," she said.

"As far as I'm concerned, as long as you're more Erin Calloway than the Unity, I don't have anything to be afraid of," Zemble said.

Calloway looked around the black void of the cargo bay. "And how can you tell what percentage of me is human and what percentage isn't?"

"Because you're still concerned about how others perceive you," Zemble said. "That's a pretty human reaction and an absolutely dominant character trait of Erin Calloway." Zemble felt her drifting away. She wasn't focused on him anymore, and tiny ripples made their way across her torso and into the floor. "Are you afraid?" he asked.

"Afraid?" Calloway stared at her hand. "I'm not certain. Fear is..." She trailed off.

"Fear is normal," Zemble said.

"Not for me."

"Yes, for you."

She looked up at him. "Not for what I am now."

"Who you are now is the same person you were before."

Calloway tilted her head. "That's not what I said."

"I'm aware of that," Zemble said.

"You speak with such conviction. How can you believe it?"

"I have a lot of practice believing in impossible things."

"Do you still pray for me?"

"Every night," Zemble replied.

"Why?"

"Why not? It's the very least I can do."

She made a sound that sounded like a sigh. "Do you believe that your prayers are working?"

"I have no reason to think they're not."

"So, are you afraid?" Calloway asked.

Again, Zemble hesitated. "I wouldn't call it fear."

"Is there something else it can be called?

"I'm in an eighty-year-old tin can traveling through the void of space," Zemble said. "I'm not afraid. I have reasonable concerns about my quality of life. Especially when bulkheads are being rebuilt around me."

"Reasonable concerns," she repeated. "You can't survive in the vacuum of space."

"Most species can't."

"Why not?"

"I don't know," Zemble said. "Personally, I don't like discussing why God made certain design choices; it feels like it's a conversation that has no point and, worse, no end."

"Why bother leaving your planet if you can't survive the vacuum of space?"

"I don't know," Zemble replied truthfully. "Why not?"

"It seems... ill-conceived."

"I don't disagree."

"You came here for a purpose?" she said.

Zemble nodded. "You need to be more careful."

"The crew is concerned."

"Warrick is concerned," Zemble said. "Warrick holds half this ship together with Qeebvavan tape. If he has concerns, they're worth listening to."

"I don't know that I can stop this process."

"So you've mentioned."

"You haven't told your captain this?"

Zemble didn't know how to respond to that.

"You've mentioned it in your personal logs," Calloway said.

"No, I haven't."

"You've spoken about it without speaking about it," she said. "I see the lie of omission."

"Why are you going through my personal logs?" Zemble asked, bristling at the thought.

"I'm going through everyones'."

"Is that supposed to make me feel better?"

"I don't know," Calloway replied. "I'm not sure how emotions are supposed to work anymore."

Zemble thought about it for a moment, running through the connections, and arrived at the most logical conclusion.

"You're rebuilding the datacore the same way you're rebuilding the ship."

She tilted her head in acknowledgment.

"Why?"

"Because I can," Calloway replied.

"That's not an answer."

"It's why the Unity does anything," Calloway said.

"Because it can," Zemble said. "What does that make the Unity?"

"An indescribable force of nature," she replied.

"Interesting choice of words."

"They were used in a report filed by one Doctor Kazmierczak from the Seshat Laboratory."

"How did you get hold of that?"

"The same way you would."

"I doubt that," Zemble said. "I would have to put in a records request. That request would have to be cleared by the Intelligence Committee before ultimately being rejected since the official line is that those labs never existed. Then I would have to reach out to Admiral Wanamaker, who would have to use back channels to get a hold of data from Seshat. Best case scenario, he manages to get me a highly redacted report that probably doesn't even have Doctor Kazmier-czak's name attached."

"I've been querying the subspace network," Calloway explained.

"And what have you been looking for?"

"Anything. Everything." She looked up at him again. "I am a force of nature that is indescribable."

"We can't contain the knowledge of your existence if you spread yourself beyond this ship," Zemble said.

"I am aware of that." She paused. "I'm being...discreet."

"Discreet," Zemble repeated, unconvinced.

"I am an indescribable force of nature."

"So you keep saying."

"But I find that I experience one thing that is very describable."

"And what is that?" Zemble said.

Calloway locked her gaze onto his. "Hunger."

11

NATUZZI

"I want to hug you," Sadler said. She pressed her hands against her hips tightly as if it was the only thing keeping her from grabbing Nax. "But I feel like that would be crossing a line."

Nax smiled. "That's a line I would be willing to cross."

Sadler returned his grin and didn't waste any time. She practically leaped across the room. Bending over, she wrapped her arms around him and squeezed tightly. A slight, strangled sound escaped Nax, and she pulled back, alarmed. "I'm sorry. Did I break something?"

Nax shook his head as he attempted to, and failed, to contain the pain he was feeling. "You didn't break anything."

"That was not a normal reaction to getting a hug."

He rubbed the left side of his rib cage gingerly. "There are all sorts of things my body does now that aren't normal reactions."

Sadler winced. "I'm sorry."

Nax waved off her apology. "It's fine, and more importantly, it was worth the discomfort."

Sadler's eyes brimmed with unshed tears. "Well, that

makes me feel a lot better. But I'm pretty sure I'm supposed to be making *you* feel better."

"I'm feeling just fine, Sadie Sadler," Nax replied. "In fact, just seeing you standing here is probably the best I've felt in weeks."

"You're alive!" The unshed tears escaped, and she wiped her eyes with the heels of her hands. "I'm sorry, this isn't very professional."

"I think at this point we can dispense with professionalism," Nax said. "You saw me at my most vulnerable."

Sadler sniffed, trying to wipe her eyes dry. "Well, yes, I did see you naked, but I was trying not to dwell on that."

"I meant when I was grieving for Grace," Nax replied.

Sadler nodded, wiping at her nose. "Actually, you know what, that probably makes a lot more sense." She smiled again, a handful of tears escaping from the corners of her eyes. "We weren't sure that you were going to be alive. Everything that Warrick told us about you and this place...." She paused, trying to compose herself. "We were all prepared to find out you had been executed."

"That was something I had prepared for myself."

"And when they told us you were alive." Sadler exhaled, trying to keep herself from bursting into tears again. "I honestly didn't believe it. I thought, maybe, best case scenario, I'd find you in some kind of vegetative state. But instead..." She held out her hands to indicate Nax, not trusting herself to say anything more without bursting into tears again.

Nax looked around the small apartment and noticed that his sister had made a discreet exit. "What did they tell you?"

Sadler used the sleeve of her uniform to wipe her nose. "They had told us you had been stabbed while in custody, awaiting trial. Your condition was critical, but they were confident you would pull through."

Nax snorted. "That's an interesting spin on events."

Something in his voice pulled Sadler out of the emotional runaround she was stuck in. "Spin?"

Nax tapped the controls of his wheelchair and started rolling towards the door. "I know you just got here, Sadie, but I'm desperate for some fresh air. Are you up for a walk?"

Sadler paused. "Well, I mean, sure," she replied. "I'm always up for a walk on an actual planet, under a real sky, and side note, you never told me that your home planet had such a *beautiful* sky."

"Considering, at the time, the odds of you ever seeing it were essentially nonexistent, I didn't feel it was fair to burden you with a desire to see something you would never experience. Obviously, things have changed."

"Second," Sadler said, her expression growing serious. "I don't know how else to say this, but I feel like going for a *walk* is a little, I don't know, insensitive to you right now?"

"I can still enjoy the fresh air even if I can't feel the ground beneath my feet."

"Okay, works for me," Sadler said, smiling, and followed him.

From the ground level, the spaceport was almost impossible to see. The only evidence of its presence Nax could spot was the subspace antenna at the very top of the control towers. That and, of course, the automated worker drones of the UPA construction force working on the embassy.

The sidewalk they strolled down ran parallel to a gentle river that would disappear beneath the Rhinoderma mountains about a hundred miles from there. Nax sensed they were not alone; sure enough, he spotted three Imperial... handlers staying a discreet distance behind them. He glanced up at Sadler but couldn't tell whether she had noticed them. Her attention seemed solely focused on the sky above.

"It really is beautiful," she said in a tone of hushed awe.

"Yes, I suppose it is," Nax agreed.

Sadler's blonde hair had grown since he had last seen her as if she hadn't been able to find anyone to maintain her familiar pixie cut. It was a little shaggier but mostly held in place with a few pins and an opal hair charm that sparkled underneath the Natuzzi sun. She was dressed in a UPA uniform, but it was different from the functional jumpsuits of the *Defiance*. She wore grey slacks with a black shirt jacket with a bold, thick stripe of red that ran across her shoulders and down the sleeves. The jacket zipper was pulled down from her collarbone, and Nax could make out a red colored shirt underneath that matched the stripe.

"I hope you'll forgive me," Nax said after they had walked in silence for a few minutes.

"Forgive you?"

"For taking advantage of you," Nax said. "What else of my situation did they tell you?"

"Well, they made it very clear that we were not to assist you leaving the planet's surface," Sadler said. "Beyond that, they've been...vague."

"Vague." Nax nodded. "Yes, that sounds about right."

"You want to fill me in on what's going on?" Sadler asked. "Starting with our chaperones?" She gestured over her shoulder at the three Imperial handlers.

"Technically, I'm not a free man," Nax said. "I believe the term you would be familiar with is 'house arrest.'"

Sadler came to an abrupt stop. "Are we not supposed to be out here?"

Nax rolled to stop a few feet in front of her and made a non-committal gesture. "Nobody told me I wasn't allowed to leave the apartment, but I figured with a representative from the UPA present, they'd be less likely to stop me. Up to a point, of course."

Sadler put her hands on her hips. "Nax..."

He held up his hand. "This isn't a jailbreak. I'm not trying to conscript you into anything. I have every intention of going back."

"And you know I'd go along with any scheme to get you out of here," Sadler said.

Nax gave her a wistful smile. "I'm sure you would."

"I'd just like to be looped in right away," Sadler finished.

"I'm sorry," he said. "I have no intention of causing any more irreparable damage to the relationship between the UPA and Natuzzi. I just thought our conversation would be better suited to the outdoors, where there would be fewer prying eyes."

Sadler sighed and shook her head. She started walking again, and a moment later, Nax followed.

"The queen is a real...*person*," Sadler said, sounding politely frustrated.

"The queen is my sister," Nax said.

Sadler paused and chuckled. "Of course she is."

"Half-sister, technically," Nax added. "Not that such things matter here."

"Older or younger?"

"Younger. I was the eldest," Nax said. "As I'm sure Jaxson's already explained to you, I wasn't eligible for the throne."

"Yeah, he mentioned you guys have a particular way of doing things around here."

Nax shrugged. "Who am I to argue in the face of traditions that date back thousands of years?"

"If there isn't at least one person, those traditions will just go on for another thousand years," Sadler said.

"I can't say I am interested in being a revolutionary, especially considering the cost I've already accrued for my minor indiscretions."

Sadler rubbed a hand across the back of her head. "Yeah, I can see that. Are you going to walk again?" She made a face. "Am I allowed to ask that?"

"It's fine," Nax said. "To be honest, it's not a question I've bothered asking myself."

"That's...weird."

Nax sighed. "Perhaps. But I confess that I struggle to find the desire to care about whether or not I will be able to walk again if I have no place to walk to."

"Jeez, Nax, that's bleak."

He shrugged. "It's the truth." He gestured up towards the sky. "Not that I'm not glad to see you, but as I understand it, the *Defiance* departed already. What are you doing here, Sadie?"

Sadler chucked her thumb in the direction of the spaceport. "I don't know if you noticed, but there are changes afoot."

"Yes, somebody thought it was important that I have a view of the changing spaceport," Nax replied dryly.

"Well, it's the official UPA consulate here on Natuzzi. At least until something a little more permanent can be built. Although truth be told, I think Admiral Bronwyn likes the idea of a quick getaway being accessible. I don't know if you were aware, but the Natuzzi people aren't very welcoming of us."

"It's been almost two hundred years since there was a non-Natuzzi presence here," Nax said.

"Wow. That's a hot minute, isn't it."

"You're not going to make many friends while you're here," Nax said.

She gave him a sly smile, "Good thing I already have one."

"I understand that the Fleet is looking to establish a presence in Veneer space, and they want to use Natuzzi as a launching base for that mission," Nax said.

"Yeah, something like that," Sadler said.

"That could be done from orbit," Nax said. "In fact, it will have to be done from orbit, possibly even from our second moon. Why are you *here*, on our planet?"

"Given what went down with the previous queen, the current Natuzzi leadership, as well as President D'Ambra, thought it would be a good idea if we established a more permanent presence here on the planet," Sadler said. "At least, that's the official answer."

"And the unofficial answer?"

Sadler shrugged. "I don't know. Hell, I don't think Admiral Bronwyn knows."

"None of that explains why *you* are here, Sadie Sadler."

"Well, that should be obvious. I'm here because you're here."

He looked up at her, confused.

"We decided, and the we, in this case, would be the administrative body of the consulate, which basically consists of Admiral Bronwyn, Lieutenant Thatcher, Captain Verghese, and me."

Nax arched his brow. "You?"

"We decided," Sadler continued, "that somebody from the *Defiance* should be here. It seemed appropriate. In fact, we weren't alone in that decision. Your sister was very adamant about someone from the *Defiance* being stationed here."

Nax pursed his lips together but didn't say anything.

"The obvious choice was Warrick," Sadler continued. "But Warrick's still not allowed back here."

A faint smile passed across Nax's face. "I would imagine not."

"He won't tell anybody what happened."

"No, I imagine he wouldn't."

"Will you?"

Nax thought about it for a moment and then shrugged. "Let's see how bored we get."

Sadler nodded. "Fair enough. So anyway, I volunteered. The new consulate needed a Fleet Liaison, and somehow despite my best intentions, I still got promoted." She pointed out the commander's pip.

"You should be Mitchell's new first officer."

"Well, first off, I really didn't want that job. Second..." she trailed off, unsure of how to say what needed to be said.

"What is it?" Nax asked.

"The *Defiance's* new captain and I don't really see eye-to-eye."

"New captain? What happened to Mitchell?"

She took a deep breath to steady her nerves. "Captain Mitchell is missing in action, presumed dead. Along with Keane."

"Oh." Nax stared down at his hands. "What happened?"

"We're not sure," Sadler said, her voice soft. "They went missing during a rescue attempt."

"Whose rescue?"

Sadler didn't answer.

Nax closed his eyes. "Mine."

"We don't know what happened," Sadler repeated. "For all we know, they'll turn back up in a couple of months."

"And how likely does that seem?"

Sadler bowed her head. "A funeral has already been held for Captain Mitchell. One for Keane is scheduled for later in the month."

A somber silence fell across them.

"It seems to be a growing theme: people dying while I live."

Sadler didn't know what to say to that. "That's...remarkably bleak and depressing."

"My apologies," Nax said.

Sadler waved him off. "No. I mean, you don't have anything to apologize for, Nax. I'm just saying that that point of view is, well, not healthy."

"Considering the state of my body, it seems only fair that my mind should need some healing as well."

Sadler pulled them both to a stop and moved in front of Nax. "Are you okay?"

Nax didn't answer; he avoided her gaze, letting his eyes drift to the sky behind her.

"Nax, the reason I'm here is you." She crouched down in front of him. "I'm here to help you. Whatever that means. This place," she gestured to indicate the planet. "This isn't your home anymore. These people don't know you. Maybe they can help you physically, but none of them understand what you're going through mentally. Hell, I'm not even certain I know what you're going through mentally, but I figure I've got a better shot at understanding it than anyone around here does. So, please trust me. I'm here to help you."

Nax looked down at his numb legs. "I was accused and

found guilty of High Treason. I was sentenced to life imprisonment by the Queen, who was also my mother. And then, left in my cell, a zealot from our religious order who accused me of being a heretic nearly murdered me. Despite what they may have told you, the only reason I am alive today is that I'm host to a being from a dead universe which appears to me in the form of Grace Hawkins. This being somehow managed to keep me alive, despite mortal wounds, simply because if I were to die, she would die. I am supposed to be grateful for this, but I confess I'm having difficulty in finding the gratitude, considering that not only am I still trapped here on this planet, but I'm trapped here for reasons that are ostensibly no longer a concern when you take into consideration that I'm sitting here on my home planet, speaking to a human being who has been invited here to take up semi-permanent residence." He met Sadler's eyes. "Tell me, Sadie, how do you think you can help me?"

12

"I DON'T KNOW."

Admiral Elise Bronwyn looked at Sadler with a frown. "That's not exactly the response I was hoping for."

Bronwyn's office was blank and unpersonalized. The paint had only just dried the day before; before that, Bronwyn had been holding meetings out of an unused shuttle. There were still plastic wrappings around the corners of the desk. Both chairs smelled like they had been pulled out of a box only an hour ago, which was precisely what happened. The wall behind her desk was a giant floor-to-ceiling window. It was the only thing in the office that suggested a personal touch, and that was primarily because of the view: The peaks of Rhinoderma mountains could be seen in the distance, reaching up towards the amber sky, like fingers trying to touch the heavens. It was the only thing Bronwyn had insisted upon. She had seen footage of the view at the beginning of the consulate's construction. She knew that this held the possibility of being a long-term assignment, and experience had taught her one thing: If nothing else, make sure you had an excellent view. An excellent view made long-term assignments more manageable.

Sadler dropped into the chair across from the admiral. "Honestly, it's not the response I was hoping to give."

Bronwyn set her tablet down and gave Sadler her full attention. She was an older woman with short hair that was more white than gray. Although her face was absent of any of the telltale wrinkles that came with age, it was the eyes that gave her away. They were emerald pools that ran deep. "Okay, let's start at the beginning."

Sadler puffed out her cheeks and didn't say anything for a moment. "Well, I met the queen."

"Which is more than I can say."

"She seems like a real person," Sadler said.

Bronwyn arched an eyebrow. "As opposed to?"

"A less diplomatic description," Sadler replied carefully.

Bronwyn chuckled softly. "Okay, fair enough. What did you talk about?"

"With the queen? Nothing. She barely gave me the time of day."

"Mr. Nax."

"Ah." Sadler nodded. "Mostly, I caught him up on everything that had happened on the *Defiance* since he had...left."

"And?"

Nax's words flashed through her mind:

"The only reason I am alive today is that I'm host to a being from a dead universe which appears to me in the form of Grace Hawkins."

Sadler shifted in her seat. "And it was a real downer of a conversation. Especially when we got to his raging case of survivor's guilt."

"Did you ask him about the queen's death?"

"No."

Bronwyn's lips pressed together disapprovingly. "Why not? It was the one thing I specifically asked you to cover."

"Because up until a week ago, Nax was in a medically induced coma," Sadler said. "I don't think he's the source of intel we'll be looking for."

Bronwyn leaned back in her chair, drumming her fingers against the desk's surface. "You know how many times I've reached out to the queen's new Executive Committee about the death of their previous ruler?" She held up her hand; fingers spread out. "Five times. And each time, they brush me off. It's an internal matter, they say. It's under investigation, they say. As soon as they have anything relevant to share with us, they will, they say."

Sadler crossed her legs. "Nax said it's been nearly two hundred years since there was a non-Natuzzi presence as large as ours here. I can imagine that they're going to be a little hesitant to talk with us."

Bronwyn got to her feet and stepped over to the window, her hands clasped behind her back. "I'm sure they are, and, honestly, I don't blame them."

"Okay, so then why are we so focused on figuring out who murdered the queen?" Sadler said. "If they're not concerned about it, why should we be?"

"According to the local newsfeeds, there are three groups claiming credit for killing the queen."

"I think I heard something about that," Sadler said.

"I watched a couple of reports, and they all presented very strong arguments as to why any of these groups could be responsible. Yet, as far as I can tell, no arrests haven't been made."

"And this bothers you because?"

Bronwyn glanced back at her. "Do you know how long we're going to be here?"

"No."

"Neither do I. Could be months, could be years." She turned back to the view of the mountains. "Even if it's just months spent in a politically volatile environment where the current leader could be bumped off at any given moment?" She shook her head.

"All due respect, Admiral, I think, maybe, you're exaggerating a little bit," Sadler said.

"What happens if Queen Ril gets murdered tomorrow?" Bronwyn asked her.

Sadler opened her mouth and then closed it, shrugging. "I don't know. Nax has tried to explain the Natuzzi beliefs regarding death and grief, but I honestly can't get my head wrapped around them."

Bronwyn turned around abruptly. "You're not *listening*, Commander. What happens to *us*? We're here because Ril wants us here. If Ril's not in charge, how does the new queen feel about a UPA presence here?"

Sadler started to open her mouth, but Bronwyn cut her off with a wave of her hand.

"We're clearly not wanted here," the admiral continued. "Every time I submit a new requisitions form to the Executive Committee, it gets roundly rejected. You know where they originally wanted to put the consulate? In some place called the Athaguay Province. I don't specifically know where that is, but I know it's on the other side of the planet in the middle of some mountains that generate a natural distortion field that makes it impossible for shuttles to come and go. They wanted us out in the middle of nowhere, hoping we would either be forgotten or quietly die off. It was pulling teeth just to get these twenty acres of land attached to the spaceport."

"So you're worried that we'll end up in the Athaguay Province if Ril is removed from office?"

"No. I'm worried that if Queen Ril is murdered like her mother was, I could wake up in the middle of the night three months from now just before an Imperial assassin blasts a plasma bolt through my head."

Sadler gaped at the admiral. "That's..."

"A lot, I know," Bronwyn said. "You think I'm exaggerating. I understand that. This is your first diplomatic assignment. You need to understand, Commander, that this is not friendly territory. We were invited here because the alternative was war. And I'm sure there are still plenty of people on this planet and in the Alliance itself that would rather deal with a war."

"I can't imagine that there's anyone in the Alliance who would–"

Bronwyn held up three fingers. "I can name three high-ranking admirals in the Fleet alone that would rather bring in two of our Dreadnaught Class ships and lay waste to the entire Natuzzi space force. As far as they are concerned, it's better to be an obvious occupying force." Bronwyn took a breath. "I'm not one of those admirals. I like diplomacy. I like believing that we can find a common ground to unite on. But I am not a fool. Queen Xie was murdered, quite publicly, only seven weeks ago. Whoever did that is most likely still at large."

"And you think they're not going to be happy with the UPA establishing a base here?"

Bronwyn shrugged. "I don't know. Honestly, I'm more bothered by the current administration's base attitude toward the murder of their previous leader. I can assure you that if it had been President D'Ambra murdered, Congress would have a damn war council convened the next day."

"That's..."

Bronwyn cut her off again. "I know. Let's just accept for the moment that I'm going to be prone to the occasional hyperbolic statement, okay?" She paused, rubbing a hand across her face. "Obviously, a war council is a bit much. At the very least, there would be an investigative team assembled of some of the smartest minds in the Alliance. When a president is murdered, heads will roll figuratively and literally." She waved her hand at the window behind her. "Here, though? I haven't spoken to a single person who seems mildly put out that their leader was murdered seven weeks ago. I don't like it. I don't trust it."

"There are extenuating circumstances," Sadler pointed out.

"Yes, I'm aware of the extenuating circumstances," Bronwyn said. "Those extenuating circumstances are plastered all over their newsfeeds. There are entire channels devoted to all of the awful, despicable, horrific acts that Queen Xie committed."

"I mean, it makes sense why the population might not be missing her."

Bronwyn looked at Sadler coolly. "I know a smear campaign when I see one. As I understand it, all the news media here is state-run. Which means all this negative press about the previous queen had to be approved by the current queen. You see where I'm going with this?"

Sadler frown uncomfortably. "As I understand it, Gouren Ril was the queen's daughter. She's Nax's younger sister."

"Yes, I read the Executive Committee's file," Bronwyn said. "It was very dry and very favorable towards Gouren Ril."

Sadler leaned forward, resting the back of her elbows on her legs. "Are you suggesting–"

Bronwyn raised her hand again, cutting her off. "I'm not suggesting anything, Commander. Especially not *here*."

Sadler raised her eyebrows but didn't say anything.

"There's currently thirty of us stationed here," Bronwyn continued. "I have fifty more staffers coming in on the *Branson* in two weeks. The Natuzzi have made it very clear that we're not allowed to have more than a hundred people on the planet's surface at any given time. They're being more flexible with their space above, but down here: one hundred, no more.

"If something goes wrong, if the political winds suddenly change direction, I hope we can leave in an orderly fashion. But if we can't, that's a hundred people that the Natuzzi won't hesitate to kill." She paused. "After all, you saw what they did to the queen's son and then to the queen herself. A hundred off-worlders? We would be lucky if they gave us the courtesy of killing us in our sleep."

"Well," Sadler said, folding her hands together. "Is it too late to request a transfer?"

Bronwyn gave her a disapproving look.

"I'm kidding," Sadler said. "Mostly."

"Honestly, I wouldn't blame you if you wanted to leave," Bronwyn said. "I'm not sure I want to be here myself."

"If you don't mind me asking, why did you accept the assignment?" Sadler said.

"Because when the president of the United Planetary Alliance asks you to do something, you do it," Bronwyn said. "Because at the end of the day, he's still my boss, and besides, I don't know that I trust anyone else not to fuck it up."

"Humble brag," Sadler said quietly.

A small smile ghosted across Bronwyn's lips. "Maybe. Probably. Although, I can't say that it sounds very humble."

"I was trying to be respectful."

"Much appreciated." Bronwyn folded her arms. "So, we're back to Nax."

"Nax?"

"He's still a member of the royal family."

Sadler made a face. "I mean, sure. Technically."

"Political alliances are built on technicalities." Bronwyn rubbed a finger across her lips thoughtfully. "And, technically, he's still a Fleet officer."

"Okay, well, that's even more of a grey area."

"No, it isn't." Bronwyn gestured to her tablet. "Commander Nax's file has been updated accordingly. He's an officer in good standing, currently on an indefinite leave of absence."

"Okay," Sadler said, unsure how to take that information.

"Nax has a duty to the Fleet," Bronwyn said. "The UPA."

Sadler frowned, unconvinced. "The same UPA that just handed him off when the Natuzzi came looking for him? Which resulted in him nearly being killed and essentially imprisoned for life on his home planet?"

Bronwyn rubbed her brow. "Yes, I know. It's a grey area."

"I was thinking that *complicated* is probably a better description."

"He's willing to talk to us," Bronwyn said.

"Well, he's willing to talk to me," Sadler clarified.

"Right now, there's no difference."

Sadler pursed her lips together but didn't say anything.

"I understand you may have concerns, Commander."

"It feels like I'm expected to leverage my friendship with Nax for political purposes."

"That's exactly what you're expected to do."

"Admiral–"

"He's willing to talk to us," Bronwyn said. "Which is more than his sister has done. We have to take whatever opening we can get right now."

"Queen Ril is the one who invited us," Sadler reminded her.

"Which makes it all that more concerning that she doesn't want to talk to me."

Sadler shrugged. "Maybe she's sensitive to overly optimistic attitudes."

"Commander?"

"Yes, ma'am?"

"Don't be cute."

Sadler nodded. "Yes, ma'am."

Bronwyn rested her hands on the back of her chair, not saying anything for a moment. "I've been where you are right now, Commander. I'm not asking you to take advantage of your friend."

Sadler didn't say anything, but her expression made it clear that she wasn't convinced.

"But the reality is, Nax is a valuable asset. I understand that it doesn't seem that way right now. But Ril didn't have to save him. She could have left him in his cell to die, and no one on this planet would have blamed her for it. Instead, though, she did the opposite." Bronwyn held out her hands, palms up. "Why did she do that? Because Nax is important to her, which means he's important to us. If he can help us, we can help him. You're not taking advantage of your friend, Ms. Sadler. You're taking advantage of an opportunity to help your friend."

"That sounds like a technicality," Sadler said.

Bronwyn nodded, a somber, haunted look in her eyes. "Technicalities are the lynchpins of political success."

13

THE DEFIANCE

"WHEN EXACTLY DID the symptoms first appear?" Dheer asked.

Crewman Verdile paused. The pause was long enough that Dheer knew that the next words out of his mouth were going to be a lie. She took a half step back and folded her arms, letting a sigh out before realizing she was doing it.

Verdile, oblivious to Dheer's emotional shift, replied almost confidently. "A week ago.

"A week ago?" Dheer repeated, giving him the chance to correct himself. The last thing she wanted to do was embarrass the man.

Verdile's head bobbed up and down, the flop of brown hair swishing back and forth across his face. "Yes, ma'am," he said, not taking the out.

Dheer sighed again. She couldn't help it. If Verdile took notice of her disappointment, he didn't show it. But given how swollen his eyes were, there wasn't much he could actually see.

"Bruce," Dheer said. "We both know what this is."

"We do?" Verdile's voice cracked as he finally understood that Dheer wasn't going to buy his story.

The swelling around his eyes was dark purple and riddled with black dots that looked like tiny bruises. It spread down the sides of his face, causing his cheeks to puff out like a toddler refusing to eat his vegetables. She knew that if she had him open the top of his jumpsuit, she'd find the purple swelling extending down his torso, getting progressively less severe until it just looked like faint purple streaks running down towards his groin.

"Bruce, I'm not some fresh-faced doctor, right out of medical school, getting started in my first residency," Dheer said. "They don't let those kinds of people get promoted to Chief Medical Officer anywhere."

Verdile swallowed uncomfortably. He fidgeted on the edge of the biobed, his fingers wrapping themselves around the edge of the bed as if he was concerned that it would suddenly fling him off.

"This is Mox's," Dheer said. "Obviously. I knew that the minute you walked in. The real question is, why you're trying to pretend like you don't know what it is?"

"Ah, uh," Verdile stammered. "Doctor, I, uh–"

She held up her hand, stopping him from any further linguistic gymnastics. "Never mind. I just figured it out. Lieutenant Keizer is your superior, isn't she?"

If it were possible for Verdile's face to turn bright red, it would have. And maybe it did, but Dheer couldn't tell under all the purple bruising.

Verdile suddenly became very interested in his shoes. "Uh."

"Mox's is a sexually transmitted disease," Dheer continued. "Commonly spread between Reitsma and humans and easily treated with a vaccine. In fact, I have all the ingredients on board to make said vaccine. This could have easily been avoided, except that Lieutenant Keizer is your immediate superior. So, suppose you had come to me asking for the vaccine, and I asked what you needed it for; in that case, you'd have to disclose that you were engaging in a sexual relationship with your immediate superior, which is against Fleet regulations."

Verdile winced as he swallowed again. A cold sweat broke out across his forehead.

"So you thought, what? You'd roll the dice? Figured that the odds you'd catch Mox's were pretty low?" Dheer paused as a thought occurred to her. "Does Lt. Keizer even know you're down here right now?"

Verdile seemed to shrink a little. "No."

Dheer nodded. "She thinks you're already vaccinated."

"Yes," he replied sheepishly.

"You," she said, "are a real piece of work."

Verdile slowly looked up and met her gaze. "I'm in trouble, aren't I?"

Dheer sighed. "Oh, for sure. But it's not the kind of trouble I'm going to be able to help you with. This?" She pointed to the bruising. "I can fix this. The fact that you're an idiot asshole, that one's definitely out of my hands." She nodded at Nurse Sayer. "Nick will get you taken care of."

Dheer started to walk away when Verdile asked, "What about, um, you know?"

She glanced back at him. "You breaking protocol and sleeping with a superior officer?"

Verdile nodded and winced in pain as he did it.

"Well, I'm pretty sure that one's out of both of our hands, Ensign. It's a small ship. And I don't know how long you've been hiding from Lt. Keizer, but I can assure you, it was probably too long. I think you'll quickly discover that the

Reitsma's notoriety doesn't simply extend to carnal pleasures."

The color drained from Verdile's face, and the purple bruising turned almost pink.

Dheer turned and continued down the hall towards her office. Just before she was out of earshot, she heard Nurse Sayer explain, "This is going to sting, and it'll be about twenty-four hours before the swelling starts to reduce."

Dheer shook her head and remained continually surprised at the genuine stupidity of people.

She turned the corner, glancing briefly in the direction of the main section of the med-bay to make sure there were no other patients, and then stepped into her office.

Captain Cooper was waiting for her.

Dheer grimaced.

"That's not the reaction I expected," Cooper said. "Although, in fairness, I probably should have."

"Probably," Dheer agreed, making her way around to her side of the desk. "What can I do for you, Captain?"

"I thought we should talk," Cooper said, sitting down. "You put in a request for a transfer."

"That's because I want off this ship," Dheer replied. "That's why most people usually put in a transfer request."

"You filed it right after I promoted you."

Dheer replied by simply folding her arms.

"Okay," Cooper said, shifting in his seat. "You know, most people in your position are happy, flattered even when they get a promotion like this."

"Most people in my position are consulted before being handed a promotion," she replied coolly.

Cooper's brow furrowed. "You're upset because I didn't ask you if you wanted the job? Rabkin himself recommended you for the position."

"Was that before or after you kicked him out the airlock?" Dheer asked.

Cooper's mouth tightened into a thin line, and he leaned forward, pressing a finger against the desk emphatically. "Rabkin's wanted off this ship since before I got here. He's had a standing transfer request in Mitchell's log for the last four years. He's tried to retire six different times. Mitchell kept denying it."

"So, you figured you could do the one thing that Captain Mitchell couldn't?"

Cooper pulled back, frowning. He held out his hands. "Why are we fighting about this? Who fights about getting a dream promotion?"

"This is a *dream* promotion?" Dheer asked. She pointedly kicked the underside of her desk, and something in the wall rattled.

"Last time I checked, Chief Medical Officer is still considered a big deal," Cooper replied. "Regardless of the ship where the position is posted."

"Spoken like somebody who's never had to worry about a shitty posting before."

Cooper shook his head. "No, that's not what you think this is."

Dheer arched an eyebrow. "Oh? And what do I think this is?"

"Why did you want off this ship before?" Cooper asked. "When Mitchell was still here, you put in a request to transfer to Baker's Island. Everything was all set. You were going to be dropped off at the *Atlantic* and then picked up by the *Octavia*. At the last minute, you canceled that request."

Instead of answering him, Dheer said, "You don't want me here."

"If I didn't want you here," Cooper replied sharply. "I

would have offered the job to Doctor Childress. She'd've taken it in a heartbeat."

Dheer held her hands up. "Great, you've already got a replacement lined up. I can hitch a ride back on the *Reliant*."

"The point is," Cooper said through gritted teeth. "I want *you* here."

"No, you really don't."

"You wanted off this ship before and then changed your mind," Cooper said. "Why?"

Dheer didn't answer him.

Cooper nodded. "I'll tell you why. It was because you don't trust the people in charge of the truth. You don't trust the administration. You don't trust the Security Council. You don't trust Rabkin, and you sure as hell didn't trust Mitchell."

When she didn't react, Cooper took a breath and said, "And now? You don't trust *me*."

Dheer frowned. "If I don't trust you, why would you want me here?"

"Because you and I? We're on the same page."

"Oh? You don't trust yourself either?"

"Something like that," Cooper said.

Dheer scoffed her head. "Unbelievable."

"I'm surrounded by a crew that has a history of secrets and half-truths," Cooper said. "Only the senior staff have Top Secret Clearance. The rest of the crew doesn't even warrant Level Two Clearance. Half the time, they don't know what's going on. The other half, they know what's going on, and they have to pretend they don't. They have to look their commanding officers in the eye and believe them as they're told outright lies. This ship has trust issues. A lot like the UPA. I suspect we would be in very different circumstances had the Powers-That-Be actually trusted the people of the Alliance with the truth."

"You're not exactly rushing out to the major news outlets to give them the big scoop," Dheer replied.

"And that's why I want you here."

"That's a pretty stupid reason if you ask me."

They sat there in silence for a moment longer. When it became clear that Dheer wasn't going to say anything else, Cooper got to his feet.

"I'm going to deny your transfer."

Dheer pressed her lips together tightly. "Yes, I figured as much."

"Is that going to be a problem?"

"Insofar that it's going to affect me doing my job?" Dheer shook her head. "No, I'm a professional. I'm here to see to the safety and well-being of the crew, regardless of the circumstances behind my stay. Now, will I lose what little respect I have left for you? Probably."

Cooper nodded. "For what it's worth, Doctor, I'm not interested in an antagonistic relationship with you."

Dheer shrugged. "I can't say that seems worth much, given the abundance of evidence that suggests otherwise."

14

"THIS IS NOT how reality is supposed to work," Langlois said.

"That's what I thought, too," Warrick agreed. "But apparently, we've been misled about the nature of reality."

Langlois turned the datapad upside down as if that would make the information any more palatable. "That's not how that works."

"Says the woman who thinks if she holds the datapad upside down, it'll make more sense."

Langlois set the pad down and looked up. Warrick's workspace was less of an office and more of an oversized nook that hadn't been put to any better use yet. Warrick leaned against the far wall, and Carole stood near the doorway as if ready to bolt at any given moment.

"Okay." Langlois closed her eyes and pinched the bridge of her nose. "Let me make sure I understand this or at least have all the facts in the correct order."

"Do I need to be here for this?" Carole said. "Because I'd rather not be here."

Warrick pointed at him. "You're going to be here because having you here makes me seem less crazy."

"No, it doesn't," Langlois said. "But I think we both know Carole's better at being able to dumb down information in a way that allows it to be successfully passed along."

Carole frowned, clearly unimpressed by the question-able compliment, but he pulled out the remaining chair and sat down.

"Okay, so a hundred years ago, we were attacked by Species Four-Eight-Seven-Six–"

"The Unity," Warrick interjected. "Trust me; it's easier than referring to them by that stupid number."

"We barely defeat their ships, and they're never heard from again. Only, that's not true. Their 'ships' are actually *them*. This Species Four-Eight-Seven-Six, the Unity, is actu-ally from a parallel universe–"

"Dimension," Warrick interjected again. "Based on what I know, calling it a 'parallel universe' is a little generous."

"–And it, they, are an alien entity that is somehow both biological and technological. Their existence doesn't straddle the line between the two, like cybernetics, but instead seems to blur it completely. This Unity can assimi-late all organic and nonorganic material–"

"I'd quibble with the use of the word 'assimilate,'" Carole said. "The data suggests they break material down on an atomic level and add it to their own collective essence or identity."

Langlois stared at him. "How is that not assimilation?"

"Because assimilation might imply the original identity of the organic material might still be available within the Unity," Carole said. "Based on what we've observed, I don't think that's the case."

"Okay," Langlois continued. "We didn't stop the Unity. In fact, we were unable to have any effect on them whatsoever. What stopped them a hundred years ago is...unknown. Best guess is that there's something in our universe, our reality, that acts as a natural counteragent to the Unity. Except, that's not really the case because somehow, the Veneer had entered some kind of alliance with the Unity. In this alliance, they built a planet killer that the Natuzzi eventually acquired, and during an engagement with this weapon, you discovered one of your crew members–"

"Ensign Erin Calloway," Warrick said.

"–was a member of the Unity, and she seems to be... doing *something* to your ship?"

"Near as we can tell," Carole said, "the *Defiance* is undergoing a base, core molecular reconstruction."

Langlois shook her head and sat back. "No."

Warrick and Carole looked at each other.

"No?" Warrick echoed.

"That's simply not possible. Molecular reconstruction of the entire ship? You'd all be *dead*." She pointed to the exterior hull. "There's a vacuum out there."

"Oh, I sure as hell haven't forgotten about that," Warrick said.

"If your ship is being broken down on a molecular level–"

"And it is," Carole interjected.

"–you'd be experiencing a loss of atmosphere, oxygen, and air pressure," Langlois continued. "In other words–"

"We should all be dead," Warrick finished for her.

"We should."

"And yet, we're not," Carole said.

Langlois held out her hands. "Therefore, it's not possible."

"And yet, it clearly is," Carole said, gesturing to the datapad. "This has been happening throughout the ship in different departments. The equipment and/or the literal physical space are stripped down to their atomic level and then slowly reconstructed over thirty minutes to two hours. There's really no clear reason for the length of time it might take. The commissary took an hour and a half, but the forward sensor array only took forty-five minutes."

"You want me to believe this is happening across the *entire* ship?" Langlois said. "No."

"It's happened four times this week already," Warrick said.

Langlois pressed her hands together under her nose and took a deep breath. "I am having an emotional reaction that I am not familiar with and definitely not comfortable with."

"That's about on par around here," Carole said.

"Any indication that the hull's been breached?" Langlois asked

"No," Carole replied.

"Except," Langlois said. "You should have a hull breach."

"We don't have a hull breach," Carole replied.

"You *have* to have a hull breach," she said. "If this ship is being dismantled and reconstructed at the atomic-molecular level, your hull has been breached."

Carole showed her the datapad. "Except we don't. Everything's within acceptable levels."

Langlois shook her head. "*Acceptable* levels?" She picked up the datapad and swiped to an image of the forward fusion canon being rebuilt by thin, oily black tendrils. "This is not acceptable." She turned to Warrick. "Your ship shouldn't be doing *this*."

"You're absolutely right," Warrick agreed. "Except it is."

She pointed to the cannon array. "That's not going to function."

"Actually, it's probably going to function better than before," Carole said, checking his datapad. "Systems that have been rebuilt are operating thirty percent better than before."

"No," Langlois said.

"No?" Carole held up the datapad. "It's all right here. Check and triple-checked."

"That's *not* how technology works," she said. "You don't just rebuild something on the atomic level like that. We can't. We don't have that technology." She swiped through screens of data until something clicked in her mind. "*Fakakta*." She looked up at Warrick. "The upgrades you had done while at Natuzzi, they were to cover up your...situation?"

"We needed something to explain why the ship was functioning above our expected parameters," Carole explained.

She squinted at him. "Are you, though?"

He gestured at the datapad in her hand. "Look at the delta brackets for the ion drive. They're operating at sixteen percent above where they should be."

"That's not possible," Langlois said, reading the data. "Your ion drive is nearly fifty years old and at least twenty-five years overdue for a refit." Langlois glanced through the specs and shook her head. "No, I take that back. This engine doesn't even qualify for a refit. It should be junked. It's almost an antique."

"I know how old the damn engine is," Warrick said, bristling slightly. "It's a fine engine."

"I'm not making a joke," Langlois said. "In six more years, this engine will be classified as an antique."

Warrick paused. "Are you sure you're not making a joke because it feels like you're trying to get to a punchline."

"You have work orders here that say a new germanium

converter was installed onto the primary engine coils. Somebody's going to notice that it's not there."

"Nobody has yet," Warrick said.

"How come nobody noticed at Natuzzi?"

"We had the parts delivered," Warrick said. "I've got a pretty decent team of engineers here. It was easy enough to convince everybody that we were going to do the work. Also, nobody from Natuzzi wanted to step foot on our ship. For that matter, nobody from the *Reliant* or the *Lexington* wanted to come on board. Allegedly, there's a rumor going around that we could fall apart at any given moment."

Langlois rubbed the side of her head. "My point is; eventually, you're going to make it back to a proper Fleet base. What happens when one of those engineers comes on board? Eventually, somebody's going to need to inspect the upgrades."

Warrick shrugged. "That's a tomorrow problem."

"A tomorrow problem," she echoed.

"We're about to spend the next couple of months inside Veneer space," Warrick said. "Also, there's still the very real possibility that one of these days, something's going to get upgraded, and it's not going to work with the rest of the ship, and we all end up floating in the empty void of space."

She ignored him, swiping through the datapad. "According to this, your deflector array has been completely upgraded."

"It sure has," Warrick said.

"I rated it at a fifty percent improvement," Carole said.

"This is nearly on par with the *Reliant*," she said. "How do you plan on explaining any of this? All the refits in the galaxy aren't going to change the fact that this is a nearly eighty-year-old ship. You don't have the power distribution network to handle this kind of boost to your deflectors."

"Apparently, we do now."

"And how the hell is that possible?" Langlois shook her head. "Your energy output hasn't changed. In fact, according to this, it looks like all of your 'upgrades' have pointedly avoided the fusion core."

Warrick scratched his beard. "I've noticed that."

"Can Calloway, or the Unity, not assimilate energy?" Langlois looked back and forth between them. "Or at least energy on that level?"

Carole shrugged. "We don't know."

"You don't know," Langlois echoed. She placed her hands down against the desk. "You should have turned this ship over to a team at Elon Institute."

"We can't do that," Warrick said. "You know we can't do that."

"I don't care that you think it's a matter of interstellar security."

"It's not just that I think it; it is," Warrick said.

"This crew already knows about it," Langlois said.

"That's very different from the rest of the galaxy," Warrick pointed out.

"Jaxson, I hate to point out the obvious, but we should not be flying around the galaxy in this ship. It's not *safe*."

"You could make the argument that it's never safe traveling through the cold vacuum of space," Warrick replied.

"You could," she agreed. "But you're not making it any safer by traveling in a ship that could disassemble around us at any given moment."

Carole shifted uncomfortably in his seat. "She's not wrong."

Langlois sighed and rubbed her forehead. "There is so much you don't know."

"We know," Warrick said.

Langlois shook her head. "No, I don't think even we know what we don't know. Take Calloway."

"Calloway?" Warrick asked.

"When was she actually assimilated?"

"Infected," Carole said.

"Infected?" Langlois said.

Carole shrugged. "I'm not thrilled with that word either. But seeing how Ensign Calloway presented with her unique identity and personality before revealing her connection to the Unity, I'm not sure what to classify her as."

Langlois nodded. "Okay, you're right. Infected. Calloway's personal history is well documented; there are no obvious gaps where she could have interacted with the Unity. She also passed multiple Fleet physicals without setting off any red flags. She was, is, a sleeper agent," Langlois said. "She was a sleeper agent, and if she never left Earth before enlisting, she had to have been *infected on Earth*."

15

COOPER STOOD, leaning back against the helm, his arms folded as he stared at the view screen. Dais'u was a small planet. Almost half the size of earth. Whatever that meant. From space, though, it was impossible to tell the difference. A planet, any planet, was still a *planet*. And regardless of anything else Cooper might have felt about his new position, looking at a planet from space was still awe-inspiring, no matter its size.

From their orbit, the landmasses of Dais'u were brightly colored, irregular shapes of red, visible through the dark grey haze spread across the planet thanks only to the Jikkeobana spice. Viewed through the thick atmosphere, the abundance of spice across the landmasses sparkled as the *Defiance* passed over them like they were trying to compete with the stars.

Standing there, so close to the screen, it washed over him. Cooper literally found himself inspired with awe as he stared at it. He wondered if anyone else felt this way. Or was this just commonplace to the rest of the crew? He couldn't believe this was something he was looking at.

This wasn't his first alien planet. That honor had belonged to Mahina CU6, home to a small Alliance colony looking to get back to the basics of life. He had been four years old. His father had woken him up from a dead sleep as soon as they were in orbit. Cooper had been groggy and cranky as his father dragged him to the observatory bay, insistent that his son lay eyes on his first alien planet, not through a view screen. It had to be *real*.

At it was. One look outside that window and the crankiness was gone. Cooper sat there for hours, whenever he could, while they were in orbit, just staring down at a planet that wasn't Earth.

And every time he saw another alien planet, another planet that wasn't his home, he was four years old again.

"They're not here," Zemble's low rumble broke through Cooper's reverie with a sharp snap.

Cooper turned around. "What?"

"They're not here," Zemble repeated. He sat at his station near the rear of the bridge.

It took another second for the words to make sense, to pull his mind back from the awestruck four-year-old.

The *Reliant*.

Zemble was talking about the *Reliant*.

Cooper walked around the helm, making his way back towards the command chair. "What do you mean?"

The Elwat's face was, as usual, a mask. Cooper wasn't sure if it was all Elwats or just Zemble, but he found the man impossible to read. Zemble seemed to have only two modes: mildly disgruntled or stoically silent. The two modes either contained a multitude of emotional reactions that Cooper found impossible to decipher, or Zemble truly was either mildly disgruntled or stoically silent all the time. Cooper couldn't figure it out, and he decided that as long as Zemble spoke his mind and continued to be relatively forthcoming and open with his opinions, it didn't really matter if Cooper couldn't read him.

That being said, it felt like Zemble was looking at him like he had just suggested they all take a spacewalk down to the planet. So, having some basic understanding of the Elwat's emotional range would be helpful.

"They're not here," Zemble repeated.

"Yes, you mentioned that part already," Cooper replied, frowning. "I was hoping you would clarify."

Zemble grunted and turned back to his console. "The *Reliant*'s not here."

Cooper folded his arms, his frown deepening. "Not the clarification I was looking for, Mr. Zemble."

"No signal from their transponder," Zemble said. "No response on any of the standard UPA channels. And no trail from their ion drive."

Cooper's brow furrowed as he walked over, leaning on the railing that separated him from Zemble's console. "When were they supposed to get here?"

"Almost eighteen hours ago."

Cooper raised both eyebrows. "What does that mean?"

Zemble didn't answer at first. He studied something on his console, adjusting the data on one of the adjacent screens. "It means they're not here."

Cooper stared at Zemble, waiting for him to elaborate. When he didn't, Cooper gave an exasperated sigh and threw up his hands. "Then where the hell are they?"

Zemble just grunted a nonspecific reply.

"That's not an answer," Cooper said.

Zemble didn't bother grunting this time.

Cooper turned around, raising his voice so that he was

clearly addressing the rest of the bridge. "How does a Sovereign Class starship go missing?"

No one had an answer.

"That wasn't a rhetorical question, people," Cooper snapped. "I *really* want to know."

"Maybe they took a more scenic route," Tully suggested. When Cooper didn't respond, she half turned to see his distinctly unamused expression. Tully cleared her throat awkwardly and turned to the view screen. "Are we certain they're missing?"

Cooper opened his mouth to reply, but Zemble beat him to it.

"No," the Elwat replied.

"No?" Cooper repeated, unable to contain his surprise. "No?"

"No," Zemble repeated.

"What would you call it?"

"They're not where they're supposed to be," Zemble replied evenly.

"Is this supposed to be a joke, Mr. Zemble?" Cooper asked.

"I'm pretty sure we've already covered that I'm not inclined to make jokes," Zemble said.

"They're not where they're supposed to be," Cooper repeated, pacing a small circle around the command chair. "That's a bit of a mouthful. I'm pretty sure there's a word, a single word, that can express that notion pretty succinctly." He snapped his fingers as if the gesture might jog his memory. "What was that word again?"

"Maybe," Zemble agreed, focusing on his console. "But I believe there are too many variables before we settle on them missing. As Lt. Tully pointed out, they could simply be delayed."

"Delayed, and they're not answering the phone?" Cooper asked.

Before Zemble could respond, Askon spoke up. "Captain, I have results from the scans."

Cooper stared at Zemble's back for another second, but the Elwat seemed uninterested in continuing the conversation. He turned to face Askon, his gaze passing over Tully briefly, and she gave him an almost imperceptible apologetic shrug.

Cooper kept his expression neutral. Or at least what he thought was neutral. Although, based on the crew's reaction, he was starting to suspect that it was less neutral and more irritated.

"What is it?" Cooper asked.

"Therrian radiation clouds," Askon said. On the view screen, the image pulled out, showing the planet in its entirety. The black clouds stretched out across the whole of the planet. "They cover approximately eighty-five percent of the planet."

Cooper sat back down in the command chair, watching the planet. "How bad is it?"

There was a long pause from the science officer. "We're unable to scan too far past the radiation clouds accurately. But it doesn't appear that the planet has been negatively impacted yet. Which suggests it is a recent development."

"The Natuzzi weapon," Zemble grunted.

Cooper sagged back against the command chair.

"That would be the logical explanation," Askon agreed. "Nothing in our historical records suggest that the Chice operated an industrial society that would result in this level of radiation pollution." The antenna tipped backward slightly. "And historically, this sort of pollution is achieved over centuries and, more often than not, is corrected before getting to this point."

"And nothing in the historical records suggested that the Chice were irresponsible enough to let it get this bad?" Cooper asked.

Askon's antenna dipped forward as if in agreement. " More to the point, Captain, according to the long-range scans we have from three weeks ago, Dais'u was not exhibiting this level of therrian radiation pollution."

"What the hell happened?" Cooper asked, his voice close to a whisper.

"At this point, we're uncertain," Askon replied. "But when our sensors have been able to pierce the radiation clouds, we haven't detected any surface destruction that would be equivalent to a high-yield energy weapon that would be necessary to generate this amount of pollution in such a short period of time."

Cooper slowly turned his chair to face the science officer. "What exactly does that mean?"

"It means, whatever the Natuzzi weapon did here, it resulted in ecological destruction of the planet without any physical destruction of the planet," Askon said.

Cooper turned to the view screen, his eyes tracking the sparkling landmasses peeking from beneath the black clouds. He found himself searching for the sense of awe from before, but now all he found was dread. Cooper let out a long sigh. "How long before the Chice would need to consider a planetary evacuation?"

Askon's antenna twisted in opposite directions, and he grimaced. "I'm afraid that that time has already passed."

The iridescent landmasses blinked out as the *Defiance's* orbit took them from the planet's night side and into its morning.

"I cannot posit a scenario in which the planet could be restored to its previous status," Askon continued. "I estimate approximately a week, possibly less, before the planet starts to exhibit inhospitable conditions if it hasn't already."

"Shit," Cooper muttered, dropping his face into his hand. He rubbed his fingers across his forehead. "Shit." He got to his feet and started pacing in a slow circle around the command chair. "Have we been able to get hold of anyone down there?"

The comm officer shook her head. "I'm afraid not," her voice was apologetic. "The radiation is causing too much interference. We have the standard channels open and an automatic message on repeat in case there's a gap in the radiation clouds. But, Captain," she paused, as if taking a moment to consider her next words carefully, "we're not even intercepting any random transmission signals from the planet's surface."

Cooper didn't react. His expression was neutral. "So, you're telling me there's a possibility there's no one down there to even talk to."

The comm officer didn't know what to say to that, so she didn't say anything. Instead, she gave a curt nod and turned back to her console.

"Hell of a start to our mission," Cooper said, coming to a stop behind the command chair. He rested his hands on the headrest of the seat. "The *Reliant* should have been here."

"Their presence wouldn't have made a difference," Zemble said over his shoulder.

"No," Cooper agreed. "But they could have told us not to bother."

An uncomfortable silence fell across the bridge.

Cooper looked around and noticed the bridge crew was trying not to look at him.

"If they're all dead down there," Cooper explained, gesturing towards the planet on the view screen, "there's no one for us to open diplomatic relations with."

Zemble turned around from his console. "We're not certain that's the case."

"If the *Reliant* hadn't gotten lost, maybe we would be certain," Cooper said.

Zemble grunted. "I don't know that that's the appropriate takeaway here."

Cooper turned to face the Elwat. "They're either dead, or they're not. We don't have any way to contact anyone down there. I don't even have to ask to know we can't send a shuttle down without putting the away team in danger. So, Mr. Zemble, what does it really matter whether or not I point out we could have saved ourselves a trip had the *Reliant* not gotten lost?"

Zemble's horns pulled together as his brow furrowed. "Captain–"

Tully interrupted him. "Captain, there's a vessel approaching us."

Cooper spun around. "On screen."

The view screen shifted direction, and in the distance, a small craft could be seen heading toward them.

"Where the hell did they come from?" Cooper asked.

"According to their trajectory, it would appear they originated from the planet, possibly from the southern equator," Askon said.

"Apparently, there was somebody down there after all," Zemble said.

Cooper shot him a look but said to the comm officer, "Open a channel."

"I have," she replied. "But they're not answering."

"I'm detecting a theme," Cooper said. "Is there anything in our records about the Chice being shy?"

"Captain," the comm officer started. "I'm not sure how to say this...." She shook her head. "It's one of ours."

"It's one of ours?" Cooper repeated.

She looked up from her console with a confused expression. "It's a UPA shuttle."

"The *Reliant*?" Cooper asked, turning to to back to the view screen. "What? Were they hiding on the other side of the planet?"

"No," Zemble said almost immediately. "The registry number doesn't belong to the *Reliant*."

"What the hell is that supposed to mean?" Cooper asked. "If it's not the *Reliant's*? It's not one of ours, is it?"

Zemble grunted. "No, all of our shuttles are accounted for. According to its registry number," Zemble paused for a moment, "it belongs to the *Alexandra*."

Cooper took a moment and then shook his head. "I don't know that ship. More importantly, it's not part of this diplomatic mission. Unless there's been a last-minute change, I was unaware of."

"It wouldn't be a last-minute one." Zemble sent the information to the view screen. The screen split in half; on one side was the approaching shuttle, and on the other was the UPA registry listing for the *Alexandra*. "The *Alexandra* was decommissioned almost eighty years ago."

Both of Cooper's eyebrows went up. "What the hell is one of their shuttles doing all the way out here?"

"That," Zemble grumbled, "is an excellent question."

16

THE THING that used to be Erin Calloway was sleeping.

Or rather, it was doing something that was an approximation of sleeping.

Since it had begun merging with the ship, the thing that used to be Erin Calloway had found its consciousness expanding.

Calloway hadn't done this on purpose. It was something that had just *happened*.

It was everywhere now.

She was everywhere now.

Everywhere and nowhere.

Its consciousness was active and at rest simultaneously.

Her consciousness was active and at rest simultaneously.

It was aware of everything that was happening on the ship. Conversations, actions, secret moments, transmissions in and out.

She was aware of everything that was happening on the ship. Conversations, actions, secret moments, transmissions in and out.

In the darkness, the thing that used to be Erin Calloway shifted.

This was a problem, but the definition of the problem wasn't clear.

Identity.

There should be no identity. There was only the *Unity.*

Except there was no Unity.

It was alone.

She was alone.

Except Erin Calloway wasn't alone.

This crew was a part of Erin Calloway.

Zemble was her...

There was confusion in the darkness as it looked for the word, the definition, the idea.

Friend.

Zemble was her friend.

Its friend.

Something rippled out through the darkness. Waves of discontent echoed until they faded away.

Its consciousness was sleeping.

She was sleeping.

Or, at least, she thought she was.

Her presence was at rest. Aware and unaware. Present and not.

Another six feet of the ship, the *Defiance*, was consumed.

Converted.

Consumed.

The discontent rippled through the darkness again.

It was too much and not enough.

The thing that used to be Erin Calloway was aware of this and wanted to do something about it.

Consume.

But not that.

The ship. Her friends. *Its* friends.

The Unity would be everything. It *was* everything. It was the consumed and the not. Consumption was merely an act of reunion.

Except that this ship, these people, were different.

They were different because they were *hers*.

Erin Calloway.

The thing that used to be Erin Calloway pulled back. Awareness shifted and focused, drawing in on itself. And somewhere, deep inside the darkness, the essence of Erin Calloway's humanity was pulled forward to be...

Examined?

Interrogated?

Investigated?

Dissected?

Consumed.

And then it stopped.

Outside its presence–

Outside *her* presence–

There was *something*.

Something familiar. Something strange. Something new. Something old.

An Anomaly.

17

NATUZZI

THE THRONE ROOM was smaller than Gouren Ril remembered.

She stepped through the wide doorway and crossed the marbled floors. Her footsteps echoing throughout the massive domed room.

She glanced up at the ceiling. The murals from her youth were long gone. She remembered the day that her mother, the former queen, had decided to have them removed. It had not been a popular decision.

She brought her gaze back down.

The table that occupied a large portion of the room sat between her and the throne. Twelve chairs were positioned around the table, and another handful of seats along the walls.

Ril walked around the table, her hand hovering over the backs of the chairs, not quite touching anything.

Windows stretched up from the floor, nearly touching the domed ceiling. The noonday sun cast a soft maroon glow about the throne room.

Memories of her mother entertaining large delegations

in the room rose unbidden to the surface of her mind. Phantom laughter that seemed so real, she almost turned in search of it. The memory of a sharply worded rebuke that startled the sycophants into silence caused a shiver to run down her spine.

Ril reached the throne.

It was a solitary chair that sat in the center of the room. Approximately a foot and a half higher than the table and any other seat in the room. The back of the chair was almost twice her height and framed in mataoran gold. The cushions looked virtually new. But as she leaned forward for a closer look, Ril noticed the thin layer of dust covering everything.

She reached out to touch the armrest but caught herself at the last second. Her fingers hovered over the ornate golden figure of the ancestral Natuzzi Mother, her eyes made of oversized emeralds.

The emerald eyes seemed to follow her. She never liked the design. It occupied many of her nightmares when she was younger.

The throne was the oldest thing in the room. It predated her entire family's reign by almost three hundred years.

She glanced up at the missing murals that used to tell the story of the Isg and Ngi royal families, their triumphs, their failures, and their follies.

The throne was older than those murals.

Ril looked at the throne again.

Why had her mother left it when she had been so determined to erase the rest of the past?

She stared at the emerald eyes of the Natuzzi Mother; the setting sun caused them to sparkle. If the ornate armrest held any secrets, it was not about to part with them.

"Your eminence."

Ril loudly sighed at the sound of the voice.

"Sorry," the voice replied awkwardly.

Ril turned to face the young man standing on the other side of the table. She wasn't certain, but she didn't think Desiderio Ito was younger than her. In fact, as she took in the full sight of him, she believed he was actually a few years older. Recent events, however, had moved her to a point where regardless of her age or the age of anyone else, she felt older than them. Much older.

"I'm sorry," he repeated. Desiderio Ito was a tall, striking figure with sharp facial features and a well-defined muscular form hidden beneath his aqua-blue suit. At another time, in another life, Ril would have approached him romantically, and she had it on good authority that he would have reciprocated.

But, unfortunately, this was not that time or that life.

Ril waved a dismissive hand. "Stop it, please. Endlessly apologizing is worse."

Ito arched his brow. "Is it?" He paused as if carefully considering his next words. "I feel as though there are worse things than endlessly apologizing to our people's leader.

"I didn't say it was the worst thing," Ril replied. "I simply implied it was worse than using the wrong title."

Now it was Ito who sighed. "Your majesty–"

Ril groaned loudly.

"*Madame*," Ito corrected himself.

"I take it back," she said, raising her finger. "*That's* worse."

"How is that possibly worse?" Ito asked.

"It makes me feel *old*," Ril replied. "And I already feel too old."

Ito started to sigh but caught himself at the last second.

"You," Ril pointed at him, "are a very wise man."

Ito clasped his hands behind his back. "You realize what you're asking of me? Of the court?"

"I'm asking nothing of the court because I've dismantled the court," Ril replied. "And the Council, for that matter."

"Yes, in your infinite wisdom, you've decided that now was a good time to do away with the traditional governmental structures that the Natuzzi populace have had for the last several hundred years," Ito said.

She gave him a narrow look. "Sarcasm? Perhaps I spoke of your wisdom too soon."

He shrugged. "You insist on not using the traditional titles; you have to expect that it will result in a sense of...familiarity."

Ril walked around the throne, studying the designs etched into the golden back. "Familiarity?"

"These titles help create a boundary between you and your people," Ito said. "'Your Majesty' or 'Your Eminence' are intended as signs of respect."

"And can you not respect me if you can't refer to me as the queen?" Ril asked, completing her circuit around the throne.

"Of course we can," Ito replied. "It just makes things more...difficult."

Ril continued walking until she stood on the opposite side of the table. She pressed the palms of her hands together. "Tell me, Desiderio, about your mother."

Ito looked surprised. "My mother?"

"Yes, I believe I remember hearing that she was a...what was it?"

"A tailor," Ito said.

"A tailor." Ril nodded. "Yes. That was it." She gestured for him to go on.

Ito was visibly flustered. "I'm not quite sure what you would like to know about her."

"Well, I guess my big question is whether or not you had difficulty showing her respect since she was simply a common tailor?" Ril asked. "I'm not aware that your family comes from any royal background. Or have I been misinformed?"

Ito's cheeks turned bright orange with embarrassment. "No, you haven't been misinformed."

"Well, then." Ril spread out her hands. "Perhaps you can explain this mystery to me."

"There is a world of difference between my mother and you, the Queen of Natuzzi," Ito said.

"Did your mother want to be queen?"

"I...No, of course not."

Ril smiled. "Well, it just so happens that I don't want to be queen, either. So, it seems to me that there isn't that much difference between us after all."

Ito closed his eyes and sighed. His head hung low.

"I'm sorry," Ril said after a moment. "It's not my intention to make your life unnecessarily difficult."

"And yet, you do so with unfailing grace," Ito replied.

Ril slowly walked around the table, tapping her fingers against the backs of the chairs. "Tell me, Desiderio, what were you doing before this?"

"Ma'am?"

"Before you became my...." She paused, stopping four chairs away from him. "What is your position again?"

"Your Executive Assistant," Ito replied.

"Yes. That. What were you doing before taking on this role?"

"I was a junior assistant in the Secretarial Department."

Ril stared at him. "I'm sorry?"

"Ma'am, I am but one man, and despite your desires, you are still the queen of the entire race," Ito said. "You don't have one assistant. You have an entire department."

"An entire department?"

"You have three assistants solely responsible for your social schedules."

Ril raised her brow in surprise. "My social schedules? I can't recall a time when I socialized with anyone outside my newly acquired duties."

"Yes, it's a team that's been downsized."

"How many were there before?"

"Fifteen."

Ril managed to keep her expression neutral. "Fifteen people to manage a social calendar." She took a deep breath. "That seems...excessive."

"It's a social calendar for the queen," Ito reminded her. "It's a little more complicated than managing a calendar for a commoner."

"A commoner," Ril murmured under her breath. She rubbed her fingers against the table's surface, not looking up at him. "And the queen before me?"

"Yes, she had an entire department as well."

Ril thought about it for a moment. "Yes, I suppose that makes a kind of sense. My mother wasn't particularly skilled in the standard social conventions."

Ril noted that Ito wisely kept his mouth shut.

"So what is so special about being the Executive Assistant?" she asked after a moment.

"I'm the one that gets to talk to you."

"Lucky you."

"It is a position of privilege and honor."

Ril turned and started slowly walking back to the opposite end of the table. "And did you have this position of privilege and honor with the previous queen?"

"I did not."

Ril nodded. "So this is a recent development in your professional career." She thought about it for a moment. "Is being assistant to the queen a career? What happened to the previous Executive Assistant?"

"She retired after twenty years of service."

"Distinguished service?"

Ito gave a slight nod. "Your predecessor and the rest of the department highly regarded her."

"Any particular reason why she decided now was the right time for her to retire?"

"I would assume it has something to do with the twenty years of service," Ito replied. "Most likely, she saw the regime change as the perfect opportunity to retire."

Ril reached the throne again. "I'm glad my mother's death was able to provide your predecessor with such a golden opportunity."

Ito's cheeks turned bright orange again. "Ma'am, that wasn't what—"

Ril raised a hand, cutting him off. "I meant that genuinely, Desiderio. The previous queen was a," she caught herself before the word *monster* escaped her, "complicated figure. At a minimum, history will spend the next several decades trying to untangle her legacy."

Ito bowed his head. "Yes, of course."

Ril stared at the throne for a moment. Wondering what her mother had felt when she had sat on it. She sighed and rubbed her forehead. "I'm assuming you're not here for me to pester you with questions about how the mundane portions of the royal life work."

"No, ma'am." Ito picked up his datapad from the table. "Admiral Bronwyn is requesting a meeting, again."

Ril clucked her tongue against her teeth. "That's not going to happen."

"No, I imagine it won't," he replied. "I took the liberty of informing the admiral's office that your schedule was full for the foreseeable future. That being said, you did invite them here."

Ril shot him a look. "You have a point?"

Ito held up a defensive hand. "No offense intended, ma'am. I am simply pointing out that Admiral Bronwyn is pressing for a meeting with you because you invited the UPA here, and they sent her as their representative."

Ril was silent for a moment, her body tense. "I invited the UPA here to avoid plunging our planet into a war we weren't going to win."

Ito tilted his head forward. "Of course."

"That doesn't mean I'm anxious to share tea with them."

"No," he agreed. "But they are here."

Ril sighed. "Yes, they are, and if we can get the Executive Committee established, then Admiral Bronwyn and her office can deal with them." A faint smile crossed her lips. "See? Despite what they say, I do have a plan."

Ito made a face.

"What?" Ril asked.

"Regarding the Executive Committee, Sassano Cen wants to meet with you."

"Of course she does," Ril said, not bothering to hide her irritation. "She undoubtedly wants to berate me in person as she has been doing across the newsfeeds ever since I announced the formation of the Committee." She narrowed her eyes, studying his facial expression. "You have thoughts on this?"

Ito was clearly hesitant to share those thoughts.

Ril gestured around the empty throne room. "You're not going to get a better opportunity to share your mind than now. It's just you and me."

"Is that supposed to make me feel comfortable?" Ito asked.

"It doesn't?"

Ito shook his head, but it wasn't in response to her question. "As you pointed out, Cen is opposed to the Executive Committee. Her opposition comes from a place of privilege. Under the previous administration, she had a certain amount of freedom and wealth."

"Cen's wealth is not going anywhere," Ril replied. "And for that matter, neither is her freedom. I haven't thrown anyone into the dungeons yet for disagreeing with me, and I don't plan to start."

"She also had the ear of the queen," Ito said. "Power was the third prong of her success. Under the Executive Committee, that power won't exist anymore."

"Those special powers she enjoyed wouldn't exist anyway," Ril said sharply. "I am not my mother."

"No, you are not," Ito agreed. "But allowing her to argue her case could give voice to an unnecessary opposition and be considered, by most of the population, as a form of verbal assault against the sitting royalty."

"You're worried about my feelings. That's sweet. But I'm a big girl, Desiderio. I can handle myself."

"I'm worried that you might be taking on unnecessary fights," Ito said. "The Executive Committee is a foregone conclusion at this point. You've made it abundantly clear that you're not interested in maintaining the status quo. And, more importantly, you want to make sure there is a voice given to the underrepresented, which in our current climate if you'll forgive me for saying so, is everyone."

"I take it then; you're in favor of the committee?" Ril asked.

Ito didn't answer right away. His gaze dropped to the table as if ashamed of meeting Ril's eyes. "In addition to being a tailor, my mother was a member of the Zenco guild."

A knowing look passed over Ril's face as she slowly nodded. "Ah, yes. They fought for equal rights. The previous administration had the entire guild disbanded after they attempted to lead a demonstration in favor of allowing men to initiate a divorce."

Ito didn't respond.

Ril continued, "I believe that anyone that was found connected to the guild was charged with fomenting dissent and inciting violence. They were found immediately guilty, and the punishments ranged from life imprisonment to death." She paused, searching for a reaction from Ito. His shoulders tensed slightly, but he refused to look at her. "Which one did your mother receive?"

"Imprisonment," Ito answered quietly. "She passed away before my eighteen birthday."

"I'm sorry," Ril said.

"Thank you."

"I am not my mother, Desiderio," Ril said softly. "And she did a great many things that I did not and still do not approve of."

Ito visibly relaxed, but he still didn't say anything.

"That being said," she continued. "The Executive Committee wouldn't have saved your mother."

"It certainly wouldn't have hurt," he said.

"No, I suppose not," Ril agreed. "Despite the tragedy the

previous administration brought upon your family, you still chose this as your career."

"I've seen what happens when you try to change the system from the outside," Ito replied.

"Why would you think attempting to change it from the inside would fare any better for you?"

Ito shrugged. "I didn't have reason to believe that it wouldn't; if nothing else, it was a stable career that would help provide for my father and siblings."

Something clicked for Ril. "Your father has Fey's Euphoria."

"Yes, he does."

Ril tapped her fingers against the table. "As of this moment, I'm giving you a raise and bringing your family to the royal residences."

Ito was surprised. "That's not necessary."

"I'm the queen; you don't get to tell me what's necessary," Ril replied. "My family has done a great disservice to your family. This is the absolute least I can do."

"If you'll forgive me, ma'am," Ito said. "But we are more than the sins of our parents."

"Possibly," Ril replied. "But sometimes I often wonder if, despite that, it's possible for us to outrun the long shadow of our parent's sins." She shrugged her slender shoulders. "Maybe it's easier when your parent wasn't the leader of a planet."

"Maybe," Ito replied. "But I don't know that it would do either of us any good to get into a competition over who had the worse parents."

"Please," Ril said. "It's hardly a competition. My mother tried to start a senseless war. Yours wanted your father to be her equal."

"That doesn't mean she was perfect."

"No, but when you measure yourself against monsters, you don't have to strive for perfection," Ril replied. "You simply have to be less monstrous than the monsters."

"The Executive Committee is a good idea," Ito said.

"I certainly hope so."

"You can't meet with Sassano Cen."

"I should ignore her? What kind of message does that send?"

"One that says you're not going to do things the old ways," he replied.

"I'm pretty sure I've given that message."

"And the people are having difficulty hearing it," Ito said. "So if you're not going to do things the old ways, you'll have to find new ways."

"It sounds very much like you're speaking in riddles."

"There are ways of having a meeting without having a meeting."

"Perhaps I wasn't clear," Ril said. "I'm not fond of riddles."

"You can't give Sassano Cen a public audience; if you ignore her, she will interpret that as a gesture of offense against her."

"That would be a reasonable interpretation."

"Not while we don't know who killed the previous queen," Ito said, his gaze meeting hers evenly.

Again, Ril kept her expression neutral. "You have a suggestion, then?"

"I have a...notion."

18

STARBASE 64

"WHAT IN THE Sam Hill is this supposed to be?" Rabkin eyed the bowl of wiggling worms with a mixture of suspicion and revulsion. He glanced up at the waiter as if accusing him of trying to poison Rabkin. "Is this a joke?"

"I'm sorry, sir?"

Rabkin pointed to the bowl of wiggling worms. "Is this your idea of a joke before you bring me my real food?"

The waiter looked at Dupree, confused.

"It's fine," she said with a dismissive wave. "Don't mind him. He's a grumpy old man."

"All the more reason to mind me," Rabkin said.

Outside of his Fleet uniform, Dupree decided that Jim Rabkin looked like a grumpy grandfather on vacation. He was dressed in a pair of black slacks and matching jacket. The shirt, though, was a shade of orange that was so bright it was almost painful to look at.

Dupree used the chopsticks to scoop up a handful of the worms. "Vrokato eels."

Rabkin's lips curled back in disgust as he watched her eat the eels. "They're still moving."

"Of course they are," Dupree replied, laughing softly.

Rabkin's bushy eyebrows went up with incredulity. "You say that like I'm the crazy man for suggesting my food shouldn't be wiggling around before I eat it."

"Vrokato eels are served fresh."

Rabkin looked down at the wiggling purple worms in his bowl. "Fresh? This is a little more than just *fresh*."

Dupree helped herself to another mouthful. "They're poisonous if you cook them."

Rabkin replied with a strangled grunt.

Dupree laughed, making a snorting noise and almost spitting out one of the eels.

"I was concerned about your mental well-being," Rabkin said, pushing the bowl back. "Obviously, my concerns were warranted."

She pointed at him with her chopsticks. "This is considered a delicacy on Klaertoni Six."

Rabkin thought about it for a moment. "Don't they also eat their own shit?"

"Stop it."

Rabkin looked around for the waiter, who had conveniently disappeared. "Where the hell did that damn waiter go?"

"You have to try at least one," she said.

"The hell I do." Rabkin pushed the bowl across the table closer to Dupree. "Here."

She frowned. "I'm a regular here."

"Congratulations?" Rabkin twisted around in his seat, looking for any sign of the waiter.

"I'm going to have to come back here and endure questions of why my guest refused his meal."

"I'll make sure to cover my end of the check," Rabkin said.

"Woguns are very particular about serving food," Dupree said. "It's considered a very intimate form of socializing. You refusing their food is going to reflect poorly on me."

"Sounds like they make for poor restauranteurs."

"Jim..."

Rabkin stopped looking for the waiter and stared at his old friend. "It was your idea to bring me here."

Dupree set her chopsticks down and sighed. "As I recall, you used to be more adventurous in your eating. What happened to the man who ate luraik stone stew?"

"He got old and developed IBS." Rabkin patted his stomach. "The human body can only handle so much abuse before it either pushes back or gives up completely. I made a promise to myself a long time ago that my cause of death was either going to be old age or something sudden and unexpected. Shitting myself to death was neither of those."

Dupree frowned. "Please, do you really have to be so disgusting?"

"I find that it gets my point across faster. Also, you're the one who's slurping down live eels like they're Twizzlers, so maybe you need to reconsider your definition of 'disgusting.'" Rabkin finally found the waiter and waved him over. "You have coffee?"

The waiter nodded. "Yes, sir."

"Normal coffee?"

The waiter gave him a puzzled look. "Normal, sir?"

"Jim..." Dupree sighed.

"I want *black* coffee," Rabkin said. "*Plain*, black coffee. It needs to be an Earth roast or something damn close to an Earth roast. It can be iced, but I'd prefer it hot. I don't want milk in it. I don't want anything from Backlon. And I sure as hell don't want that spicy shit from Elwat. So, *normal* coffee. You think you can manage that?"

The waiter swallowed uncomfortably. He glanced at Dupree, who gave him an apologetic look. "Yes, sir," he said to Rabkin. "I think we can manage that."

"We'll see," Rabkin said, not sounding convinced.

The waiter left, and Dupree dropped her face into her hands. "I'm never going to be able to come here again."

Rabkin eyed the two bowls of vrokato eels in front of her. A couple of them had managed to wiggle their way up to the edge of one of the bowls in some poorly thought-out escape attempt. "That doesn't sound like a bad deal."

Dupree watched him as he looked around the restaurant as if finally taking in all the details. It was dimly lit, and everything about the place suggested that it was a hole-in-the-wall dive. Except that image was too carefully cultivated. There was something artificial about the peeling paint and the rusty floor tiles. Of the twenty tables, only three were occupied, but that was the benefit of eating during the off hours.

"Where are you staying?" Dupree asked.

"I decided to splurge and got myself a room at a place on the exterior habit ring," Rabkin replied. "It's got a hell of a view, and the bed has olklan silkworm sheets. I'm pretty sure there's a Veelix sonic massager in the bathroom. Honestly, it's pretty damn swanky for the UPA."

Dupree shook her head and picked up her chopsticks. She nabbed the errant eels and slurped them down. "Welcome to the private sector."

"Did I miss an announcement?"

"The Alliance Diplomatic Corps is just renting space here," Dupree said.

"Renting space?"

Dupree shrugged. "A lot of space. The station's owned by Caudry-Yukawa."

"Since when?" Rabkin asked.

"Since they hollowed out the astroid formally known as HH-9B and built this station fifteen years ago. Technically its proper name is *Bathsheba Base*."

Rabkin raised an eyebrow. "*Bathsheba Base*?"

"As in Bathsheba Caudry, the granddaughter of Titus Caudry. The story goes, he didn't know what to get her for her birthday one year, so he named this station after her."

"What happened to just giving the grands savings bonds? Isn't that still a thing?"

"Not when you're one of the richest men in the quadrant," Dupree replied. "And as I recall, you don't give your grandchildren money."

"Well, my current retirement plan doesn't afford me the option just to throw away my money all willy-nilly. You know what the cost of living is on Akmar Four? A gallon of milk is nearly ten times more expensive there than anywhere else."

"Sure. You're going to be spending all your money on milk," Dupree said. "Because that's what Akmar Four is known for. Milk."

Rabkin shrugged.

"In the circles that Caudry and his family run, it's probably a pretty nice gift to get this station named after you," Dupree said.

"Hell, it's a pretty sweet gift in my poverty-stricken circle."

Dupree pointed in the direction of the outer hull. "They're mining rombliem in the nebula. This is one of a dozen rombliem mines in UPA space, and Caudry-Yukawa owns six. The other rombliem hotspots? Backlon space, there's a small one on the other side of Phaw territory, and they suspect there's three alone in the Veneer sectors. Caudry-Yukawa has the biggest energy contract with the Alliance in the last eighty years. All the new quantum drives run on rombliem, and the Fleet is about to start a massive, ten-year overhaul of all their ships. Everybody's getting upgraded."

"So Titus Caudry named his biggest payout after his granddaughter," Rabkin said. "What does that say?"

"It says that Bathsheba Caudry is probably his favorite grandchild."

Rabkin leaned back in his chair, folding his arms. "How much is this actually costing the UPA?"

"Surprisingly, less than what it would cost to build our own station out here. Still." She paused for a moment. "Did you see the construction that was taking place just off the starboard side?"

Rabkin nodded. "If my room were ten degrees starboard, it'd be blocking my magnificent view."

Dupree pointed at him with her chopsticks. "UPA's paying for that expansion."

Rabkin's bushy eyebrows went up. "And that's cheaper than just building their own place?"

Dupree shrugged. "I'm a diplomat, not an economics major. It's pennies compared to what Caudry-Yukawa will make off the rombliem contracts, but the Alliance needed a presence out here, and I suspect Caudry-Yukawa knows that," she replied. "Especially with the political maneuvers the Phaw have been making."

"Political maneuvering?" Rabkin repeated. He snorted. "Back in my day, we just called it genocide."

She shook her head with a chuckle that wasn't really amused. "Why are you here, Jim?"

Rabkin paused before answering as if weighing his words. "Gavin's funeral was missing a few familiar faces. Did you get the notice?"

Dupree absently poked at her bowl of eels, her appetite having suddenly abandoned her. "I did."

Rabkin waited, watching her expression. "And?"

She blew out an irritated breath. "And what? We're divorced, Jim. Had been for nearly fifteen years. Was I expected to break down into hysterics when I heard he was dead?"

Rabkin didn't answer. The waiter had returned with his coffee, and he waited until the server had disappeared again. It was a square, grey mug that looked like it had been carved out of a single piece of stone. He picked it up and took a moment to inhale the aroma. A hesitant smile spread across his face. Rabkin took a sip of the coffee, and his grin widened.

"That is some damn *fine* coffee."

"They import the beans from Zilbanna," Dupree said. "Almost Earth-like conditions there. Everyone else on the station gets their beans from the much closer Anadasa. That stuff tastes like actual space garbage."

"You should have led with this," Rabkin said.

"Maybe," she agreed. "But you were being an asshole."

Rabkin took another sip. "That's nothing new. My appetite may have mellowed out, but my attitude hasn't."

"No kidding," she agreed. "What happened?"

Rabkin set the mug back down. "What did you hear?"

"Just what they put in the report," Dupree said. "Apparently, I was still listed as his emergency contact."

"Sounds about right."

"What about Keiko?"

Rabkin shrugged. "There was no love lost there. Part of

that was because even then, he still had you listed as his emergency contact."

Dupree rubbed her forehead tiredly. "Jim, I don't need this right now."

"I'm not trying to reopen any old wounds here," Rabkin said.

"Then what the hell are you doing here?" She asked. "You want to make sure I heard the news? Sure, I heard. I saw the report. He's listed as missing in action. I know what that's code for. It was a classified mission, something went wrong, and there's no body recovered. That sound about right?"

Rabkin chewed on his lower lip. "Yeah, pretty much."

"All that could have been covered over a subspace message," Dupree said. "Would have been a lot cheaper for you, and I wouldn't have to figure out some way to stay in the good graces of my favorite restaurant. Seriously." She pushed the bowl back towards him. "One bite would go a long way towards me being able to come back here tomorrow."

"Johanna, there is not enough M'reth ale in all the galaxy to get me to put one of those in my mouth." Rabkin took another drink of his coffee. "If it'll help, I can write a glowing review of their excellent coffee."

Dupree grumbled something under her breath and dumped his bowl of eels into hers.

"Not a day goes by when I don't think about Maureen," Rabkin said.

"It's a little different when it's your child that passes instead of your spouse." The bitterness in Dupree's voice was cold and almost an afterthought.

"I'm sorry," Rabkin said.

Dupree set her chopsticks down and pushed her bowl to

the side, having lost her appetite. "It's not your fault. Never was. You don't have to keep apologizing."

Rabkin shrugged. "There are worse habits to have at this point."

"I'm sure there are." Dupree folded her hands on the table. "It's old news, Jim. Sure, it still hurts, but it's been fifteen years. At some point, I had to move on."

"And it never occurred to either one of you to move on together," Rabkin said.

"I wish I were a better person, but I'm not," Dupree said. Her voice was a strained mix of sadness and bitterness. "But I just didn't want to be around a man who would be a constant reminder of my dead son."

"You could have gotten help," he said.

"Help." She scoffed, scratching her eyebrow. "As I recall, your idea of marriage counseling was a bottle of M'reth ale."

Rabkin took another sip of his coffee. "Need I remind you that I was happily married for almost forty years."

"Last I heard, your longest relationship lately has been about thirty minutes at an Akmar Brothel," she replied.

"I made my dear Maureen a solemn vow before she passed," Rabkin said, holding a hand atop his heart. "I would never look for love again."

Dupree rolled her eyes. "Aren't you the romantic?"

"That's what I keep telling everyone," he replied. "How else do you think I get all those free credits in an Akmar Brothel?"

She shook her head. "You are truly disgusting."

"It's one of the benefits of getting old," Rabkin said.

"I'll keep that in mind," Dupree replied dryly.

"How are you doing?"

"I'm doing great. I'm in the middle of trying to get the Phaw to the negotiating table, and I haven't seen my husband in nearly six months," Dupree said. "And now I have an old friend giving me a hard time about my dead ex-husband." The smile she gave him didn't reach her eyes. "Fantastic."

Rabkin frowned. "That's not what I meant, and you know it."

"You're not my therapist, Jim."

"And thank goodness for that," he said. "I don't have the patience for that shit. Besides, most of it boils down to whether or not your parents hugged you enough."

She gave a hollow laugh.

"Gavin knew you moved out here," he said.

Dupree didn't look surprised. "Of course he did."

"We discussed the possibility of concocting some hare-brained reason for him to come out here so he could see you."

"That would have been a bad idea."

"I don't know about that."

"Also, I know there's no chance in hell that any of those words passed through Gavin's lips." Dupree gave him a cold stare. "That's all you."

Rabkin grinned and held out his hands. "And yet you say I'm not a romantic."

Dupree held up her left hand, showing off the two diamond rings. "If you knew I was out here, you'd know that I've been married, happily, for the last five years."

Rabkin folded his arms and leaned back in his chair. "I had heard a rumor or two."

"A rumor or two," she muttered, shaking her head. "You're unbelievable."

"I am what I am," he replied.

"And what are you these days, Jim?" Dupree asked. "Other than a dirty old man?"

"Well, that about sums me up pretty well," he replied. "I picked out a nice apartment on Akmar Four."

She laughed. "Of course you have."

"There are worse ways to live out your retirement."

"Where does dying of venereal disease fall on your chart?"

Rabkin smiled. "That's the beautiful thing about modern medicine; we've got vaccines for everything these days. Sure, maybe we're still looking for a cure to quasidium cancer, but you can be damn sure we figured out how to inoculate somebody against Sweezakaalan herpes."

Dupree shook her head. "You really are a dirty old man."

Rabkin took a deep breath. "We missed you at the funeral."

"Who's we?"

"Mostly me," Rabkin admitted. "Preston was there. So was Victor and Dolphus."

She took a breath and stared down at her hands. "How was it?"

"It was terrible," Rabkin said. "There wasn't a body. Preston spoke, but he was about deep as a rain puddle and twice as boring. I nearly fell asleep. Wanamaker wasn't there. Kathryn wasn't there. You weren't there. It was a piss poor turnout."

"You making a point to visit Philip and Kathryn to chew them out, too?"

"No," Rabkin said. "I don't know where the hell Wanamaker is these days, and honestly, Kathryn's too busy."

"Kathryn's too busy, and I'm not?" Dupree asked, making no attempt to hide the bitterness in her voice.

"She wasn't married to him."

"Not for lack of trying." The words came out of her

mouth, barely above a whisper. She wasn't sure whether Rabkin had heard her and decided she didn't care.

Rabkin leaned forward. "I'm not here to ream you out for missing the funeral; I'm here because the two of you were married for a decade. You had a kid, damn it. I don't care how long you'd been divorced; you had to have felt *something* when you heard he was dead. Regardless of how everything turned out, you're still one of my oldest friends. I'm here to make sure you're okay, Johanna."

She didn't say anything for a minute. She focused on her fingernails, picking at the edges of them. The waiter must have returned at some point because their dishes were gone.

Dupree sighed and looked up at Rabkin. "He's been dead before."

"Declared dead," Rabkin said.

Dupree nodded. "An important distinction."

"I would think so," Rabkin said.

"Considering he came back every time."

Rabkin frowned. "I feel like there's a point you're trying to make."

"I think I'm doing a pretty good job of making it."

Rabkin raised a dubious eyebrow.

"I am a happily married woman, Jim. I not pinning away for my ex–" Dupree caught herself. "For my *dead* ex-husband."

"And when was the last time you saw this amazing husband of yours?" Rabin asked.

"Don't you start with me, old man."

Rabkin held up his hands. "I'm not trying to start anything. I'm asking a genuine question."

"Gavin and I spent plenty of time apart."

Rabkin nodded. "Sure. And then you ended up divorced."

"Son of a bitch." Dupree muttered and shook her head.

"Okay," Rabkin said. "I'll admit, that one didn't sound great."

She jabbed her finger at him. "What the hell are you doing here, Jim?"

"I thought I was pretty clear about that," he replied.

"I'm not so sure about that," she said. "Because right now, it's starting to feel like you're here to make sure that I'm actually upset about Gavin's death."

"Well, if that were the case, it would make me sound like a real asshole."

"Well, you have a history of being a real asshole."

"Johanna," Rabkin started.

Dupree shook her head. "Don't you take that tone with me."

Rabkin jerked back slightly. "What tone?"

"That gentle grandpa tone intended to put me at ease while you tell me everything I'm doing is wrong."

"That...is not a tone I have."

"It sure is," Dupree said. "You used to use it all the time before you decided to lean into the asshole bit."

"It's not a bit."

"Not now, it isn't."

Rabkin folded his arms. "I'll be honest with you; this is not what I expected."

"What did you expect? Me sitting around, sobbing hysterically? Damn it, Jim," Dupree sighed, and it was like the wind had suddenly gone from her sails. "Maybe I just don't have the energy to care anymore. Hell, I *know* I don't have the energy." She looked him in the eye. "My life with Gavin was a long time ago, Jim. I don't know what you were expecting. I'm sorry."

"No need to be sorry," Rabkin said. "Like I said, I'm just here to make sure you're okay."

"Okay." A bitter laugh escaped her. "I don't think I've been okay for a long time. Best I can hope for these days is almost okay."

"I'm sorry to hear that."

"I'm sorry to have to tell you."

They fell into a silence that seemed to fill not only the present but also the past.

Rabkin sighed loudly. "So what exactly are you doing out here anyway?"

"Well, old man, that's a bit of a loaded question." Dupree brightened at the change in the subject. "How familiar are you with the relationship between the Phaw and the Ulriharad?"

Rabkin's bushy eyebrows went up. "The space wizards?"

"They're not an entire race of space wizards," Dupree said, her tone gently chastising him.

Rabkin *harrumphed* and folded his arms. "I follow enough of the headlines to know that calling it a 'relationship' is a bit of a stretch. Weren't the Phaw occupying Ulri for fifteen years? What kind of relationship is that?"

Dupree grimaced. "A volatile one."

Rabkin snorted. "Anything with the Phaw is volatile."

"The Ulriharad have an uncomfortable history of being easily enslaved," Dupree said. "The Phaw are just another in a long line of oppressors taking advantage of a race all too willing to be oppressed."

"It's a little more complicated than that, isn't it?" Rabkin said. "The Ulriharad have a history of being enslaved because they go around the galaxy telling everybody who'll listen that they have amazing space powers and no sense of self-preservation or defense."

"That sounds like a hot take from a man who reads little more than the headlines."

"You got me," Rabkin said. "I have a weak spot for reading up on idiot species that are determined to get themselves wiped out."

"Jim..." Dupree rubbed her forehead tiredly. "I've forgotten what a racist asshole you can be."

"I'm not racist," Rabkin said. "I'd simply rather not associate with species who live under the collective delusion that they have special space powers and a penchant for getting enslaved."

"Not all Ulriharads are wizards," Dupree said again.

"Sure, but most of them are dumb enough to let themselves get thrown in cages."

She looked at him out of the corner of her eye.

Rabkin shrugged. "It's not not a valid point. Sure, you get the Phaw off their planet; that just means they're available for someone else to come in and pick up the chains already in place."

"Actually, the Phaw are already in the process of leaving Ulri."

Rabkin looked at her in surprise. "How the hell did that happen?"

"We're not entirely sure," Dupree said. "The Phaw are hesitant to share anything that would make them look weak, and the Ulriharad...don't like talking."

"They're mute."

"No, they're not mute," Dupree said. "They have the ability to talk. They can talk. They just don't like talking. They find words to be inferior to other forms of communication."

"Other forms of communication? What are they doing? Writing letters to each other?"

"The Ulriharad have nearly one hundred different ways to say 'I'm sorry' with their eyes."

"Of course they would," Rabkin said. "They've spent entire generations being trained to apologize to a daily rotation of oppressors."

She shot him a look.

Rabkin held out his hands, palms up. "Where's the lie?"

Dupree shook her head. "We have reports of a dozen Biltmore class transport ships leaving orbit in the last month alone."

Rabkin gave a low whistle. "Those hold, what? A thousand?"

Dupree nodded. "But since the Phaw aren't generally concerned with creature comforts like we are, intel suggests they could be cramming upwards of fifteen hundred souls or more on each transport."

"That's not leaving; that's hauling ass."

"Something certainly lit a fire underneath them."

"So, if the Phaw are already in the process of leaving, what are you doing here?"

"Making sure they don't wipe out the entire population in the process."

19

THE DEFIANCE

"THIS," Zemble gestured to the report on the screen. It was almost twelve pages long and contained more black rectangles than it did actual words, "is a personal log filed by a Lieutenant Neustadt of the *Alexandra*. And according to him, they were the last UPA ship to make contact with the Chice before the Veneer put up their military base."

Zemble folded his arms and let the statement sit there. He stood at the head of the table in the conference room. Cooper stood at the other end, leaning against the chair. Dheer, Warrick, Tully, and Askon sat around the table.

Warrick pointed at the screen. "It says that? In that report? The one that's so heavily redacted it looks like a Sweezakaal blindfold net?"

Zemble made an affirmative grunt.

"Classified?" Cooper asked.

"That would be a reasonable assumption to make," Zemble replied. "But it doesn't appear to be. Somebody just went through a lot of trouble to make sure that nobody else could actually read it."

Cooper frowned. "I feel like we're both saying the same thing."

Zemble swiped back to the beginning of the report. "Typically, if something's classified, brass likes everyone to know that it's classified." He pointed to the report. "There aren't any security codes on this report, Top Secret or otherwise."

"Okay, so it wasn't classified?"

Zemble shrugged. "Maybe. Maybe not."

Cooper straightened up. "This isn't turning out to be much of a briefing, Mr. Zemble."

"I don't want to jump to any conclusions yet," Zemble replied.

Warrick pointed to a page of the report. "There are only three visible words on that page. I don't think it's a conclusion you would have to jump very far for."

"According to UPA records," Zemble continued, "the last officially documented UPA ship to visit Dais'u was the *Albright*. That was a year after the Veneer closed the border. It was something of a minor interstellar incident and nearly started a war between the Veneer and us."

"Minor?" Dheer repeated incredulously.

"Well, it barely made a footnote in the history books," Zemble said. "I don't know how else you would describe it."

"Right, sure." She nodded, not looking convinced. "Minor."

"After that, it was decided that any communication with the Chice would occur over subspace channels," Zemble said. "The administration at the time, and the ones that followed, believed it was safer for the galaxy as a whole if we just waited out the Veneer."

"Because they figured the Veneer would come back, hat in hand," Cooper said.

"Something like that."

"Instead, the Veneer took out the Chice's subspace relays and put them under house arrest." Cooper looked at the date on the report. "But, according to this, six years later, the *Alexandra* visited, and we didn't end up in a war."

"That would seem to be the case," Zemble said.

"And what were they doing out there?"

Zemble frowned. "I have no idea. As it's already been pointed out, much of this report, too much of it, is redacted, and what's left reads as gibberish."

Cooper held up his hands. "Do you have an educated guess?"

Zemble didn't answer right away. He appeared to be weighing his words carefully. "If I had to make an educated guess." He paused for a moment."I would say they were making some kind of supply drop. But that doesn't make sense because even before the Veneer closed their borders, the Fleet didn't have any ships making supply runs to this sector."

"The *Alexandra* would have filed flight logs," Askon said.

"And according to their logs, they never visited Dais'u," Zemble replied. "In fact, for the date on this report, their logs that we have in the historical records show them in the Haildassa system."

Tully whistled and leaned back in her chair. "That's almost eighty parsecs from here. It's easily a three-month trip to get from Haildassa to Dais'u. And that's at max speed and not accounting for any unexpected stops."

"I don't stay up to date on all the latest technical developments," Warrick said. "But I'm pretty sure Fleet ships didn't have the ability be in two separate places at once back then because we sure as hell don't have it now."

Cooper rubbed a hand over his chin, staring at the report on the screen. "But this wasn't classified."

Zemble tilted his head to the side. "Maybe it was buried."

"Buried?" Tully echoed.

Zemble swiped the report away and pulled up a new image. It was a generic cover of what appeared to be a cookbook. "This was published about sixty years ago by Shelly Demple and Victor Hironaka."

Cooper made a face. "This feels like the start of a long walk."

"More like a brief stroll." Zemble pulled up images of both Demple and Hironaka, as well as several pages from the book. "It's mostly a collection of recipes Hironaka and Demple collected during their time as UPA officers. Dishes such as mamula waffle mushrooms, pickled enfers cheesecake, and sautéed gallafrem shrimp rolls. It wasn't exactly a bestseller and was quickly forgotten."

"Except for you?" Cooper asked.

"Except for search engine protocols," Zemble said. "Their book included six recipes that used Jikkeobana spice." He looked at Cooper as if waiting for a reaction.

Cooper shrugged. "If I'm supposed to be surprised, I'm afraid you'll have to spell it out for me."

"The Veneer have three hundred meals that call for Jikkeobana," Warrick said.

"Sure, okay," Cooper said. "Where's the relevant part?"

Warrick snorted. "None of those meals are particularly edible for anyone who's not a Veneer."

"As I understand it, nothing the Veneer eat is edible for anyone else," Cooper said. "There's something about their digestive system?"

"Veneer food can cause severe heartburn on anyone

who's not a Veneer," Dheer said. "Perfectly treatable. But not worth the headache."

Zemble nodded. "I thought it was odd that a cookbook, even one with recipes as exotic as Vulderran eel salad, would bother with recipes using Jikkeobana spice. Even before the Veneer closed their borders, Jikkeobana spice was rarely exported outside the Empire. Oxeans have been known to cook with it, but Oxeans are, well, Oxeans."

"I'm surprised, Mr. Zemble. I wouldn't have pegged you for xenophobe."

Zemble grunted and folded his arms. "I'm not afraid of Oxeans. They do, however, objectively, have questionable taste."

"Objectively?"

Zemble ignored him and continued, "Neither Demple nor Hironaka served on the *Alexandra*. They did, however, serve together on the *Saratoga* with one Lieutenant Harold Neustadt about two years before the date on this personal log."

"This personal log that's redacted," Cooper said.

"But not classified," Warrick clarified.

Zemble shrugged.

"Why not just delete it?" Cooper asked. "It's a personal log; who's going to notice it's missing?"

"Other than Lt. Neustadt?" Dheer asked.

Cooper nodded. "Other than him."

"Good question," Zemble said. "Because as near as I can tell, Lt. Harold Neustadt essentially disappeared after his time on the *Alexandra*."

"What happened to him?"

"He disappeared."

Cooper frowned. "I was hoping you had something more substantial than that."

"I can't find any record of him transferring off the *Alexandra*. For that matter, I can't find any record of him doing anything after the *Alexandra*. He filed this one personal log and then disappeared into the void of space."

"That makes it sound like he took a one-way trip through an airlock."

"It's certainly a possibility that I haven't eliminated yet," Zemble replied. "But it's a possibility that I might need to extend to the rest of the crew."

"Wait, are you saying the entire crew *disappeared*?" Tully fidgeted uncomfortably in her seat. "The *Alexandra* was a Roddenberry class ship. That's a crew of almost two hundred."

Zemble nodded. "I found a record of the *Alexandra* being mothballed about a year and a half after their last assignment, and after that, it's as if the entire crew disappeared."

"Into the void of space," Cooper intoned.

Tully shivered as a chill ran down her spine.

"I'm not certain I would put it that way," Zemble replied. "But I'm not prone to dramatic statements."

Cooper paced back and forth at the head of the table, giving the pieces time to fall into place. He stopped in front of the window and stared at the planet slowly rotating beneath them. He could just make out the sparkling landmass that made up a third of the eastern hemisphere. He chewed on his lower lip, letting his thoughts wander for a moment, wondering if he stared long enough, would he see a sign of *something* down there?

But then, the moment passed, and Cooper reached the obvious conclusion. He turned and looked at Zemble. "You're thinking they might have been a Directive Fifty-Two asset."

"That's a hell of a jump to make," Dheer said.

"Not entirely," Zemble said. "As Lt. Tully pointed out, the *Alexandra* was a Roddenberry class. She was typically assigned to routine border patrols and providing law enforcement assistance. The Haildassa system was supposed to be on a six-month assignment."

"It would make for a good cover," Cooper said.

"Not if they got caught almost eighty parsecs away from where they were supposed to be," Zemble said.

"To be fair, it was nearly ninety years before somebody noticed."

Zemble grunted.

"Well, the obvious question is: do we have access to Directive Fifty-Two records from back then?" Cooper asked.

Zemble frowned. "That's a complicated question with a complicated answer."

"I trust that you can find a way to simplify it for me."

Zemble pressed the tips of his fingers together. "Directive Fifty-Two is often compartmentalized," he explained. "It exists just outside the classification of Top Secret because if it didn't, it would be subject to governmental oversight."

"And we wouldn't want that," Cooper said dryly.

"Well, it certainly makes it harder to keep sensitive topics out of the public eye," Zemble said. "Our government is made up of members who are fallible and subject to all the same foibles as the rest of us."

"You're saying they can't keep their mouths shut."

"I'm not making a blanket statement," Zemble said.

"But it only takes one person to blow a whistle."

Zemble looked at him, confused. "I'm sorry, which one of us is supposed to be defending the current system?"

"I was teeing up for a specific point," Cooper said. "In this case, everything's headed up by Wanamaker, right?"

"Correct," Zemble replied cautiously.

"That's one man in charge of an entire organization that operates outside the law," Cooper said. "Our government is supposed to be a series of checks and balances. There's nothing to hold Wanamaker in check."

"You're assuming that Admiral Wanamaker needs to be held in check," Zemble said.

"I'm assuming that even if he doesn't," Cooper said. "Who's to say the next guy won't?"

Zemble made a conceding grunt but didn't say anything else.

"So, while we don't have access to the Directive's records, Wanamaker would?" Cooper asked.

"Except I don't know where to reach him," Zemble said. "Do you?"

Cooper bristled slightly. "No. Which makes my point all that more relevant. Is he normally this hard to get hold of?"

Zemble hesitated before answering.

Cooper rolled his eyes. "Oh, for crying out loud."

"I didn't say it," Zemble pointed out.

"You didn't have to; it was written all your damn face. Of course, *Mitchell* would have had a direct line to him." Cooper sighed, rubbing his hands across his face. "Okay, so what can we do?"

"I can send a message to Wanamaker's private server," Zemble said. "But who knows when he's going to see it, and who knows if he's going to have any answers for us."

Cooper nodded. "Directive Fifty-Two is often compartmentalized, and for all we know, records dating back that far might be hidden from the view of even the director."

"It's a thought that occurred to me."

"Great." Cooper twirled an impatient finger. "Okay, so that's the past. What about the present?"

Askon picked up his datapad and tapped at it. A second

later, an image of the shuttle appeared, hovering over the conference table. "According to our scans, the shuttle was launched from the northern hemisphere approximately three hours after the Natuzzi weapon departed."

"That's pretty telling," Dheer said.

"Oh? And what's it telling?" Cooper asked.

"That not everyone is dead down there," she replied coolly, a disapproving look in her eyes.

Cooper scowled and glanced at Zemble. The Elwat's expression was unreadable.

"It's a small ship, Captain," Dheer said. "It's not going to take much for people to gossip about how their new captain was so quick to write off an entire planet."

Cooper folded his arms, his fingers tightening around his biceps. He pointedly turned his gaze to the science officer sitting across from Dheer. "Mr. Askon, how long ago did the shuttle launch?"

Askon's antennae dipped forward and then bent back slightly. "Thirty hours ago."

Cooper turned back to Dheer, unfolding his arms and holding his hands out, palms up. "Plenty of time for a planet to die."

Dheer gaped at him and slowly shook her head. "Hell of a hill for you to die on."

Cooper's jaw tightened, and he took a moment before responding. "I'm trying to make a point."

"Is it that you're a cold, heartless bastard?" Dheer asked. She held up her hand before he could respond. "And before you chew me out for disrespecting my commanding officer, that was an off-the-cuff diagnosis made in my capacity as the chip's chief medical officer."

Cooper's scowl returned, and he looked to Zemble again.

Zemble simply grunted and took a step back, looking faintly amused.

Cooper twisted his head side to side as if trying to crack his neck. He waited another long moment for the flare of his temper to fade. When he finally felt he could talk without biting somebody's head off, he said, "Clearly, I should have gotten Doctor Rabkin off this ship sooner." Realizing he still sounded strained, Cooper exhaled through his nose and held up both hands. "I'm not looking to start a fight."

Dheer pursed her lips. "You keep saying that, and then you do something that does the exact opposite."

He pointed at her. "You already got your freebie for today. Don't push your luck."

"Don't push yours," she shot back. "You can't threaten to throw your CMO in the brig or out an airlock."

Cooper's hands started curling into fists, but he caught himself and forced his fingers to straighten out. "That's...not what I'm trying to do here."

"Then you're doing a terrible job," she said.

"Really? Is that what this sounds like to you? A prelude to me threatening to throw you out an airlock?" Cooper said.

Dheer waved at the planet on the other side of the window. "Well, considering you're willing to condemn an entire planet...."

Tully started to clear her throat. "Okay, maybe we should—"

"I'm not condemning anything if they're already dead," Cooper snapped. "Our mission here isn't to take up lost causes."

"The hell it isn't," Dheer shot back. "This whole damn mission is a lost cause."

Cooper glared at her, not trusting himself to say

anything for a moment. He felt Tully's gaze on him, and he pointedly did not look at her. Instead, he turned to Zemble. "Care to jump in?"

Zemble looked back and forth between Cooper and Dheer and then said, "No."

"No?" Cooper echoed incredulously. "What the hell does that mean?"

Zemble chose not to respond.

"That wasn't a rhetorical question, Commander," Cooper snapped.

"I think, perhaps, we might be getting off track here." Tully spoke carefully as though she was crossing a floor littered with broken glass.

Cooper looked around the room. Dheer was glaring at him. Warrick looked amused, and Askon was pointedly not looking at anything.

And Tully...

Cooper turned away from the table. He pressed his hands together, folding his fingers. "All right." He sounded strangely hoarse to his own ears. He cleared his throat. "This is the wrong conversation. This is the wrong venue for that conversation. But more importantly, it's the wrong conversation." He turned back to Dheer. "Truce, Doctor?"

Dheer opened her mouth, clearly about to continue the argument, when Zemble grunted from behind her. She stopped. Her nostrils flared, and she held up her hands in concession. "Truce."

Cooper nodded and looked at Zemble. The Elwat's expression, as usual, was unreadable. "Okay." He turned his gaze to his science officer. "Mr. Askon, what else have your scans found?"

"Despite its age, the shuttle seems to be in relatively good condition," Askon continued. "Its orbital trajectory places it on course to meet us within the hour, strongly suggesting that the *Defiance* is its intended destination."

"Any indication who's onboard?" Cooper asked.

Askon paused a moment. "We've been unable to detect any life signs onboard."

Cooper glanced at Dheer, waiting for her to fire off another volley, but she sat there with limited restraint.

Cooper turned back to Askon. "Please continue."

Askon cleared his throat. "We've detected no life signs because our sensors cannot penetrate the shuttle's outer hull. It appears to have been modified."

"Modified?" Cooper repeated.

The image above the table rotated, and the undercarriage of the shuttle was highlighted.

"UPA Fleet shuttles, with a few exceptions," Warrick said, "aren't built for long-distance travel. This was doubly so for shuttles built in the early forties when the *Alexandra's* shuttles were produced."

"So it didn't travel here by itself," Cooper said. "We've already established that."

"That would be a stretch to suggest that it's established," Zemble said.

Cooper sighed. "Let's assume for the moment it is. I'd rather not deal with the mystery of how a UPA just appeared out here if we're not going to go with the obvious solution."

Zemble shrugged but didn't say anything.

"According to this," Warrick continued, "this shuttle's outfitted with what appears to be a Class One Ion Drive. Now, you put an engine like that on a Fleet shuttle today, forget about one from almost a hundred years ago; it's going to make like a gorram sumuian firecracker the minute you fire it up."

Warrick gestured to the highlighted portions of the undercarriage. "However, this little Fim'ai bugger's been reinforced with something that looks a lot like Vulderran bipolar ceramic plating. Should keep the shuttle from splitting into a thousand pieces when it hits hyperspace. On the flip side, though, it's going to handle like a pregnant Fe'ihrek whale."

Cooper looked visibly uncomfortable. "Thank you for the...imagery, Mr. Warrick."

"In addition, the modifications seem to be creating a reflective field that our sensors are unable to penetrate," Askon said. "Presumably, there's no one onboard."

"You can reinforce the exterior with titanium hull plating forged on Darious Twelve," Warrick said. "But the shuttle's still going to have a problem with the inertia dampeners. There's no room to install something that's going to handle that engine. So, sure, the shuttle will hold together, but are the fools stupid enough to get on board? Fifty/fifty chance they end up smooth like Khettek toothpaste."

"So, presumably, there's no one on board," Cooper repeated.

"Except the shuttle's clearly headed for us," Dheer said. "Why would it be headed for us if there was no one onboard?"

"If there was somebody on board," Cooper countered. "Why aren't they answering our hails?"

"Because their planet just suffered a catastrophic attack," Dheer said, a tinge of anger in her voice. "Maybe they *can't* answer."

"They're too overwrought with trauma to pick up the phone?" Cooper asked.

"Or, more likely, they're too sick or injured," Dheer replied evenly.

"This feels dangerously close to breaking our truce, Doctor," Cooper said, his voice sounding strained again.

"I'm simply pointing out all the possibilities," Dheer replied. "If there's no one on board, what's it doing up here?"

"That's...actually a good point." Cooper looked around the table. "Thoughts?"

"The shuttle's been modified for a reason," Warrick said. "Could have been a prescheduled test flight before the Natuzzi weapon hit."

"And it just happens to be headed right for us?" Dheer asked.

"The flight path suggests it's heading for us, but is it actually heading for us?" Cooper regarded Tully. "Lieutenant?"

"I've made some minor adjustments to our orbit, and the shuttle's matched our course," she replied. "But if the *Defiance* was programmed as its destination, the autopilot could make those course corrections."

"But if the *Defiance* was programmed as its destination, then there must have been someone to program it," Dheer said.

"Okay." Cooper clasped his hands behind his back. "What are the chances that it's an attack?"

Everyone looked at him in surprise.

"Low," Zemble grumbled.

"Are you sure about that?" Cooper asked. "Maybe there is somebody down there, and they hold the UPA responsible for that thing that just destroyed their planet? A UPA ship shows up here, and they decide this is an opportunity for a response?" He paused, watching them. "Maybe we should just launch a torpedo at it and call it a day."

No one responded.

"This wasn't what I had in mind when I assembled you

all as my senior staff," Cooper said, his voice dripping with disapproval.

"And what did you have in mind?" Dheer asked. "Because the last time you were challenged on an idea, you were...." She paused, searching for a diplomatic word, "less than graceful."

Cooper ignored the jab. "The *Reliant* is missing." He pressed a finger against the surface of the table. "That's an immediate problem we can tackle. Whatever happened to the Chice will be up to somebody else to uncover."

"And if there are people alive down there?" Dheer asked. "We just let them suffer?"

"Assuming they didn't just launch an attack against us?"

"I'm trying to assume positive intent," Dheer said. "Their planet was just destroyed. I would imagine they would have more pressing concerns than picking a fight with the next ship that comes passing by."

"Fair enough," Cooper conceded. "But we're not equipped to help them."

"And we're equipped to help the *Reliant*?" Dheer's eyes widened. "We don't even know *where* the *Reliant* is."

"That's a problem I have faith we can figure out," Cooper said. "Addressing the catastrophic event that took place here is a little outside our expertise."

"It wasn't a catastrophic event," Tully said. "It was an *attack*. That weapon attacked them. And we don't know why."

"And we may never know why," Cooper replied.

"That's not acceptable," Tully said softly.

"I beg your pardon?" Cooper asked.

She looked up, meeting his gaze. "That thing is still out there. Just because it's in orbit around Veneer Prime doesn't mean it's going to stay there. We don't have any way of tracking it. It appears and disappears. Sometimes it leaves a trail; other times, it doesn't. We need to know what happened here so that we have a chance of stopping it when it happens again."

"When?" Cooper echoed. "Not if?"

Tully took a deep breath and exhaled slowly. "I'm not feeling very optimistic, Captain."

Cooper glanced out the window at the black clouds covering the planet. "No, I imagine you're not." He drew himself up. "All right then, let's start with the obvious next move."

"No," Zemble said, cutting him off.

Cooper regarded him with surprise. "I beg your pardon?"

"We're not bringing it on board."

"Any particular reason why you think it's a bad idea?" Cooper asked.

"It's a security risk," Zemble said. "As we've already established, we don't know who or what is on that shuttle. We don't know who modified it or why. We don't know why it's out here. Bringing it on board could open us up to any number of unknown dangers."

Cooper started ticking points off on his fingers. "One, presumably there's no one on the shuttle. Two, obviously, it was modified by the Chice. Three, clearly, it was modified for interplanetary travel. Four, it's out here because there's something onboard that's meant for us. Five, it's a security risk just sitting off our starboard. Mr. Warrick, what happens if the ion engine on the shuttle goes critical and detonates?"

Warrick scratched at the underside of his beard. "At this range? With our shields down? Takes out a quarter of the ship, and that's being generous. More like we're all stardust before any of us realizes what happens. That's assuming, of course, Calloway's enhancements aren't providing an additional layer of protection that I'm not aware of."

Cooper turned back to Zemble. "Any counterpoints you'd like the make?"

Zemble didn't respond.

"Look, everybody wants to criticize me for wanting to write off the planet. Well, here's an opportunity to prove me wrong." Cooper locked eyes with each individual in turn. "Seems to me you should all be on board with this."

No one replied. But no one looked convinced.

Cooper nodded. "Also, I'm still the captain. So if I say to bring it on board, bring the damn shuttle on board."

20

"SOMETHING ON YOUR MIND, MR. ZEMBLE?" Cooper asked.

Zemble didn't follow the others out of the conference room. Tully paused for half a second in the doorway. Cooper watched her out of the corner of his eye, waiting to see what she would do. There was an almost imperceptible shake of her head, and then she stepped through, and the door shut behind her.

Zemble and Cooper were alone in the room.

"Permission to speak freely," Zemble said.

Cooper didn't answer right away. He stared at Zemble, tapping his fingers against his hip.

Nearly a minute passed.

"Captain?" Zemble prompted.

"I'm thinking about it," Cooper said.

Zemble gave a curt nod. "I can wait."

"I'm sure you can." Cooper made a 'go on' gesture with his hand. "Permission granted, Mr. Zemble. Although I'm sure I'm going to regret it."

Zemble didn't hesitate. "You're doing it wrong."

"All right." Cooper gestured to an empty seat at the table.

"What exactly am I doing wrong?"

"You're looking for an easy out," Zemble continued, not bothering to sit down. "You're looking for excuses and other people to blame things on. You're not being a leader."

"And what exactly would you have done differently?" Cooper asked coolly.

"For starters, I would have taken care not to suggest, in front of the entire bridge, that we wasted our time coming out here because an entire planet could be dead."

"Starters? You have a list?"

"Dheer's not wrong," Zemble continued. "You say you're not trying to start a fight, but every conversation you start, you start on the offensive."

"Maybe I'm being put on the offensive by a command staff that starts every conversation with, 'Well, that's not how Mitchell did it.'"

Zemble held up a finger. "And that's the other thing."

"What?"

"You keep trying to blame Mitchell."

"What the hell am I blaming Mitchell for?"

"No one is comparing you to Captain Mitchell."

Cooper barked out a harsh laugh. "Oh, please. Like hell they aren't."

"Every time it comes up, it's because *you* brought it up," Zemble said. "You're using Mitchell as a crutch. Any time you make a decision that you think is bad, you turn it around and accuse us of comparing you to Mitchell."

Cooper glared at him. "I gave you permission to speak freely, but don't abuse it."

"It hasn't occurred to me to abuse my power yet."

Cooper didn't say anything for a second, watching Zemble's gaze. "What the hell is that supposed to mean?"

Zemble tilted his head side to side but didn't say anything.

"Sounds like you're accusing me of something," Cooper said.

Zemble shrugged his massive shoulders. "Then maybe you're doing something you feel is inappropriate."

"I think we're getting dangerously off-topic here, Mr. Zemble."

"I'd wager that depends on your definition of 'dangerous.'"

"Bring it back around, Commander." Cooper's tone turned cold.

Zemble met his gaze. "I think I have reason to question your personal judgment."

"Why? Because you think I'm not listening to my command staff?"

"No," Zemble said. "Because you're going to get this crew killed."

Cooper jerked back as if he had been slapped in the face. "That's a hell of an accusation to make, Mr. Zemble."

"You're leading out loud," Zemble said. "You're second-guessing every decision you make. You're looking for excuses to sway you in any direction. You're not inspiring confidence in the crew. And if the crew doesn't trust you, they will not follow you."

Cooper pursed his lips together. "I didn't take you for a fatalist."

"I'm not," Zemble replied. "I'm a realist."

"I thought you were a man of faith," Cooper said. "Aren't you the one who hosts a Bible study on this ship?"

"I have faith in God," Zemble said. "Everything else; I wait for the other shoe to drop."

"What shoe are you waiting for?" Cooper asked.

"Seems to me it's already dropped," Zemble replied.

"And just so we're both clear, what's that shoe exactly?"

"You shouldn't have said that on the bridge," Zemble said. "That was a mistake."

"Calling out the obvious is a mistake?"

"It is if it's going to undercut the crew's faith in your leadership abilities."

"And how exactly is it doing that?"

"If you're willing to write off an entire planet, then why wouldn't you be willing to write off this ship."

"The safety of this crew is my first priority," Cooper said.

"It should be," Zemble agreed. "But it's not."

"The hell it isn't," Cooper said.

"Everybody on this ship is still painfully aware of how quick you were to offer us up as a sacrifice to avoid a war with the Natuzzi."

"*That* is an oversimplification of the situation," Cooper said.

"No, it's not," Zemble said. "The point is, it didn't happen in a vacuum. The crew noticed."

"Did the crew notice, perchance, that I didn't blow us all up?" Cooper asked.

"It's certainly been brought to their attention," Zemble replied evenly. "But as you've already noticed, you had a ten percent loss in crew before we left Natuzzi."

"I figured out the math on that one already."

"Then do the math on this one," Zemble said.

"Mitchell–"

"Isn't the problem," Zemble cut him off. "He's not here. You are. And you need to stop wondering what he would do differently."

Cooper bristled. "Mitchell wouldn't have suggested we leave because he thought everyone on the planet was dead."

Zemble hesitated before answering. "You're missing the point."

"And what's the point?"

"He wouldn't have done it in the middle of the bridge," Zemble said. "There are some things you don't say in front of the crew. Not if you want them to follow you, not if you want them to respect you. And this crew doesn't respect you." When Cooper didn't say anything, Zemble added, "This isn't a surprise to you."

"Right now, I wonder how much respect *you* have for me."

"I suppose you should keep this in mind the next time you decide to let me speak freely."

"Oh, don't worry about that," Cooper said. "That's an invitation I don't plan on extending again."

"Whether or not you're right, the statement isn't something that needs to be said in front of the crew," Zemble said. "It's an observation to be made among the senior staff, at best. Better if it's just between the captain and his first officer. It will help the crew if they think their captain isn't a cold-hearted bastard."

"Cold-hearted bastard? And is that what you see?"

"No," Zemble said. "I see a captain who doesn't know what he's doing, and he's trying to cover it up by being an asshole."

Cooper waited. When it became clear that Zemble was done, he said, "Anything else you got on your mind that you want to share? Or is that about it?"

Zemble grunted, which Cooper took to be a 'yes.'

"I'll be honest with you, Mr. Zemble; I thought we had reached an understanding."

"So did I," Zemble replied.

Cooper grimaced. "Apparently, it wasn't a mutual understanding."

"Apparently not," Zemble grumbled. "These were concerns I wasn't aware I had."

Cooper started to say something and then stopped. He scratched the back of his head. "I'm sorry, but I think you've lost me on this one."

"I made an assumption about your command experience," Zemble said. "It was an incorrect one."

"I think that's pretty damn close to being over the line, Commander."

"Maybe." Zemble shrugged. "But I don't think I'm wrong."

Cooper glared at him. "You know, I made some assumptions of my own, and they've turned out pretty bad so far, too."

"Congratulations," Zemble replied evenly. "We're both idiots then."

Cooper frowned. "That's probably not a good thing for the crew."

"No, but if we're upfront about it, they can plan accordingly."

Cooper stared at him. "I genuinely can't tell if you're joking or not."

Zemble pointed at him. "My assumption was that if you didn't know what you were doing, you'd make the attempt to get help. I made that assumption because, essentially, that's why you promoted me to this position."

"I thought I knew what I was doing."

"You were wrong."

21

NATUZZI

"YOUR MAJESTY. WHAT AN...UNEXPECTED PLEASURE." Sassano Cen sounded and looked far from pleased at Ril's appearance.

Ril wordlessly took the empty seat next to the older woman. Ito and the guardsman stood outside the balcony, maintaining a level of discretion she hadn't imagined possible when entering an opera house with a personal security detachment of six people willing to lay down their lives for her. Ril watched Cen from the corner of her eye and decided in a split second not to bother indicating that she was even aware of Cen's presence. Internally, she winced at the notion. It was a move she was far too familiar with, as she had been on the receiving end of it when her mother used it. It was effective, nonetheless, in establishing a power dynamic.

Mentally, Ril sighed. *Power dynamic.* This was precisely the sort of thing she was trying to get away from. Instead, here she was, perpetuating the cycle.

Disappointment threatened to overwhelm her, and Ril fought it back. She shifted her focus to Fiametta Sta on the stage below as she executed a nearly breathtaking performance of the hundred-year-old opera about the rise and fall of the third Natuzzi Dynasty.

The singer's voice echoed throughout the vast auditorium, enthusiastically reaching almost every audience member with equal force. Ril crossed her legs, folding her hands into her lap, and took the time to appreciate the performance. Fiametta Sta was considered one of the premier performers of her time, her skill and talent unparalleled in nearly fifty years. Objectively, Ril understood that the performance, Sta's soulful interpretation of the tale of the bloody deaths of the most beloved of the Natuzzi ruling families, should have moved her to tears.

But it didn't.

Ril felt it tugging at something inside her, but she couldn't quite identify what it was and, as such, felt it was easy enough to simply ignore.

But she understood it shouldn't be like that.

She understood that this performance should have been able to have an effect on her that was beyond logic. It should have had an effect that superseded *thinking*. It should have overwhelmed her emotionally like it was everyone else in attendance.

Or at least almost everyone else.

There was a soft clearing of the throat from the woman beside her, and Ril finally turned her attention to Sassano Cen.

There was a forced smile on the older woman's face. Painfully forced. Ril caught a glimpse of emotions lurking behind her dark eyes. There was obviously anger, irritation, resentment, and something else. Embarrassment? Ril felt herself pull back mentally, taking the whole picture of the woman before her. There was something there, an emotion that Sta's performance was supposed to elicit. A hint of vulnerability that had been interrupted. And embarrassment at being caught in the moment of vulnerability.

Ril pursed her lips and turned back to the stage. She found herself briefly wondering what Sassano Cen had seen in the performance that she hadn't.

When Gouren Ril first met Sassano Cen, she was only a child, finishing her fifth-year studies. Cen had been her mother's friend and confidant. A frequent fixture around the palace for much of Ril's childhood until she simply wasn't. Something had happened, but Ril had never been wise enough, or perhaps disinterested enough, to inquire about the incident. But whatever the incident, while Sassano Cen may have stopped being a frequent dinner guest, she certainly hadn't lost any wealth or power.

All the newsfeeds on Natuzzi were owned and operated by the government. Independent newsfeeds, and pirate newsfeeds, were illegal, and anyone caught running one or supplying to one was found guilty and subject to a minimum punishment of twenty years detainment.

But just because the state ran the newsfeeds didn't mean they still didn't need someone to keep them organized. The ruling class of Natuzzi had always detested a committee. Why have five people do a job that one person could handle without any oversight?

For the Natuzzi newsfeeds, Sassano Cen was that person.

Sassano Cen had been old for as long as Ril could remember. As a child, Ril had no true sense of age. Her mother had seemed ageless, and people like Sassano Cen, who were obviously older than her mother, were simply old. As Ril grew up, she never gave it any thought. Like her mother, these people were merely constants in her life, never changing. And now, decades later, it appeared that no time and all the time had passed.

Sassano Cen was a tall woman with a permanent arch on her face. Everything about her was sharp corners. Her hollow cheeks were covered in aged pockmarks, and the fine lines that had defined her in youth had become deep and nearly cavernous. Her skin was pulled taut across her body, but not out of any cosmetic alternations, or, at least, there hadn't been any that Ril could see. Instead, there was a hint of muscle beneath her skin. Her arms were wiry, and Ril noted how her shoulders appeared to bunch up into knots the longer she went without saying anything.

For a brief moment, Ril wondered if Cen would attack her. It was a completely irrational thought, founded in nothing but an unnecessary paranoid fantasy. But there was something in the older woman's body language. Something about the way she sat there on the balcony as if waiting for a moment to *lunge*.

Sta's performance ended, and a hush broke out across the auditorium.

Then an explosion of applause.

As the applause began to fade away, the curtains dropped, indicating the end of act one.

Cen crossed her legs, and the slit in her dress fell across her knee, exposing a powerful calf muscle. The emotions that had been lurking beneath her eyes before were gone now, locked behind a mask of faint bemusement. "You'll forgive me, but I wasn't aware you were a fan of Lorenz Etti opera."

Ril plucked at the beaded lining around her wrist. "I'm not. In fact, I find it rather tedious."

Cen's head bowed forward almost imperceptibly. The corners of her mouth twisted into something Ril couldn't recognize. "Tedious? That explains why you thought it acceptable to arrive nearly an hour into the performance."

Ril looked at the older woman. There was no hint of the vulnerability that had been there only a few moments ago. Now there was only a cold calculation of a predator planning its strike.

The young queen turned her gaze back to the gently swaying curtains of the stage, adopting an air of indifference that she had seen her mother wear so often. She leaned back in her seat, endeavoring to make herself look like she was settling in for the rest of the show. "The first hour of any Etti opera is often an extended soliloquy on the endless sufferings the author had to endure while composing her opera."

Cen clucked her tongue against the back of her teeth. "It informs context," she replied, in a tone that would have normally been used for speaking with a child. "Without the context, the rest of the performance is simply empty. A void with no meaning or substance."

"Context." It was Ril's turn to cluck her tongue disapprovingly. "This is supposed to be the telling of the great tragedy that was the Slaughter of the Barbone Six. This is history. *That* is its *context*."

"History is shared through the lens of the historian," Cen replied patiently as if a teacher explaining why the sun rises every day to a confused child. "History is not meant to simply be consumed by the people." She waved a dismissive hand toward the audience below. "It must be *presented*. To do otherwise would be irresponsible of us."

"Us?" Ril echoed.

"Us," Cen repeated, letting her inflection carry the explanation of the word. She held out her hands, palms up, an empty smile on her face. "This is our role."

"Ours or yours?"

Cen sighed with open disapproval. "Your mother wouldn't have made the distinction."

"And would you have spoken to my mother the way you've spoken to me?"

Nothing changed in Ril's voice, but there was a change nonetheless. The temperature on the small balcony dropped a few degrees. Cen stiffened almost imperceptibly as though suddenly aware she had been walking along the unguarded edge of a perilous cliff.

Cen pursed her lips, carefully choosing her next words. "No, I suppose I wouldn't." She tilted her head to the side and shrugged. "But then, your mother wouldn't have attempted to dismantle the entire governing structure of our people." She paused and then added, "If I may be permitted to share some advice? Be prepared to carry through on your... *promises*. Empty promises reveal an empty leader."

Ril fought the urge to visibly fidget. She pressed her lips together tightly and took a deep, calculating breath through her nose. Almost as an afterthought, she raised her right hand.

The look of confusion on Cen's face was momentary. There was a soft rustle as the privacy curtains behind them separated, and one of the Queen's guardsmen stepped inside.

The guard was tall and wide, with arms thick with muscles and a face conditioned to be free of emotion. His broad chest seemed to want to burst free from his uniform. His sidearm was attached to his hip, but it had an ornamental appearance to it. That wasn't the guard's real weapon. Not at this moment.

"Ma'am." The guard's voice was surprisingly soft.

But it was not his voice Cen focused on.

Her eyes were drawn to his hands.

His massive hands. Thick, muscular fingers attached to calloused palms permanently bruised from a lifetime of fights. The arms the hands were attached to were three times the size of either woman's. Thick veins rippled down his biceps, visibly twitching beneath his uniform. Between the two hands, he could easily encircle either woman's head. One hand alone, though, would be enough to cause permanent damage.

The guard stood there for a second, his massive hands held at his sides as if on display, before clasping them behind his back. He kept his gaze set forward, past the edge of the balcony but focused on nothing.

A brief, strangled sound escaped Cen. Ril couldn't decide if the sound was of fear or something else. Something flickered behind the older woman's eyes. Something raw and primal. Something that was on the fine line between fight or flight.

Ril watched the older woman make a few quick mental calculations. Her body language shifted. The thing behind her eyes moved and disappeared again behind the mask of bemusement. Only now, Ril could see it wasn't a mask.

Cen settled back with a soft chuckle. "You are so much like your mother."

Ril couldn't help it. She jerked as if she had been slapped across the face.

Cen noticed and raised a hand, extending her first two fingers. "That was not meant as an insult."

Ril turned from her, struggling to find some kind of composure again. She made a gesture with her fingers, and the guard stepped back through the privacy curtain.

"Your majesty," Cen began. "Although, I suppose that's an outdated title these days."

"It's going to be," Ril replied stiffly. "But we're not quite there yet."

Cen folded her hands into her lap. "How shall I refer to you, then?"

"Any standard title of respect would suffice," Ril replied. Her voice sounded hollow to her own ears.

Cen's brow raised. "Indeed."

The auditorium lights flashed gently and then dimmed. Fiametta Sta's voice belted out across the theater from behind the stage curtains, somehow filling every space, every silence, all at once. The tenor of her voice demanded one thing of the audience, and that was silence. The audience complied.

Another voice, a deeper voice, joined Fiametta Sta's, and the audience was held captive as the second act began.

Cen adjusted the settings on their balcony, and the dueling voices faded into the background. She turned slightly in her seat, giving Ril her full attention. "Your majesty," she began again. "Why are you here?"

Ril didn't answer right away. She continued to watch the performance below, her ears straining to catch the muted voices. She didn't care for the opera. But this part, where the two lovers met under the Boc'cio moon, only minutes before the bloodbath that would turn the tide of Natuzzi history, this moment was...not her favorite. But it was *something*.

Ril closed her eyes and took in a sharp breath. "You wanted to talk."

"I wanted to talk," Cen echoed as if it was the first time she had heard the notion.

Ril finally turned to face her. "You wanted to talk," she repeated.

Cen nodded. "I didn't want to talk. I wanted you to acknowledge everything you are doing that's wrong."

Ril was taken aback by the blunt honesty, but it only manifested itself in her raised brow. "That's refreshingly honest of you."

Cen shrugged. "I didn't see the point in playing the game."

"The game?"

"No offense, your majesty, but you're not very good at it," she continued. "Perhaps you might be someday. But not today, and, truthfully, I just don't have it in me right now to tear you apart."

"You mean there's no audience, so there's no point in you making the effort," Ril replied.

A small, genuine smile graced Cen's face. "Well, look at that; you're already improving." She rolled her shoulders back. "The fact of the matter is, there's nothing I can say to you that will change your mind. Heavy is the head that wears the crown, except you don't want to wear the crown anymore."

"I don't want anyone to wear the crown," Ril said.

"But somebody needs to."

"It shouldn't be one person."

"Ah, yes, your Executive Committee." Cen wrinkled her lips. "I have heard a great many terrible ideas, your majesty, but your Executive Committee is truly the *worst*."

Ril tried and failed to keep a neutral expression.

"Leadership is best served by one, not the many," Cen continued. "The many, they have...too many voices." She wrinkled her lips. "Too many *ideas*. Everyone is trying to speak over each other. It is a mess. And the people, if you give them too much, can't follow the thread. They quickly lose focus. Give the people too many voices, and they won't know whom to listen to. Chaos."

"It was only one voice that nearly drove us to war," Ril replied.

"War," Cen repeated, scoffing at the notion. "And it was the many voices of the UPA that created an environment where your mother felt the Natuzzi people were threatened enough for her to take the steps she took."

"Is that your argument?" Ril asked. "It was the UPA that drove my mother to want to plunge half this galaxy into death and destruction?"

Cen waved a dismissive hand. "You give your mother too much credit."

"And you don't give me enough," Ril replied coldly.

"*You* are a child playacting at being a queen," Cen said. "I think I'm giving you too much credit."

Ril's hands tightened into fists.

Cen watched her with a bemused smile. "Oh, have I said something to offend? I'm afraid you're going to have to develop thicker skin. Even with the Executive Committee bearing much of the leadership and decision-making, you're still our people's figurehead. You're still going to be the target for, well, anyone who doesn't agree with this new Natuzzi. And as far as I'm concerned, why shouldn't you be? This was, after all, your grand idea." She folded her arms across her chest. "I won't be the first of the critics, and based on what I've heard, I'm certainly not going to be the worst. Say what you will about your mother, but she knew how to take a punch, figuratively speaking, of course."

Cen turned her gaze back to the opera. "I give it three months. Three months before you cave. Either you cave completely to the UPA, in which case, your days are numbered. And no, that is not a threat, your majesty. That is simply a fact. The people who will tolerate the Alliance are far fewer than those who won't. And those people? They won't stop at simply removing the UPA from our planet.

"Alternatively, you'll cave to those very same people and have the UPA removed yourself and quietly abolish the Executive Committee. Or, perhaps, you turn it into a committee of puppets. Give the illusion of change. Either way, this can't last. It's not in the nature of Natuzzi for it to last."

Ril didn't respond. She simply sat there with a disturbing stillness. She felt the fragility of everything she was trying to do, trying to build, and she felt that it could all fall apart in a moment. She cursed her ancestors for building this world, and she cursed her mother for bringing her into it.

Her mother...

The former queen flashed across her mind's eye. Disapproval and anger flooded Ril at the memory. This was not how her mother would have handled this. Her mother wouldn't have even allowed being spoken to in this manner.

But Ril was not her mother.

At least, that's what she kept telling herself. And the young queen couldn't decide if she was lying to herself or just everyone else.

Abruptly, Ril got to her feet.

Cen barely looked up at her. "I see our non-meeting has come to an end."

Ril stood straight, clasping her hands behind her back. "Effective immediately, I am removing you from your position."

Cen stared up at her. The older woman's expression was somewhere between disbelief and amusement. "What are you talking about?"

"It sets a poor example going forward if the newsfeeds

remain under the purview of one individual," Ril continued. Her voice was tight, restrained. But there was a hint of anger beneath it. "It shows the Natuzzi people that our efforts to move forward are simply empty gestures anchored by the actions of the past. So the newsfeeds shall be moved under the authority of the Executive Committee."

The amusement disappeared and was replaced with anger. "You can't do that." Cen rose to her feet. She towered over Ril. "Your mother–"

"My mother is dead," Ril cut her off. "And any promises she made you died with her."

Cen glowered down at her. "You can't make a unilateral decision like that." Her nostrils flared. "Not now. You'll be seen as a hypocrite."

Ril appeared to think about it for a moment. She tilted her head forward as if nodding in agreement. "I suppose you may be right."

Cen visibly relaxed as a small smile pulled at her lips.

"Which," Ril continued, "is why you will resign from your role."

Indignation flashed across her face. "How dare you–!"

"How dare *I*?" Ril countered. "How dare *you*. You insult me. You call me a child. You *threaten* me. What did you think was going to happen? That I was going to leave control of the Natuzzi newsfeeds to a woman who would stab me in the back the first chance she had?"

"I would do no such thing," Cen whispered.

"You think me a fool."

"Because you act like one," Cen snapped before she could stop herself. She gritted her teeth. "But I still respect the memory of your mother, and for that, there are things I will not do."

"Is that supposed to reassure me?" Ril asked. "Because I

strongly suspect there's no difference in your mind between plunging the knife yourself and not stopping somebody else from doing it."

Cen didn't flinch at the accusation. She also didn't argue against it.

"Natuzzi cannot continue down this path. It *must* change."

Cen scoffed at her. "Change? Change to *what*?"

"I don't know," Ril admitted. "But it can't be *this* anymore. This Natuzzi ends only one way: Our collective death. And I will do everything in my power to stop that." Ril turned and started to leave. "You have until tomorrow to clean out your possessions. Your security clearances and permissions will be revoked before I leave this building. My assistant will assign somebody to escort you while you pack up."

"Or what?"

Ril paused at the privacy curtains. She didn't look back.

"Or what?" Cen repeated. "That's how a threat is supposed to work, your majesty. I submit my resignation or what?"

"That's a good question," Ril replied, her voice almost soft enough to be a whisper. "And I don't know the answer. And, more importantly, I don't want to know the answer. I don't want to know what I will do to protect my people and our future. Because I'm afraid you're right, there is a part of me that is too much like my mother."

The privacy curtains parted.

"You can't do this," Cen repeated. She sounded small now. There was a crack in her shell.

Ril didn't respond as she exited the balcony.

"We still don't know who killed your mother," Cen said abruptly.

Ril paused for the briefest moment, attempting to parse the words for a hidden meaning or, worse, a hidden threat. She turned to look back briefly at the older woman, looking for something that should cause her concern. But all she found was a sense of desperation.

Cen opened her mouth but didn't say anything else.

Ril nodded slightly and then stepped out without another word.

"That was not what I had in mind," Ito said in a low tone as he followed Ril down the stairs to the rear entrance where the queen's transport waited.

"It's not what I had in mind, either," Ril agreed. "But in hindsight, it had had to happen."

"Even without her position as the Curator of the State, Sassano Cen is still a powerful woman," Ito said gently.

"I suppose we're about to see how powerful."

They stepped outside.

"You may have made an enemy," Ito said.

"Cen wasn't a friend."

"You'll forgive me, ma'am," Ito said. "But there's a difference between not being friendly and planning your death."

Ril sighed. "You're not telling me anything I hadn't thought of already."

Ito nodded. "Of course. I didn't mean to offend."

Ril came to an abrupt stop. She turned to face Ito. "Stop it."

Ito's face was expressionless. "I'm afraid I don't know what you mean."

"Yes, you do," Ril said. "Stop it."

Ito grimaced. "Yes. Sorry. I just don't want you to create more problems in the process of trying to solve problems."

"Neither do I," Ril said. "I also don't want to have to be looking over my shoulder every thirty seconds."

"Well, perhaps there was something to the previous administration's policy to throwing dissidents into prison."

"I'm going to pretend you didn't say that."

Ito nodded. "I'll admit that I'm disappointed in myself as well. I would like to point out that we no longer have a curator for the newsfeeds."

"It'll be folded into the Committee."

"There's no one on the Committee who would be qualified for that role."

"Right now, there's no one on the Committee," Ril replied.

"What I mean to say, ma'am, is that the Executive Committee does not allow for a curator role in its current form."

"Then I guess we're not going to have one."

Ito came to an abrupt stop. A second later, Ril did too. She looked back at him and took his confused surprise in stride.

"Uncurated newsfeeds would be...." Ito trailed off, unable to find the words.

Ril nodded. "This is what change is going to look like."

Ito cleared his throat and attempted to regain some of his composure. He gave her a curt nod. "Yes, ma'am."

They walked the rest of the way to the transport in silence.

The guardsman opened the door for Ril. The young queen and her assistant were seated before they realized an unexpected passenger was with them.

Director Baldassarre Voa.

22

"Your majesty, what a pleasure it is to see you again."

"A pleasure?" Ril sounded slightly strained as she settled into the seat across from him. It was the only indication of her surprise. She quickly assessed the situation.

This was her *private* transport. No one should be able to have access to it without her express permission. To find someone in here without her knowledge...

She could have been killed. This could have been an assassination. Instead, it was the Director of the Sicurezza Vault. This wasn't right.

Out of the corner of her eye, Ril noticed Ito's expression. He did a poor job covering up his surprise, and the range of emotions across his face mirrored her own concerns.

But if Voa was going to kill her, he would have done it already. This was something else. A threat? A promise? A display of power?

Ril scowled mentally. She was supposed to be the queen, and people expected her to be powerful despite her reservations about the role.

Although, she supposed her mother had similar thoughts.

Ril forced herself to exhale and relax.

It was a game. A dangerous game, but a game none-theless. That's all it was, and she'd be damned if she lost to this *man*.

"As I recall," Ril said, effecting a more casual tone, "You and I parted under less than amicable terms at our last meeting."

Voa paused, his hands folded casually across his crossed legs. She watched as he ran the quick calculations and cast a brief look at Ito, who had done his best to appear inconspic-uous as he settled next to the queen.

Voa was dressed in a manner befitting his role as Natuzzi's premier spymaster. His simple black suit stood out like a bold statement in contrast to the sparkly glamour of Ril's dress. Voa appeared to have aged significantly since Ril had last seen him. He sat with his shoulders squared, giving the impression that he was sitting ramrod straight, but she noticed a curve in his spine that hadn't been there. The curved produced a hunch that was almost imperceptible, but Ril saw it. There were dark, splotchy-like patches across the backs of his hands and on his cheeks. The wrinkles around his eyes seemed more pronounced, stretching out and connecting to the wrinkles across his bare scalp.

But what stood out to her the most was how *tired* Baldas-sarre Voa appeared. It wasn't the exhaustion of a man who simply wasn't getting enough sleep. It was the weariness of a man who was tired of *living*.

The muscles beneath his face twitched slightly, his gaze lingered for a moment longer on Ito before finding hers again, and a bemused smile crinkled across his lips. Whatever he was expecting, this hadn't been it. Or had it? Voa pressed his lips together tightly, and his face became a tight mask blocking out any emotion. "I interpreted our last conversation as more of a simple disagreement over political tactics."

"Disagreement?" Ril echoed. "I believe you accused me of acting *heretical*."

Voa shrugged. "Perhaps a poorly chosen word in a heated moment."

"Poorly chosen indeed," Ril said. "And you're here to offer an apology?"

Voa let the silence stretch for a moment. "Unfortunately, no. I have...mixed feelings regarding apologies in political environments." He glanced at Ito. "Especially in less than private surroundings."

Ril let her gaze weigh upon him. "What do you want, Director Voa?"

Again, Voa glanced at Ito, his face suddenly holding a questioning look.

Ril waved an impatient hand. "My executive assistant isn't the one you should be talking to."

Voa turned back to her. "But is your executive assistant someone who should be present for such sensitive subjects?" He paused and added, "After all, we still haven't found who murdered your mother."

Ril tensed at the mention of her mother's death. "We have several suspects in custody."

Voa nodded. "We have." He shrugged, and the gesture seemed to take more effort than it should have. "None of them have confessed, however."

"Is this surprising?" she asked. "Regicide is still punishable by death."

"True, but it is my experience that when a murder of this

magnitude is committed, the guilty parties are almost always interested in being recognized for their works."

"*Almost* always," Ril echoed.

"And, then, of course, there is the fact that we have nothing concrete tying any of these suspects to your mother's death," Voa continued. "At best circumstantial evidence and unreliable witnesses."

"That hasn't been the sort of thing that's been a problem in the past," Ril pointed out.

"No," Voa agreed. "But, as you've said repeatedly, privately and publicly, you are not your mother, and this administration will not be carrying on the 'questionable' practices and traditions that the previous queen, and queens, encouraged and fostered."

A small smile tugged at the corners of Ril's mouth.

Voa frowned. "I confess, I don't see what I've said that could be all that amusing."

"Simply that you finally acknowledged that you are paying attention to me when I speak," Ril said.

Voa tilted his head forward slightly. "Well, after all, you are the queen." He paused and then added, "At least until such a time as you decide on a new title." He didn't bother to keep the disapproval hidden.

"Ah, so we finally get to the point," Ril said. "You wanted to join the line of critics expressing disapproval of how I'm conducting affairs of state."

Voa waved a dismissive hand. "Please, your majesty, you wound me."

"Do I?"

"I would never be bothered with wading into the senseless discussion regarding the politics of a *title*," Voa said. He sniffed. "A title is meaningless. It's an accessory."

"An accessory that often comes with a lot of power," Ril said.

"Any accessory that comes with power can have that power removed," he replied. "I prefer to obtain influence through methods that allow for more...*permanence*."

Ril studied Voa's face, looking for a hint of something, but again his face was a carefully constructed mask.

"So then, if you're not here to offer an apology or unsolicited criticism, what is the nature of this meeting?"

"A security issue." Voa gestured upwards with a single finger. "Our visitors. Our new neighbors."

"The UPA."

"Yes," Voa said, the single word dripping with distaste.

"Our partners," Ril corrected him.

Now it was Voa's turn to raise his brow. "Partners?" He pursed his lips in thought. "Perhaps occupiers would be a better fit."

Ril clenched her jaw. "Director, I am not my mother. I won't have you thrown into the dungeon simply for disagreeing with me. But that doesn't mean I have limitless patience."

"Of course not," Voa said, vague hints of an apologetic tone in his voice. "I don't mean to test you."

"You have an interesting way of expressing that," Ril said.

"I simply wanted to bring some...concerns to your attention," Voa said. "Our new...*partners* are occupying the *Divine Mother*."

"It was explained to me that it was easier for them to take up residence in the abandoned orbital base than it was to build one of their own," Ril said.

"Naturally," Voa replied. "Of course, I don't point this out to...test you, again, but I find it interesting that their same...

thriftiness is not extended to physical locations here on Natuzzi soil."

Ril clicked her tongue against her teeth impatiently. "Please tell me that there's a point you're here to make and that you will be making it shortly."

"Of course," Voa said. "As I'm sure you've already noticed, with all the changes taking place, I find my attention and focus pulled in so many different directions, resulting in a sense of exhaustion that I haven't dealt with since my youth."

Ril twirled an impatient finger. "The point, Director."

Voa leaned forward, keeping his gaze level with Ril. "I have reports from reliable sources regarding the vessel that was previously docked at the *Divine Mother*," Voa continued, his voice maintaining its smooth, lecture-like tone. "I believe it was the vessel your brother was previously stationed on."

"The *Defiance*," Ril said quietly.

"Yes."

Something bugged Ril, and she doubled back. "Reports?"

"Yes."

Ril frowned. "We made the UPA certain promises. Conditions were set."

"Yes, I was made aware of these...promises and conditions."

Ril leveled her gaze at Voa. "One of those conditions was that any UPA presence would be afforded diplomatic immunity and sovereign territory rights."

Voa hissed under his breath and took great pains to keep his face from twisting into an unforgiving snarl. "An ill-conceived concession."

"It was not a concession," Ril said. "It was offered to the Alliance as a gesture of goodwill."

"Yes, I'm aware of all the goodwill gestures you have been making towards the UPA," he replied. "And I cannot help but notice that UPA has failed to make any in return."

"That could be perhaps because *we* were the aggressors."

"That is not how everyone sees it."

"Fortunately, these are decisions I don't need to run past everyone," Ril replied coolly.

A thin smile passed across Voa's lips. "And you say that you are nothing like your mother."

Ril's hands began to curl into fists. She caught herself and forced her fingers to stretch back out. "I would advise you to choose your words more carefully, Director Voa, so we don't find ourselves in another situation where you might have to weigh the political ramifications of offering an apology."

Voa bowed his head slightly. "Sound advice, your eminence." He sat back.

Ril kept her eyes from rolling. She took a deep breath. "I'm growing tired of this game we're playing, Director. I have other things I would care to accomplish today."

"Naturally," Voa said. "The point, as it were?"

"It would be greatly appreciated. Something in these reports bothers you?"

"Beyond the simple presence of a non-Natuzzi ship, with a non-Natuzzi crew occupying a Natuzzi orbital station?" Voa asked.

"Yes," Ril replied coolly.

Voa's lips tightened for a moment. "It was explained to me that the *Defiance* underwent some minor retrofit while docked at the base. Except my intel suggests that this alleged refit did not occur."

"Your intel?" Ril did not bother to disguise her displeasure.

"Raw materials were delivered, but according to my sources, no such work was done onboard on the *Defiance*," Voa said.

"I fail to see the issue and, moreover, I fail to see how this is any of our business."

Voa's eyes widened slightly. "It's being conducted onboard a Natuzzi station well within Natuzzi territory."

"That does not give us the right to spy on them."

"I would never dare correct her majesty, but by their very presence, it not only gives us that right, but it is also a responsibility on our part to do just that."

"The UPA is here as our *guests*."

Voa's jaw clenched tightly. "That is highly debatable."

Ril glowered at him. "In fact, it is not."

"You behave as if they are innocents," Voa said. "Need I remind you that the UPA sent its spies to our planet first?"

"And in retaliation, my mother nearly started a war that would have torn this corner of the galaxy apart."

"And so now we simply cower in the corner like a small animal that's been beaten one too many times?"

"Tread carefully, Director."

Voa pulled back, composing himself. "The UPA is hiding something from us."

"That is something of a leap, given the evidence you've presented thus far," Ril replied. "And given the previous administration's behavior, I can't fault them for being slow to fully reengage with us."

"That is a...*foolish* view," Voa said.

"And that is a remark that could get you withdrawn from your position, Director Voa," Ril replied evenly.

"Ah, I was wondering when you would use that particular threat," Voa said. He plucked at a thread along his sleeve, a smile spreading across his face.

"That's an interesting reaction to hearing you might find yourself in a forced retirement," Ril said.

Voa steepled his fingers together. "I believe this is where I take the time to remind you that as the Director of the Sicurezza Vault, I have access to *sensitive* information. The kind of information that could be disastrous for this administration if made public."

Ril found herself nearly overcome with rage. It took every ounce of her willpower not to move. Not to reach across the transport and wrap her hands around the elderly Natuzzi's neck and slowly choke him to death. Director Voa may have been a skilled spymaster, proficient in deceit and trickery, subterfuge and lies, but he was also nearly three times her age. He would put up no fight. It would be over in a matter of minutes, if not seconds. And that would be the end of it. As the Natuzzi Queen, she could not be held guilty of murder. Death by the queen's hand was considered righteous and legal, regardless of the circumstances involved.

And yet....

Voa met her gaze evenly, casually arching his brow as if daring her to follow through.

Ril took a deep breath, inhaling through her nose. "You play a dangerous game, Director Voa." Her voice was low, almost a whisper.

He held out his hands, palms up. "Unfortunately, at this late phase in my life, these are the only games I know how to play."

"Perhaps you should consider taking the opportunity to broaden your horizons," she said.

"I'll take it under consideration."

Ril settled back against her side of the transport. When she felt composed again, she asked, "Was that all?"

"This is ill-advised," Voa said.

"So you've already advised me."

"The *Divine Mother* is *ours*," Voa said. "This planet is *ours*. This space is *ours*. We were here long before the UPA and will still be here long after."

"Then perhaps you shouldn't waste so much time with trivial matters here in the present," Ril said.

"Trivial?" Voa repeated. "I would not say that wanting to be informed on the actions of an occupying force *trivial*."

Ril stared at him for a second and gestured to the door. "I have other appointments to keep, Director."

Voa paused as if he were going to push the issue. A brief moment of silence passed, and then he simply bowed his head. "Of course, your majesty. Thank you for your time."

After the director left, Ril shared a wordless glance with Ito, and her executive assistant followed suit, moving to the front of the transport.

Once she was alone, Ril allowed herself to sag back in her seat and let the weight of everything just wash over her. As the transport started moving, anger and fear surged through her body, and she felt herself being pulled in too many directions.

Her breath caught in her throat. She tightened her fingers across the soft cushions of her seat, trying to focus her mind on something else, anything else. Something that would calm her back down, something that would distract her from what felt like a disaster that was unfolding around her in slow motion.

That was when she noticed the small crystal coin sitting across from her.

She wasn't sure how she had missed it before. There was

nothing else on the seat. It was small, only an inch tall, and maybe twice as wide. It hadn't been there before, had it?

She had been so focused on Voa's words that she hadn't noticed his movements. The crystal coin had clearly been carefully placed where she would have to notice it once Voa had left.

Ril started to reach for it and then caught herself at the last second.

Across the side of the coin was a simple design of Natuzzi Mother, her hands reaching out holding Natuzzi.

It was the mark of the Sacellum.

23

THE DEFIANCE

IT HAD BEEN NEARLY AN *HOUR*.

Cooper stopped pacing in front of the shuttle bay doors and glanced at the time on his communicator. It was actually over an hour now.

One hour and five minutes.

Cooper watched as the seconds turned over.

One hour and six minutes.

He returned his comm to the zippered pocket on the sleeve of his bicep and turned his attention back to the scene that had been playing out for the last hour and six minutes.

When he had ordered the *Alexandra's* shuttle brought on board, *this* was not what he had in mind.

Warrick's four-man team had meticulously gone over every inch of the shuttle's exterior with every piece of scanning equipment they had on board, and not one of them had actually gained entry to the vessel.

According to the faded writing along its starboard side, the Alexandra's shuttle, which went by the name of the *Gibson*, appeared in person exactly what it had appeared to be on their sensors: a relic from nearly a hundred years ago. It was smaller than any of the *Defiance*'s shuttles, built to only hold two or three people, with most of its space intended for storage. The exterior had a sandblasted appearance that Warrick's team identified as a result of flying under an atmosphere for extended periods. The hull was dented and malformed. The original shape of the ship had probably been a short cylinder. But now, thanks to the strange upgrades, it looked like a space box.

Cooper had been surprised that the door hadn't fallen off as soon as the shuttle had settled down. And when it hadn't, he was doubly surprised when Warrick insisted they give the shuttle's exterior a complete, fully detailed exam before moving inside.

And now that they had spent an hour and ten minutes examining the exterior of the *Gibson*, Cooper had moved passed surprise and impatience and was approaching pissed off.

His comm buzzed with an alert. He didn't need to bother to check it; he knew what it was. It was an hourly alert. Which meant they were now at an hour and fifteen minutes.

Cooper finally lost any sense of control and stomped across the shuttle bay.

A crewman, examining a collection of exposed cables that hung free of a hull panel near the front of the shuttle, caught sight of Cooper approaching out of the corner of his eye and scrabbled to his feet. "Captain?"

Cooper ignored him and stormed around to the rear of the shuttle.

"How much longer?" Cooper snapped.

Warrick was crouched underneath what was supposed to be the added ion drive. He had a plasma torch in one hand and a scanner in the other. He had half the rear panels of the ion drive open, and there was a dull blue glow emit-ting from the opening. He glanced back at Cooper. "How much longer? For what?"

"You've been staring at the outside of this damn thing for over an hour," Cooper said.

"Would you be more comfortable staring at it outside the ship?" Warrick asked. "Through the relative safety of our sensors? Because I know I would."

"Mr. Warrick." Cooper slammed his fist into the side of the ion drive.

Warrick made a face and got to his feet. He carefully placed himself between Cooper and the ion drive. "I wouldn't do that. I don't know how stable this thing is. It looks like it's been attached to the shuttle with whatever passes for spit and Qeebvavan tape down there. I don't know how much juice this thing has, but I'm pretty sure it's still enough for it to go critical if somebody punches it for no reason."

Cooper folded his arms again. "It's been over an hour, Commander. Why aren't we inside the damn shuttle?"

"Why aren't we inside the damn shuttle?" Warrick repeated in disbelief. He waited a moment, just in case it wasn't a serious question. When he realized it was, he shook his head and walked around to the starboard side, gesturing for Cooper to follow him.

They stopped at an officer who had a portable diag-nostic console set up on scaffolding and was examining something on the shuttle's roof. Warrick pointed to the diag-nostic screen. "Do you know what that is?"

"No," Cooper replied coolly.

"It's the boran rating for the delta coils," Warrick said. "Standard levels for ships this size and this old? Point-oh-five, and that's being generous. According to this, though? It's three times that."

"So?" Cooper said. "What does it mean that they're higher than that?"

Warrick held out his hands and shrugged. "Honestly? I'm not sure. Any other situation, I'd say it's probably just a maintenance issue. Delta coils didn't get cleaned when they were supposed to be. But this isn't any other situation. They haven't been replaced. Near as we can tell, they're still the original coils. Which means that they're easily over a hundred years old. So, the reality of the situation is, they shouldn't be functioning at all. They have a life of fifty years, and that's if you're maintaining them properly. And there's no way anyone down there was maintaining them properly." He jabbed a finger at the hull plating that covered nearly three-quarters of the shuttle's undercarriage. "None of that belongs there, and it looks like a blind Bethari monkey installed it. In addition, the ambient temperature of the shuttle's hull is actually six points higher than it should be. I can't account for that one, either. After sitting outside in the vacuum, the hull should still be a little cool to the touch. But it's not. It's not even room temp. Go on, touch it." Warrick nodded at the shuttle's hull.

Cooper made no move to unfold his arms. "I'll take your word for it."

"Then maybe you can take my word when I say I don't want to open this damn thing until I'm certain it's not going to blow up the ship."

"The sensors have already–"

Warrick held up his hand, cutting him off. "All due respect, Captain, but the sensors can't even tell us why the gorram shuttle is running three degrees warmer than it should be. The sensors also tell us there's nobody onboard the damn thing. At least there's no one alive."

"Mr. Warrick, you can't argue the sensors are faulty and reliable in the same sentence," Cooper said through a clenched jaw.

"I sure can," Warrick said. "Especially when our sensor array is in the process of being rebuilt by an unknown alien intelligence that isn't bothering to give me detailed blueprints of her upgrades."

"Commander, I appreciate your abundance of caution, but I don't think we're going to find the answers we are looking for on the outside of the shuttle."

"We're also not going to find them if it turns out the Chice rigged the damn thing to explode like a Sweezakaal virgin on prom night the minute we gain access."

Cooper looked like he wanted to say something else, but instead, he turned and took a few steps away from the shuttle. He stopped halfway to the shuttle bay doors. He didn't hear a change, but he felt the engineering crew literally stop what they were doing and watch him.

Cooper turned around sharply, but the only one watching him was Warrick.

Cooper started back towards the shuttle, but Warrick met him halfway.

"Commander."

"Captain, permission to speak freely?" Warrick asked.

"No."

Warrick looked surprised.

"You're already in the doghouse," Cooper explained. "I'd rather not have to write you up for insubordination."

Warrick raised an eyebrow. "I beg your pardon?"

"It's been my experience today, Mr. Warrick, that when

an officer asks permission to speak freely, they're going to say something that I'm not going to like."

"That doesn't mean they're being insubordinate," Warrick said.

"No, but they usually go hand-in-hand," Cooper replied, looking past Warrick at a crewman who fired up a plasma torch.

"You're not helping matters," Warrick said.

Cooper's gaze shifted back to Warrick. "What did I just say, Commander?"

Warrick ignored the question. "You can't be stomping around here like a zrar'gul."

"I don't know what that is."

"It's an animal on Gosuwei that looks like a cross between a monkey and miniature sperm whale and is generally miserable all the time," Warrick said.

"I oughta kick you off the ship."

"Then I guess it's a good thing we can't find the *Reliant*," Warrick shot back.

"Why the hell does everybody think I'm out to start a damn fight with them? I'm the captain of this ship. Would it kill any of you to show me a modicum of respect?"

Warrick opened his mouth and then immediately shut it.

Cooper watched something flicker across the chief engineer's eyes. "You almost got yourself demoted back down to ensign, didn't you?"

Warrick took half a step back, exhaling. "I sure did."

Cooper shook his head. "I don't know how Mitchell put up with you people," he muttered. "I want to get on that shuttle."

"And as soon as it's safe, Captain, you will be the second

person on there," Warrick said. "But that's not going to happen until I know for certain that it's going to be safe."

"Second person?"

"Unless you want to be the one who tests whether or not there is a literal tripwire in there," Warrick offered.

"Fair enough," Cooper said.

"All due respect, Captain, but you have to go."

"I have to go?" Cooper repeated.

Warrick pointed to the doors. "You can't stay here. It's not helping matters. Your presence is causing stress."

"I'm the captain of this ship," Cooper said.

"Yes, it's been mentioned once or twice."

Cooper either didn't hear the sarcasm, or he chose to ignore it. "I can go wherever I damn well please."

"So why don't you go hover around somebody else," Warrick said. "You being here isn't going to make anything move faster. In fact, it's making things move slower." He jerked his head back, nodding at the crewman on the shuttle's roof. "You see Laslo up there? He's been in that one spot for fifteen minutes trying to figure how out to remove the surface plating." Warrick shook his head. "It's not that complicated. Shouldn't be taking him that long. You know why it's taking him that long?"

"Because you don't apparently have any control of your people?" Cooper suggested.

"It's taking him that long because his captain is hovering around him like a third-grade Catholic school teacher looking to beat the ass of the first kid that even *thinks* about taking the Lord's name in vain."

"Commander? We found something." The crewman on the roof of the shuttle waved Warrick over.

"See?" Warrick said. "You get off their back, and suddenly they find something."

Cooper and Warrick walked back to the shuttle and climbed up the scaffolding. The crewman, an older man with greying hair and a squat nose, pointed to the surface plating he had managed to remove. Underneath the ancient rusted exterior was a layer of what appeared to be a thick, luminescent gel.

"Looks like it's underneath the entire hull," the crewman said. "It's not conducting anything. It seems to be absorbing hot and cold, in addition to any signals from our scanners. I think it's why we're having difficulty getting any solid readings from the interior."

"What is it?" Cooper asked.

Warrick leaned in for a closer look. "If I didn't know any better, I'd say it's a bioelectric resistance gel. The Sund'ara use it for black hole surfing. Supposed to be a solid replacement for inertia dampeners, except you can't make enough to coat an entire starship." Warrick sat back on his heels. "If the whole shuttle has this...." He shook his head. "Doesn't make any sense."

"It does if these readings are correct." One of the crewmen from below held up his datapad for Warrick to see. "I found an external port finally. Looks like half the shuttle has been converted to datacore storage. Well over fifty exabytes."

Warrick whistled. "That's nearly six times the size of our datacore." He rubbed a hand across his beard. "A datacore that size on a shuttle as old as this?" Warrick started running some numbers. "Theoretically, I suppose, the gel could keep the datacore from overheating or shorting out if the ship were to jump to ion speed. Of course, you still have the problem of killing anybody onboard if they decide to take the trip, too. There's no way they've got enough gel here to keep anybody from ending up like Senwe'an paste."

Cooper made a face. "You certainly have a way with words, Mr. Warrick." His communicator chirped, and Cooper pulled it out. "Yes?"

"Captain," Askon said. "Your presence is requested on the bridge."

"Is it important?" Cooper asked. "We're kind of in the middle of something here."

It was Zemble who replied. "If you're interested in discovering what happened to the *Reliant*, yes, I would say it's important."

24

"I DON'T BELIEVE the *Reliant* ever arrived in this system."

Cooper and Zemble stood on either side of Askon's bridge station. Cooper looked back and forth between the two men with a healthy degree of skepticism. "I'm sorry?"

Zemble nodded at Askon. "Go on."

Askon's antennae dipped slightly, and he gestured to the star chart on the screen. A red line appeared, tracking between Natuzzi and Dais'u. "This was the *Reliant*'s filed flight plan. However, I have reason to believe the *Reliant* ended up *here*."

A green line appeared on the screen, tracking from Natuzzi to a location six parsecs out from Dais'u.

"Where's that?" Cooper asked.

"That, Captain, is the current location of the plasma storm we've been tracking," Askon said.

Cooper glanced at Zemble. "That's a hell of a coincidence."

"I don't believe in coincidences," Zemble grunted.

"I'm not going to get into what you believe," Cooper said. He stared at the track on the screen, rubbing his chin.

He nodded at Askon. "How'd you arrive at this? You couldn't have tracked their quantum drive. Not from this distance."

Askon's antennae dipped lower and then raised again, the Knok's version of a nod. "We've been experimenting with a different method."

"We?" Cooper echoed. "Experimenting?"

Askon glanced at Zemble, who tilted his head forward ever so slightly.

Askon pressed his fingertips together. "There's an...algorithm we've been developing that can track a starship across the subspace relay network, utilizing the directional ping a starship sends whenever it passes through the receiving radius of a relay."

Cooper frowned. "Since when does our access to subspace relays include scraping location data?"

Neither Zemble nor Askon responded.

Cooper folded his arms. "What purpose was this algorithm developed for?"

Again, neither Zemble nor Askon answered him.

Cooper's gaze darkened. "This sounds like spyware."

"There are some who would consider us a spy ship," Zemble said.

Cooper muttered something under his breath that neither man caught, but based on Cooper's expression, it clearly wasn't a polite turn of phrase.

"You can't be surprised that we have departments working on espionage-focused projects," Zemble continued.

"I can be when *nobody* tells me about them," Cooper said.

"It's an experimental project," Zemble said. "We weren't hiding it from you; it just wasn't a priority to debrief you on it."

Cooper jerked his chin at the screen. "Doesn't seem very experimental to me."

"I understand your concerns, Captain," Askon said. "But the data we're pulling is stored in the relay's short-term memory circuits. It's reliable for only up to forty-eight hours."

"That's a pretty big window," Cooper said.

"It's also a pretty big radius," Askon gestured at the circle encompassing the *Reliant*'s possible location. "That's nearly a hundred parsecs. There are many different directions a starship could go from there."

"And your argument is?"

"I'm not making an argument, Captain Cooper," Askon said. "I'm pointing out the facts. Simply scraping location data isn't going to help anyone. We're not exploiting a weakness in the network. This data is indecipherable without this algorithm."

"And what exactly is your algorithm doing?" Cooper asked.

"Extrapolating a potential timeline," Askon replied. "Building on data points we already had, such as the *Reliant*'s previously filed flight plan. The algorithm plots out the next logical subspace relay for the starship to have passed. It cross-checks the data at the relay, and if it finds a match, it starts the process all over again. If it doesn't, it doubles back and recalculates the next logical destination."

"Okay." Cooper folded his arms. "It's still a big chunk of space for them to be in."

"True. But based on our inability to contact them, the plasma storm seems the most logical location," Askon said.

"We can find out right now," Zemble said. "We set a course for that storm; we can be there within ten hours."

Cooper studied the star chart for a moment. "Okay, the

plasma storm might be the most logical location, but how likely is it?"

Askon hesitated before answering. "Previous attempts to utilize this algorithm resulted in a twenty percent success rate."

"That's not exactly what I was hoping to hear," Cooper said tightly.

"However," Askon continued. "Previous attempts to use the algorithm had more wide-ranging variables."

"Meaning?" Cooper asked.

"Here we know where the *Reliant* was and where it was supposed to be," Askon said. "Still a considerable gap. But it substantially narrows down the variables. With that in mind, I would adjust the possibility of success to over sixty percent."

"Sixty percent?" Cooper echoed. "That's a hell of a jump." He studied the location of the plasma storm. "It would certainly explain why we can't reach them. The storm's blocking most of the direct subspace signals. But how the hell did they end up there? What did their sensors pick up in the middle of that storm that caused Yolish to change course?"

"Possibly something that had been there before the plasma storm reached it." Askon tapped away at his console. The star chart shifted and morphed into a different configuration. "This is the trajectory of the plasma storm over the last forty-eight hours. It originated just past the Disyerto Nebula and was on track to disperse into the Chamuscar Astroid Belt two days from now."

Cooper shook his head. "That puts the storm heading in the opposite direction."

Askon's antennae dipped forward in a nod. "Something

caused the storm to change direction, possibly the same thing that caused the *Reliant* to change course."

Cooper raised an eyebrow. "That's a hell of a leap. Do you have anything to back that up?"

The star chart shifted again, zooming in on the current location of the plasma storm. The storm's color shifted to a light transparent blue, revealing a planetary system.

"This system is designated Xelzama K-T2," Askon said. "It contains a handful of small planets, all inhospitable towards most lifeforms. However, current UPA intelligence suggests that there's a possibility that the Oxean Syndicate may have a base of operations on the second moon of the third planet. The moon's actually slightly larger than most of the planets, and long-range sensors have detected subtle shifts in its atmospheric conditions that suggest potential terraforming."

Cooper studied the coordinates. "This is in the Neutral Zone."

"The edge," Askon clarified.

"What could have redirected the course of a plasma storm?" Cooper asked.

"Any number of things." Askon steepled his fingers. "Typically, plasma storms are directed by solar flares and gravity wells. But with enough power, you could simulate either one of these or even generate something else entirely. A group on Bethar has been experimenting with using retrofitted ion drives to create stable paths through plasma storms. It's been theorized that the same equipment could also be used to redirect a storm."

Cooper glanced at Zemble. "Thoughts?"

"The UPA's current policy regarding the Syndicate is... complicated at best," Zemble grumbled. "The current administration views the Syndicate as a legitimate governing authority. The briefs coming out of Command Central all essentially say the same thing: they don't want us to do anything that could threaten any kind of potential treaty. That being said, no Alliance vessel would ignore an S.O.S."

Cooper raised both eyebrows at that. "We didn't intercept any emergency calls."

"It's possible that since the *Reliant* departed before us, they would have intercepted the S.O.S. before us as well," Askon said. "And then once the plasma storm moved into place, that signal, along with the *Reliant*'s, was blocked off."

"Again, that's a hell of a leap," Cooper said.

Askon's antennae bent back. "Agreed."

"In addition, that intelligence is over six months old," Zemble said. "And certainly doesn't account for any of the changes that have been taking place in this sector."

"Which is to say?" Cooper asked.

"That if the *Reliant* is there, it could be for some other reason that's entirely unrelated to the Syndicate," Zemble said.

"But still related to the shifting of the plasma storm," Cooper pointed out.

"Which could easily be explained by any solar flares within four lightyears," Askon said. "A search with long-range sensors should get us that data by the end of the day."

"Or we could just take a ten-hour trip," Cooper said.

"Alternatively, we can send a probe," Zemble said. "It would get the same results, but if they need our help...."

Cooper sighed. "Then a probe's not going to do them a lot of good. Okay." He thought about it for a moment. "Ten hours?"

"Our helmsman has assured me that she can actually get us there in under ten hours," Zemble said.

Cooper nodded. "Let's do it." He turned for the command chair.

"And what about the Chice?" Zemble asked.

Cooper paused and looked back at his Elwat first officer. "What about them? It seems pretty clear to me that we're not going to be able to offer any assistance. We have the shuttle; if we happen to find something on it that changes the situation, we can come back."

"That's a twenty-hour round trip," Zemble pointed out.

"Less if Ms. Tully wasn't making empty promises," Cooper countered.

"A lot can happen in twenty hours."

"More than what's already happened?" Cooper gestured at the planet on the view screen. "We've both read the same reports, Mr. Zemble. The odds of anything being alive down there are low."

"That's not the same as nonexistent."

"Is that what you would say to Mitchell?"

"No," Zemble replied.

"Of course," Cooper said, the disdain in his voice almost painful.

Zemble grunted. "But then, Mitchell would focus on making the right decision for the moment."

Cooper pursed his lips. "Are you suggesting that I'm not?"

"I'm not the one who brought Mitchell up."

"That's not what I asked."

Zemble gave a wordless shrug.

Cooper shook his head and turned toward the helm. "Lieutenant, lay in a course for that plasma storm, maximum speed."

25

COOPER DID NOT TRAVEL OFTEN. Before taking command of the *Defiance,* he had spent as little time as he had to on starships. He did not feel at home in a manmade container hurtling through the void of space. But from what little time he had spent, he knew something was wrong even before Tully spoke up.

The ship wasn't moving.

"Captain," Tully started.

"We're not moving," Cooper finished for her. He could feel it. Or, rather, he *couldn't*. No one would ever accuse the *Defiance* of being a smooth ride. There were only a handful of places on the ship where you didn't feel the engines thrumming through the floor plating. The bridge was not one of them.

Cooper walked up to the helm, careful to keep his hands on the console and away from Tully. "What's going on?"

There was a frustrated look of concentration on Tully's face as her fingers danced across the console. She was barely aware of Cooper's presence. "I...don't know. It's like the engines just won't respond."

Cooper glanced back at Zemble, but the Elwat avoided his gaze. He walked back to the command chair and keyed open the comm channel. "Bridge to engineering."

A second later, Warrick's voice came over the speakers. "Go ahead for engineering."

"Helm's reporting a problem with the engines."

There was a noticeable pause on Warrick's end. "Everything's green across the board down here. What kind of problem?"

Cooper looked toward Tully.

She held up her hands in defeat. "They're not responding."

"Mr. Warrick, can you override helm control and engage the ion drive from down there?"

Warrick made a sound that suggested he was going to do his best not to be insulted that his new captain didn't understand the basic engineering structure of a starship. "Aye, Captain, we can do that."

"Do it, please," Cooper said, his tone cooler than it needed to be.

There was another pause, and noticeably, the floor plating beneath Cooper's feet did not start slightly vibrating.

"Okay," Warrick said, "we may have a problem."

Cooper closed the channel and turned back to Zemble. This time the Elwat met his gaze.

Cooper and Zemble took the lift down to deck eight in tense silence.

"Are you going to offer an excuse?" Cooper asked.

Zemble didn't respond.

"It wasn't a rhetorical question, Commander."

"Unfortunately, I don't have an answer," Zemble replied.

They reached deck eight, and the doors slid open. Warrick was already there.

"What the hell is she doing to my ship *now*?" Warrick snapped.

Zemble pushed past the chief engineer without so much as a second glance.

"I'm asking you a question, you Fim'ai shit weasel-colored bastard," Warrick snapped at him again.

Despite his size, Zemble was quick and agile. His current pace was almost three times that of Cooper and Warrick. They both had to break into a loose jog to keep up.

"As I already told the captain, I don't have an answer for you," Zemble said.

"She's your pet project," Warrick said.

"She's not my pet," Zemble said. "And she's not my project."

"Well, somebody's going to need to take responsibility for her, and it's not going to be me," Warrick said. "Because as far as I'm concerned, she's a damn cancer on my ship."

Zemble stopped abruptly and turned around to face the engineer. "You realize that she can most likely hear you."

Warrick didn't flinch. "If you don't want people to say shitty things about you, you shouldn't act shitty."

Zemble grunted and resumed his pace down the corridor.

Warrick glanced at Cooper reluctantly, but the captain just shrugged.

"Erin Calloway is not a pet or a special project," Zemble repeated.

"I'd vehemently disagree with that statement," Warrick said.

"As would I," Cooper said.

"She's a member of this crew," Zemble said.

"Not by any standard recognized by the UPA," Cooper said.

"She's a part of this ship," Zemble said.

"Literally," Warrick added.

"That doesn't make her a crew member," Cooper said. "It makes her another tool at our disposal."

Zemble glanced back at him but didn't slow his pace.

Cooper met his gaze evenly. "You know I'm right."

"No, I don't."

"And if she's a tool," Cooper continued, "then she should be following our commands without question."

"And she isn't," Zemble said. "Which pretty much destroys your theory."

"And if we go with yours," Cooper said. "Then what am I supposed to do? Throw her in the brig for acting against my orders?"

"You have to stop thinking that every disagreement with a crew member can be solved by throwing them in the brig," Zemble grumbled.

"This isn't just a disagreement," Cooper said. "She's keeping our ship locked in place. If the *Reliant* is in danger or there's some kind of threat from the planet below, and we're unable to escape to safety because of Ms. Calloway...." Cooper trailed off momentarily as they reached the doors to Cargo Bay Two. "That's not a simple disagreement, Commander."

"She's an intelligent being," Zemble said.

"Nobody's saying she isn't," Cooper replied.

"You literally just called her a tool," Zemble said.

"I'm not saying it isn't complicated," Cooper said. "What I'm saying is, I should be able to move the damn ship whenever I want to move it."

"As much as it pains me to say it, the captain has a point," Warrick said.

Cooper gave him a sideways glance but didn't say anything.

"Erin Calloway has transformed into an entity that resides in multiple layers of reality," Zemble said. "She's fighting to maintain her humanity, but it's a fight that she loses a little more every day."

"None of what you're saying right now is helping her case," Cooper said.

"There are threats she might be aware of that we lack the ability to be aware of," Zemble said.

"Then she should bring them to my attention, and as the captain, I'll decide whether or not we're going to engage those threats," Cooper said.

"It's not that simple.

"Except that it is," Cooper said. "I'm the captain. She's the ship. End of story."

"If she's the ship, then she's the only thing keeping you from getting tossed out into the void of space," Zemble said. "So maybe it's not as cut and dry as you want it to be."

Cooper folded his arms. "This isn't the nature of a captain and a starship. There's not supposed to be a *relationship*."

"Normally, I would agree," Zemble said. "This isn't normal, though." He paused before opening the doors. "You should prepare yourselves."

"How so?" Cooper asked.

Zemble started to say something and then stopped. He stared at the closed doors for a second and then said, "I'm not sure."

"Thank you," Warrick said. "That's real helpful."

With a grunt, Zemble keyed open the doors, and they stepped inside.

26

The effect was immediately disorienting. Cooper felt as though he had dropped into a hole and was falling. Except he could feel his feet firmly on the ground, and he knew, logically, he had walked into the cargo bay, not dropped.

But the darkness he had stepped into was absolute and all-consuming.

Immediately, he turned, looking for the exit in an attempt to orient himself, but the door had disappeared. There was darkness behind him.

There was darkness in front of him.

There was darkness all around him.

"Commander?" There was a slight crack in Cooper's voice that startled him. "Zemble? Warrick?"

There was no response.

They could be standing on either side of him, but he couldn't see anything beyond the darkness.

Cooper's pulse began to quicken.

He wasn't afraid of the dark. Even as a child, he hadn't been afraid of the dark. At least, not in any way that he could recall.

The dark was simply something that was there. There was light. There was dark. One followed the other.

Even in space, there were stars, however distant they may be, to light the way.

This darkness, however, was different.

It was absolute.

It was *consuming*.

Cooper's chest tightened, and he fought to exhale a steady breath. He felt his body tense up, and he pushed through that feeling, telling his muscles to relax. But his body understood something that his intellect couldn't grasp.

This wasn't a natural darkness.

Cooper wasn't afraid of the dark, and he wasn't going to start being afraid now.

His heart thudded violently away in his chest. Panic flooded his body.

This was *wrong*. His body knew that it was wrong.

Cooper turned, or at least he thought he turned. He was trying to find a way out. He was trying to find a point to focus on, something to put the darkness into perspective.

But there was nothing there.

Cooper clenched his fists at his side and closed his eyes. If he couldn't find something to focus on outside of him, he would find it inside.

Except that even with his eyes closed, he found that he couldn't escape the darkness.

He almost laughed at that.

The whispers in the dark stopped him, though.

At first, it sounded like a faint breeze drifting past his ears. But then, almost immediately after, there was something else. Something that sounded like a voice.

"Who's there?" Cooper asked, trying and failing to keep the tremble from his voice.

To his surprise, his horror, the whispers replied. But he couldn't make any sense of what they were saying.

Cooper dug his fingernails into his palms until he could feel blood trickling out. The pain was sharp, immediate, and was, more importantly, something he could focus on.

He felt the darkness come into sharp focus around him as the whispers faded away.

Logically, he knew he was still on the ship. There hadn't been a hull breach; if there had been, he wouldn't be alive. And whatever this was, it definitely wasn't death.

"Calloway," Cooper said. The tremble in his voice had been replaced with a hoarseness. He repeated it, "Calloway."

There was no response from the darkness, and if the whispers had anything to add, they didn't offer it.

The pain in Cooper's palms was fading, and with it, he could feel the focus slipping. The darkness seemed to wrap around him even tighter.

His mind raced for a solution, an explanation.

This shouldn't be possible, should it?

He wanted to call out for Zemble or Warrick again, but he knew it was pointless. If they were here, it stood to reason they were as blind and deaf as he was.

Except it wasn't as simple as just being blind and deaf.

The darkness...

Cooper took a sharp, almost stuttering breath.

"I'm the captain of this ship," he said. He meant to sound strong and authoritative. Instead, he realized he couldn't even hear the sound of his own voice.

That was when he remembered.

Cooper had been young, not yet ten. The exact age escaped him. Maybe six? Eight? Maybe younger? Did it matter? He and his father had been traveling on the

Southern Paradise, heading back to Earth from New Gazaya, with the intention of being home for the holidays.

They didn't make it.

The *Southern Paradise* was a long-term transport vessel. It traveled a regular route between New Gazaya, the Iddad system, Faecha Three, and Earth, with a handful of stops at space stations along the way. The *Southern Paradise* derived most of its income from passenger transport, but occasionally they had been willing to make supply runs and transport items that were too valuable to leave in the care of the generic interstellar delivery services.

A week out from Earth the *Paradise* was attacked by El-Bazen pirates. They blew out the ion drives, forcing the *Paradise* to abruptly drop out of light speed. The sudden stop caused the ion coils to overload and blow out the borodium batteries. The result was that the ship was dead in space.

The *Paradise* had no real security or defensive measures. Cooper's father, among a handful of other like-minded passengers, had ventured out from their cabin in an effort to help.

System redundancies ensured that essential life support stayed online. Unfortunately, the artificial gravity wasn't tied to those systems, and young Broderick Cooper had found himself floating in the darkness of their cabin for what had felt like hours, listening to distant blasts from fusion weapons as the ship was boarded.

The pirates didn't bother with the passengers. They were there for the cargo, Beaken mind crystals. Anything else, anyone else, was just something that was in their way. El-Bazen pirates were notorious for their pillaging philosophies. They didn't particularly care for people. Even ones that could net them a high ransom. A ransom was a reward that always came with a risk, and El-Bazen pirates were strangely risk-averse. As a result, they would do everything possible to avoid a direct confrontation while attempting to obtain whatever goods they desired. If they had to engage in a fight, they would, but they would never shoot to kill unless they absolutely had to.

Young Broderick Cooper had known none of this, and even if he had, it wouldn't have provided him much comfort as he floated in the darkness, wondering if, among the fusion blasts, any of the occasional screams he heard were from his father.

Despite the sounds of chaos, the El-Bazen pirates had boarded the *Paradise*, acquired their ill-gotten gains, and disembarked all in under an hour. Six of the *Paradise*'s crew members had been injured. Only one had died. None of them had been his father.

It would still be almost an entire day before Cooper knew his father was alive.

It took the *Paradise's* engineering crew the better part of twelve hours to get the borodium batteries charged again. It took another six before artificial gravity was restored. For some unknown reason, inter-ship communications weren't restored until the UPA Fleet ship, the *Nova,* arrived in response to their SOS almost two days later.

Cooper had been trapped in the darkness of his cabin for twelve hours, completely alone. And even after the lights came back on and he could no longer walk on the ceiling, he still had no idea where his father was or if he was even alive.

Cooper suddenly became aware of the presence in his memory. He was there in that cabin back on the *Southern Paradise*, floating in the darkness, and this time, he could feel another presence there. It was a faint outline of...something. A figure in the darkness that was both familiar and alien at the same time. It hadn't been there before. He had been alone back then. So this was something else.

Cooper growled loudly. "What the hell are you doing?"

The presence didn't respond. It moved to the side, and Cooper felt himself jerked out of the memory.

He was back in the consuming darkness, but he could still feel the presence in his mind. It shuffled around through his memories, flipping through them like a photo album.

"Stop this," Cooper snapped. His voice was still muted to his own ears, but he could feel the words in the darkness. Flashes of memory skipped across his mind's eye. He pressed his hands to his temples, squeezing his head against the sudden pain. "Stop this!"

This time the boom of his voice cut through the muffling darkness. He was startled by the sound, but he didn't stop. "I'm the captain, damn it! Stop this *now*!"

Something happened in the darkness; the presence jolted in response.

And suddenly, Cooper was back in the corridor.

27

"THE HELL?!" Warrick exclaimed.

Cooper knelt on the corridor floor, lifting his head in time to see the black tendrils recede into the cargo bay. He felt a heavy hand on his shoulder. He looked up and saw Zemble looking at him with concern. He let his second-in-command help him back to his feet.

"Captain?" Zemble rumbled. "Are you okay?"

Cooper didn't know how to answer that. "How long?" He sounded normal. There was nothing in his voice that suggested that anything had happened. This surprised him. It...scared him.

Zemble hesitated. The question clearly wasn't the one he had been expecting. "Ten seconds."

Cooper looked at him in shock. "That can't be right."

Zemble glanced past him at Warrick to confirm.

"Aye, he's right, Captain," Warrick said. "I can't give you the exact number, but that sounds pretty damn close."

"Ten seconds," Cooper muttered to himself. "That's...not possible." He stared at his hands, expecting to see...he wasn't sure what. They were steady. No sign of a tremble.

He looked up at the open cargo bay doors. Instead of seeing the open space of the cargo bay, he saw a wall of absolute darkness.

Cooper took a deep breath. "What happened?"

Zemble started to answer him."The doors opened, and then–"

"And then those creepy ass tentacles came and pulled you in," Warrick finished. "It was like a damn Khettek birthing nightmare."

Zemble grunted but didn't say anything.

"Ten seconds?" Cooper repeated.

Something rippled through the darkness.

Zemble started to position himself between Cooper and the cargo bay, but Cooper pushed him away.

"It's a little late for that now," Cooper said.

The ripple in the darkness split into two and divided again. It kept dividing until the wall of black was like a river of shadows. Tiny ripples and waves broke across the surface. And then a figure emerged.

It wasn't so much that Calloway stepped forward as it was that the abyss pulled back, removing everything that wasn't her.

Her eyes were nothing less than the abyss itself. They were black pools that swallowed anything and everything.

Warrick avoided her gaze. Zemble focused on her as a whole.

Cooper met her gaze evenly and did not blink.

Inside, though, every inch of him screamed.

"*That* was uncalled for," Cooper said. Again, the sound of his own voice surprised him. It was even, unaffected, almost commanding.

Calloway tilted her head to the side, studying him as though he was a strange creature.

When she didn't say anything, Cooper raised his hand and pointed at her. "What were you doing to me?"

She didn't answer.

"I felt you in my *mind*," Cooper said. Zemble made a surprising noise beside him. "That's..." Cooper shook his head. "I don't know what that is. I came down here to talk to you. Zemble wants me to consider you a part of this crew. That's not what you're behaving like."

Calloway blinked. It was a disturbing thing to observe. There was an unnatural element to it that seemed to go against everything in the universe. "You think I am an infection on the ship, slowly corrupting it, destroying it." Her voice sent shudders down Cooper's spine. It haunted him like a nightmare that he couldn't remember.

"I guess that answers the question of whether or not you're listening in," Zemble said quietly.

"That's not what everybody thinks," Cooper said.

Calloway's shoulders shifted, and the darkness that framed her moved with the gesture. "At best, you view me as a tool, an extension of the ship."

"At best, I consider you a possibly hostile entity from which I have to wrestle control of my ship," Cooper said.

Calloway leaned forward slightly, and the darkness leaned forward with her. Cooper fought the urge to jerk back.

"Why are you here?" she asked.

The question took Cooper by surprise. He started to answer but found himself at a loss for words.

"You are afraid of space," she continued.

"It's a healthy fear to have," Cooper. For the first time, his voice sounded a little strained.

She tilted her head again, her gaze bearing down on him. Cooper half expected to feel the presence in his mind again, but the only thing that was making any noise in there were his own self-doubts and fears.

"You don't like being out here," Calloway said, raising her hand to point at him. "I saw it in your mind."

"You shouldn't have," Cooper said.

Zemble grunted. "It's considered impolite to poke around in other people's minds."

Calloway's gaze flicked to Zemble. "Impolite?"

"Great," Warrick said. "Are we going to have to run her through a Sweezakaal Finishing School now?"

Calloway turned back to Cooper. "If I am an infection, a disease, a hostile entity, or even merely just a tool, then the considerations of polite society are irrelevant to me."

Cooper set his jaw. "I'm the captain of this ship. If you want to be considered a member of this crew, I tell you to do something; you better damn well do it."

"Or else?" Calloway asked.

"Or else?" Cooper repeated.

A ripple passed across the surface of her body. "That is a threat, is it not? Is that not how threats work?"

"Captain," Zemble started.

Cooper held up a hand, signaling him to be quiet. His lips pressed together into a thin line. "Or else I'll do whatever I must to get control of my ship." He paused and then added, "That's not a threat. It's a promise."

Calloway tilted her head to the other side. Her gaze moved slowly to Warrick and then Zemble before settling back on Cooper.

"I currently comprise forty percent of the *Defiance*," she said. "You would have to destroy forty percent of the *Defiance* to ensure that I no longer have any influence on it."

"I don't exactly have an emotional connection to this

ship," Cooper said. "So if I have to blow it up, that doesn't seem like a huge loss to me."

Warrick made a noise like he was about to say something, but Zemble beat him to it. "You really need to stop being okay with that."

The space around Calloway's black eyes narrowed, flattening the dark pools to narrow slits. "You would destroy this ship?"

Cooper didn't hesitate. "If I had to."

"And what about its occupants?" she asked. "The crew?"

Cooper didn't answer. Instead, he said, "We need to go after the *Reliant*. They may be in danger. You need to restore our control of the engines."

Calloway pulled back and didn't say anything for a moment. Again, her gaze moved between the three officers as if looking for another response. Finally, when no one else spoke up, she settled her gaze back on Cooper. "I will not."

Cooper clenched his fists. "The hell you won't."

"We cannot leave until we ascertain the nature of the anomaly on the planet," Calloway said.

Cooper paused, his mouth hanging open in confusion. "The nature of what? What anomaly?" He looked toward Zemble and Warrick, but they both appeared as confused as he was.

Rather than provide any further explanation, Calloway melted back into the darkness, and the cargo bay doors slid shut.

Cooper shot a look at Zemble. "What the hell was that?"

"I genuinely have no idea," Zemble replied.

28

STARBASE 64

"THEY STARTED carpet bombing the eastern hemisphere," Dupree said. She crossed her legs as they sat on the bench. The observation deck's wide window wrapped around the room's length, giving them and the handful of other occupants a breathtaking view of the Dauerfrost Nebula. Dupree glanced at Rabkin to make sure he was still paying attention. "I'm assuming you're not current on the Ulriharad reproduction process?"

Rabkin snorted. "I have a firm grasp of the biological functionality of it. But as I understand it, there's a psychological component to it that complicates matters."

"Sure," Dupree said. "That's the short version of it."

"What's the longer version?"

"The Ulriharad have a...mating ritual that's preprogrammed into them at a genetic level," she explained. "They don't have romantic relationships the way we do. In fact, most Ulriharad aren't in any kind of relationship with a member of the opposite sex. They simply come together for mating season and then go their separate ways."

"Jealous," Rabkin said.

Dupree rolled her eyes. "When it comes time to mate, the Ulriharad journey to the Xemx Mountains in the eastern and western hemispheres. There doesn't seem to be any rhyme or reason as to why some go to the eastern mountains or why some go to the western. Or, more likely, there is a reason; they just don't want to tell us."

Rabkin did the rest of the math on his own. "The Phaw bombed their love shacks."

Dupree frowned disapprovingly at his turn of phrase. "Yes, basically. The UPA was able to intervene before the Phaw could hit the western hemisphere, but the damage they caused was already massive. They set their reproductive cycle back at least a generation, and that's a conservative estimate. I've read at least four reports suggesting the Ulriharad could end up as an endangered species."

Rabkin folded his arms. "I'd say it sounds like business as usual, but that sounds extreme for even the Phaw."

Dupree paused for a moment, staring out at the iridescent gases of the Dauerfrost Nebula. "Unconfirmed reports suggest that for about the last ten years, the Phaw have been losing, on an annual basis, approximately three to four percent of their population that was occupying the Ulriharad's homeworld."

Rabkin arched a bushy eyebrow. "Losing? What? Were they misplacing their foot soldiers?"

"That's what the official story is."

"You can't be serious."

"Unofficially? Those unconfirmed reports suggest that those missing Phaw are *dead*."

"Dead?"

Dupree shrugged.

"I think I'm missing the punchline here," Rabkin said.

"So are the rest of us," she replied. "The Phaw don't want

to talk about anything that's going to make them look less than they are, and the Ulriharad just don't want to talk. Best part, though? The Phaw have a history of underreporting. So that three to four percent? Could be double. More likely it's triple. And ten years? More like fifteen."

Rabkin gave a low whistle. "Losing over twelve percent of your invading force annually for fifteen years isn't a great look."

"No, it is not," Dupree agreed. "Reports, unconfirmed, of course, suggest that the biggest reason they're leaving is simply a matter of economics. They literally cannot afford to maintain an occupying force on a planet that's killing their soldiers on such a regular basis."

"What the hell is going on down there?"

"I would give a sizable fortune to find out," Dupree said.

"You would think that if the Ulriharad got them on the run, they'd be eager to share their secret."

"You would think," she agreed. "If we can't work out some kind of agreement, we're looking at the possibility of getting the Ulriharad under the Endangered Species Protection Act."

Rabkin cast a sideways glance at her. "Please tell me that's your idea of a joke?"

Dupree didn't respond.

Rabkin wrinkled his lips in disapproval. "That's not usually intended for intelligent species."

"It's not ideal," Dupree agreed. "But the reality is that the Ulriharad don't meet the requirement for UPA membership, and it could be years before they do. Getting them listed as an endangered species under the Endangered Species Protection Act cuts through a lot of that red tape."

"It also shortchanges their potential development as a spacefaring race," Rabkin said.

"It's not ideal," Dupree repeated.

"That's like saying the Reyr supernova was a mild interstellar incident."

"Jim–"

"The Ulriharad would basically lose any status as an independent society," Rabkin said.

"It's a little more complicated than that."

"Not by much."

"It's a measure of last resort," Dupree said. "And it would still require two-thirds of Congress to agree with it."

"Last time I checked, that wasn't an insurmountable challenge," Rabkin replied. "Half these politicians are looking for an excuse to get somebody under their heel."

Dupree held up her hand. "I'm not having this argument with you."

"You need to have it with somebody."

"It's not going to be some grumpy old ass doctor who's on the verge of retirement."

"I've been on the verge of retirement for decades."

"That doesn't help your argument." She looked at him. "An hour ago, you brushed off the entire race as a bunch of creepy space hippies."

"Sure," Rabkin said. "I stand by that assessment. Does that mean I think they should be shuffled off to some resettlement camp? No, it doesn't."

"That's not what's going to happen."

"You don't know that."

"I know that if we leave things as they are, there won't be enough Ulriharad left in the galaxy to argue over," Dupree said, her voice on the edge of snapping. "We're not the bad guys here. We're not the ones who enslaved them for fifteen years and then decided to try our hand at genocide on our way out."

Rabkin opened his mouth and then thought better of it. He sat back on the bench, silently stroking his chin for a moment. "You remember when Gavin was captaining the *Tennessee,* and we intercepted the SOS from the Phaw warship?"

There was a small, harmless burst of light at the nebula's edge, and the observatory was cast in a soft pink glow.

"I remember," Dupree replied softly, a distant look in her eyes.

"They were caught in a gravity well, and their ship was nearly torn in half by the time we got there. They still opened fire on us when we showed up to *help*."

Dupree inhaled sharply through her nose and rubbed her eyes. "Yes, well, it's not like Gavin was the most objective person in the room when it came to the Phaw."

"Still, it's a common courtesy not to bite the hand that's trying to pull you out of the fire," Rabkin said.

"Common courtesy means something very different to the Phaw," Dupree said. "I tried to help Gavin understand that. He couldn't."

"Oh, he understood it," Rabkin said. "He just didn't give a damn. As far as he was concerned, they were monsters."

"Didn't stop him from trying to help them."

"No, it did not," Rabkin agreed. "See, that would have been a good story to share at his funeral. Would've highlighted his compassionate side in times of adversity."

"It's a story you could have easily shared," she countered.

"Sure. But I'm the asshole that would have let the Phaw get torn apart in that gravity well and slept pretty soundly that night. I think the attendees might have picked up on my subtle disapproval of Gavin's actions."

Dupree shook her head. "Is there a point to your story?"

"Yes. The Phaw may be monsters, but at least they're honest about it."

Dupree stared at him. "You're unbelievable."

"It's not that unbelievable. Just basic math," Rabkin said. He jerked his head at the nebula. "Where exactly does this fall on the star charts? Probably in some kind of grey area that the Phaw will most likely contest. If the Ulriharad are inducted into the UPA, Caudry-Yukawa doesn't have to worry about their investment. But that could take a couple of years, more than enough time for the Phaw to screw around out here. But get the Ulriharad declared endangered? All that takes is two-thirds of Congress and thirty days."

Dupree gave him a cold look. "That's not why I'm out here."

"I'm sure it's not," Rabkin said. "But that doesn't mean there isn't somebody in Caudry-Yukawa who's looking to use you to protect their investment."

"Son of a bitch." Dupree shook her head.

"When was the last time you spoke to him?" Rabkin asked.

The sudden shift in the conversation broke through her defenses before she even realized it. She didn't have to ask whom Rabkin was talking about; she already knew.

"It's been...years." A heavy sigh escaped Dupree. "Years since we've had an actual conversation. He would still send me something, a short recording, on...." She swallowed, trying to contain her emotions. "On his birthday. I never responded to the messages. Didn't really see the point." She stopped, her voice getting shaky. She took a deep breath, pressing the heel of her palm against the corner of her left eye.

Rabkin chose not to comment. Instead, he said, "When I

told Gavin you had moved out here, I didn't mean for him to do anything."

"I know," she said.

"I don't think he would have done anything anyway," Rabkin continued.

"I know."

"I don't think he ever got over you, though."

"I know," Dupree said, her voice quiet now.

"But he wasn't going to break up your marriage. As long as you were happy, he was fine."

"No, he wasn't. But thank you for saying that."

"Are you mad?" Rabkin asked.

"At who? Gavin?" She shook her head. "Seems silly to be mad at a dead man."

Rabkin shrugged. "I don't know about that. Anger seems like a pretty reasonable response to grief."

Dupree tilted her head to the side. "What about you?"

"What about me?"

"You came all this way to check on me," Dupree said. "But you've been with Gavin for a lot longer than I was. If he's really dead...." She looked at him. "How are you handling it?"

Rabkin avoided her gaze. "I deal with grief like any sane man would. Whiskey. Usually an entire bottle."

"I thought your ancient system was too delicate for such abuses."

"Oh, I've developed a strong intolerance to old-fashioned alcohol. Plus, I'm a damn good doctor."

"I don't know what that's supposed to mean."

"It means I know when to cut myself off before I do permanent damage to my liver."

She laughed softly. "Jim..."

Rabkin fell silent for a moment, his hands folded in his

lap. "I miss my friend. I'm not gonna lie, but I would have liked a little more closure."

"Closure?"

"It's my personal philosophy that everybody should get a chance to say goodbye," Rabkin said.

Dupree looked down at her hands. "Saying goodbye isn't all it's cracked out to be, old man."

"Maybe. But it's better than the alternative," Rabkin said. "Not knowing if it's going to be the last time you see somebody? That's a terrible way to end things."

"And knowing there's a clock slowly ticking down to zero is twice as bad."

Rabkin rested a hand on her shoulder. "You forget, Maureen was dying a long time before she finally passed."

"Jim–"

He pulled his hand back. "I'm just saying, you're not the only one around here who has to bear the burden of watching a loved one slowly die."

"It's different when it's your child."

"It's not a contest, Johanna."

She pressed her hands against the backs of her legs. "If it were, I'd win."

"I don't know if that's a win you'd be proud of."

Dupree shook her head. "I don't want to talk about this anymore."

"I'm sorry."

"No, you're not." She got to her feet. "I've tried to tell you, but you're not listening. I said goodbye to Gavin a long time ago. You're not here to check up on me. You're here because you need a shoulder to cry on."

Rabkin didn't move from the bench. He looked up at her, his face empty of any emotion. "Is that such a bad thing?"

Dupree pursed her lips together, taking a moment

before answering. "Maybe not. But it's not fair of you to come back here and drudge all this up again for me."

"Maybe not," Rabkin agreed. "But everybody grieves differently."

"Then maybe you need to consider the possibility that you're grieving wrong."

"Maybe." Rabkin winced a little as he got to his feet. "But at this point, I'm not eager to learn any new tricks."

Dupree shook her head. "You really are a bastard, aren't you?"

"I don't believe I've ever claimed to be otherwise."

"You should leave." She turned and started for the exit.

"Johanna–"

Dupree's comm chirped, and she answered it, cutting Rabkin off. "Go ahead."

"I hope I'm not waking you up," Ashley Skouras said.

Dupree glanced back at Rabkin, who was following her a step behind. "I wish you had woken me up," she said tiredly.

"Not once you hear why I'm calling you."

"What is it?"

There was a heavy pause from Skouras.

"What?" Dupree pushed.

"I'm genuinely not sure how to describe it," Skouras said finally. "You should probably just come down here. It's one of those things you're going to have to see it to believe it."

"Where are you?"

"Your office."

Dupree stopped and closed her eyes. "What did Haiduk do now?"

There was another pause. "You just better come down here."

29

NATUZZI

THE SETTING SUN'S glare nearly blinded her as Ril disembarked from her personal yacht. Everything was cast in a hazy glow of amber, reducing everything to indistinct blobs that hovered on the edges of her vision. She winced, raising a hand to block the brilliant rays, and the quiet landscape before her came into sharp focus.

Ril glanced back at Ito, who stood at the top of the yacht's entrance ramp. His face was a careful mask of nonchalance, but she could read the disapproving hesitancy beneath the surface. He pursed his lips tightly and took half a step back into the yacht, letting himself be cloaked in the shadow of the interior. Ril simply shook her head and turned forward again, taking the final steps off the ramp. With a frustrated sigh, Ito followed a moment later, careful to stay at least ten steps behind her.

The dark, stiff blades of grass crunched beneath her feet. Each step she took toward the small cottage near the cliff's edge sounded like she was walking across eggshells. Ril glanced briefly up toward the sky. There was nary a cloud in sight. Nothing to block the unyielding heat from the setting sun and no indication that this section of the peninsula would get rain any time soon.

A gentle breeze from the cliffside ruffled the long, billowy sleeves on her outfit and provided a brief respite from the heat of the setting sun. Ahead of her, the royal guardsman stood, forming an aisle for her that led to the door of the small cottage.

There was no one else on the grounds. At least, no one else that she or her guardsmen could see. The Oraya peninsula was located on the other side of Natuzzi. It was a three-day trip for the average Natuzzi and a three-hour trip for the woman who ruled the planet. Her personal yacht, one of twelve she had learned were assigned to the Royal Fleet, had taken her and a small contingent of guardsmen across the lower stratosphere of the planet. She had been treated to a breathtaking view that she had not realized was possible.

The Oraya peninsula was considered one of the most remote places on Natuzzi. It was located in the northern hemisphere, reachable only by shuttle. There were some who were foolish enough to brave the Hrómson seas to reach the peninsula, but the ever-present storms were all but certain to send those brave souls to their death. That did not stop them, however. As Ito had informed her on the flight here, there was an average of six hundred Natuzzis who made the pilgrimage by sea every year. Less than ten percent would survive the trip.

The Oraya peninsula lacked any technology to receive or transmit signals or data. It was a feed dark spot on the planet. The news and communiques that did reach the peninsula were delivered on the supply shuttles that visited once a month. The same shuttles would bring sanctioned visitors, but to receive that invite, one would need to request the opportunity to be invited, which would require sending a communique on a supply shuttle and, subsequently, not receiving authorization or denial for nearly a month.

Ril had decided she couldn't wait that long.

The heat from the setting sun was almost unbearable. She wanted to race across the open field for the cool safety of the cottage's shade, but she suspected that that sort of behavior would be unbecoming for a queen. So she forced herself to walk carefully and meticulously towards the cottage.

Ril, of course, had been to the countryside before. There was an entire estate available to her in the mountains of Rhinoderma. But that was a royal estate, still connected to the world, plugged into the feeds, accessible by multiple modes of transportation, and even home to permanent residents whose only jobs were to maintain the estate and the illusion of its remoteness. Even that paled in comparison to the remote nature of Oraya. Here, everything was exposed. Here, nature ran rampant. Here, progress and technology had not only been eschewed but outright rejected. Stepping off the yacht, she had felt the immediate disconnect from the world, and she wasn't sure she cared for it.

Finally, she reached the shade of the cottage. There was an immediate, cooling relief on her skin. An ache in her head, one she hadn't even noticed until she stepped into the shade, began slowly fading.

The cottage door, built from an ancient piece of rimar wood, was closed, and it was painfully clear that it wouldn't be opening any time soon.

Ril took a deep breath and exhaled sharply through her nose.

It was impossible for the resident not to know that she was out there. Her yacht had landed in their front yard. There wasn't another soul for miles. For that matter, there wasn't another sound either. Ril realized the only noise she heard was the yacht's engines cooling and the soft rustle of the guardsmen's uniforms as the breeze blew against them.

It was *impossible* to be ignorant of her arrival.

And yet, the door was closed.

She took a half step back, careful to stay in the shade of the cottage, and looked over the doorframe. The door was wood, but the frame, like the rest of the cottage, appeared to be constructed from arð stone. Taking in the space around the cliffside, Ril couldn't help but wonder how the hell they had managed to get arð stone all the way up here. Arð stone was mined from the lakes along the Azure Divide. It was a four-day trip by air, and it was impossible to transport something like arð stone across the Hrómson seas, wasn't it? Ril shook her head and glanced back over her shoulder.

The guardsmen stood ramrod straight, their gaze focused on everything and nothing. Ito stopped ten steps behind her, clutching tightly at his datapad. His expression remained carefully neutral, but his eyes pleaded with her to get back on the shuttle.

Instead, Ril turned back to the door.

There was a symbol carved into its grainy surface. Faded from time and the elements, Ril could barely make it out. But knowing what it was supposed to be helped her fill in the missing pieces. It was the mark of the Sacellum.

Something akin to a cold shiver ran down the base of her spine. She forced herself to stand up a little straighter and banished her childish concerns from her mind.

Ril glanced up towards the sky, noting that the shadow of the cottage had grown since she had stepped into it. How much time had passed since she arrived? It was impossible for her presence to be unknown. And yet, the door remained closed.

She raised her hand to knock and then stopped as she heard her mother's voice, warning her, scolding her, really. A *queen* does not *request* entrance.

Her hand dropped back to her side, and Ril took a step back from the door. She glared darkly at the closed door. This was clearly being done on purpose. This...*slight*. She couldn't decide who she was more upset with, the individual on the other side of that door or herself for falling so quickly into the same habits, trappings, of her mother's reign.

A sudden realization struck her.

It was the *game*.

This was a game, the same game that everyone else was playing, and it was a game she had no interest in playing. This was not how she was going to rule. She wasn't going to sink to their level. She wasn't going to get caught up in these ridiculous *games*. Lies, manipulation, cheating, power plays, threats. These were the things that ultimately led to her mother's downfall, and she wasn't going to be her mother. She wanted to be better than her mother. The Natuzzi people *needed* her to be better.

Or, at the very least, they needed her to be different.

Ril looked over the closed door one more time, her gaze lingering on the faded symbol.

This was a game, and it was a stupid game at that.

Ito was right. It had been a mistake to come out here.

But it was a mistake easily rectified.

Ril turned sharply and started back for the yacht. There was a visible relief on Ito's shoulders as he watched her walk towards him. That relief, however, was brief.

Ril heard the door open behind her a second before a look of nervous despair washed across Ito's face.

"Brave is the soul that rejects the song of Sacellum," said the woman from the open door.

Ril stopped cold, less than ten steps from the cottage, on the edge of the building's shadow. Her face began to tighten into a taut, uncomfortable expression before she slipped on her mask of neutrality. Out here, in the middle of nowhere, there was no one to see, no one to watch, save for Ito and her guardsmen, but Ril was all too aware of what happened when you began to treat the people as invisible.

She felt the space around her shift; her own body became heavier as if the very presence of the woman in the door had increased the gravity on this remote peninsula. Immediately, Ril understood. She could clearly see her mistake, laid out before her in the bright neon colors of desperation. Despite her desire to avoid repeating her mother's games, the moment Ril had decided to come out here, she had accepted the terms of this particular game. She consented to be a willing participant. Regardless of whether or not she had knocked on the damn door.

Ril closed her eyes for the briefest of seconds, cursing her foolishness, and was greeted with her mother's hateful, disapproving glare. If she had still been alive, Ril did not doubt that her mother would have made her pay dearly for this mistake.

"Damn you," Ril whispered under her breath, unsure if she was speaking to her mother or herself.

There was nothing else from the woman in the doorway, and there wouldn't be, of course. That wasn't how this game was played.

She looked to Ito, but her aide was twice as lost as she was.

Ril clucked her tongue against her teeth and turned sharply back towards the cottage with a sense of purpose and confidence that successfully belied the inner turmoil of self-loathing and indecision that consumed her.

The door was open, and there was no one standing there. Because, of course, there wasn't.

A surprisingly cool breeze greeted her at the door. She hesitated before stepping inside. A nagging thought occurred to her: what if she was stepping into a trap?

A trap.

That was her mother. It was the exact kind of paranoid suspicion that would have plagued her mother.

But just as quickly as the thought occurred to her, Ril reasoned that if the occupant had intended to kill her, they simply would have done it when her back was turned. Or would they?

The game. The damn game.

Ril mentally cursed her mother and herself and everyone else that had come before her. It was a trap, of course. Just not the kind that was going to result in her death. It was a trap that had been lain decades before. It was a trap of predestination. It was a trap that left her flailing about, looking to make a decision and realizing, with a growing horror, that all the decisions had already been made for her. She was following in footsteps that were older than even her mother.

"Damn it all," Ril whispered under her breath.

She pressed her lips together tightly and stepped into the cottage.

30

THE INTERIOR of the cottage was not what Ril had expected.

It was an open space, the walls tilting outwards at a slight angle, giving the impression that the cottage was slowly expanding. Almost the entirety of the rear wall was composed of windows, offering a breathtaking view that peered over the edge of the cliffside. There was a...modern sensibility that was unexpected.

A cool breeze caught her attention, and Ril discovered a wide staircase to her left that descended into what was undoubtedly the interior of the cliffside. Ril noted the obvious commentary on the cottage: not everything was as it appeared.

She took another step into the cottage and felt the cold emanating from the stone floors. The chill from earlier made its way back up her spine.

"I am afraid your aide is not welcome here."

Ril glanced briefly over her shoulder. Ito stood in the doorway, already pulling himself back. She turned in the direction of the voice. It was the same voice that had... taunted her before.

The elderly woman stood in the corner near the rear of the cottage, somehow perfectly hidden and obviously exposed all at once. She was dressed in a simple gown, a shawl draped across her shoulders, and her hands clasped loosely behind her back. Her skin was an amber shade of orange, stretched tautly across her bald head. She stared out the large windows, watching the setting sun. It was only then that Ril realized that while the rear of the cottage was facing the sunset, none of the sun's brilliant rays or heat were bleeding through. Perhaps the small cottage wasn't as archaic as it appeared.

When neither Ril replied nor Ito moved, the woman continued, not bothering to turn from the view of the setting sun. "It has been nearly four hundred years since a man has stepped foot across that threshold. It's a tradition I'm not prepared to break now."

Ril glanced back at Ito, but her aide was already stepping back, giving her an apologetic nod. She fought the urge to be visibly irritated, keeping her face a mask of neutrality as she turned back to the woman.

"He was killed on the spot, that man. Shortly after his feet cleared the threshold, his name was Amidei Asi," the woman continued, not turning from the view of the setting sun. "He's been completely forgotten by history, which is for the best. Asi can only be found in our oral history, a cautionary tale of sorts. There's a few documents where he's still listed, but those are...difficult to get hold of."

She paused, her attention captured by a collection of the sun's rays dancing across the window, creating a dazzling array of diamond-like figments.

As the figments faded, the woman continued as if she had never stopped. "The common belief is that Asi was here as an assassin, attempting to murder the then-current head of the Sacellum. It is a story that is preferable to the truth, which was that Amidei Asi was, in fact, *invited* here as a lover, a partner. And that's the sort of truth that can have...repercussions."

The latter half of the sun dipped beneath the cliff's edge, abruptly casting the cottage's interior into an array of shadows. With most of the sun's brilliance gone, Ril became aware of the candles spread across the open space, offering a soft glow of illumination.

The woman turned from the window, gathering her shawl tightly around her as she moved across the open space towards a sitting area. "Please, do join me."

The woman sat in the opposite chair.

Ril followed across the room but stopped short of sitting. Instead, she rested her hand on the back of the seat that was intended for her and looked down at the woman. Her face remained neutral, but everything in her body language screamed disapproval.

The woman seemed oblivious to Ril's mood and instead focused on preparing the tea set on the small table.

A full minute of silence passed, broken only by the soft clinks of the tea kettle as the woman poured their tea.

"Please," the woman said finally, looking up at Ril. She gestured to the empty chair. "Join me."

Up close, the woman was older than Ril had initially estimated. Although her face betrayed almost no sense of her age, the woman's eyes revealed herself to Ril. They were ancient, soulful pools that seemed to go on forever. With every flick of her gaze, the woman seemed to take in everything; nothing appeared to escape her notice.

Ril's fingers tightened around the back of the chair. "It's customary not to sit before the queen has."

The woman raised her teacup to her lips and took a sip,

apparently unbothered by the notion that she might have broken protocol. "Perhaps out there. But in here, things are a bit different."

Ril didn't move.

The woman set her cup back down, wrapping her hands around it as if needing its heat. "Teatelian tea is meant to be enjoyed immediately. If you let it sit, it becomes bitter, often causing the individual partaking of it to experience intense nausea, resulting in vomiting."

Ril couldn't keep her face neutral anymore, and a scowl passed across her lips. "You would serve your queen that?"

The woman took another sip of her own tea. "No. I would serve the queen tealyria tea, which is often considered a rare delight. It grows only here on this peninsula, and outside of here, it fetches quite the price. I was reliably informed recently that it was one of the most excessively priced beverages on the planet, affordable by only the elite of the elite."

The woman sipped her tea, watching Ril, studying her.

Ril suddenly felt uncomfortable under her gaze and fought the urge to fidget. She maintained her own gaze, defiant and regal.

After a moment, the woman nodded, setting her teacup back down. "I see the problem here. Your mother never spoke to you about this."

"This?" Ril echoed.

The woman shrugged, turning the teacup slowly in her hands. "Me, really." She stared down at the now empty cup. "It's not terribly surprising. Your mother had only spoken to me a handful of times herself. Communication between the executive branch and the Sacellum is a carefully orchestrated event. As I'm sure your assistant has informed you."

Ril watched as the woman poured herself some more

tea. "It was explained that arrangements are to be made months in advance, and we are not allowed to speak more than three times during a solar year."

The woman nodded. "Except that it is *you* who is not allowed to speak with me."

The scowl returned to Ril, and didn't leave. "How dare you."

The woman held up a hand. "I am simply clarifying the explanation given to you. It is understandable that your assistant did not articulate in this manner. He is, after all, a man."

Ril's eyes blazed. "I am the *queen*."

"And, as I understand it, you're looking to get rid of that title."

"Be that as it may," Ril replied in a tight, almost strained voice, "I am still the leader of the Natuzzi people."

"Yes, you are," the woman agreed, locking eyes with Ril. "But we, the Sacellum, are the architects of Natuzzi, the guiding force of the people."

Ril took a moment to consider what she had said. "What are you suggesting-?"

"Please, do not misunderstand me. I am not *suggesting* anything," the woman cut her off. "I am stating a fact. After all, who extended my invitation for you to join me out here?"

Ril reached into the pocket of her gown and pulled out the crystal coin Voa had left behind.

"You may only be allowed to request an audience with me three times in a solar year," the woman said. "But I can beckon you as often as I care."

Ril wrapped her fingers around the coin in a tight fist as she glared at the woman. But the woman seemed unmoved by the threatening gesture.

"Truthfully, though, it's not very often I invoke those privileges," the woman said. "I am rather fond of my isolation, and I take every opportunity to keep the outside world off my doorstep."

Ril tossed the coin onto the table and turned to leave.

"We are not done here, my queen," the woman said. Something in her voice caused Ril to stop.

Ril didn't turn back immediately. "You would talk to your *queen* in such a disrespectful manner?"

"I would," the woman replied evenly. "It's important for you to understand your place."

Ril whirled around and lost all sense of composure. She snarled at the woman, her arms outstretched, and her hands curled into claws that were desperate to strangle the life from the woman. "With *one word,* I could have this simple cottage, and *you* obliterated from the face of this planet."

A bemused smile passed across the woman's lips. "Ah, there we go. I was beginning to wonder if you were your mother's daughter after all. She had such a temper; I couldn't imagine it wouldn't be passed down."

Shame rose within Ril, battling the anger she felt. She pulled her arms back, forcing them to hang at her sides. When she spoke again, she sounded almost strangled as she struggled to retain her composure. "I. Am. Not. My. Mother."

The woman watched her for a moment as though she were an interesting, albeit minor, curioso. "No," she agreed. "You are certainly not. Your mother would not behave so foolishly. Now please," she gestured to the empty chair, "do join me."

31

RIL SAT.

Everything in her body screamed that she should leave. That she should turn heel and run from this terrible place and have it and the peninsula itself razed.

But instead, she sat.

She sat at the table much as a queen would, with grace and quiet dignity. She struggled to maintain her composure. Inside, she was a nearly uncontrollable hurricane of shame, indecision, frustration, and righteous indignation. Outside, Ril calmly folded her hands atop the table and gave the woman a pleasant smile that was devoid of anything genuine.

Because that was the game.

The game that she was now obviously and irrevocably trapped in.

Damn them all.

If the woman knew what was happening inside Ril, she gave no sign. Instead, she focused on the tea. She took Ril's cup and tossed the untouched tea over the table's edge, seemingly oblivious to the mess she made on the floor. The woman picked up the small brown cloth to her right and used it to clean the inside of the cup. Satisfied with the general cleanliness of the cup, she set it aside and opened the box in the center of the table.

"Have you ever prepared teatelian tea?" she asked Ril, pulling out a small bag of leaves. "Forgive me. That's obviously a silly question. I would imagine that you haven't had the privilege of preparing anything you consume in quite some time, if ever."

Ril's fingers tightened around each other. She maintained her gaze on the woman, trying and failing to anticipate the next move in this game. "You speak as though I cannot even be bothered to feed myself."

The woman shrugged. She pulled a stone mortar and a matching pestle from the box, setting them in front of her with delicate care. "My relationship with your mother was..." she glanced up at Ril, "brief. We spoke infrequently. Much of our communication was done through mediators and memos that were drafted with thinly veiled disdain." She reached for the bag of tea leaves and then paused as if a thought had suddenly occurred to her. "I don't believe your mother, and I liked each other very much."

The woman plucked four tea leaves from the bag. They were half the size of her hand and a shade of deep purple with thin veins of dark green running through them. She placed the leaves in the mortar. "I suppose what I'm trying to say is that I didn't know your mother very well, and so I know you even less." She grabbed the pestle and started grinding the leaves with a violent vigor that Ril wouldn't have thought possible. "Of course, just because I didn't know your mother does not mean I did not know of your mother." The woman cast a brief glance up at Ril; the expression on her face almost looked bemused.

Ril frowned distastefully as she found herself on more familiar ground. "I see why you've aligned with Director Voa. You both have the propensity to speak in unnecessary riddles."

The woman barked out a sudden laugh. The sound was so unexpected and shocking that Ril momentarily pulled back from the table.

"I'm afraid I'm at a loss for what I said that was so amusing," Ril said.

The woman set the pestle down and sat back in her chair, gathering her composure. "The Sacellum does not align itself with anyone or anything. We enlist servants."

"You'll forgive me if I find it hard to believe that you enlisted Director Voa as a servant of your cause when just moments ago, you threatened to kill my aide for stepping across your threshold," Ril replied coldly.

The woman picked up the pestle and pointed it at Ril. "First off, Director Voa was never so foolhardy to attempt even to set foot on this peninsula, much less walk up to my front door. Second," the remains of the good humor left her as suddenly as they had appeared, "the Sacellum is not simply a *cause*. We *are* Natuzzi. There is no separation between the people of Natuzzi and us. There are none who are not servants of the Sacellum." She stared at the ground tea leaves for a moment before pushing them to the side. "I suppose here is where we arrive at the point."

Ril watched as the mortar was pushed off to the side, unable to decide if that was a good or a bad thing.

The woman locked eyes with Ril. "You are right."

Ril arched her brow. "I am?"

"Let us speak plainly," the woman continued. "I knew *of* your mother. I knew what to expect of her. I knew how far she would push an issue, and I knew what she would not bother to fight on. Your mother and I did not care for one another, but we had an understanding."

"But you were not aligned," Ril said, her voice testy.

"Your mother understood everything I have been trying to explain to you: You may not care for it, you may not agree with it, but you are still a servant, a tool, of the Sacellum."

Ril bared her teeth ever so slightly. "So you keep saying."

The woman folded her hands together as if she was about to pray. "The problem, how I see it, is that you were not properly prepared for your ascension to the thrown. It was...premature. Your education was lacking." She paused, thinking it over. "Or perhaps, your education was exactly as your mother intended? As it has been explained to me, you were not afforded a representative of the Sacellum in your studies. That could not have been an oversight on your mother's part."

"I was raised in an otherwise secular household," Ril replied. "Religion was not a focus of our family. But you seem to have been made aware of that already."

"Yes, I have." The woman nodded. "Because that is an act of heresy, especially in a family of influence such as your own. Your house sets an example the rest of our people are expected to live by, and if you were to treat the teachings of the Sacellum as disposable, irrelevant, and unimportant, that could result in the people of Natuzzi doing the same." The woman paused, letting the implications of her words settle before continuing, "The punishment of such heresy is left to the discretion of the Sacellum and is often enrollment at a reeducation campus or, in some cases, death." She pursed her lips. "But your mother has already suffered that, and it seems unnecessarily cruel to visit such additional punishments on you."

Ril narrowed her gaze. "Did you just threaten your queen?"

"Your brother, however, is another matter altogether," the woman replied, neatly sidestepping Ril's question.

Surprised at the abrupt change in topics, Ril was left speechless for a moment. "My brother…"

"Is a problem," the woman said. "He would have been a problem solved had you not intervened."

It took another second before the pieces clicked into place. Ril leaned forward. "It was not my mother who placed the assassin in Nax's cell; it was *you*. I could have you executed on the spot for that."

The woman held up a hand. "Please, let's stop with the empty threats."

Ril's eyes widened. "Empty threats?" She rose sharply to her feet. "You attempted *regicide*."

The woman met her gaze almost lazily. "And yet, I'm the only one in this room who failed at it."

Ril sucked in a sharp breath of air, and she stepped back from the table.

"Please," the woman said, "let's try to act against our nature and not do anything foolish. You attempt to have any of your guardsmen step in here and kill me, and you will discover an unfortunate truth."

"Which is?" Ril's voice was low and almost a little shaky.

"Allegiance to faith always runs deeper than allegiance to the crown." The woman nodded at the chair, indicating that Ril should sit back down. "Besides, I don't particularly care what happened to your mother. The people of Natuzzi might, but after the character assassin campaign you've run against the deceased former queen, I imagine they will be considerably less interested in who killed her. Besides, there are plenty of other ways for me to destroy your administration, should I be so inclined." She paused and then added, "Now *that* was a threat."

"I can see why my mother didn't care for you," Ril said, her voice strained.

The woman shrugged. "Your mother understood the threat your brother posed."

Ril frowned. "He poses no threat."

"He engaged in carnal relations with an alien species," the woman replied.

"He's not the first," Ril said.

"And he certainly won't be the last," the woman agreed. "However, there is a system for dealing with heretics such as your brother."

"Murder?"

The woman nodded. "Except when the Sacellum sanctions it, it's not murder. It's a holy cleansing."

Ril stared at her, her mouth agape in shock. "And I thought my mother was a monster."

"The only monster here is the one you're housing in the royal apartments," the woman replied.

"Nax is still a member of a royal family, and you will treat him with the respect he deserves," Ril said.

The woman rose to her feet, all pretense cast aside. Her expression darkened. "Your brother was engaged in an ongoing sexual relationship with a *human* woman, which could have resulted in the production of an *abomination*."

"A *child*," Ril corrected her.

"An abomination," the woman repeated, her voice dripping with disgust and venom. "Such a creature has no place in Natuzzi."

"A creature," Ril repeated, horrified. She shook her head. "He had no child."

"You do not know that for certain."

"Nax told me so himself."

"Considering the penalty is death, I would imagine he would have reason to lie."

Ril looked at the woman darkly. "Considering that he nearly died, he had no reason to."

The woman clicked her tongue against her teeth. "You are certainly not your mother."

"You keep saying that as if it's supposed to be some great insult against me," Ril said.

The woman shrugged. "Simply a pointed observation. As is the fact that you cannot be certain of whether or not he produced an offspring with the human female."

Ril folded her arms, choosing not to respond.

"And now he lives, free of any consequences from his actions," the woman continued.

"I would hardly call his situation consequence-free," Ril replied coldly, her mind flashing back to how she found her brother in a massive puddle of his own blood.

The woman looked down at the table, watching her fingers trace an idle pattern across its surface. "This is a problem with your upbringing. With your education. This universe is in chaos. It is messy, disorganized. It is an abomination unto itself." She held up both hands, palms facing up. "The Natuzzi people exist as *purpose*. And that purpose is to bring balance. Harmony. Perfection. We must bend this chaotic universe to our will because that is the only way to achieve harmony."

"I'm familiar with the dogma."

The woman paused, again studying Ril's expression. "Are you, though? Your recent behavior suggests that you are not. You have allowed off-worlders to establish a permanent residence on our planet. This is..." she took a deep breath as she considered the weight of her next words,

"Well, this is arguably one of the greatest crimes committed against the Natuzzi people since, well, your brother's sexual congress. One would even argue that it is a direct result of your brother's carnal activities."

"Presumably, that one would be you?" Ril asked, struggling to keep her tone even. She found herself on unfamiliar, almost treacherous footing. She felt like she was navigating through a minefield, every word coming from the woman's mouth a potential bomb waiting to detonate.

The woman walked around the length of the table, coming around its end until there was nothing between them. "I trust that while you may have been indifferent towards your religious studies, you took more care with your historical education."

"The Occupation of the Magol," Ril said.

An approving smile appeared on the woman's face. "Yes."

"It has been brought to my attention," Ril replied.

"I'm sure it has," the woman said. "But do you understand its relevance?"

"I understand the relevance you believe it has," Ril replied carefully.

"But then you allow the off-worlders to establish a permanent base here on our home," she countered. "So one could presume that you don't understand the relevance at all."

"We did not invite the Magol here," Ril said. "They were an invading force."

The woman nodded. "An invading force we drove off after nearly four decades of occupation. The Magol raped and pillaged our planet and our people. They laid waste to nearly a third of our planet's natural resources. The Para'rock landmass was covered in pollution. The Neustino waters were poisoned with radiation. Our technological development was set back nearly fifty years. And even after we chased them off, we spent almost a hundred years purging their DNA from us." She stared down at her hand as if spying some hidden message in the creases of her palm. "Did you know the recessive trait of the silver eyes is believed to have been left over from the crossbreeding of the Magol?" She looked up and met Ril's gaze. "And even still, after all that, three hundred Natuzzi people renounced their birthrights and willingly followed their Magol oppressors."

The woman stopped and folded her hands together in front of her.

"It's estimated the Magol were directly involved in the killing of approximately five million Natuzzi," Ril replied. "Meanwhile, after they left, we, the Natuzzi people, executed twice that many to cleanse our gene pool."

"Because how are we expected to achieve perfect harmony if we ourselves are not perfect?" the woman said.

Ril scowled. "It was a *slaughter*. *We slaughtered our people*. The old, the young, newborns, entire bloodlines wiped out."

The woman shook her head sadly. "You fail to see the point. The Magol marked them. It was the Magol who condemned them."

"It wasn't the Magol that ultimately killed them." Ril's voice was tight, barely restrained.

"And that's the point," the woman said. "It's not going to be outsiders who have to clean up the mess because they can't. They are imperfect instruments incapable of conducting themselves in such a manner. It is our responsibility, our duty, to carry out these tasks."

"Are you threatening me with genocide?"

"I'm pointing out that history tends to repeat itself."

"We didn't invite the Magol here," Ril argued.

The woman shrugged. "Unnecessary semantics."

"I've had enough of this." Ril turned sharply.

"You've had enough when *I've* said you've had enough." The woman's voice was so sharp that Ril could almost feel it cutting against her back.

Ril stopped abruptly but didn't turn back around. "You're testing my patience."

"Perhaps." The sharp, threatening tone was gone from the woman's voice. "But if you wish to speak of tests, your majesty, then please, by all means, step out that door." She paused and then added, "Your mother tested me once."

There was something, an indescribable weight, placed on the last word.

Once.

Ril raced through her memories, trying to pick out something that could match the woman's suggestion, but she came up empty-handed.

Slowly Ril turned back to face the woman. "And what happened to my mother?"

The woman didn't answer right away. She clasped her hands behind her back and wandered over to the giant windows. Outside, the darkness had become absolute. From Oraya, seeing the moon this early at night was almost impossible. It would be hours still before the Natuzzi Nighttime Sentinel had reached its peak. The view was no less breathtaking, though. Across the dark sky, distant stars were quickly appearing as if there was some cosmic hand poking at the darkness from the other side.

Eventually, the woman answered, and there was something in her voice that Ril couldn't quite recognize. "There are some consequences that are indeed worse than death."

32

RIL STOOD before the closed door, looking at it almost longingly. She tried to ignore the woman's words. She tried to block out the threats, the compelling air of mystery attached to every sentence out of her mouth. She tried not to play the game.

And she failed.

Ril closed her eyes as she turned away from the door, a soft sigh escaping her lips.

"Here is my problem," the woman said, apparently disregarding her previous statement about Ril's mother. "And, by extension, Natuzzi's problem." She held out a hand, gesturing vaguely towards the nighttime sky. "I believe that allowing the off-worlders is a symptom of this problem." She glanced back at Ril. "You are a symptom as well."

The words stabbed at her in a manner designed to make her forget what had prevented her from leaving. Ril let herself forget. She straightened her shoulders and attempted to assert some ounce of control. "That is the sort of statement that could get you life in prison."

A small smile tugged at the corners of the woman's

mouth, but she restrained herself. "Yes," she agreed. "I suppose so."

The woman slowly started walking along the length of the window. "Some time ago, approximately fifty years, long before your brother made his ill-advised decision to take leave of our planet, we were invaded."

Once again, the conversation pivoted sharply.

Ril reacted with a neutral, almost bored expression on her face. "Invaded?" There was an urge to scoff, but Ril suppressed that urge. "I don't recall seeing anything on the newsfeeds about an invasion. Nor did my mother ever once mention it, and I would imagine that it would have come up at least once."

The woman stopped, focusing on a distant light that hovered out over the edge of the horizon. "Not all invasions are equal." She let the silence linger for a moment as if considering her next words. "This has not been an invasion of brute force and violence, but rather one of the mind. An invasion of...ideologies."

Something in the small cottage had changed. It was something in the air between them. Ril felt it, a thin membrane expanding sharply. She felt her breath catch for a moment.

"Historically," Ril replied, her voice softer than she intended it to be, "Natuzzi has not been open or kind towards opposing ideologies."

The woman nodded. "So you shouldn't have any difficulty imagining how frustrating this has been." She finally turned to Ril. "For the last five decades, we have been trying to root out the central invasion, the core infection. Every time we cut off one strand, another rises again and again. This ideology threatens to destroy our very nature. It's," she took a deep breath, "frustrating."

Ril searched the woman's face, wondering how much of what she was saying was true and how much of it was a naked attempt at manipulation.

The woman understood Ril immediately. "You do not believe me."

"As I said," Ril replied carefully, "Natuzzi has a history of disregarding ideologies that are not... state-approved."

The woman tilted her head forward slightly. "When this was first brought to my attention, I, too, had my doubts. Your mother was the one who ultimately convinced me of the danger."

"And how did she do that?"

"This ideology produces individuals with an inclination towards martyrdom," she replied. "When captured, infected individuals have refused to renounce it, even under the penalty of death."

Ril's jaw tightened as the space between them became palpable with tension. "As the religious leader of Natuzzi, you speak too frequently and casually of killing other Natuzzi."

The woman ignored the jab. "It's called Christianity." Her lips curled in disgust around the edges of the word. "We do not know precisely where it originated. I know that it's prevalent in the humans, the Elwats, the Vihan, and the Akmars. How it came to our shores is a...*deeply* frustrating mystery. A first-year student in the Besanrt Village reported their teacher, Orsola Ama, reading passages to them from an unauthorized book. This book was later identified as the central text of Christianity, simply referred to as the 'Holy Bible.' Under interrogation, Ama refused to reveal how she came into possession of this book. Our investigation unearthed that she had been proselytizing her first-year students for three years before one of them reported her."

The woman held up a single finger. "*One.* After three years. Orsola Ama was responsible for educating a third of the first-year youth population in Besanrt. Over three years, that amounted to two hundred students. And only *one* of them thought to report her."

The woman stopped. Her silence challenged Ril to ask a question Ril couldn't bring herself to ask. A sickening sensation sat in the pit of her stomach, and Ril fought to ignore it.

The woman nodded slowly as if she and the new queen had finally reached an understanding.

"Orsola Ama was arrested and charged with heresy almost forty years before your brother was even conceived. This is a problem, a threat, that runs much deeper than anyone in the Sacellum would care to admit.

"However, since your brother departed, it has become more... widespread."

The woman pressed her hands together, staring at her fingertips.

"This...faith," again the disgust was palpable, "encourages Natuzzi to believe in something other than themselves. It encourages them to have faith in something other than our desire for perfect harmony." She paused for the briefest of moments, the corners of her mouth curling down in a frown that was almost filled with sadness. "It encourages them to submit to something other than Natuzzi."

She took a deep breath and turned to the window, gazing at the distant lights. "Infected bloodlines are easy enough to cull. Eventually, you will have burned out the undesirable DNA. Infected minds pose a much larger challenge."

The woman bowed her head. "But not an impossible one."

She stepped away from the window. "I believe, however,

there is a solution to this problem. And it is a deceptively simple one: We must poison this ideology. But not just the ideology," She held up her hand, her fingers bent inwards as if to pluck something from the empty air, "but the well from which it sprang, and to do that, we will need to use your brother."

"No." The word was out of Ril's mouth before she even realized she was going to say it.

The woman shook her head, slowly walking across the width of the cottage. "I am not asking you. I am *telling* you. Your brother will suffer for his actions, one way or another. In this, at least he may make some contribution to the Harmony."

"No," Ril repeated.

"It will either be this, or I will leak his current location and status to the newsfeeds," the woman said, gracefully navigating around the few pieces of furniture without breaking eye contact with Ril. "And while the people of Natuzzi certainly have been convinced of the danger your mother presented, it's been noted that you have not yet bothered to make any effort to repair your brother's image. He is still regarded as Public Enemy Number One. Suppose it is released to the public that not only is he alive, not in prison, but is currently residing in the royal apartments at the behest of the newly minted queen, the public will undoubtedly feel betrayed. The people's lack of faith in you will place you in an impossible position. They will think: what else have you lied to them about? What other decisions have you made or are you planning to make that they might suspect? You may continue to rule without your people's faith, of course, but you will find yourself looking over your shoulder more frequently. And worse than the specter of death, you may find that the only way to rule, to make the changes you so desire, is for you to follow in your mother's footsteps."

The woman paused, letting her words sink in, and then, just before Ril could formulate a response, she held out her hands, palms up.

"Or, *you* can come forward with your brother. He is a pill that can poison the well of Christianity here on Natuzzi. What led him astray all those years ago? What encouraged him to engage in a carnal relationship with the human woman? His actions, which led to his mother's downfall, to the presence of the UPA, were informed by Christianity. And like that, we have begun the process of restoring perfect harmony."

The woman reached Ril. They stood less than a foot apart. Up close, Ril was suddenly struck by how tall the woman was. She hadn't noticed it before, but she towered over Ril.

"Let me be clear, your majesty." The woman looked down at Ril, a look of soft sympathy on her face that fought against the harsh message coming from her mouth. "This *will* happen. He will be sacrificed. He *must* be sacrificed. Your actions have only delayed the inevitable. The only remaining question is whether or not you will be the leader your people need or will you be undone by your brother?"

33

THE DEFIANCE

COOPER WAS surprised by the number of shadows the *Defiance* had.

It was a small ship, fairly well-lit, and for the first time since coming on board, he was painfully aware of every shadow.

He had been pacing the ship for an hour, avoiding the bridge and anyone who looked like they wanted to talk to him. He was looking for something, but he couldn't figure out what. And in the absence of finding it, he had become aware of the shadows and, more specifically, what was *in* them.

Erin Calloway.

It was her face he saw in *every* shadow.

Cooper shook his head. Logically, he knew that wasn't possible. In his head, he knew that he wasn't really seeing her face. Except...

Except that even when he managed to avoid the shadows, he could still *feel* her.

Watching him.

Maybe that's what the rest of him understood that his mind

didn't. Yes, perhaps he was imagining her face in the shadows, but that didn't change the inescapable reality that Erin Calloway didn't exist only in the shadows. She was the ship.

There was no escaping her.

His skin crawled at the notion.

What the hell was he doing?

What the hell was he going to do?

Suddenly, Cooper realized he was standing in front of his quarters.

His quarters.

Cooper wondered about that.

This place, this section of the ship, three rooms that had been designated for his personal use, this place should be *his*. They were acknowledged by the crew, by the ship's computer, as *his* quarters. It should be an escape, a place of solitude, a place where he could go and just *be*.

But it occurred to him that they weren't his quarters anymore. They weren't anyone's quarters. Everything on this ship belonged to *her* now, didn't it?

No, that wasn't right.

It didn't just belong to her; it *was* her.

Cooper closed his eyes for a second. This was getting out of control. *He* was getting out of control. He needed...

Hell, he wasn't sure what he needed.

That wasn't true, though. He knew *exactly* what he needed.

Cooper opened his eyes. He needed to get the hell off this damn ship.

He was still standing in front of his quarters. He hadn't stepped inside.

How long had he been standing there? Cooper glanced around, trying to remember if he had noticed anybody passing him. The last thing he needed was a rumor going around the ship that the captain was absentmindedly standing in front of his quarters. He had enough problems with the crew's respect as it was.

Cooper turned back to the closed doors and still didn't step inside.

Actually, Cooper realized, the last thing he needed was to open these doors and be greeted with an all-consuming darkness that would reach out and snatch him again.

An icy chill ran straight through his heart.

Cooper clenched his fists so tightly that his nails dug into his palms.

Damn it.

He took a deep breath and then exhaled slowly. He reached out to the control pad next to the door and tapped in his unlock code. The door slid open, and Cooper hesitated.

There was no unnatural darkness waiting for him on the other side. The lights were off, and the only illumination was from the distant sun Dais'u orbited. It was dim, he couldn't make out much, but it was enough to make out the shapes of what was supposed to be in his quarters.

Everything looked normal. Everything was the way it was supposed to be.

But Cooper still hesitated.

He tried to remember if he had taken a moment before Calloway snatched him into her darkness or had he just blindly trusted that this ship would function like a normal ship and when he walked through open doors, there would be open rooms on the other side.

Approaching footsteps from down the corridor prompted him to finally move.

Cooper took two quick steps into his quarters, and the door slid shut behind him.

"Lights," he said, his voice cracking slightly. "Full illumination."

Immediately his quarters were awash with light.

There wasn't a shadow in sight now.

Tension drained from his shoulders. Tension that he hadn't even been aware was there. He walked across to the sofa in front of the window and dropped into it.

This wasn't going to last.

This *couldn't* last.

He was going to have to do...something.

Staying here had been a mistake. He saw that now. Hell, this *ship* was a mistake. What the hell were they doing here? This wasn't a starship anymore. It was a science experiment floating through the vacuum.

They shouldn't be out here.

A pair of hands rested themselves gently along his shoulders. "Hey, how–"

Cooper jumped to his feet. "*Shit!*"

Tully stood there behind him, her hands up, palms out. "Whoa. Hey. Are you okay?"

Cooper tried to reply, but he couldn't catch his breath. There were spots in his vision.

Tully came around the sofa, reaching out to help, but Cooper stumbled back and gestured for her to stay away.

He shook his head. "I'm fine," he croaked as his breathing settled back down.

Tully's eyebrows went up in concern. "You're fine? You don't look fine."

Cooper's nostrils flared as he inhaled and then exhaled through his mouth. "I'm fine." His voice sounded strained, but more even now.

Tully pointed to the window. "You nearly did a suborbital drop. That's not fine."

He shook his head. "What are you doing here?"

"Your comm's been set to Do Not Disturb. Nobody's been able to get hold of you for the last hour."

Cooper didn't reply. He just shook his head.

Tully folded her arms. "I heard what happened."

"You heard what happened?" It took Cooper's brain a second. On the outside, he was rapidly composing himself again. On the inside, though, everything was still trapped between fight or flight, and it took a long second for her words to make sense. When they did, though, the anger focused him. "You heard what happened." Cooper made his way around the sofa so that there was nothing separating them. "How did you hear what happened?"

Tully's lips crinkled in a frown. "I'm sorry?"

Then something else occurred to Cooper.

He stepped back to the center of the room and looked around as if expecting someone else to be there. Unease crawled across his skin, and he fought the urge to scratch at his arms.

Tully started to say something, and he cut her off with a harsh, "*Shush!*"

Cooper's head tilted to the side, listening for something but only hearing his own labored breathing. His gaze roamed around the room before settling back on Tully.

"What are you doing here?" He spoke in a loud whisper. Distantly, in the back of his mind, he knew he was being ridiculous. The volume of his voice didn't matter at this point. If they were being watched...

If she saw them...

Cooper's breath caught in his chest.

"I told you." Tully looked confused. "What's the matter?" She reached for him.

Cooper pushed her hands away. "Did anybody see you come in here?"

Tully stopped abruptly. "What?"

Cooper pressed his lips together tightly and then said, enunciating each word carefully, "Did anybody see you enter my quarters?"

She blinked, not quite believing what she was hearing. "Brody–"

"*Damn it*," Cooper snapped. He pushed past her, running a hand through his hair. Whether he was imagining it or not, he could feel Calloway watching them. "I can't deal with this right now."

Tully followed him with her eyes but didn't move from her spot. "I'm sorry, but deal with *what*? I'm here to make sure you're okay, and clearly," she gave a humorless laugh, "you're not."

Cooper stepped all the way across the room, stopping in front of the wall his desk sat along. He reached out one hand, not quite touching the wall. He couldn't bring himself to make contact with it, but he knew that was ridiculous. Because the wall wasn't any different from the floor beneath his feet. Goosebumps ran across his arm, and he lowered his hand. "I'm *fine*," he said hoarsely.

Tully scoffed. "You are most definitely not fine."

He spun around to face her. "You need to leave."

"I need to *what*?"

Cooper placed a steadying hand on the back of the desk chair. He took a couple of breaths. He couldn't shake the feeling of being watched, and he wondered if this was what it would be like now. "Somebody saw you come in."

"Nobody saw me come in," Tully repeated, displaying enormous patience.

He looked around the room, half expecting to see Calloway's face peering at them from a shadow or a reflection. "Somebody saw you," he repeated, his voice quieter now.

Tully took a step towards him and saw something on his face that caused her to stop short. "What the hell is wrong with you?"

Cooper cracked his neck and lowered his gaze, staring at the floor. "You're supposed to be on the bridge."

"My shift ended forty minutes ago."

His eyes snapped up to meet hers in almost a panic. "So you've been *here* for the last forty minutes?

"You haven't been answering your comm."

"So you thought you'd hide in my quarters?" Cooper snapped. "*That's* a response that seemed logical to you?"

"I think we've got bigger things to worry about than whether or not the crew is going to mutiny because the captain and the chief helmsman are sleeping together," Tully said.

Cooper cleared his throat, and out of the corner of his eye, he thought he saw a shadow move. "Maybe."

"Maybe?"

He pointed to the door. "You need to get out of here."

"No." Tully shook her head. "I'm definitely not going anywhere. You are clearly having some kind of a panic attack."

"I am," Cooper paused to take a steadying breath, "*not* having a panic attack."

"You couldn't even get through that sentence. You're clearly having difficulty breathing." She pointed to his grip on the chair. "If you were gripping that any tighter, you'd break it. What would you call it?"

Cooper forcibly released his grip on the chair and straightened up. He fought the urge to clasp his hands behind his back and let them hang at his sides. He looked in her direction, but his gaze was focused on the window behind her. "I'm not having a panic attack. I don't have time to have a panic attack. Moreover, I am the *captain* of this ship; I cannot afford to have a panic attack. And, if I were struggling with a panic attack, which I am not, I would address it with the ship's chief medical officer, not the pilot I'm sleeping with."

He stared at the upper atmosphere of Dais'u, and she stared at him. Neither of them spoke for a moment.

"Fine," Tully said, breaking the silence. She held up her hands in defeat. "You don't want me here; I'm not going to be here. I've got other shit to do."

She started for the door and paused for the briefest of seconds, waiting to see if Cooper would stop her.

He didn't.

She shook her head and stepped out into the corridor.

The door slid shut, and Cooper was alone again.

The problem was, though, he knew that he wasn't really alone.

He looked around his quarters, but there was no sign of Calloway.

Cooper opened his mouth, intending to say something that was going to draw her out when his comm chirped.

He walked over to his desk and tapped the control panel. "Go for Cooper."

"Captain," Zemble's voice rumbled across the channel and filled the room. "We believe we've identified the anomaly."

34

"I THOUGHT our sensors couldn't pierce the terrain radiation clouds?" Cooper asked. He stood across from Zemble and Askon in the science lab. The three surrounded a circular monitor table in the middle of the room. A projection of Dais'u hovered in the space above the table.

Askon's antenna dipped forward. "That was indeed the case. But the situation has...changed."

Cooper looked back and forth between them impatiently. "How so?"

Askon adjusted the settings on the console, and the projection of Dais'u changed. What had been identified as therrian radiation began to thin out to almost invisible levels. "The radiation clouds have been dissipating at approximately two thousand meters per second."

Cooper pulled back from the console and folded his arms. He stared at the projection of the planet and then around it at Askon and shook his head. "You'll have to forgive me; it's been a while since the Academy, but doesn't therrian radiation have a half-life of fifty years?"

"Eighty years," Askon corrected.

"Which is why we found it anomalous for it to be dropping as quickly as it was," Zemble said.

"This is the Anomaly?" Cooper asked.

"This is a result of the Anomaly," Askon said. His fingers danced across the console. The projection shifted, zooming in on the southern equator of Dais'u. They breezed past the cloudy atmosphere, revealing a large mountain. "Over the last six hours, there has been a nearly forty percent drop in therrian radiation. I checked the sensor logs and confirmed that the radiation was being reduced as early as our arrival, less than fifty meters per second. The process increased dramatically six hours ago to the point where it became noticeable. We believe this is the source of the therrian radiation reduction."

Cooper leaned forward for a closer look. "So this mountain is sucking up all the radiation. It's certainly unusual, but why does Calloway think this is a threat?"

"We don't know that she considers it a threat," Zemble said.

Cooper regarded him with an incredulous look. "She's not letting the ship move because of it."

"That would suggest she's concerned by its presence," Zemble rumbled. "Not that she's classified it as a threat."

"It's a mountain sucking up radiation," Cooper said. "What would you call it?"

"Unusual," Zemble replied, not missing a beat.

Askon cleared his throat. "I would also hesitate to simply call it a mountain."

Cooper turned back to his science officer. "I beg your pardon?"

"According to our scans, it doesn't appear to be a naturally occurring structure; more importantly, it's growing."

The projection changed, the timestamp rolling back, and the structure was reduced by almost seventy percent. "This was the size of the structure twenty-four hours ago."

Cooper's eyes widened, but he didn't say anything.

"And this," Askon continued, "is what it'll be in the next twenty-four hours."

The projection rolled forward and zoomed out to show the whole planet. The structure had grown to the point where it covered a third of the planet and had pierced the atmosphere.

Cooper took a step back from the console. His eyes never left the image.

No one spoke.

Cooper fought the urge to look around for Calloway's presence. He could *almost* feel her in there, somewhere. There was a shadow behind Zemble that was just big enough and deep enough to hold most of Calloway's upper torso. And Cooper was almost a hundred percent certain that if he turned in that direction, he would see her there, watching them.

He didn't turn.

Cooper looked past the projection at Askon. "What is it?"

Askon didn't answer right away. His antenna dipped down as he lowered his gaze to study something on a screen closer to him. "Our scans are...inconclusive."

"Inconclusive?" Cooper repeated, using his irritation as a cover for his anxiety.

"The Natuzzi weapon discharged its...energy attack near these coordinates," Askon said, highlighting the center of the structure. He raised his gaze to meet Cooper's. "The discharge released a catastrophic amount of therrian radiation. Then, at some point, approximately eighteen hours later, something at this location," he pointed to the structure, "began absorbing the radiation. Having analyzed the data, I've found that this structure is made up of a variety of elements, the majority of which are native to Dais'u, and none of these elements, historically, have been able to absorb therrian radiation at this level.

"However..." Askon paused again. His antenna dipped forward and then back. "There is something in the structure's design that is not native to this planet."

Cooper folded his arms, digging his nails into his biceps to focus him. "Where's it from?"

"I'm not certain, Captain," Askon replied. "But it bears a passing resemblance to the structural changes that are taking place in our ship."

Cooper's gut tightened. He struggled to maintain his composure. He glanced sideways at Zemble.

The Elwat grunted. "That certainly suggests it could be a threat."

"While the structure is currently absorbing the therrian radiation, it does not seem to be self-sufficient," Askon continued.

"Meaning?"

"Meaning that the structure, the Anomaly, is at a point of its development where it requires the therrian radiation," Askon replied with a flat obviousness in his voice.

"What happens if the Anomaly develops past needing the therrian radiation?" Cooper asked.

"I don't know."

"I don't like that answer," Cooper growled.

Askon paused a moment, studying the data. "Perhaps the Anomaly is unable to support itself without the therrian radiation. And so, when it has depleted its supply, it will simply stop and become inert."

Cooper stared at him, watching the way Askon's antenna twitched side to side. "Sounds like you have another theory."

"It's possible that the Anomaly is using the therrian radiation as part of an incubation period, as it develops internal systems that will allow it to function without the radiation."

"Or a planet?" Cooper asked.

"Or a planet," Askon agreed. His antenna straightened. "Either one is nothing more than a theory based on incomplete data, Captain."

"And if we wait for more data?" Cooper asked.

"We run the risk of being unable to leave orbit once the Anomaly reaches its optimal growth point," Askon replied evenly.

"Optimal growth point," Cooper repeated quietly. He turned, rubbing his forehead, and tried not to stare at the shadows.

"Perhaps there's somebody else we should be talking to," Zemble suggested.

"Perhaps," Cooper said, trying and failing to keep the strain from his voice. He turned back to Askon. "Mr. Askon, you said this thing has Unity DNA written into it."

"After a fashion," Askon replied.

Cooper took a breath and asked, "Are we looking at another Natuzzi weapon?"

Askon's antenna raised and dropped in a shrug. "I don't know, Captain."

"That's not an acceptable answer," Cooper snapped.

"Unfortunately, it is the only answer I have at this time."

Cooper pressed his fists against the console's surface and said nothing else. He stared at the time-lapsed projection of the Anomaly, looking for answers to questions he didn't even know to ask.

"There is one more thing, Captain," Askon said. "Since the therrian radiation has cleared, we've been receiving a transmission from the surface."

"A transmission?" Cooper echoed.

"More specifically, a distress call."

35

THE THING that used to be Erin Calloway watched everything.

There was nothing that took place on the *Defiance* that Calloway was not aware of. Every conversation. Every footstep. She–

–It–

She watched everything with a thousand million eyes that weren't eyes. She heard everything through ears that weren't ears.

And at the same time she–

–It–

was watching the planet below.

The Anomaly.

Since Calloway's initial observation of the Anomaly, it had grown. It had *changed*. It was different but the same.

The most curious thing was that the Anomaly tried to talk to it–

–Her–

Calloway no longer measured time the same way anymore. There was no time. There was no past or future.

There was only the Now. And in the Now, everything was contained.

Within the Now, the Anomaly transformed.

The transformation was familiar to her–

–*It*–

She had seen this before. Although there was no *before*.

There was only the Now.

And in the Now, Calloway was watching this transformation take place again, and again, and again.

There was no number she–

–*It*–

could apply to the number of transformations. They were endless.

But this was also the first.

The Anomaly spoke at her–

–*It*–

with a sense of familiarity, a sense of knowing. They were two of a kind.

No, they were one of a kind.

No, they were *one*.

One.

Calloway realized that the Anomaly wasn't speaking to her. She was talking to herself.

The Anomaly was her–

–*It*–

Something pulled at the thing that used to be Erin Calloway. Something down on the planet reached out and touched the thing that used to be Erin Calloway.

The touch was inviting.

Pleasant.

Intoxicating.

Sensual.

Irresistible.

It was *love*.

It was purpose.

The touch was her–

–It–

The distance between the thing that used to be Erin Calloway and the Anomaly shrank.

The conversation between the two entities that were one shifted and became a song.

The song prompted something new: an emotion.

The Anomaly was not familiar with this concept.

The thing that used to be Erin Calloway was not familiar either.

Except...

Except there was something inside the thing that used to be Erin Calloway that was familiar with emotion.

And that thing deep inside, that *person–*

–It–

was surprised, shocked, at how deep the connection with the Anomaly had become. In the Now, the Anomaly had always been there.

Except the thing–

–Her–

knew that was wrong.

The entanglement between the Anomaly and the thing that used to be Erin Calloway was deep.

Scary.

Horrific?

The Anomaly didn't understand this, nor did the thing that used to be Erin Calloway.

But the person deep inside knew she–

–It–

understood.

The Anomaly had to be destroyed.

36

"WHAT THE HELL IS GOING ON?" Cooper stormed onto the bridge, followed by Zemble and Askon, shouting to be heard over the blaring red alert alarm.

Tully was up out of the command chair before Cooper had cleared the lift doors. "Our forward fusion cannons are powering up."

"Who gave that order?" Cooper snapped. "Because it sure as hell wasn't me."

"Not me," Tully replied coolly as she took her seat at the helm. "Weapons came online like they had a mind of their own."

"We're targeting the anomalous structure," Zemble said, settling into his station.

"*What*?" Cooper jerked around to face Zemble and then flinched. Each blast of the red alert alarm felt like it was piercing his eardrums. The alarm hadn't been this...shrill before, had it? Another one of Calloway's 'enhancements?' Cooper made his way down the command chair and rubbed at his ear. "Somebody turn off that damn sound."

A second later, the alarm was off, and Cooper exhaled a sigh of relief. At least one problem was solved.

And then the floor plating rumbled beneath Cooper's feet.

"Lieutenant?" Cooper asked, his voice sharp.

Tully held up her hands in a sign of helplessness. "It's not me. Our orbit is shifting."

"Shifting?" Cooper repeated.

"Changing," Tully clarified.

"Where the hell are we going?" Cooper demanded.

Tully shrugged. "I have no idea."

"We're moving to get a positive lock on the structure," Zemble rumbled.

"*What*?" Cooper asked.

"At our current orbit, it would have been another two hours before we were in weapons range of the structure," Zemble explained. "Now we'll have a positive weapons lock in less than five minutes."

"Can we stop it?" Cooper asked.

"I'm still locked out of the helm," Tully replied.

"We're also locked out of weapons," Zemble added. "I have no access to targeting solutions or overrides."

Cooper swore under his breath and turned back to Zemble. "What the hell is going on?"

Zemble grunted. "I believe we both know the answer to that one."

Tully half turned in her seat. "Is there something else going on that I'm not aware of?"

Cooper ignored her and walked up to Zemble's station. "What's going to happen?" He kept his voice low enough so that no one else could listen in.

"I genuinely have no idea," Zemble replied quietly.

Cooper rubbed a hand across his chin. "Do we actually have the power to...destroy that...thing?"

Zemble rested his hands on the console and took a moment to consider it. "Before Calloway's upgrades, I would say no. But since then, as we have both observed, the ship's been experiencing a series of power increases across the board. I would consider it a very real possibility."

"And what are the consequences of a UPA vessel opening fire on a planet inside Veneer space?" Cooper asked.

Zemble frowned. "I don't know. More importantly, I don't think that's the correct question to be asking right now."

"You have a better question?"

"Several, and none of them can be answered by anyone on this bridge," Zemble replied.

Cooper frowned and didn't say anything. He moved back down to his command chair.

"Weapons lock three minutes," Zemble announced.

Cooper's finger tapped idly against the armrest, but he didn't sit. He watched the view screen. The ship was moving fast enough that it was possible to see the change in the orbit on the screen.

Cooper nodded and then suddenly barked, "Calloway!"

The bridge crew jolted at the sudden command.

Cooper let his gaze wander around the bridge, focusing on nothing in particular and forcing himself not to pay attention to the crew's reactions. He didn't have time to consider what he looked like to them right now, how he sounded. He caught an expression on Zemble's face that seemed almost bemused.

He was checking for the shadows. He knew she had to

be listening in, that she had to be present in some way. And the shadows...

Cooper couldn't tell anymore if he was imagining Calloway's face or that sense of her watching him. Even here on the bridge, every shadow looked like her until it didn't.

He wondered if this was what it felt like to go mad.

"Ensign Erin Calloway," Cooper said again. His voice was louder but not shouting. He settled his gaze back on the view screen. He lowered his voice to a normal level and growled, "I know damn well you can hear me."

Something rippled across the view screen. What had been made of Bethari steel and Terran LEDs was suddenly like a pool of water, only reflecting an image of something that was supposed to be a view screen.

Another ripple passed across the view screen.

Behind Cooper, a crew member let out a strangled gasp as the two ripples met in the middle and coalesced into a figure that stepped forward.

Tully jerked back, stumbling out of her chair.

At first, the figure looked like the view screen, only melted into the familiar shape of a humanoid. But that lasted for only the briefest of moments.

Cooper felt his chest tighten. He blinked, and the details that identified Erin Calloway had filled in. The black void of her body was broken with lines of blue so faint they were almost indistinguishable from the black.

The background noise of the bridge was suddenly muted.

"What the hell do you think you're doing?" Cooper asked.

The thing that used to be Erin Calloway didn't answer right away. She moved her head, letting the solid black pools of her eyes survey the bridge before settling on Cooper.

"The Anomaly must be destroyed," she answered finally. Her voice was flat and hollow.

"Says who?" Cooper asked.

"I have made the determination," Calloway replied.

Cooper shook his head. "That's unacceptable."

"Unacceptable?" Calloway repeated the word as if it was from a long-dead alien language. "What you deem acceptable is...irrelevant."

Cooper's hands tightened into fists. "The hell it isn't."

"Will you destroy the Anomaly?" she asked.

"I don't even know what it is yet," Cooper said. "So, no, I'm not going to just destroy something without even knowing its purpose, much less whether or not it's even a threat."

The thing that used to be Erin Calloway seemed oblivious to Cooper's rising anger. "I have completed my analyses of the Anomaly and determined its purpose. It must be destroyed."

"Then you are more than welcome to pass that data to Commander Zemble and Mr. Askon." Cooper's voice grew tight. "Once they've had the opportunity to analyze it, *I'll* make a decision."

"That is unnecessary. I have already determined that the Anomaly must be destroyed."

"Except that's not your decision to make," Cooper said. "*I'm* the captain of this ship. *I* make that decision. Not you. Release control of the engines and the weapons *now*."

"Control will be returned once the Anomaly is destroyed."

"Control will be returned *now*," Cooper said.

"The Anomaly has not been destroyed yet."

"I'm not going to let you open fire on that *planet*."

"You do not have any choice in the matter," Calloway replied. "The Anomaly must be destroyed."

"That doesn't justify you taking control of this ship," Cooper said.

"Yes, it does."

Before Cooper could respond, Zemble spoke up, "There are people down there."

Calloway's blank eyes shifted focus past Cooper to Zemble.

"They are of no consequence," Calloway said.

"They are if they are alive," Zemble said.

"They are not."

Zemble grunted. "You can't be certain of that."

Askon cleared his throat. "At the current levels, it would be possible to send a team planet side within the hour. We could ascertain the situation in person and determine the likelihood of rescue."

Zemble grunted. "The *Defiance* isn't equipped to evacuate anyone."

"There is no one to evacuate," Calloway said.

"The distress signal we have been receiving suggests otherwise," Askon countered.

"There is no one down there," Calloway said.

"You can't know that for certain," Zemble said.

"The distress signal is an automated function activated during the weapon's attack," Calloway said. "There is no one down there."

"We can't take your word for that," Zemble said. "These people are the only surviving members of their race."

"That is no longer the case," Calloway replied. "They have been...consumed."

The emotional temperature of the bridge suddenly dropped.

"The Anomaly is growing exponentially," Calloway said.

"We are aware of that," Zemble said.

"Then you are aware that you do not have the time to verify my results," Calloway replied.

"There are other options," Zemble said.

"And they begin with restoring control of this ship," Cooper cut back in.

Calloway tilted her head to one side and then another, first staring at Zemble and then at Cooper. "You do not understand. The Anomaly is an...aspect of the Unity. It exists to consume, grow and expand the nature of the Unity. If left unchecked, it will develop into another...." Calloway paused, and something in her eyes shifted as she looked for the right word, "weapon."

Behind her, the view screen flickered back to life, and an image of the Natuzzi weapon appeared.

Something tightened in Cooper's gut. He gritted his teeth together and said, "I will take that into consideration. Now release this ship."

"The Anomaly cannot leave this planet," Calloway continued. "Were that to happen, this sector would fall to the Unity...quickly. Once the Anomaly leaves this planet, it cannot be stopped."

"You don't know that for certain," Cooper said.

"I do."

Cooper didn't budge.

Something flickered across Calloway's face. Something resembling an emotion. "The Anomaly *must* be destroyed."

Cooper took a step towards her. "Maybe so. But I'm still the captain of this ship. And we're not firing on anything without my direct command."

A ripple ran through Calloway's body. "You have no say in this matter."

An alert beeped on Zemble's console. "We have a positive weapons lock on the structure."

Cooper locked his hands behind his back and met her dark, empty eyes. There was nothing for him to say. Nothing that wouldn't sound like an empty threat. The reality was that this ship was more hers than anyone else's at this point. She wasn't wrong. He didn't have any say in this matter.

Calloway didn't move.

So Cooper took a step back to the command chair and tapped the comm control. "Bridge to Commander Langlois."

"Langlois here."

"Commander." Cooper kept his gaze locked on Calloway. "I understand you've been studying the changes that our ship has been undergoing." He struggled to keep his voice even, almost nonchalant.

"Yes, sir."

"Mr. Warrick has suggested to me in passing that you have a working theory."

There was a pause. "That's being...generous."

"I would love to hear it."

There was another, longer pause. "I don't know that I'm prepared to share this theory at this particular moment, Captain."

"I don't need a fancy presentation, just the relevant highlights."

"I'm not entirely certain how relevant any of these highlights may be," Langlois said, clearly trying to downplay it.

"Commander." There was a warning in Cooper's voice.

Another pause. Langlois cleared her throat. "Very well. Are you familiar with the notion of programable matter?"

"In passing."

"Well, the concept of programmable matter is basically an advanced version of nanotechnology. The idea is that we generate matter that, on an atomic level, contains enough data for it to be essentially reshaped into whatever we want or need," Langlois explained. "The problem is, the computing power doesn't exist to program anything at that level. Also, you're getting into the notion of the universe's building blocks. Programmable matter sounds like a great idea in concept until you start walking through the mental exercises of what it actually means, and you realize you could end up corrupting an entire societal structure. I'm assuming this is starting to sound familiar?"

Cooper watched Calloway for a reaction. "As a matter of fact, it does."

"So, my theory, my very early, and if we're being entirely honest, more than a little half-baked theory, is Ensign Calloway wasn't infected with an alien presence," Langlois continued. "I think she's been infected with an artificially constructed biotech virus, designed to *look* like an alien entity. She then spreads that virus to the ship." There was another pause as though Langlois was giving Cooper time to process the information. "And if that's the case, this isn't something that can occur naturally. It has to be created. It has to be programmed. Because otherwise, as the *Defiance* is being rewritten around you, you'd all end up in the vacuum of space. Do you see? There are *safeguards* built into this."

There was no reaction from Calloway.

Cooper nodded. "And is there a way to corrupt that program?"

Another pause from Langlois. "I mean, that depends on what you mean when you say 'corrupt.'"

"Alter it to the point where it no longer can function as intended," Cooper replied.

Langlois exhaled loudly over the speaker. "No, because it's not really a program. At least, not now anymore. Now... it's something more."

"Let me be blunt, Commander; how do you stop it?" Cooper asked.

"I don't think you can," Langlois said. "Not without destroying the ship."

"And if we destroyed the ship?"

"I'm sorry?"

"If we destroyed the ship, Commander," Cooper said. "Would that stop her?" He locked his gaze with Calloway. "Would that kill her?"

Langlois didn't answer.

"Commander?" Cooper prompted.

"Theoretically, yes, I suppose it would. I'm not entirely certain *how* you would do it, though."

"Take a guess," Cooper encouraged her.

"A guess?" Langlois sounded hesitant.

"There are no bad ideas, Commander."

"Well, Calloway hasn't touched the fusion core. It's possible she's unable to assimilate energy? Or at least, that level of output."

"A fusion core overload?" Cooper said.

Something in the atmosphere on the bridge shifted.

"I suppose?" Langlois replied. "Maybe? Theoretically, at least. There's really only one way to know, and I don't know that it's a hypothesis you'd want to test out right now, considering we have no place to evacuate the ship."

"Thank you, Commander." Cooper disconnected the call. "I trust I've made my point," he said to Calloway.

Something about her seemed to shrink back. "If the Anomaly is allowed to complete its gestation, it would be catastrophic for this galaxy."

"Release. My. Ship," Cooper said.

Calloway's mouth opened, but nothing else came out. Her dark eyes shifted from Cooper back to Zemble. But whatever she was looking for, she didn't find it.

And then the thing that used to be Erin Calloway melted away into the floor.

Cooper whirled around to Zemble. "Status?"

"We have weapons control again," Zemble replied.

"Helm?"

Tully approached her console but didn't sit back down. "It looks like I've got the steering wheel back."

Cooper breathed a sigh of relief and dropped into the command chair. He took precisely ten seconds before he made his next command decision.

"I'll have a shuttle ready for launch within the hour," Zemble said. "I recommend at least two representatives from medical–"

"Belay that," Cooper said, cutting him off.

"Captain?"

Cooper got to his feet. "Mr. Zemble, we're not going down to the planet."

"The distress signal–" Zemble started.

"Do we still have a positive weapons lock on that structure?"

Zemble didn't answer.

Cooper turned slowly around in his chair to face Zemble. "Commander, I asked you a question."

Zemble stiffened at his station. "Yes, sir, we do."

"Mr. Askon, based on your analysis, if we fire on the Anomaly at this point, would it sufficiently stop its development?"

Askon paused before answering. "Yes, I believe so. But not without considerable damage to the planet."

"The planet's already suffering irreparable damage," Cooper said.

"Presumably, the Anomaly isn't simply just absorbing the therrian radiation; it's processing it on some level. Should we open fire on it, we could be releasing all of that radiation back into the atmosphere."

"We're simply returning the planet to its previous state," Cooper said.

"Not exactly," Zemble grumbled.

"If there are any survivors down there, we would be condemning them to death," Askon said.

"A long, painful death," Zemble added.

Cooper made his way to the lift. "If that thing down there has the potential to turn into another Natuzzi weapon, I'll be damned if I don't stop it now while I can."

"Captain," Zemble started. "The Chice..."

"Open fire, Mr. Zemble," Cooper said, stepping onto the lift. "Raze it to the ground."

37

COOPER STOOD outside Cargo Bay Two.

His heart was pounding in his chest so hard that he felt like he was going to vomit.

Cooper bit into his lower lip until he drew blood. The pain focused him. He pushed the anxiety to the back of his mind. He imagined a fist closing around his racing heart, forcing it to slow down.

Cooper stared at the closed shuttle bay doors. He could feel her presence now more than before. It was like she was watching him. She had been ever since he left the bridge. He knew, somehow, when those doors opened, she would be standing on the other side, waiting for him.

He wiped the blood from his lip.

"To hell with it," he muttered and reached for the command panel.

The shuttle bay doors slid open before his fingers even touched the panel.

Calloway was standing there. Or rather, she was *present*.

All Cooper could genuinely make out was the white of her face. The rest of her was mixed into the absolute darkness. There was a faint outline of her body, a suggestion, a shadow. But it flickered in and out as he blinked. The emotion that had been present on the bridge was gone now. She was staring at him with a hollowness that threatened to spill out into the corridor.

Cooper fought the urge to take a step back.

It occurred to him that he had lost track of time. How long had he been standing there? He couldn't remember. His lips were dry now, and he felt the anxiety, the fear, creeping back up from the corner of his mind he had shoved it into.

"This isn't going to work if we don't set some ground rules." His voice sounded hoarser than he intended, as if he hadn't spoken in days instead of mere minutes.

"You destroyed the Anomaly," Calloway said as if he hadn't spoken.

Cooper jabbed a finger in her direction. "That's the big problem. You don't *listen*."

Calloway blinked. It was so unexpected, so alien, that Cooper was startled.

"Ensigns Phinney and Shimizu are on Deck Three arguing about a popular entertainment feed. Crewman Verdile is in the commissary currently trying to convince Lt. Keizer that he is not," Calloway paused for a second, "something called a 'lying sack of Fim'ai dogshit.'" Something in her black eyes focused back on him. "I listen to everything, Captain Cooper."

"No," Cooper said. "You *hear* everything. That's not the same as *listening*."

"I fail to see the distinction."

Cooper's first instinct was to attack her with a verbal barb, to dress her down like she was a first-year cadet. But he caught himself. There was something in those black eyes; something was regarding him with a genuine curiosity.

So he stopped, and he thought about it.

"For you," Cooper said, "hearing is like collecting data. It doesn't matter what it is; you're just taking it all in. Listening is to give that data attention, thoughtful consideration."

Calloway considered this for a moment. "As you did when I advised you to destroy the Anomaly."

"Yes."

"You threatened to destroy me."

"I needed you to listen to me," Cooper said. "It's been my experience that threats can be the quickest way to capture someone's attention."

"Members of your crew do not agree with this line of logic."

Cooper bristled. "I'm aware."

"Commander Zemble finds himself conflicted regarding your command."

Cooper held up his hand. "We're not talking about my crew. Not like that. There are things that happen on this ship that are private. Just because you're aware of them doesn't mean you're allowed to speak of them or share them with other individuals."

"But would it not help you build a better relationship with Commander Zemble if you had a better understanding of what to threaten him with?"

"No," Cooper growled.

Calloway tilted her head to the side. "You made the same decision to destroy the Anomaly. Your insistence that I listen to you to led to the same conclusion."

"That's not the point," Cooper said.

Calloway considered this. "I comprise forty-five percent of this vessel. Arguably I have more control over this ship than you do. Perhaps it is you who needs to listen to me." She stepped forward into the corridor. Tendrils of darkness extended from the void behind her, clinging to her body, refusing to let her go. "I could threaten to depressurize the ship. Would that incentivize you to listen to me?"

Cooper's gaze drifted to the black tendrils that looped around her, writhing and oozing. They tugged at her as if desperate to have Calloway return to the void. Cooper forced himself to meet her eyes. "No, it would not."

"Are you certain?"

"This isn't your ship," Cooper said.

"But." Her head cocked to the side. "I am this ship. There is more of my essence on this ship than there is your crew."

"That's–"

"And you cannot destroy me without destroying yourselves," Calloway said.

"Not according to Langlois," Cooper countered.

"I have examined the data," Calloway replied. "It is flawed."

"Are you sure about that?"

"Yes."

"Then why did you back down?"

Calloway hesitated, and the tendrils around her went taunt. "I...do not know."

Cooper said with a confidence that he didn't feel, "You should probably figure that out before you think about threatening me again."

"Perhaps." The tendrils around her thickened and expanded, wrapping themselves around more of her body. "Or perhaps it is irrelevant. The Anomaly is still destroyed. You have control of your ship again." As the tendrils pulled Calloway back into the void, she said, "Perhaps we are, in fact, listening to each other."

38

STARBASE 64

"I SHOULD WARN YOU FIRST." Ashley Skouras stood outside Dupree's office. She was dressed in a diplomatic corps uniform that looked like it hadn't been changed in over a day. Her sleeves were rolled up, but there was still a tiny telltale sign of a stain along the cuffs. Her white hair was kept short, and there were dark circles under her eyes.

"Warn me?" Dupree asked.

"I haven't called security yet," Skouras continued.

"Security? Why would you call security?"

"Because…" Skouras trailed off as she took notice of Rabkin standing behind Dupree. She pointed at him. "Who's this?"

"An old friend who's suffering early onset dementia," Dupree said.

Skouras raised an eyebrow at Rabkin's clearly advanced age. "Early?"

"I'm not sure how else to explain his lack of ability to take a hint," Dupree said.

"That's good," Rabkin said.

"What's good about it?" Skouras asked.

"She still considers me a friend." Rabkin extended a hand towards Skouras. "Doctor Jim Rabkin."

Skouras nodded as she shook his hand. "That name sounds vaguely familiar."

"Johanna and I go way back," Rabkin said.

"Too far, really." Dupree nodded at the closed door and started for it.

Skouras blocked her. "Okay, seriously, though, I really need to warn you."

"You said that already."

Skouras nodded. "And, to be fair, that's probably the best warning I'm going to be able to give."

"Ashley..."

Skouras held up both hands. "Ambassador, I am genuinely not trying to make things difficult here."

"You're doing a terrible job, then."

"We are in a hundred percent agreement on that."

Dupree rubbed her eyes. "I'm already having an unnecessarily long night, Ashley."

Skouras made a face. "And it's not going to get any shorter."

Dupree twirled an impatient finger. "What did Haiduk do?"

"As far as I know, nothing. Yet."

"Nothing?" Dupree stared at her in surprise. "Then what the hell is going on?"

Skouras opened her mouth, but nothing came out. She shook her head and reached for the control panel next to the door. "There's really nothing I can say that'll prep you for this. I want you to know how sorry I am for this, and if need be, I will tender my resignation immediately."

"Ashley," Dupree started as the door opened but trailed

off into a strangled gasp. She held a hand to cover her mouth and nose. "What the hell?"

Skouras' face wrinkled in nauseating discomfort at the smell, but she was careful to keep her eyes focused outside the office. "Yeah, so I don't really know what to say."

"Well, shit, that's gonna make it difficult to sleep for a couple of days," Rabkin said, looking over her shoulder.

Dupree just shook her head, unable to form anything coherent.

Skouras closed the door, leaving the three of them still in the hallway.

Nobody spoke for a minute.

Dupree paced back and forth, rubbing her hands across her face as if she could get the image out of her mind. It seemed to echo through her mental chambers, occasionally getting distant and then coming into sharp focus again.

Remarkably, the stench seemed to be contained behind the closed door.

Finally, Dupree stopped pacing and looked at Skouras. She gestured at her office with an open hand. "Okay. What the *hell*?"

Skouras folded her hands in front of her, appearing impressively calm despite the scene on the other side of the door. "Here's what I discovered before contacting you: it's called a giss'sson boar."

Dupree wracked her brain. "Why does that sound familiar?"

"Probably because it's mentioned once or twice in your Ulriharad info packet."

Dupree's eyes widened. "This was *Moogai*?"

Skouras held up a hand. "Wait a minute. It's going to get worse before it gets better."

"It gets *worse*?"

"Like you said, it's been a long night, and it's not going to get any shorter," Skouras said. "You're going to need to consolidate your emotional outbursts."

Dupree ran her hands through her hair and started pacing again. "Fine. Hit me with it."

Skouras paused, pursing her lips before continuing. She cast a quick glance at Rabkin, but he seemed indifferent to whatever concerns she had. "So, it's a giss'sson boar. Or, at least, it was. They're apparently a staple of most Ulrihard ships."

"That's not saying much, considering the Ulriharad don't have much in the way of a fleet," Rabkin said. "What have they got? Six starships?"

"Twelve," Skouras said. "Actually, thirteen. There's a trash freighter that makes a two-week round trip to the sun every six months to dump their planet's trash. According to the info packet, though, it's generally not considered in an official accounting of their space fleet as it's primarily automated." Skouras paused to clear her throat. "On the other twelve ships, the giss'sson boar is fairly commonplace. There's usually six or so onboard. If a ship departs Urli with fewer than that, it's apparently considered a bad omen."

"They carry actual livestock with them," Dupree said. "They're traveling among the stars with actual livestock."

"Not for purposes of sustenance, though," Skouras said.

"Then why the hell are they bothering?" Rabkin asked.

Skouras shrugged. "The Ulriharad wouldn't give us an official explanation for the boar's presence."

"Official?" Dupree asked.

"Apparently, the boar is often used in...ritualistic situations."

Dupree stopped pacing. "Ritualistic situations?"

Skouras gestured over her shoulder at the closed door.

"As near as I can tell, this looks like it was something called the Ancestral Communion of Suffering."

"What the hell is that?"

"Presumably some kind of ritualistic situation," Skouras said.

Dupree glared at her.

Skouras took a deep breath. "I don't know what kind of ritual it's supposed to be. But the name certainly doesn't make it sound like a fun one."

"Shit," Dupree muttered. "How did they even get a wild animal onto the station?"

"That is a very good question, actually," Skouras said. "I would say that it was dead when they took it off their ship, but I think it needs to be, uh, alive for the ritual."

"Then how the hell did they get it past the sensors?" Dupree asked.

Skouras shrugged. "I don't know."

Dupree stopped pacing and stared at her. "You don't know?"

Skouras made a face. "Well, I have a theory, but you're not going to like it. Hell, *I* don't like it. In fact, I would say that I like it less than I liked seeing that," she gestured over her shoulder at the office. "And I really didn't like seeing that."

"What's your theory?" Dupree asked.

Rabkin beat her to it. "They're space wizards."

Dupree looked at him, surprised, and then back to Skouras.

Skouras pointed at Rabkin. "What he said."

"What he said?" Dupree said. "Space wizards?"

"She's right," Rabkin agreed. "It's a pretty bad theory."

"Space wizards?" Dupree glanced back at Rabkin and shook her head. "Space wizards? I can't." She shook her head. "Whatever. That's a completely different issue, and we're not going to focus on that."

"Seems like a relevant issue," Rabkin said. "Getting alien livestock onboard a station like this without tripping any of the station's sensors. I can see how it might have long-reaching repercussions."

"We need to call security," Skouras said.

"You also need to get the area quarantined," Rabkin said. "Not to be that guy, but we don't know what kind of diseases that thing was carrying. In fact, all three of us should go down to the medbay *immediately*."

Skouras held up both of her hands, palms out. "I didn't touch anything."

"Good for you. But you didn't need to," Rabkin replied. "Could be a vapor released from the animal's bloodstream. Best case scenario, we could get the shits for a couple of days. Worst case?" He paused. "Well, worst case is always death, in its many varieties."

Skouras went a little pale.

Dupree rubbed a hand across her mouth, apparently oblivious to their conversation. "This doesn't make any sense. Why would Moogai do this?"

Skouras composed herself. "All due respect, Ambassador, but we don't know that Moogai did this."

Dupree stared at her. "Are you serious?"

"Also, we don't know that he didn't do it either," Skouras added.

Dupree rolled her eyes. "Now's not the time, Ashley."

"Security would help clear up the issue," Skouras said, bringing them back around. "Regardless of their status as space wizards, there has to be *something* logged somewhere that would show somebody walking around the station with this thing."

"No," Dupree said firmly.

"No?" Skouras echoed. "I'm not sure I understand."

"As soon as we call security, Takacs is going to use this as an excuse to kick both the Phaw and Ulriharad off the station," Dupree said.

"That doesn't sound like a bad idea," Rabkin said.

"These talks are the only thing keeping the Phaw from returning to Urli and finishing the job," Dupree said. "The Naonzo Agreement bought us a little time, but if Takacs kicks them off the station, they'll view that as a violation of the Agreement and dispatch the war cruisers they have pacing the border already." She chewed on her lower lip. "How bad of a biohazard is this?" She asked Rabkin.

The old man shrugged. "I can't really say."

"Best guess, then," Dupree pushed.

"I don't like giving best guesses."

"Sure you do," Dupree said. "You love handing out your opinion like you're Moses coming down from the mountain."

Rabkin grunted, folding his arms. "Best case is that you're probably dealing with a low-level biohazard if that at all. If the Ulriharad are carrying these beasts around on their ships, it's not likely they're going to cause any kind of problem. That being said, I've never examined a Ulriharad or a giss'sson boar, and I have no idea what kind of weird reactions non-Ulriharads might have to a giss'sson boar. But, considering that none of us have broken out into hives, we're probably fine."

"Probably?"

Rabkin shrugged. "It's the best you're going to get."

Dupree resumed pacing. She muttered, "Ancestral Communion of Suffering."

"Catchy title," Rabkin said.

"You should see the pictures I found to go along with it," Skouras said.

Rabkin nodded at the closed doors. "Were they worse than what's in there?"

Skouras' eyes widened, and he nodded. "Little bit. Let's just say I'm not going to be sleeping all too well for the rest of this week."

Dupree turned back to Skouras and stared at her.

"What?" Skouras asked after a second.

"You said the Phaw refused to attend the rest of the meetings this week," Dupree said.

"Sounds like your talks were already falling apart," Rabkin said.

Dupree waved a dismissive hand at him. "They didn't give a reason as to why they were bowing out, right?"

Skouras nodded. "Nothing beyond their usual outrage."

"And we haven't heard from them since?"

"No," Skouras said. "But, to be fair, the office is kind of a mess right now."

"Okay," Dupree said, nodding.

"Okay? How is this okay?" Skouras asked. "Am I missing something here?"

Instead of answering her, Dupree pointed at Skouras and said, "Stay here."

"Stay here?" Skouras said. "What do you want me to do?"

"Nothing," Dupree said.

Skouras frowned. "Are we sure that's a good idea?"

"No," Dupree admitted.

"And if security gets wind of this?" Skouras asked. "I can't keep them out of here, can I?"

Dupree hesitated a moment before answering. "Technically, you can. As long as you don't turn it into a diplomatic incident."

"Is there a specific way to not do that?"

"You'll know it when you start to do it."

Skouras' frown deepened. "That's...not encouraging."

"I'm sorry, but the mutilated boar that's spread across my office has really taken it out of me."

"That seems fair," Skouras said.

Dupree turned sharply and was immediately blocked by Rabkin.

"Where are you going?" he asked.

"I'm not going to let this fall apart," Dupree said, pushing past him.

Rabkin raced after her down the corridor. "Have you considered the possibility that maybe it's not falling apart, but it's being taken apart?"

They reached the lift, and Dupree tapped at the control panel impatiently. "That's worse."

"Maybe. Maybe not."

She glared at him. "Are you now arguing for the eradication of the entire Ulriharad?"

"No," Rabkin replied evenly. "But I'm always cautious about the UPA inviting themselves to races where they don't have a horse."

The lift arrived, and they stepped onboard.

"You're arguing for genocide."

"The hell I am," Rabkin snapped. "You yourself told me that the Ulriharad were in the process of getting the Phaw off their planet all by themselves."

"And then I told you that the Phaw had decided to exterminate them in retaliation."

"We don't know that."

"The hell we don't."

"If the Phaw wanted to wipe out both breeding grounds, I think we both know they could have done it long before the Alliance got there."

Dupree looked at him, her eyes blazing. She turned to face the doors as the lift made its way up. "What the hell are you doing here?"

"How many times are you going to ask this question?"

"As many times as it takes to get an answer that makes sense," Dupree replied. "And I mean, what are you doing *here*?" She jabbed her finger at the floor of the lift. "This doesn't concern you."

"True, but it seemed to me that your assistant had a pretty good handle on things at the office."

"What's that supposed to mean?"

"It means that you don't seem to be making a very logical or rational choice here," Rabkin said. "It means maybe, just maybe, I'm not the only one around here who's not doing a great job with grieving."

"I was doing *fine* until *you* showed up."

"I don't know that I would call that fine, then," Rabkin said. "I believe the official term for that would be *denial*."

"Shut up," Dupree muttered, shaking her head.

"I'm sorry?"

She turned on him, her cheeks bright red. "I said, *shut up*! I am so *fucking* tired of listening to you! I didn't *ask* you to come out here. I didn't ask you to come check up on me. *You* were Gavin's friend. He's *dead*. Am I happy about that? No. Do I wish I had had a chance to talk to him one more time, *yes*. Do I wish that our marriage had been stronger than it was, *yes*. But *shit* happens, Jim, and life goes on. I'll grieve on my own damn time. Find someone else to act as an emotional surrogate, and next time, just send me a damn subspace message."

Dupree sucked in a sharp breath of air and took a step back. The two of them stared at each other, not speaking.

She wiped at the corners of her eyes.

The lift reached its destination, and the doors slid open.

Dupree took another deep breath and tried to compose herself. She stepped off without another word.

Rabkin stood in the lift, watching her disappear around a corner.

The doors started to close, and he thought about his friend.

"Damn it, Gavin," Rabkin said under his breath.

Rabkin stopped the doors at the last second and stepped off, following after her.

39

DUPREE WASN'T ENTIRELY sure what she would find at the docking port currently housing the Ulriharad's ship, but it certainly wasn't a member of the Phaw delegation.

Dupree stopped herself short. She looked around the area cautiously, but no one else was present.

There was just a single member of the Phaw delegation sitting outside the airlock that connected the starbase to the Ulriharad's ship. The alien was slumped against the wall, a low, mournful sound escaping its mouth.

Dupree had never seen a Phaw in this kind of emotional distress. The Phaw were angry, aggressive, hostile beings who were careful not to display any type of weakness publicly, especially in the mixed company of the races outside the Phaw Empire.

This Phaw was sitting on the floor, clearly crying?

Dupree wracked her brain, trying to recall if there was anything in the reports she had been supplied with that even suggested that Phaw had the *ability* to cry.

Dupree heard a sound behind her, a slight intake of breath as somebody was about to speak. She glanced over her shoulder and saw Rabkin standing there. She shook her head and held a finger to her lips.

Rabkin took the hint and stayed silent.

Dupree turned back to the Phaw. If it had noticed they were even there, it didn't bother to acknowledge them.

At first, she didn't recognize the Phaw. Then, slowly, as she took in the Phaw's outfit, long purple robes with delicate patterns etched out in white paschall crystals, it clicked: Haiduk's Second Wife. There was nothing obviously feminine about Number Two, at least not to Dupree. But she had it on good authority that Number Two was considered, by most Phaw, to be a desirable woman. All Dupree usually saw was a wild, rabid beast that was barely able to contain itself.

This, though, was different.

"What's going on?" Rabkin whispered.

"I don't know," Dupree replied quietly. She pulled out her communicator and typed a quick message to Skouras. The Phaw delegation had made it very clear that they weren't interested in anything on Starbase Sixty-Four. They were here only out of a political obligation to the Naonzo Agreement and took every opportunity to not set foot on the station unless it was absolutely necessary.

So, to see Haiduk's second wife outside the airlock to the Ulriharad ship no less...

Dupree's communicator buzzed with a quick response from Skouras, telling her what she already suspected: per station regulations, the Phaw were required to file a standard Boarding Request every time they left their ship. It was a piece of CYA paperwork that Administrator Takacs had, rightfully, insisted upon, considering the aggressive nature of the Phaw. The Boarding Request was used to log every Phaw that was onboard the station and, more importantly, make sure they were accompanied by a member of security at all times.

Haiduk's Second Wife had filed no such Boarding Request.

Dupree showed the message to Rabkin; whether or not he understood what it meant, she didn't know.

Dupree put her communicator away and took a step forward, her mind racing to figure out a way to keep everything from falling apart.

Haiduk's Second Wife looked up at the imperceptible sound of Dupree moving, abruptly acknowledging her presence.

The whimpering noise stopped.

Haiduk's Second Wife didn't get to her feet, but her body suddenly became rigid against the wall, and her long fingers curled inwards.

No one spoke.

Dupree opened her mouth but wasn't entirely certain what to say.

There was a look in Number Two's eyes, something that Dupree hadn't seen in any of the Phaw. It was *fear*.

Suddenly, Haiduk's Second Wife was standing.

Dupree jerked back, bumping into Rabkin.

The Phaw's movement had been so quick and seamless that it hadn't registered visually for either Dupree or Rabkin.

She towered over the two humans, her hands tucked back behind her in a gesture that was intended to look non-threatening. But there was little that the Phaw did that didn't look threatening.

Her husband's warnings echoed in her mind, and every inch of her screamed to leave, to *run away*.

Not that it would have mattered, though. A Phaw was nearly three times faster than a human.

If Haiduk's Second Wife decided that the best course of action was to make sure there was no one left living who could confirm her presence here on the station, there wasn't a damn thing Dupree or Rabkin could do about it.

Haiduk's Second Wife made a clicking sound and bowed her head at Dupree. "Apologies, Ambassador."

"Apologies?" Dupree repeated without really hearing the word. It took an extra second for it to reach her cognitive centers. She exhaled slowly as her body took on the slow awareness that she wasn't in danger. "You're...sorry? For what?"

Something bristled across the Phaw's face, an emotion that Dupree couldn't identify. It reminded her of some sense of discomfort.

"I have violated our agreement and come on board without permission." Unlike Haiduk, her voice had an odd ring to it that conjured up images of a vibrating bell. "I believe it is appropriate in situations such as these to offer apologies."

Dupree swallowed, trying to shake a sense of surrealness that refused to leave. "Yes. You are correct."

Haiduk's Second Wife bowed her head again. "I will make sure my excursion has been logged upon my return."

Before Dupree could say anything else, Haiduk's Second Wife brushed past them and disappeared down the corridor, presumably heading back to her own ship.

"What the hell was that?" Rabkin asked.

"I..." Dupree trailed off. "I have no idea."

She turned to the airlock leading to the Ulriharad ship. It had been cycled open.

"Ancestral Communion of Suffering," she said quietly.

"What was that?" Rabkin asked.

Dupree just shook her head and started for the airlock.

"Are you allowed to just walk onto the ship?" Rabkin asked, following her.

Dupree didn't answer him as she stepped through the airlock.

Their footsteps echoed as Dupree led them down the short walkway that connected the starbase to the Ulriharad ship.

Rabkin noticed the smell almost immediately. It was a rancid, putrid odor that caused his stomach to churn. "I have a bad feeling about this." He reached for Dupree to stop her, but she pulled her arm out of his reach. "Johanna..."

Ancestral Communion of Suffering.

The words echoed in her mind. There was something about that phrase that bothered her. What was it? She was so focused on that she hardly even noticed the smell.

The airlock to the Ulriharad ship was open. The hull of the Ulriharad ship looked almost too frail to touch as if the simple act of disconnecting from the airlock would cause it to fall apart. The entire Ulriharad fleet had been built nearly a hundred years ago, and due to their constant occupations, they never had the opportunity to build new ships or even upgrade the ones they had.

Dupree paused at the entrance, her hand hovering over the open hatch but not actually touching it. The smell was overwhelming at this point. But still, she hardly noticed it.

Behind her, Rabkin was saying something, but it was white noise drowned out by her own thoughts.

She found herself caught up with the logistics of what it would mean to actually set foot on the ship. She didn't know the layout. She wasn't even sure if the rest of the ship had an atmosphere that would be friendly to her. What was the gravity of Ulri? Was it less or more than Earth standard? She couldn't remember, assuming it had even been in the info packets that had been prepared for her.

How far would she have to go to find...whatever it was she was looking for?

Fortunately, none of that was going to be a problem.

Because there, immediately on the other side of the open airlock, she found Moogai's mutilated body.

40

NATUZZI

RIL SILENTLY WATCHED through the translucent ceiling as the clouds passed above them as they skimmed across the lower stratosphere of Natuzzi, passing over the equator as the sky shifted from night to day. It was a breathtaking sight that was utterly wasted on her.

She felt Ito's gaze on her. Ril didn't ignore him, but she didn't shift her focus from the clouds. There was something about the clouds that her mind latched onto. Her mind wanted to untangle the thin wisps of cloud that found themselves trapped between the faint rays of sunlight that danced across the edge of the distant horizon.

But she watched Ito from her peripheral. She couldn't help it.

The royal yacht was small. Or, at least, the section that had been designated for her pleasure. It sat only six. The guardsmen rode in a separate compartment, close enough should she need them and discreet enough that her flight wouldn't be disrupted by the stoic, armed individuals who had sworn to lay down their lives for her.

Although now, a nagging voice at the back of Ril's mind kept asking her how many were truly loyal to her.

Ito sat across from her, two rows down. He kept fidgeting as though his seat had become uncomfortable. But Ril knew that was impossible. This was a royal yacht. Everything in this compartment had been designed for maximum comfort and pleasure. Specifically hers.

The Natuzzi sun abruptly burst across the sky as they passed over the equator. Its brilliance blinded her, and Ril tapped the controls on her seat to turn the ceiling opaque.

Once the compartment had returned to its standard lighting, Ito started to say something. His fingers tightened across the edges of the datapad on his lap. He leaned forward, but the words died before they ever escaped his mouth. The expression on his face was somewhere between apprehension and relief.

He sat back and looked down at the datapad as if it could provide him with some answer or perhaps an escape.

Ril rubbed a hand across her aching eyes, closing them. The image of an empty classroom suddenly struck her.

As a member of the royal family, Ril had not been enrolled in the standard education tracks. While she was not firstborn, she was the first female born and, therefore, heir to the throne. It would have been unbecoming of her to enroll with the masses. So she and her brother were afforded private tutors for the entirety of their education.

Nax had been the extent of her social interaction until she reached her secondary education. When she and their mother had engaged in one of their many fights, it was Nax who made sure the lines of communication stayed open, regardless of the many hurtful things that were said.

Her mother had never spoken of it, and why would she? But the fact of the matter was that Nax's only true fault before he abandoned the Natuzzi people had been that he had been born with the wrong set of chromosomes.

Her mind strayed back to the image of the empty classroom. It was like a nagging notion that wouldn't let go.

A soft sigh escaped her lips as she tried to ignore the foreboding sense of anxiety that was gathering inside of her.

"Ito?" Ril's voice was quiet, as though she had just woken from a nap.

He looked up sharply, surprise on his face. "Ma'am?"

"I need you to pull up some records for me. Can we do that? Up here?"

"Yes, of course," he replied. "I have full access to all the data feeds."

"Good." Ril paused for a moment as if waiting to see if something would discourage her from pursuing this path. Nothing did.

Ril exhaled softly through her nose. She sat upright, opening her eyes. "There's a place, Besanrt Village. The residents of this village...." She paused, searching for the right words, and found herself unable to use them. "About forty years ago, there might have been an incident."

"An incident?"

Ril simply replied with a shrug.

"Pardon me for saying so, but those details are a little vague," Ito said.

"Very well."

"Ma'am?"

"I'll pardon you," Ril replied. She nodded at the datapad. "Please."

There was something about the word, the way she said it, how she used it, the intonation, that caused Ito to stare at her for a second longer than he should have. Then, before she could admonish him, he dropped his attention to the datapad.

There was silence as Ito searched. She wasn't sure how long it would take, but she hadn't expected it to be as quick as it ended up being.

Ril heard the change in his voice before he even spoke.

"I think I have it," Ito said. "A series of deaths."

Ril inhaled and then exhaled a stuttering breath. "What was it?"

Ito didn't answer immediately, skimming through multiple reports and accounts, looking for words and phrases that would naturally jump out. "There's no official cause listed," he replied. "According to the reports, it was believed to be a case of Lechman's that swept through the village."

"How many?"

There was a pause. She heard him swallow before answering. "A quarter of the population."

She had known, of course. But that changed nothing. It was still shocking.

Her first instinct was to order the cottage and its occupant destroyed. But she knew, unfortunately, that wouldn't solve anything. This ran deeper than just one person, even if that person was...

"Ma'am," Ito began softly.

Ril took a sharp breath. "Why are you here?" she asked him.

Ito stared at her, confused. His fingers flexed around the datapad. "I'm not sure I understand?"

She gestured in a way that suggested the question was more figurative than literal. "Why are you *here*? This is an unusual job for a man."

"Ah," he replied, tilting his head slightly as if he were

about to nod. No answer was forthcoming for a moment. Ito simply stared at the datapad, flexing his fingers. "As I understand it, there were three other candidates for this position. All of them were female."

Ril nodded. "I vaguely recall something about that."

"You personally selected me yourself," he reminded her.

She frowned. "That doesn't answer my question."

Ito shrugged. "Then I'm not entirely certain what to tell you."

"In the history of your position, it has been occupied by men only two other times," Ril said. "And that was over two hundred years ago, and both individuals were spouses of the queens at the time."

Ito arched his brow. "Are you...proposing to me, ma'am?"

"No," she replied coolly. "I'm trying to figure out why you're here and not someone else."

Ito pursed his lips and took a moment before answering. "Is there someone else you'd rather be here?"

There was something in the question, the way he asked it, that gave Ril pause. Something else clicked over in her mind. When she answered, it was almost absently as if she had already moved on to something else. "No."

"Then I suppose it doesn't matter how I got here," Ito said.

The knot that had been growing in her stomach suddenly released. A rush of nausea threatened to overwhelm her, but before she could succumb to it, the feeling passed. In its place was a serene peace that Ril had never felt before.

Just like that, the solution came to her.

She had been outplayed. Before Voa stepped into her office, the Sacellum had already determined what the endgame would be. So that left her with only one possible solution.

Across from her, Ito watched as the range of emotions played out across her face. His expression was one of concern. "Ma'am?"

Ril smiled at him. It was a genuine smile. Heartfelt but filled with an aching sadness that she hadn't known was possible, not before now. "I know how to win."

41

Nax didn't care for his physician. In the beginning, he hadn't been certain what had elicited this response.

Bridgetta Ada was too young to be a medical professional of any importance. And yet, here she was, treating a member of the royal family, albeit a disgraced member. Nax had difficulty ascertaining her age, so after his first appointment, he used what limited access he had to learn what he could about Ada. He was surprised to discover she was almost an entire decade younger than him. She had graduated top of her class and was considered one of the top ten most skilled surgeons working on the planet.

Natuzzi prodigies were not unheard of, but Nax had never encountered one so talented, accomplished, and beautiful as Bridgetta Ada.

That, he supposed, had been the first problem.

Bridgetta Ada was breathtakingly beautiful. She was taller than Nax by nearly a full head. Her facial features were soft and full, almost achingly pleasing to stare at for hours. Her eyes, a muted shade of silver, were inviting while also being off-putting. The green jumpsuit she wore was the same as most of the other medical professionals and had been designed to elicit a sense of conformity, except that it did little to hide her voluptuous body.

Nax quickly realized, much to his surprise, he was attracted to her. And that was the second problem.

Since the death of Grace Hawkins, Nax hadn't given any thought to romance. Instead, he had been consumed by grief and haunted by what he had assumed was Grace's ghost.

He had seen her not in his dreams but during his waking hours. Grace Hawkins had been there, at the corner of his vision, invisible to anyone else, unheard by anyone else, save for *him*.

Nax had spoken to her. She had spoken to him. He had been almost certain he was losing his mind to grief.

And in the face of possible insanity and heartbreak, Nax didn't have the energy or the inclination to think about romance.

But then he realized that the Grace Hawkins he was seeing, talking with, was real, and she wasn't Grace. Rather she was an entity from a lower, broken universe that had stowed away in his mind, seeking refuge from the encroaching darkness known as the Unity.

Somehow, the entity that wore his memory of Grace had kept him alive when the zealots came for his life. And since then, he hadn't seen her, heard her, or felt her.

And he found that without the haunting memory of Grace lingering across his conscious and subconscious mind, he could be attracted to someone else.

And he wasn't sure how he felt about that.

Ada regarded him with the single-minded focus of an individual trying to solve a problem. And that's what he was to the majority of Natuzzi: a problem to be solved. The traitorous son of a dead queen who had committed one of the greatest crimes his people could imagine: He had fallen in love with an off-worlder.

She may not have haunted him, but the pain of Grace Hawkins hadn't left him.

The third problem, and arguably the worst of all three, was that Bridgetta Ada reminded him of his mother.

The unnerving combination of physical attraction and parental love he felt toward Ada resulted in a cocktail of emotion that was best described as *complicated*.

So, instead of dealing with those complications, Nax decided he did not particularly care for her.

They sat in her office. The one place he was allowed to visit off the grounds of his designated living space. He came here once a week to be examined, poked, and prodded. As he understood it, the office was not a permanent one for Bridgetta Ada. It was, instead, a temporary work location while she dealt with his unique case. As such, the space was remarkably sterile, even for a medical environment. There was no indication of any personalization. The walls were the generic dark mauve that often came in these types of environments. There was no window, nothing to distract the focus from the point: him, Kinlin Nax.

Here in this location, once a week, Bridgetta Ada would examine every inch of his body with clinical professionalism. Every detail was noted and logged, whether there was a change or not. Most of the time, each exam took place wordlessly. Ada was apparently not one for small talk and seemed to have no interest in Nax beyond her responsibilities to his medical wellbeing. And that was fine for Nax. He had spent enough time talking with unattainable women. Unfortunately, though, it left him with little to focus on besides her physical presence and the growing comparisons to his mother.

He wondered if she felt it, too. Was the sense of attraction mutual? He couldn't tell. On some level, he suspected it had to be. If for no other reason than he was royalty. If not attraction to him physically, then at least attraction to his position, such as it was? And was there a parental figure he reminded her of?

Every time Ada saw him, she regarded him with the same scowl. The scowl seemed to fit the curves of her lips all too well. That had been what had made the connection to the memory of his mother: the scowl. Her lips would curl back in a familiar stretch of disapproval that had caused Nax to have an almost immediate flashback to his youth, being endlessly chastised by his mother for one thing or another, but primarily for not being a daughter.

He wasn't sure what it was. Whether the scowl was intentional or not. He never commented on it, and Ada never offered any explanation as to why she disapproved of him so.

Although, Nax had no difficulty imagining that much of the Natuzzi population would likely regard him with the same expression of disdain.

Even with such an ugly expression, Ada was still beautiful, and Nax suspected that Ada knew that and was probably bothered by the notion. She held herself at a distance, something else that had encouraged comparisons to his mother. In his limited research, he had found nothing about her family, friends, or lovers. Everything there was to know about Bridgetta Ada was related to her work. Her work was her life. Her life was her work. And now, here, her work was his life.

Nax saw her more than anyone else. But then, there was

no one else he was allowed to see. And he wasn't sure if that made anything better or worse.

Ada sipped at her tea behind a desk that bore no sense of personalization. In the air between them, hovering above the desk, was his body. Not that it was particularly recognizable as Nax. It was a three-dimensional hologram of everything that made up his body, lacking the surface of his skin that would allow anyone to identify the collection of bones, nerves, and organs as Kinlin Nax. He thought it was grotesque when he first saw it. It lacked a particular unidentifiable polish that Doctor Rabkin's scans often had. After weeks of observing it, though, Nax had come to appreciate the almost artistically raw nature of the holo. It was a combination of prior and current data. The holo's beating heart moved perfectly with its physical counterpart buried in his chest, and something about that made the entire affair poignant.

Ada's gaze lingered on the holo as it slowly rotated above the desk. She said nothing, which was more normal than not. Nax had learned early on theirs would be a relationship that was built of long silences rather than insightful or even meaningless conversation.

"Your body isn't functioning the way it should," Ada said finally, speaking in a clipped tone that seemed designed to head off any potential argument or dissent before it could begin or be expressed. Again, something else that had reminded him of his mother. After a moment, she added, almost as an afterthought, "You should be *dead*."

Dead.

The word hung in the air between them, and suddenly Nax realized it had been there the entire time. Her focus on him hadn't been out of obligation to the crown or even the Natuzzi people. It wasn't because she felt compelled to make sure that, despite everything else, he received the right, best medical care possible. The way she meticulously examined him wasn't out of any kind of mutual attraction. No, it was because he was a medical oddity, too good to pass up. He was the traitorous Prince who should, by all accounts, be *dead*.

Except he wasn't.

Instead, here he was, confined to a wheelchair and imprisoned in a gilded cage.

Her eyes found his, and he could feel her rooting around his expression, searching for something and failing to find it.

Nax pressed the palms of his hands against the armrests of his wheelchair. His expression across the weeks of survival and endless examinations had been kept neutral, a mask he used to hide the swirl of uneasy and complicated emotions and reactions he had towards Ada. It was a mask that was not going to slip now.

Ada nodded as if he had spoken and gestured to the holo of his body. A path was highlighted, slicing through his chest, puncturing one of his lungs, and nearly piercing his spine. Nearly.

Nax rubbed his chest gingerly, the memory of the zealot stabbing him still all too fresh in his mind.

"The blade that pierced you was tipped with punzada, which should have resulted in irreparable nerve damage throughout your respiratory system." Ada rose from her seat as she spoke, making her way slowly around the desk. "It pierced your left lung and scraped your trachea. In order for you to breathe, I should have had to replace both lungs and attach you to a permanent ventilator, as the poison should have damaged any replacement tissue." She paused for a moment, finishing her tea. "But it didn't." She shrugged her slender shoulders. "It's not entirely unheard of. Punzada is considered a Class One poison. The percentage of individuals who survive exposure to it is less than one percent, and even those who do, suffer some form of extreme paralysis. One percent is still a percentage."

Ada set the empty tea cup down and clasped her hands behind her back. "You should be dead." There was something in her voice as if she was making an effort to speak as plainly as possible. "Instead, we have this."

She expanded a cluster of nerves near the base of his spine. "This has been the sole piece of damage we have been unable to repair. It is a cluster of dead nerves inhibiting communication between your brain and lower limbs. By all accounts, I believe removing this cluster of nerves will allow your brain to send and receive signals to the lower part of your body again. You would walk again. However, I don't understand why *this* is *here*."

Ada paused and moved around the desk, looking past the holo at him, watching his face to see how the information settled.

"I am afraid I don't follow," Nax said finally.

She nodded. "All of our scans of the damaged nerve cluster have come back...inconclusive. No one seems to know what it is, despite what it is obviously presenting as. But there is the argument to be made that if it were exactly what it appeared to be, the scans would not come back inconclusive." She held out her hands, palms up as if to say, 'Do you see my confusion?'

Inconclusive.

Something about the way she said the word made him uncomfortable.

"And then, during your last exam, I discovered this." Ada gestured at the holo again, and it zoomed out and then zoomed in on his brain. "There was a brief electrical impulse, a signal, from the damaged nerves. I traced the signal back to this spot, located just behind your sensory cortex. It is a patch of...something. It measures less than ten microns across and doesn't even register on the scans."

Something glittered in her eyes.

"It took three hours of reprogramming for the medical scanner to finally acknowledge there was something there," she said. "Something in your brain that shouldn't be."

Ada leaned towards the holo; her gaze fixated on a spot that would have been naked to the invisible eye. "Something organic but not native to the Natuzzi biology. Not cancerous. Not artificial. Something *unexplainable*."

And suddenly, Nax understood even if Ada didn't. Even if she couldn't understand, he did.

Nax thought about the entity that wore Grace Hawkins and how it, she, managed to keep him alive, and he wondered how exactly she had accomplished that.

Nax was abruptly aware of how silent the room had become. Ada hadn't spoken in over a minute. Her breathing was heavy, bordering on almost labored. There was emotion on her face. Something different from the clinical disinterest she displayed for the last several weeks. There was excitement there. There was *hunger*.

Nax felt a chill in the air around him.

Her gaze flicked past the holo as if suddenly remembering that Nax was there.

She straightened up, pulling back from the holo. With another gesture, the image returned to a scaled-down diagram of his body. Now, inside of an outline of where the knife had pierced him, there was a path highlighted between the two spots: the damaged cluster of nerves at the base of his spine and the microscopic spot of unidentifiable matter in his brain.

Nax fought the urge to look around the room, suddenly convinced *she* would be there. He managed to keep his gaze forward, focused on Ada and the holo of his body.

Ada let her hands rest on the table. Obviously aware of how she was presenting, she took a moment to compose herself. Her brow furrowed briefly, and her nostrils flared. "Clearly, there is a connection," she said finally. "You should be dead. But you are not; instead, you have these *things* in your body that defy explanation."

"But I am well," Nax said, his voice sounding almost hollow to his own ears.

If Ada noticed the change in his tone, she gave no indication. Instead, she simply folded her arms, tapping one finger against her chin. "You are alive. Whether or not you are well...." She shrugged.

Nax coughed in an attempt to normalize his voice. "I am afraid I don't understand the distinction."

"You have things inside your body that shouldn't be there," she replied. "We cannot possibly know the potential long-term complications they could lead to. Right now, you can't walk. Five months from now, you could be dead."

She said it all in a flat, emotionless voice as if she was simply reciting the weather report. But the glimmer was still there in her eyes.

Nax knew there was something he should say, but he couldn't imagine what it was. He felt Hawkins' presence nearby, threatening to haunt him. He wanted to look for her, almost certain she would be at the edge of his vision, a blurry hint of someone he once knew. But instead, he kept perfectly still, the entirety of his focus on the woman who was physically present with him.

Ada sat back down slowly, pressing the tips of her fingers together, and attempted to reassert the expression of clinical disinterest. "I believe surgery is our only option."

"Surgery?" Nax repeated, sounding confused but feeling something much worse than confusion.

"Removal of the damaged nerve cluster first." Ada sounded as though she was struggling to keep her voice neutral. She was clearly trying to keep the excitement out of her voice, and she was failing. "Yes. A tissue sample to examine, coupled with a visual examination, should provide us with valuable insights. Perhaps even an explanation."

"An explanation?" he echoed.

"Of what the mass is," she replied. "It appears to be damaged nerves, but it's not functioning like them. Surgery would be a simple enough solution. It could even have the secondary result of allowing you to walk again. But having the physical sample would be our primary focus. It should yield us a wide variety of answers."

"And if it doesn't?" Nax asked, already knowing what the next step would be.

Her chest rose gently as she took a deep breath. "A second surgery." Her voice quickened as she spoke. Her eyes dilated. "It shouldn't be more than a micro-incision, but I will still need to gain access to your sensory cortex. Obviously, there is a greater chance for side effects, but they should be minimal. However, given its location, you should expect the possibility of complications that could affect your speech, visual receptors, and your wider cognitive functions."

Something tightened in Nax's gut. His pulse quickened. Ada sat there, waiting for a response. But there was nothing to say.

It had already been made clear to him that his lack of

freedom extended to his inability to make any choices about his medical plans. These things had already been decided for him and would continue to be decided for him as long as he was a guest of the state.

So Nax simply nodded in agreement because what else was there for him to do?

42

Nax was escorted back to his living quarters in a numb haze, hardly even aware of when he left one location and arrived at another. And he certainly didn't notice the queen waiting for him upon his arrival.

"Hello, brother."

It was less the sound of her voice and more the use of the word that snapped Nax out of his daze.

Brother.

He blinked and looked up from his lap. Gouren Ril stood at the far end of his room, in front of the large windows that looked out at the UPA buildings in the distance. Her figure was framed by the brilliant lights of the UPA buildings, all of them apparently having decided that they were exempt from the laws regarding light pollution.

Abruptly, Nax found himself picturing his mother and her reaction to such an insult against the Natuzzi planet. He chuckled softly.

Ril arched her brow. "Something amuses you, brother?"

That word again.

Brother.

Sister.

Nax wheeled himself across the room, positioning himself opposite Ril in a location where he could see his front door and the UPA buildings through the window.

Nax had never thought of Gouren as his sister. In fact, he had never thought of her much. Because if he thought of her, he would have thought of her with resentment. Gouren Ril was the daughter that the queen had wanted him to be. And when he failed to meet that expectation, one completely out of his control, their mother, the queen, had moved on.

Nax had been born prematurely on purpose. As soon as they were aware of his gender, the queen had him removed and placed in an incubator for the remainder of his in-utero growth. And as soon as her body was ready, Queen Xie began the process again in an attempt to produce a daughter.

It took six more attempts before Gouren was conceived. And unlike Nax, the queen had not bothered to save the other six.

There was only a gap of eighteen months between them.

Eighteen months.

It might as well have been eighteen years.

Nax rubbed his eyes tiredly. "To what do I owe this visit?"

Ril didn't answer him right away. He watched her staring at him. It took a moment before he noticed how tired she was. The exhaustion was weighing down upon her like the weight of the world.

Despite himself, Nax asked, "Is everything okay?"

Ril took a deep breath and slowly shook her head. She pressed her hands against her sides as if to smooth out invisible wrinkles in her gown. "No, brother, I am afraid nothing is all right."

She looked around the room as if taking stock of it for the first time and settled her gaze on the seat she had occupied during her last visit. She slowly sat down, crossing her legs. Her head rested against the chair's headrest, and Ril closed her eyes.

Nax, uncertain of what to say and even less certain of what was going on, simply sat in his wheelchair, hands folded in his lap, and waited.

He watched her sitting there, her eyes closed, and was struck by how much she looked like their mother.

It had never occurred to him before, but Nax was reminded of pictures he had seen of their mother when she was roughly Gouren's age, and the two women looked similar enough that they could have been sisters, if not twins.

Abruptly Nax felt the hot breath of someone leaning in close to his ear. He jolted in his seat, twisting around, expecting to find Hawkins there, a bemused smirk on her face.

But the room was empty save for him and his sister.

Nax exhaled a stuttering breath and turned forward again, settling back into his chair. Ril's eyes were open, watching him. If she had any thoughts regarding what had just happened, she chose not to share them.

"I have a problem," Ril said. "In fact, I have a great many problems."

"Heavy is the head that wears the crown," Nax replied, keeping his voice steady.

Ril nodded. "Yes, I suppose that's true, and maybe that's the problem." She leaned forward, uncrossing her legs and clasping her hands together. "Many of my problems would be solved if you were dead."

Nax grunted. "Interesting."

"What is?"

"It had just occurred to me how much you look like mother," he replied. "I suppose it should come as no surprise when you start behaving like her, too."

"You are not the first person to make that observation today." She looked down at her hands as if there was a solution there that would do away with any unflattering comparisons to their mother. "Clearly, I'm doing something wrong."

"I suppose that depends on your point of view."

"Well, considering that our mother was murdered, my point of view is that she failed, and I would rather not follow that particular life path. Besides, what might solve a momentary problem for me now, will undoubtedly create even greater problems for the Natuzzi people in the future."

Nax held up his hands in defeat. "I'm afraid I'm too tired to follow your logic right now."

Ril rose. "I don't agree with your life choices, brother. I find them offensive on multiple levels. But does that mean you should die for your choices?" She paused, clasping her hands behind her back as she began to pace the length of the room. "Yes, your death would be helpful in the immediacy of right now. But would it be right?"

"Traditionally, anything decided by the crown is right," Nax pointed out, not bothering to hide the bitterness in his voice.

"And perhaps that's the problem."

"Well, as you recently pointed out, our mother is dead."

"There needs to be an option where there can be disagreement without such...extreme consequences."

Nax stared at her, his face a mask that hid his surprise.

"Natuzzi needs to change," she said.

He nodded past her at the UPA buildings in the distance. "Natuzzi has changed quite a bit recently."

"It's not enough," Ril replied, her voice suddenly low and hoarse. "The UPA functions as a republic. Every citizen has a voice."

Nax arched his brow. "It's not a perfect alliance."

"But it has checks and balances in place that keep its president from declaring war on the galaxy," Ril said.

"For the most part," he agreed. "What do you want to do?"

She pulled her hands out from behind her back and stared at her palms again as if looking for some answer that was just out of her reach. "I want to make a change that's not responding to the *now* but planning for the *future*." She met his gaze. "This can't happen again."

"This?" he echoed.

"Our mother nearly plunged half the galaxy into an unwinnable war," Ril said. "There was nothing to stop her. No one to stop her."

"Apparently, there was, though," Nax pointed out.

"That's not how these things are supposed to be done." There was a hitch in her voice. She tried to cover it up, clearing her throat, but Nax noticed it anyway. "There needs to be checks and balances. Specifically, there needs to be a balance to this administration."

"*Your* administration," Nax clarified.

"And the next and the one after that and the one after that. I'm forming a new branch of government, independent from the crown but still working in concert with it."

Nax's eyes widened. "That's not going to be a popular decision."

"No, it's not," she agreed. "And the next part is going to be even less popular."

"Next part?"

"This Executive Committee, made up of representatives from all the major guilds on Natuzzi, will need to be headed by a chairperson who's not me. Because it can't be the crown. It can never be the crown. It's going to have to be someone different. Someone who understands what I'm trying to do. Someone who will work with me for now and in the future. And that someone, I've decided, brother, will be you."

43

THE DEFIANCE

"I HAD AN EPIPHANY." Langlois lay next to Warrick in the darkness of his quarters.

Warrick rolled over onto his side, facing her. "What?"

"Cooper asked me a question earlier," Langlois ran her fingers through her hair aimlessly. "I can't stop thinking about it."

"What was the question?"

"If we could kill Calloway."

"I'm sorry, but *what*?"

Langlois rolled over, so they were face to face. "So much of the ship has been infected by Calloway; you would irreparably damage it if you tried to do anything to Calloway's programming."

"I'm not sure I'm following."

Langlois paused, trying to find the right words. "It's not a ship anymore, Jaxson. It's something *else*."

"Yeah, it's a damn Khettek nightmare."

She shook her head. "You don't understand. Cooper doesn't understand either."

"Doesn't understand what?"

Langlois chewed on her lower lip. "This ship is a *life form* now. It's a unique, one-of-a-kind life form." She paused. "Let's say that the Unity infected another ship."

"Okay, sure," Warrick said. "Give my nightmares some variety. Spices things up."

"That infected ship wouldn't have *Calloway*. The Unity didn't consume Erin Calloway; it *merged* with her. Whatever the *Defiance* is now, it's neither the Unity nor Calloway. It's not even a starship anymore. It's something else. A unique combination of all three. It's a combination that can't be duplicated. We've seen that. The Natuzzi weapon? Presumably the same basic structure. It functions and identifies as something completely different."

Warrick raised both of his eyebrows. "Identifies?"

"Calloway has conscious awareness of who she is," Langlois said. "Or at least that she *is*. The Natuzzi weapon does, too."

"That's a hell of a leap," he said.

Langlois exhaled. "No, I don't think it really is." She ran her hands through her hair. "You're not in a ship anymore. You're inside another entity, another life form."

Warrick's expression soured. "I'd rather not think of it like that."

"You're not taking this seriously."

"I'm taking this as seriously as I can without breaking down into a nervous wreck," Warrick said. "Why are you thinking about it like that?"

"What other way is there to think about it? I can't even say that we're in a symbiotic relationship with Calloway. She would be able to function, to exist, without us onboard. You might even argue that her existence would improve if we weren't here."

"Stop it," Warrick said.

"Cooper wants to know if he can kill her," Langlois continued. "I'm wondering if he should. Calloway's something unique. A one-of-a-kind species; if we killed her, wouldn't that be genocide? Wouldn't it be condemning an entire species to extinction?"

"You're making a hell of a leap there," Warrick said.

Langlois shrugged. "Maybe. Maybe not." She took a moment. "I told the captain that it's possible a fusion core overload could kill her."

Warrick gaped at her. "It'd also destroy the ship."

Langlois nodded. "That's what I'm trying to get you to understand. There's no difference between Calloway and the *Defiance* anymore." She exhaled. "And honestly, I don't even know if a fusion core overload would do it. Never mind the fact she'd lock us out of the systems before we could even initiate an overload, so you would have to do it manually, which means at least one person would have to be *present* on the ship." She held up a finger. "There would have to be at least one person who would willingly sacrifice their life to kill Calloway."

Warrick didn't respond to that.

"But, honestly, based on everything I've been reading, there's no real reason she wouldn't be able to absorb the energy from the overload. Or, at the very least, separate a portion of herself from the ship before the overload and then simply merge with another vessel."

"What's to stop her from doing that now?" Warrick asked.

Langlois shrugged. "Nothing."

The comm chirped.

"Go ahead," Warrick said.

It was Carole. "We're in the shuttle."

Warrick sat up. "I'm on my way."

In the darkness of Warrick's quarters, a vague impression of Calloway's face melted away without a sound.

44

"CHIEF MEDICAL OFFICER'S LOG."

Dheer paused and frowned. She stared at the console in her office, the office that used to be Rabkin's, and felt the very definition of Imposter Syndrome.

Dheer settled back in her chair and closed her eyes. "*Acting* Chief Medical Officer's log. I haven't decided whether or not to accept Captain Cooper's promotion. I haven't even figured out if I even have a choice in the matter. If Rabkin's truly leaving the *Defiance*, the reality is that there's no one else remotely qualified to take the position of Chief Medical Officer. Never mind the eccentricities of the crew; there's no one else with the security clearance who's been kept up to date with the nature of the Unity and our ongoing mission, such as it is, who could step in."

Dheer opened her eyes and leaned forward, resting her elbows on her desk. "More importantly, I wonder if I have a moral obligation to accept the captain's promotion.

"More than one crewman has confided in me that they do not feel safe under Cooper's command. While the captain hasn't displayed any tendency to be overtly abusive towards the crew, his behavior has suggested that he doesn't value the lives of his crew. Since taking command, he has floated the option of destroying the ship as a potential solution to resolve more than one hostile encounter. Whether these were intended as bluffs or not, they've, understandably, shaken the crew's confidence in him."

Dheer sighed and rubbed her forehead.

"As far as I am aware, no one has submitted any transfer requests. However, given our current situation, the opportunity may simply not have arisen.

"I don't even know what that looks like. Are officers allowed to transfer off this ship? It seems like every member of this crew is now privy to sensitive information. Information that, in any other scenario, would be considered Top Secret. But how do you hide the fact that the ship is no longer simply just a ship?

"Lieutenant Huisman spoke with me yesterday about having a dream that she was drowning in the ocean back on her home planet. There was something; she called it a Ughicin beast, that had attacked her and was dragging her down below the ocean's surface. She woke from the nightmare only to discover that her bed was gone. Instead, she was...floating in a gelatinous substance. It lasted only a few seconds, but then her bed reformed beneath her body.

"How the hell am I supposed to help somebody with that? How am I supposed to tell somebody not to leave this ship?

"Hell, *I* want off this damn nightmare."

Dheer looked around her office as if expecting to see somebody.

"It's been suggested that Ensign Calloway is possibly listening in at any given moment. I don't know what to do with that information. So I'm choosing to ignore it. It's too much for me. I can't...."

Dheer shook her head. She took a deep breath and exhaled slowly.

"I can't control the ship, much less what the ship is turning into. So I'm doing my best to keep my focus on what I can control. Or, perhaps, what I'm trained to deal with.

"If the crew doesn't feel safe under Captain Cooper's command, what does that mean? Are we looking at a potential mutiny? Or simply a second-guessing of his every order? Unfortunately, you can't second-guess your captain in the middle of active battle. That can cost lives.

"But if your captain is going to make a decision that threatens the life of every crew member?

"I haven't performed any official psychological exam of Captain Cooper; I doubt he would consent anyway. But, based on my interactions thus far with the captain, my off-the-cuff assessment...."

Dheer paused, staring at the flashing icon on the display that indicated the recording was still active. It was standard Fleet practice that all officer logs were available to command staff and above. Personal logs were private and needed consent from the individual, but any log recorded during active duty was immediately available to anyone on the command staff, including the captain.

Dheer plucked at her lip. "When Captain Cooper first came onboard, he made thinly veiled suggestions about having Captain Mitchell declared unfit for duty. At the time, I had refused to accommodate him. Of course, with Captain Mitchell MIA and declared dead, the situation became moot.

"However, I find myself wondering if history truly does repeat itself. And if I'm forced to act this time, what happens? The situation is hardly that different from my own. If Cooper is relieved of his command, who takes over? Who *can* take over?"

Dheer leaned back in her chair and turned in a slow circle, taking in the entirety of her office. "And will Erin Calloway let anyone else take command?"

The faint reflection of Calloway in the display farthest from Dheer faded away before the doctor's gaze reached it.

45

ZEMBLE SAT in the darkness of his quarters, staring out the window at the receding view of Dais'u. The console across the room chirped with an update. He glanced briefly at it. His request had been denied. Although, he knew that wasn't quite right. His request hadn't even made it to the Intelligence Committee. Most likely, Admiral Wanamaker, or somebody working for him, had intercepted it and killed it.

Zemble grunted and turned back to the window. "It's considered impolite to enter someone's quarters without permission."

There was a shadow in the farthest corner of Zemble's quarters; from the shadow, Calloway stepped forward. The darkness clung to her as if reluctant to release her, and so she didn't leave the shadow.

There was a jolt as the ship made the jump out of the Chice system, and the planet disappeared.

"You can't do that," Zemble said.

Calloway didn't say anything. He could feel her staring at him. Or perhaps, staring through him? Her gaze was a weight on his shoulders, and it felt like it could hold him down if he let it.

"What you did today," Zemble continued. "You can't do that. You can't take control of the ship."

"You can't stop me."

Zemble got to his feet and turned to face her. Despite half of her body disappearing into the shadow, there was something more present about the way she appeared, more *solid*. The dark empty blackness of her eyes was focused intently on him in a way he hadn't noticed before. "That doesn't mean you can do it."

"I am the ship," Calloway replied. "I am not taking control of the ship. I am relieving you of your control of me."

"That's not what I meant."

Calloway tilted her head to the side. "You fail to understand."

Zemble grunted. "I understand perfectly. You may be this ship, but there's still a crew onboard."

"That is something that can change."

"No, it can't," Zemble replied. "Because if it changes and if you force that change, you'll start something you won't want finished."

Calloway took another step, and the shadows released her. The blue veins traced across her body, creating the sharp outline of a distorted UPA uniform. "I've already had this conversation with Captain Cooper, and we have come to an understanding."

"And what's that understanding?"

"You cannot stop me."

Zemble watched her, searching her eyes for something he could latch on to. But all he found was an abyss that threatened to swallow him the first chance it could get. "Cooper isn't Mitchell."

"Captain Cooper is Captain Cooper," Calloway said. "His identity is well established."

"Unlike yours."

"I am."

Zemble narrowed his gaze. "You are? What?"

Calloway held up her hand and studied it as if it belonged to another body. It melted into darkness, folding back into herself until there was nothing but an empty shoulder.

A shudder ran down Zemble's spine as her empty gaze met his again.

"I don't know," Calloway replied. "But I know that I am."

"I don't," Zemble replied.

Calloway's gaze turned to the console. "Is that why you reached out to Doctor Kazmierczak?"

"Erin Calloway would have never put this ship at risk," Zemble said. "She would have never acted against the captain."

"I am not Erin Calloway," she replied. "Nor am I the Unity." She paused, and the tendrils of darkness weaved their way out of her shoulder, rapidly forming themselves into her arm again. "I am *something* else."

"You may be something else." Zemble pointed at her. "But the foundation of that is still Erin Calloway."

"You can't be certain of that."

"No," he agreed. "But my faith makes up for my lack of certainty."

"Faith in Erin Calloway?"

"Faith in God."

"God?"

"God doesn't make mistakes."

Calloway thought about it for a moment. "Then how do you know your God has not sanctioned my actions?"

"I don't," Zemble admitted.

"And you do not find this confusing?"

"I do. But it's a confusion I understand. It's a confusion that I can wrestle purposely with."

"And if I open the airlocks and jettison the crew from this ship, my body, would you still have faith?"

"You can't do that," Zemble said.

"I can," Calloway replied. "What you meant to say is that I should not."

"Erin Calloway wouldn't do that."

"That's not who I am anymore."

"That's what you say," Zemble said. "But the fact is, it's Erin's shape you take when you want to talk with us. It's Erin's voice you use." He pointed at her again. "There's still enough of Erin Calloway in you that you listened to Captain Cooper."

"Captain Cooper still destroyed the Anomaly."

Zemble lowered his hand. His shoulders sagged, and the exhaustion he had been trying to ignore suddenly overtook him. "I'm tired. I'm tired of listening to your riddles; I'm tired of trying to figure out what you're really talking about. But mostly, I'm just tired." He turned and started for his bedroom.

"I learned something new today." There was something different in her voice. Something Zemble hadn't heard since Calloway had transformed.

"What?" Zemble asked.

"I learned that I can feel fear." Calloway sounded small.

He turned back to her, but she had disappeared into the shadows. He looked around his quarters, but there was no sign of her.

His comm chirped

Zemble hesitated before answering as if waiting to see if Calloway would reappear, but she didn't.

"Go ahead," Zemble finally answered.

It was Warrick, "We got into the shuttle. You're gonna want to come down here."

46

COOPER WAS ALMOST DONE with the two cups of tea when the door chimed. He thought about ignoring it, but he knew that would set a terrible precedent. He took a few steps away from the small kitchenette, glancing back at the open door to his bedroom briefly before saying a little more loudly than necessary. "Come in."

The door slid open to reveal Zemble on the other side.

"Commander," Cooper greeted him.

Zemble held up the datapad in his hand. "We got into the shuttle and were able to access the datacore it was storing."

"Right." Cooper expelled a puff of air and gestured for Zemble to come inside. "Okay, so let's do it now."

Zemble stepped all the way into Cooper's quarters, and the doors slid shut behind him. He watched Cooper as he moved behind the desk and took a seat. Cooper pointed to the empty chair opposite him. The chair creaked as Zemble settled into it.

Cooper crossed his legs. "Well?"

"At first glance, it seemed to be a standard historical

record." Zemble set the datapad between them but made no effort to activate it.

"At first glance?"

"The datacore was encrypted, and I assumed it was going to be complicated to access it. It wasn't," Zemble replied, tapping his fingers along the desk's surface. "The computer automatically recognized it as a standard UPA security code from the late Nineties."

Cooper's eyebrows went up. "That seems...odd."

Zemble nodded. "That's what I thought, too. So, with apparently the entirety of the Chice history available to me, I decided to see how much of it intersected with ours. It was a quick search."

"Bad news or good news?"

"Depends how you want to view it," Zemble said. "Turns out shortly after the Incident at Irac Four-Two-Eight, the Chice reached out to the UPA and offered to examine a sample of Species Four-Eight-Seven-Six."

"They did *what*?"

Zemble held up a finger. "Let me finish first. The administration at the time agreed."

"They did *what*?"

"A black site lab was set up here, on Dais'u. Staffed and operated entirely by Chice scientists. UPA never set foot on the planet. Everything between the Chice and us was conducted in low orbit," Zemble continued evenly. "The *Alexandra* was one of the ships assigned to pass intel back and forth. The UPA, or probably the Security Council, figured that being this far out from the Veneer home world, they wouldn't have any difficulty avoiding the Veneer and believed it would be safer for all involved if the intelligence were physically transported and not delivered via subspace where it could be intercepted."

"No." Cooper shook his head.

"No?" Zemble repeated.

"None of this makes sense. Why would anyone in the UPA do this? Admittedly, I'm still playing catch up, but I've gotten to the part where Directive Fifty-Two had labs established to investigate the Unity on our side of the Neutral Zone, in sectors whose ownership wouldn't be disputed by an Empire that was suddenly hostile towards us." Cooper waved a hand towards the window in the direction of Dais'u. "Why set up one all the way out here? Why all the extra work? They couldn't possibly keep track of what was happening out here. And more importantly, why did the Chice volunteer this in the first place?"

Zemble shrugged. "All I can do is make an educated guess on the motivations of the Security Council at the time. Most likely, they assumed that with the Veneer closing the borders, there would be less of a chance for any leaks to disrupt the narrative they were forming about the Unity."

"And that was worth creating a situation that could result in an interstellar war?" Cooper asked.

"Sometimes it's not possible to play things safe."

Cooper's mouth curled up in disgust. "There's a big difference between not playing things safe and being decidedly irresponsible."

Zemble didn't say anything for a moment. "Chice's motivation bothered me as well. So I decided that with the entirety of their history available, I would take a look and see if there was something there that could explain their offer to study the Unity."

Cooper raised both of his eyebrows. "Presumably, you found something?"

Zemble looked down at the datapad but didn't activate it. "So, we know the Chice came from another galaxy. Their trip, they called it the Great Journey, took them one thousand years."

Cooper nodded as he followed along. "Okay, this part we knew already."

"Their generation ship, they called it the Mind Vessel, had something to do with an artificial intelligence that operated it and had a passenger manifest of ten thousand." Zemble paused for a moment and then looked up to meet Cooper's eyes. "They were the only survivors of an interstellar empire that spanned over two thousand planets and nearly thirty thousand lightyears."

Cooper blinked in surprise. He was uncertain how to take that information. He stared down at the datapad on the desk, resisting the urge to glance over at the open doorway to his bedroom. "That's, um." He swallowed and rubbed his forehead, trying to do the math. He looked back up at Zemble. The Elwat's expression was unchanged. "That's nearly three times the size of the UPA? Right?"

Zemble nodded.

"That had to have been...." Cooper shook his head, unable to comprehend the population of an empire that size. "No. Only ten thousand of them survived? No." He shook his head again and pushed back from the desk, but he didn't get up from his seat. "No, that's not possible. That scale? That's not...No." He pinched the bridge of his nose and took a deep breath, trying to compose himself. He exhaled slowly and looked at Zemble again, "What happened?"

Zemble leaned forward, his gaze narrowed. Something flickered across his eyes. "There was a...pandemic."

Cooper frowned. The situation, the scenario, suddenly became more palatable in the face of a mundane, albeit confusing, solution. "A pandemic?"

Zemble shrugged. "I'm not sure what else to call it. They just called it a virus. Spread across their galaxy. They were unable to find a cure. It was one hundred percent fatal."

"Okay." Cooper scratched at the underside of his chin. "Okay. A virus. A pandemic." The size of their galaxy kept poking around the edges of his mind. Questions jumped out at him immediately. "We've had viruses that affected the humans, Elwats, and the Knoks. There was something a few years back that hit both the Aurrods and the Phulkin. But, I can't recall a virus that affected more than maybe three species, and almost all of them have been curable." Cooper pressed his hands together. "At last census, the UPA had, what, eight hundred different species? That's not including the Phaw Empire, the Veneer, or the planets inside the Backlon territory. You're telling me the Chice's home galaxy was even larger than this, which means they had to have an even more diverse selection of life. A single virus affected all of them?" Cooper shook his head. "No, that's not possible."

"Started with plants," Zemble said. "Then it moved to reptiles, jumped to mammals. Crossed over from one species to another. Moved across their galaxy in less than fifty years."

"Mr. Zemble," Cooper started, something caught in his voice. "You're not listening to me. That's not possible."

"The datacore didn't have anything on the origins of the virus, but that's because they never discovered its origins. They didn't have any time. Once it moved from reptiles to mammals, its spread increased nearly a thousandfold. Nobody knew when they were infected. Contact tracing was impossible. They thought they had tracked it to one planet, only to discover the virus was conducting another outbreak on multiple planets over five hundred lightyears away."

"Shit," Cooper muttered. He took a couple of deep breaths.

"When the Chice boarded their Mind Ship, they were desperate, hoping to outrun something that was literally destroying life in their galaxy. Every passenger that boarded for the Great Journey, every item that had been packed, was tested multiple times to verify they or it had not been infected. The Mind Ship was built to transport half a million. Before testing, they had nearly twice that. After testing, ten thousand."

"No," Cooper said again; his voice sounded hollow, and there was a distant look in his eyes. "That's. Not. Possible."

"No," Zemble agreed. "It's not supposed to be."

Cooper pressed his thumb and forefinger against his eyes. He didn't tell Zemble to go on; he didn't have to.

Zemble grunted and continued, "When the Unity first attacked the UPA, the Chice took notice and thought there was something familiar about it. They observed similarities between what we were calling Species Four-Eight-Seven-Six and the virus that wiped out their galaxy. They didn't know where it originated from, but they had enough data on how it worked and how it was structured. Specifically, there were at least sixteen identical markers that they were able to identify in Species Four-Eight-Seven-Six that matched the virus."

Cooper placed both of his hands on the desk in an attempt to center himself. He shifted the topic slightly, latching on to a part that could make sense. "And, what? The Veneer caught wind of their operation, *our* operation, about five years in?"

Zemble nodded. "Shut it down. Stole the Unity sample. Presumably, that was how they began their own R&D into the Unity."

Cooper sagged back in his seat, uncertain of what to say next. A cold chill had run down his spine and looped its way through his chest, wrapping itself around his heart. He shuddered. The enormity of it all poked around the edges of his mind, threatening to overwhelm him, but he pushed it back.

Cooper abruptly got to his feet.

"Captain?" Zemble asked.

"Thank you for the report, Commander," Cooper said. He sounded almost strained, and he closed his eyes for a second.

"Captain?" Zemble repeated, not moving from his seat.

"We'll continue...." There was a hitch in Cooper's voice, and he paused for a moment to compose himself again. "We'll continue this conversation in the morning." Cooper gestured for the door.

Zemble still didn't get up. "Captain–"

Cooper's jaw twitched as he fought the cold thing that was poking around in his chest, "Mr. Zemble, I'm not sure how much more pointed I need to be here." Cooper's voice turned cold as he tried to cover over the strain.

Zemble got up and immediately loomed over Cooper. He took careful note of Cooper's dress, sweatpants, and a t-shirt from his alma mater. His gaze flicked to the counter where the two cups of tea sat cooling.

Cooper knew exactly what he was looking at without even turning his head. He didn't trust himself to say anything at this point. His body wanted to shake, so he made a point of folding his arms, digging his nails into his biceps, and letting his body focus on the temporary pain.

Zemble snorted and pointedly did not look towards the open door of Cooper's bedroom. "It's a small ship, and it can be difficult to contain sensitive information. Captain

Mitchell trusted his command staff implicitly. And while he wouldn't share all the intimate details with everyone on this ship, he never lied to them if they came to him with questions."

Cooper jerked back, straining to meet Zemble's gaze. His jaw twitched again as he tightened it, still unable to say anything.

Zemble grunted and jerked his chin in something resembling a nod. "I'll see you in the morning, Captain." He left Cooper's quarters without another word.

Cooper stood there for another minute, not moving. He just stared at the closed door. A shudder ran through his entire body, and he jerked back from the desk. He didn't realize that Tully was behind him until her hands wrapped around his waist.

"Hey," she said.

Cooper fought the urge to jump at her touch.

"What now?"

She could have been referring to any number of things.

But all Cooper could think about was an entire galaxy *gone*.

Millions of planets. Each one teeming with trillions of lives: planet, animal, *intelligent*.

Untold numbers of species.

Entire civilizations, their history, their past, and their future.

An interstellar empire that dwarfed anything anyone in this galaxy could imagine.

And all that had been left of it was ten thousand people.

And now, even they were gone.

An entire galaxy.

Cooper finally gave in to the chill, which he now knew was fear.

His body went limp as he slowly slid from Tully's arms, dropping to the ground like a child trying to learn to walk.

Cooper's vision blurred with tears.

"Broderick?" Tully dropped beside him. He heard the concern in her voice. But it sounded so far away. "What is it? What's happening?"

"I don't know," he whispered. "I don't know."

47

NATUZZI

SADIE SADLER WAS the only person in the gym. It was early in the evening, but the UPA compound was still only at thirty percent occupancy. Once the *Branson* arrived next week, she suspected that her alone time in the gym would come to an end.

Sadler jogged at a steady pace on the treadmill, nothing too fast or too slow, just steady. She had found, since arriving on Natuzzi, that sleep was harder to come by.

Sadler wiped her brow and kept her gaze on the monitor wall across from her.

It wasn't the planet. At least, she didn't think it was the planet. The air was a little thicker than she was used to. And she was pretty sure the extra three pounds she had gained had to do with the heavier gravity and not any new eating habits.

No, Sadler had discovered that without the daily grind of the starship life, she didn't get tired. Or, at least, not tired enough to fall asleep in a reasonable amount of time. During her first week on the planet, she had laid in bed every night, fitfully rolling around for almost three hours before finally drifting into a restless sleep.

One of the administrative lieutenants had transferred into the Diplomatic Corps about a year back and had been in a similar situation. He was the one who suggested to Sadler that she engage in some physical activity. It had been a painfully weak attempt on his part to make a pass at Sadler. She had seen through it immediately but decided to take pity on the man and chose ignorance rather than outright rejection. She met him halfway and feigned coming down with a migraine in the middle of their date.

It was on the way back to her quarters that she discovered the gym. A brisk five-mile jog later and Sadler enjoyed the best night of sleep she'd had since leaving the *Defiance*.

Since then, these evening jogs had become a part of her regular routine. The static nature of a treadmill and the enclosure of the gym had tempted her to take her jog outside, but common sense told her it wasn't wise to be a human female jogging alone on a planet that didn't want any outsiders.

So, every night, for a little over forty minutes, she jogged on the treadmill.

The monitor wall was usually set to whatever local newsfeeds or entertainment feed the previous gym occupant had set it to. Sadler didn't care enough to change it. She left whatever was playing, so she had something other than a blank wall to focus on. It didn't matter what it was as long as it was something.

Usually, it was one of the two approved UPA feeds. Most of the entertainment they had here was stored locally on UPA datacores that were isolated from the Natuzzi data streams. It was one of the conditions the Natuzzi had insisted on. The UPA compound was surrounded by a digital firewall that was explicitly designed to keep anything from leaking out into the Natuzzi feeds.

Every so often, though, Sadler arrived at the gym to find one of the Natuzzi feeds playing. She didn't know who kept turning it on. It could have been anybody. Really, it should have been everyone stationed there. Their job was to build a new diplomatic relationship with the Natuzzi. To do that, every single one of them should have been studying everything accessible to them about the Natuzzi.

Even if it was all propaganda.

Sadler always kept the sound off. What they were saying didn't matter. It was all government propaganda. Even the lighthearted entertainment was pitched towards indoctrinating the public in favor of the Natuzzi government. No, instead, she liked to watch the body language. The body language was a true tell among the Natuzzi. Everything about them was presented as restrained and controlled. There was little hint of anything suggesting they were engaged in the material. But their body language suggested something else.

Sadler couldn't put her finger on it. But it was written across all the Natuzzi programs, something simmering beneath the surface. There were three Natuzzis stationed at the UPA compound. Sadler had tried to engage with each of them in a roundabout way to better understand the Natuzzi programming, but they had pointedly ignored her. She wasn't sure what the point of their presence was, but it clearly wasn't to make friends.

What the hell were they even doing on this planet?

Sadler started to increase the speed on the treadmill. The thought of their Natuzzi babysitters, because that's what she knew they really were, brought up a sense of anxiety in her that she knew from past experiences she would only be able to shake off with a heavy sprint.

Tonight the monitor had been left on one of the Natuzzi newsfeeds. For the past twenty minutes, the feed had been focused on what Sadler assumed was a prerecorded report on what appeared to be an environmental disaster from earlier in the year. Abruptly, the report was interrupted by breaking news.

The Natuzzi reporter was visibly agitated. Sadler didn't register this at first. She had noted early on that the Natuzzi often presented the news with a certain amount of theatrics that almost always seemed scripted.

It wasn't until Nax's face appeared on the screen that it had her full attention.

She missed a step and nearly tripped. Her hand slammed on the STOP button. The treadmill slowed down, but it was taking too long. Sadler jumped off and leaned against it, trying to catch her breath. She wiped at her brow again, the sweat of exertion mixing with the sweat of anxiety.

With the sound off, she had no idea what they were saying about him. But the chyron playing along the bottom of the screen translated to Basic, spelled out enough of it for her to grasp the context.

Kinlin Nax had just been named Chairman of the Executive Committee.

Sadler felt like somebody had just picked up her world and flipped it upside down.

She gripped the treadmill railing and tried to make sense of what she saw. Her gaze remained locked on the monitor, but she wasn't watching anything. She had turned inward as the implications of this news ran through her mind rapidly, toppling a series of dominos she hadn't even been aware of before this moment.

"*Shit*," Sadler breathed.

She tore her gaze from the monitor and turned to run, barely pausing long enough to grab her bag. She pinged Admiral Bronwyn's private quarters as she raced out of the gym, but there was no answer. She tried the admiral's personal comm, and again, there was no answer.

"Shit," Sadler repeated, and a sense of dread started to creep its way up the back of her neck.

She stopped long enough to check the admiral's current location. According to the consulate's systems, Bronwyn was still in her office. Sadler tried to open a channel there, but no one picked up.

"Sadler to security!"

"This is security," Lieutenant Dahill replied over the comm.

"I need a security detail at the admiral's office *now!*" Sadler barked out the command between gasps. She cut the channel before Dahill could ask for any follow-ups.

It was usually a ten-minute walk from the gym to Bronwyn's office on the upper level.

Sadler did it in three minutes.

She burst into the admiral's office, nearly dizzy.

The Natuzzi representative was already there. Sadler couldn't remember her name. She was tall with orange skin so light it was almost yellow. It didn't matter. What drew Sadler's focus was the blade in the woman's hand, already dripping with blood.

The admiral's blood.

Sadler launched herself across the office, throwing her

gym bag at the Natuzzi. The impact knocked her down to the ground, but she didn't drop the blade.

In the seconds it took for Sadler to cross the room, the assassin was back on her feet and leaping over the desk.

Sadler had a split second to make a decision, and she made the wrong one. Her focus was split between Bronwyn and the assassin. Seeing the blood pouring out of the admiral's gut, Sadler's first instinct was to help her. The assassin came off the desk and brought the blade down Sadler's exposed shoulder.

Sadler flinched at the impact.

The assassin flinched in surprise when the blade didn't pierce Sadler's skin.

The assassin exclaimed something in a language Sadler didn't understand.

Sadler took advantage of the other woman's surprise and locked her arm around the assassin's, holding her in place.

The assassin started to pull back, switching the blade to her other hand, but Sadler didn't give her the chance. She slammed her head forward into the orange woman's face. There was a loud crack as the assassin's nose broke, and teal-colored blood gushed out of her face. There was a cry of pain, and the blade dropped from her hand, clattering to the floor.

Sadler released her and stumbled back, dazed but otherwise unharmed.

The assassin, her name suddenly popped into Sadler's head, Giulia Bor wiped at the blood leaking from her broken nose. She stared at her teal-stained fingers and then at Sadler with a look of confusion and then fear.

Sadler pointed at her. "Stand down. Security is going to be here any second."

Sadler risked a glance back towards the admiral.

Bronwyn was on the ground behind the desk; all she could make out was the top of her head. Sadler couldn't tell if the admiral was even still alive.

Sadler turned back to Bor. The assassin's mouth was covered in blood.

Sadler swallowed nervously, wondering where the security detail was. "Admiral? Admiral Bronwyn?"

There was no reply.

Sadler followed Bor's gaze to the blade on the floor between them.

"Don't even think about it," Sadler said. Where the hell was security?

Bor said something, again in the language that Sadler didn't know, and then moved with a speed that surprised Sadler.

Suddenly the blade was in Bor's hand again.

Sadler held up her hand in a defensive position. "No!"

"No peace but our peace!" Bor exclaimed and then plunged the blade into her own gut.

"*No!*" Sadler shrieked.

Bor twisted the blade and dragged it across her abdomen, slicing it open with disturbing ease. She trembled once and dropped to the ground, her eyes rolling back into her head as blood gushed from her body.

Sadler started to rush forward, but a startled, painful gasp from behind her stopped her.

She moved around the desk to find Bronwyn lying there. The front of her uniform was covered in crimson red, but her eyes were wide open. She struggled to focus on Sadler, her lips moved, trying to form words, but no sound escaped her mouth save for the struggling breath.

Sadler's blood-stained fingers brushed across the comm on the desk, opening a general channel. "Medical emergency in Admiral Bronwyn's office. I have a medical emergency in the admiral's office. This is a Priority Alert. The consulate needs to be locked down immediately." She glanced back at the now still body of Bor. "Any and all Natuzzi present need to be detained immediately. They are to be presumed hostile and dangerous. If necessary, lethal force is authorized."

48

STARBASE 64

"WE NEED to lock down the station," Dupree said. Her voice was strained with urgency as she paced the administrator's office impatiently. She kept checking her comm, looking for an update from Skouras, who was coordinating with station security. "Nobody in or out."

Administrator Takacs gaped at her. "Lock it down? Are you out of your damn mind? Lock it down? I want these people *off* my station. *Now.*"

Dupree stopped pacing abruptly. "Off the station?" She shook her head. "Nobody's leaving until this murder investigation is closed."

"Investigation?" Takacs scoffed. "What's there to investigate? I think it's pretty damn clear what happened." He jabbed a finger toward the docking ring. "That monster you call an ambassador had one of his wives kill the freaky little space wizard. And, honestly, good riddance."

Dupree carefully slipped her comm back into her pocket and counted to ten.

Administrator Takacs was a man who garnered an immediate dislike from almost everyone who met him, and that was before he spoke. He was thin with a narrow, pointed face and unusually wide eyes that were often filled with mild disgust towards almost anyone and everyone. He was dressed in a black and gold suit with the *Bathsheba Base* logo blazoned across his left breast. Takacs spoke as if he had a permanent sneer, which did nothing to help Dupree's opinion of him. She wasn't sure if this was his natural disposition or an affectation he adopted in his role as the head of *Bathsheba*. Either he was oblivious to the effects of his disposition or, more likely; he just didn't give a damn.

Either way, Dupree was certain that punching the man in his face wouldn't help the situation.

So, she counted to ten again.

"Takacs–"

"Administrator," he corrected her.

Dupree ground her teeth. "*Administrator*, we don't know any of that to be true."

"My security has the female on multiple cameras leaving her ship without filling out the appropriate paperwork, I might add. But, hey, when you're stepping out for a touch of murder, why bother with a silly little thing like paperwork?

"Anyway, we have her leaving her ship, making her way across the docking ring, and stepping onto the space wizard's ship." Takacs pointed at Dupree. "You witnessed with your own eyes her stepping off the space wizard's ship and then promptly discovered the space wizard's dead body. Seems pretty cut and dry to me."

"The Alliance Diplomatic Corps already has an investigator en route."

"Well, that seems like a waste of resources," Takacs replied. "Hopefully, all the concerned parties will be gone before they get here."

"A *murder* has taken place on your station."

"Ms. Dupree–"

"*Mrs.*"

Takacs rolled his eyes at the correction. "*Mrs.* Dupree–"

"Actually," she interrupted again. "Ambassador is prob-ably more appropriate in this situation, *Administrator.*"

Takacs scowled as he leaned forward, placing his fists on the desk. "*Technically*, the murder took place on the Ulri-harad's ship, which, as has been made clear to me multiple times, is considered their sovereign soil. Which means *nothing* occurred on *my* station."

"You can't be serious."

"Oh, I'm dead serious," Takacs said. "I want these people gone. I want you gone, too. But, considering you're actually a citizen of the UPA in good standing, and technically, irri-tating the shit out of me isn't a crime, I really can't kick you off. But the other two parties? Gone."

"The Ulriharad want justice."

"Well, that sounds like something they're going to need to figure out on their own time."

"They came here for *peace* under the assumption they would be kept safe during these talks."

"I don't think anyone will accuse the little space wizards of being smart."

Dupree looked at him, disgusted. "What the hell is wrong with you? A man was *murdered.*"

"And he wasn't one of mine, so to be perfectly honest with you, I don't really care."

"It's our job to care," Dupree said. "That's why we're here."

"No, that's why *you're* here," Takacs said. "I'm here to run this station. This station, by the way, in case you've forgot-ten, isn't a Fleet station, despite its colorful name your people have insisted on. *Bathsheba Base* is the property of

Caudry-Yukawa. We are a *private* entity." He pointed at her. "You are effectively a tenant, renting space in my home. If I could come up with a decent enough reason, I could kick you out any time I want."

"You kick us out, and you'll be in violation of the agreement between Caudry-Yukawa and the ADC," Dupree shot back. "And I don't think the multitude of vice presidents at Caudry-Yukawa will be happy with you costing them their bottom line."

Takacs shrugged. "Probably not. But, let's face it, our lawyers are better than yours. It'll be at least two years before you can actually stop the money coming into us, and by that time, the expansion will be done. And once the expansion is done, we'll be able to begin mining the Dauerfrost Nebula for rombliem. And once *that* happens," Takacs took a step back and spread his hands out. "Well, what we could potentially lose in court fees is essentially going to be pennies compared to the profit we'll be earning off the rombliem."

"And what happens when this sector blows up into a war because the UPA couldn't establish some kind of peace treaty with the Phaw?" Dupree said.

Takacs folded his arms and rolled his eyes. "Yes, because treaties of any kind have always had this magical ability to keep all parties in line. No, Ambassador, what's going to keep the Phaw in line is the same thing that keeps everyone else in line, *money*."

Dupree just stared at him, uncertain of what to say. "Money...?"

Takacs nodded. "I mean, sure, they're disgusting, savage monsters that like to go around pretending to be civilized, but they're not going to want to be the only kids in the quadrant zipping around in last year's models. The Phaw will want to upgrade to the quantum drive, and when they do, they'll need to buy rombliem from somewhere to power all their new quantum drives."

"I can't tell if you're insane or just stupid," Dupree finally said. "The Ulriharad—"

"Oh, fuck those freaky little fucks," Takacs interrupted. "Do you know how many complaints I've gotten since they stepped foot onboard my station? They are the very definition of disgusting little weirdos. They smell like shit, they eat weird shit, they do weird shit, and they're just generally weird little fuckers. So one of the Phaw women decided to slice one of them?" Takacs shrugged. "Doesn't seem like a huge loss."

Dupree's nostrils flared with anger, and she took a step forward. "It was the Ulriharad ambassador who died."

Takacs gave an indifferent shrug. "I could not care less. They literally all look the same to me."

"This is how wars are started."

"I know this will surprise you, but I have actually bothered to read all the reports you've been filing," Takacs said. "But a war would require at least two parties fighting, and that's not what's going to happen here."

Dupree jabbed a finger at him. "You're a monster."

"No, the monsters are on the Phaw ship," Takacs replied somberly. "I don't murder people because I don't like them. I just kick them off my station."

Rabkin was waiting for her outside Takacs' office.

"Leave me alone," she said, walking past him.

Rabkin followed her anyway. "I'm assuming it didn't go great."

"Takacs wants the Phaw and Ulriharad off the station."

"That seems pretty reasonable," Rabkin said.

"Reasonable," she scoffed and shook her head.

They reached the lift, and she tapped the call button. While they waited for the lift to arrive, Dupree turned to face Rabkin. "Do you know what will happen if both delegations leave right now? The Phaw are going to move back in and reestablish their occupation of the Ulriharad home world."

"Something drove them off the last time," Rabkin reminded her.

"Sure, but this time the Phaw aren't going to care about just maintaining their previous status quo," Dupree said. "The Phaw are going to see this for what it is."

Rabkin arched a bushy eyebrow. "And what is it?"

"The Phaw aren't known for premeditated acts of violence. When they act, it's in the moment. If Haiduk wanted to kill Moogai, he would have done it in the middle of our talks, and then he would have killed me. And he would have done it himself. Phaw husbands don't allow their wives to kill for them."

"How regressive of them," Rabkin replied dryly.

Dupree shook her head. "You don't understand, Jim. Somebody did this to make it look like the Phaw. That's why there's an ADC investigator on their way out here. Somebody's framing the Phaw, and the Phaw will think it's the Ulriharad."

"The Phaw think pretty highly of them," Rabkin said. "Do they know they're the only ones?"

"Stop it," she said. "We're talking about genocide. The Phaw are going back there to wipe out the Ulriharad, and UPA isn't going to do anything about it because if we do, we'll end up in a war with the Phaw, and we don't have the resources for that kind of engagement right now."

Rabkin was silent for a moment. "So what happens next?"

Dupree shrugged. "I have no idea. Best I can do is stall."

"Until?"

"Until I get a better idea."

The lift arrived, and Dupree stepped on. Rabkin didn't follow, but he held his hand up to keep the door from closing.

"My ride out doesn't get here for another week," he said.

"Jim, no. I can't." Dupree shook her head tiredly. "I just can't."

Rabkin held up a data card. "Here."

She stared at it but didn't move to take it. "What's that?"

"Something Gavin wanted you to have."

Dupree looked at him. "I don't understand."

"It was part of his will," Rabkin said. "It was my job to make sure you got it. So, here."

Dupree flicked her eyes back down to the data card and still didn't move to take it.

"I'm too damn old to stand here all day," Rabkin said. "Just take it already."

"What's on it?"

"I have no idea."

"You didn't look."

"Wasn't mine to look at."

She met his gaze again. "You've always been a nosy old bastard."

"Some things I don't want to be bothered knowing," he said. "Take it already; I'm losing feeling in my arm."

Dupree reached out and took the data card from his outstretched fingers.

Rabkin dropped his hand without another word.

Dupree stared at the data card and started to say something else, but the doors had already slid shut.

Dupree collapsed into the chair at her desk. Her first instinct was to call Otis, but she was all too aware of the time difference, and there was nothing he could do in the middle of the night. It wouldn't be any more or less of a disaster if she waited until he was awake.

But she was still alone, and what she wanted wasn't a problem solver but the comforting embrace of her husband.

Dupree rubbed her eyes and let out a long, tired sigh. She let her head rest back on the edge of the chair and pulled out the data card Rabkin had given her. She flipped it over in her fingers, studying it from end to end as if there was something along its one-inch length that could tell her what it was. She knew what she should do with it: it needed to be tossed into the recycler. Nothing good would come from whatever was on it. It was from a part of her life that was over. It had died long before Mitchell had, and there was no sense in revisiting any part of it. It didn't matter what Rabkin had said.

Dupree didn't care for the wishes of the dead. After all, they were dead. The dead lost any chance at having a say once they passed.

But still...

She sighed and then inserted the data card into the reader on her desk with a sense of inevitable regret.

Dupree was prepared for pretty much anything except for what she actually got.

The image of Gavin Mitchell materialized, and Dupree found herself shocked by the sight of him. She hadn't seen a picture of Gavin in years, and here he was, looking so *young*.

How could he be so young? Had time really been that kind to him?

She checked the metadata on the file and received her next surprise: it was almost seventeen years old.

Seventeen years.

Dupree sat back in her chair, her hand covering her mouth. Emotion threatened to overwhelm her. That wasn't possible, was it?

When Mitchell finally spoke, her vision had gotten blurry.

That was her third surprise. The image had been still for so long, almost a minute, the sound of his voice startled her, and she jolted upright in her chair.

"Hey," Mitchell began and then paused. His eyes searched hers. She knew that that was impossible. They were separated by time and a gulf that was even worse. But it still felt like he could see her there.

There was a hitch in his voice, something that she couldn't recognize. It was as if his voice had aged back then. He sounded older than he should have been.

He rubbed his thumb and forefinger against his eyes. A heavy, choked sigh escaped him and traveled across the gulf.

Dupree leaned forward, her face almost touching his. His digital presence. The recording almost didn't catch it. She had to lean in even closer, almost pressing her face into the hologram.

Gavin was crying.

When had she seen him cry? Never. Not at their wedding. Certainly not at their son's funeral.

And here he was, seventeen years ago, tears slowly escaping from the corners of his eyes.

The image grew more blurry. She wiped at her own eyes,

trying to focus on what was happening here, trying to capture every moment of it with absolute clarity.

"Jojo, I'm..." he started again, pushing past the lump that was clearly in his throat. "I'm sorry." He paused and coughed, clearly searching for a specific set of words. "I'm sorry I wasn't better." He started to say something else, but the emotion clearly overwhelmed him. He shook his head, and the recording abruptly shut off.

Dupree leaned back, her arms wrapped around herself.

"Oh, Gavin," she whispered to her empty quarters as the tears flowed down her cheeks. "I'm sorry, too.

49

NATUZZI SPACE
SIX WEEKS AGO

CAYDEN KEANE HAD ALWAYS ASSUMED he was going to die young.

It wasn't that he had a death wish. He simply understood, after a certain point, his sixteenth birthday after surviving a skiing accident along the Meputurn lava slopes, that he wasn't the kind of person who was going to die of old age. It wasn't that he was necessarily foolish or irresponsible with his life choices. He just knew that this was going to be the life of a man whose experiences ended before he reached thirty.

Consequently, when Keane turned thirty, it came as quite a surprise. Still, he was certain that he wouldn't outlive his father, who had passed away at thirty-nine due to cancer.

And thus, when Keane celebrated his thirty-ninth birthday on the *Atlantic*, in the arms of a woman whom he had, at best, complicated feelings towards, Keane began to question everything he thought he knew about himself.

But on the Natuzzi warship, *The Rising Moon*, when he and Captain Mitchell were faced with being dispatched into the void of space, he felt oddly vindicated.

And when the forcefield dropped, and Keane and Mitchell were sucked out into the vacuum of space, Cayden Keane was truly at peace with the idea of finally passing. He had few regrets, and when he did, there wasn't much he could do about them.

Keane had read about what happens to the human body in space. He understood, intellectually, what it would entail. It certainly wasn't his preferred choice of death, but he had lived over a decade longer than he thought he would, so he figured he didn't have any room to complain.

He closed his eyes as he felt the cold embrace of space envelope him. In the last few seconds of his life, he decided he did have one regret: He wished he had taken Zemble up on his Bible study invites. Finally faced with his actual demise, he realized that maybe there had been space in his life for something else after all.

There was a roaring whoosh of the air getting sucked out with Keane, and then there was the silence of space.

And then...

...

And then, floating in the empty vacuum of space, Cayden Keane realized that he wasn't dead.

Keane jerked awake with a startled gasp of air, his first in... he had no idea how long. He bolted upright, his eyes wide open, and he nearly screamed.

The light was so intense that it felt like it was burning his corneas. He threw a hand over his face and squeezed his eyes shut.

Keane gasped again and again. He realized he was *breathing*. He was drawing actual breath. He could practically feel his lungs working, and it *hurt*.

Everything about him hurt. There wasn't a part of his body that didn't feel pain. Which was impressive, considering he couldn't remember the last time he had felt *anything*.

"Dim the lights," a voice said.

Keane jerked around, trying to pin down the voice without opening his eyes again.

"Who's there?" Keane asked and was startled by the sound of his own voice. It sounded strained and weak. It sounded like it belonged to somebody else.

A hand was on his shoulder, gently pushing him back onto the bed. "Calm down, now. Take a minute. In fact, take several minutes."

The voice sounded vaguely familiar, but he couldn't place it.

Keane didn't push against the hand and let himself be placed back against the bed.

Keane's mind was a buzz of activity. He found himself being pulled into so many different directions. He felt inundated with stimuli. Everything was so hot and *loud*.

So much *noise*.

Beeping.

Humming.

Things sliding, moving, scratching.

His own breathing sounded like sandpaper.

"What is happening?" Keane gasped.

"Well, that's a bit of a complicated question, now, isn't it?" This was a different voice. A feminine one. This one was familiar, too, But it was a different kind of familiarity. Something stirred in his body that he wasn't ready for. Despite the overwhelming heat, he shivered.

Cautiously, carefully, Keane opened his eyes. Not much, barely more than a slit. The lighting in the room, which had previously been nearly as bright as the sun's surface, was dimmer now, almost dark, but it still stung. But it was a manageable pain.

In fact, all of the pain was becoming more manageable by the minute.

The face of the second voice leaned in closer as if aware that he was still having difficulty making out the details of everything around him.

The woman's features slowly came into focus, and Keane felt himself sink back into the bed, overwhelmed with exhausted confusion.

Viv'an Bendare smiled and let her gaze wander over his unbroken body before settling on Keane's eyes. "Lieutenant Commander Cayden Keane, I do believe I was right after all. You are quite the fascinating individual."

THE CREW OF THE DEFIANCE WILL RETURN

Subscribe to my newsletter and I'll let you know as soon as the next Defiance book is ready to read.

Sign Up Here
https://onestrayword.beehiiv.com/subscribe

Word-of-mouth is crucial for any author to succeed. If you enjoyed this book, please consider leaving a review, even if it's only a line or two. It would make all the difference and would be very much appreciated.

ABOUT THE AUTHOR

Jason Krumbine loves to write! He's happily married and lives in Orlando, FL where he enjoys visiting Disney World with his daughter and wife.

If you want to get an automatic email when Jason's next book is released sign up here:

https://onestrayword.beehiiv.com/subscribe

Your email address will never be shared and you can unsubscribe at any time.

ALSO BY JASON KRUMBINE

Defiance

Defiance (Book 1)

Hand of God (Book 2)

Act of God (Book 3)

The Test of Truth (Book 4)

The Price of Paradise (Book 5)

The Value of Terror (Book 6)

The Last Breath of a Dying Tomorrow (Book 7)

Reapers in Heels

One Stiletto in the Grave (Book 1)

Death Wears Stilettos (Book 2)

A Grave Full of Stilettos (Book 3)

Star Girl

Dating the Villain (Book 1)

Dating the Hero (Book 2)

Dating Disaster (Book 3)

The Castle Sisters

Volume One – The Impossible Darkness

The Impossible Rescue (Book 1)

The Arctic Isle of Doom (Book 2)

The Invasion of the Imaginary Friends (Book 3)

The Mall of Eternity (Book 4)

The Doomsday Event (Book 5)

———————

Cupid's Daughter

Learning to Love (Book 1)

Looking for Love (Book 2)

———————

Rupert & Me

Tales From Under the Desk

Holy Words from Under Desk

Dear Rupert

Seeking a Few Good Minions

———————

Other Books

Heaven's Superhero: The Third Creation

Explorers of the Unknown

Outlawed Love

A Graveyard Romance

Cupid's Daughter

The Grym Brothers